# WHEN THE MISSOURI RAN RED

Novels by Jim R. Woolard

WHEN THE MISSOURI RAN RED

RAIDING WITH MORGAN

RIDING FOR THE FLAG

THUNDER IN THE VALLEY

THE WINDS OF AUTUMN

BLOOD AT DAWN

# WHEN THE MISSOURI RAN RED

JIM R. WOOLARD

www.kensingtonbooks.com

KENSINGTON BOOKS are published by

Kensington Publishing Corp.
119 West 40th Street
New York, NY 10018



All Kensington titles, imprints, and distributed lines are available at special quantity discounts for bulk purchases for sales promotion, premiums, fund-raising, educational, or institutional use.

Special book excerpts or customized printings can also be created to fit specific needs. For details, write or phone the office of the Kensington Special Sales Manager: Attn. Special Sales Department. Kensington Publishing Corp, 119 West 40th Street, New York, NY 10018. Phone: 1-800-221-2647.



Library of Congress Card Catalogue Number: 2021936515

ISBN-13: 978-1-4967-3406-8
ISBN-10: 1-4967-3406-8
First Kensington Hardcover Edition: October 2021

ISBN-13: 978-1-4967-3408-2 (ebook)
ISBN-10: 1-4967-3408-4 (ebook)

10 9 8 7 6 5 4 3 2 1

Printed in the United States of America

# A NOTE FROM THE AUTHOR

Most of us would assume a war that ended almost a hundred and sixty years ago would be considered "old" history. But as I revised this book in the summer of 2020, nothing could seem farther from the truth.

The Civil War remains to this day the deadliest conflict in American history, with some estimating the total civilian and soldier casualties to be three quarters of a million. It was the most economically disastrous for some regions in the South, which would not recover for generations. It was the first war to be captured by the new technology of photography, the images of war and carnage published in newspapers throughout America and the world: a phenomenon the modern American is all too familiar with, but which must have been a terrifying shock for readers at the time. It was the first time civilians far removed from violence were actually able to *see* the carnage of war.

And most importantly, the Civil War abolished slavery in the United States of America.

To this day, our thoughts and emotions of the Civil War are volatile, and it remains one of the most controversial episodes in American history, as evidenced this summer, when we as a nation publicly reconciled with how we remember that history.

This novel is based on actual events The state of Missouri was torn apart by the Civil War. Anti-slavery, free-state Kansas Jayhawkers like Quantrill raided the slave state of Missouri and killed and robbed Confederate supporters holding slaves, along with fellow Unionists who were for saving the Union but not for abolishing slavery. In addition to Rebel sympathizers populating parts of the state, willing to die for the Southern cause, there were large numbers of Missouri Bushwhackers like Bloody Bill Anderson who had no sympathy for either side and raided and killed for personal gain and revenge against anyone who had ever slighted them.

This local civil war played out in the midst of the armed conflict of regular Union and Confederate armies numbering in the thousands. In my research, I discovered the simple truth is that the violence of the Old West of later years was never as wild and deadly as Civil War Missouri.

As I work in comfort from my home, it can be hard to imagine the pervasive violence that overran our nation for four bloody years. But by writing this book, I'm hoping to rekindle our imaginations and knowledge of that past yet so relevant war. What is most important is how we remember that conflict for the future.

Jim R. Woolard
Newark, Ohio
January 2021

# PROLOGUE

*This old world can tempt a young man still wet behind the ears into great danger till he learns to watch out for his own well-being. One of those temptations nearly resulted in my being shot to death, at the mere age of seventeen, on August 6, 1864.*

*Gunshots rang out that summer morning right after Laura Kellerman, the particular lass for whom I bore much affection, walked past my uncle's hotel on the opposite side of Ohio Avenue. Her lavender parasol identified her beyond doubt; and rightfully fearing for the raven-haired, blue-eyed female who shadowed my nightly dreams, I dropped my broom, bolted out the hotel's front door, unarmed and heedless of my future, and was greeted by a wild bullet not intended for me.*

*I felt a searing blow to the head above my right ear. Knocked senseless, I tumbled off the hotel's porch and landed flat on my backside atop the hardpan surface of Ohio Avenue. Shouts rent the air about me. Those loud words didn't register while my stunned brain scrambled to make sense of what was happening.*

*A throaty panting and the splatter of wet slobber on my cheek stood out first among the jumble of noise assaulting my ears, which meant my hound, Shep, had followed on my heels as he always did. A distinct, close-by yell was the next thing to force its way into my ringing skull:*

*"Hey, Bub!"*

*The calling of my childhood nickname enticed me into opening my eyes despite the pain, and there, staring down at me from atop a dun-colored horse, with a pistol in his hand, was the hate-distorted face of my half brother, a face I hadn't seen for seven years. I cringed when Lance cocked the pistol, aimed it at me, and, with a mean smile twisting his bearded, scarred features, pulled the pistol's trigger.*

*The bullet wasn't meant for me. Without so much as a whimper, the panting Shep collapsed on my chest. Lance leaned from the saddle. His mean smile widened. "Didn't want you to forget me, yuh runty little shit."*

*With that insult, Lance's body straightened and he raked the dun with his spurs. The startled horse lunged forward and the edge of his left front hoof pinched the flesh above my left knee. Fresh pain snagged my breath, and with a fading glimpse of the tip of a lavender parasol and the crown of a black-haired head accompanied by a female scream, I lost consciousness, remembering later someone, it had to be me, muttering, "You should have killed me, Lance."*

*How I came to be in such a dire fix and what happened afterward may interest you, dear reader, for my story recalls not only personal adventures that to this day enthrall even the man who survived them, but it also tells how the War of the Rebellion had the mighty Missouri running red with blood, made heroes of cold-boned killers, and left scars on both victor and vanquished.*

*Bear in mind as you thumb through my pages that I will journey to my grave thanking the good Lord every night for teaching me the love of a faithful woman is to be cherished, true brothers in arms never desert you, no matter the color of their battle flag, and fighting for a lost cause need not be the final measure of a man's worth.*

*Hoping my feeble prose will enlighten the recent past for those of you in the body public desiring to separate truth from rumor and falsehoods regarding certain wartime events . . .*

*Your faithful servant,*

*Owen Wainwright*

# PART I

# PREPARING FOR WAR

# CHAPTER 1

THE SIX DAYS THAT FOLLOWED MY ENCOUNTER WITH THE DUSTY SURface of Ohio Avenue were a jumble of pain, spells of hot fever followed by bone-numbing chills, short periods of blurry wakefulness, and frightful nightmares. I slowly became aware I was abed in my sleeping room next to the alley door of the Wainwright Hotel. I distinctly remember the piercing pricks of Dr. Franklin Gribble's needle as he knitted together the edges of the lengthy gouge in the skin of my skull. I slept through the scalp shaving that preceded the buttoning up. Then there was my aunt and stepmother, Emma Wainwright. She hovered over me with a damp cloth to sop my sweaty brow when the fever gripped me and with a handy blanket when my teeth chattered.

The pain of my stitched scalp, the bullet groove in the bone of my head, and the hurt arising from the hoof-clenched, swollen flesh of my trampled thigh persisted like constant toothaches, forcing me to bite my lip to keep from shouting out whenever I so much as twitched anywhere. Though I had no diagnosis from Dr. Gribble to confirm it, I suspected in my more lucid moments the nightmares besieging my fretful sleep were birthed by the brain-jarring strike of Lance's bullet. Scary dreams of whippings by my father, Lucien Wainwright, roused a tingling feeling in the narrow, ridged scars lining my back ribs. During a feverish spell, I swear I felt Lance's hands round my neck as I relived his near drowning of me in the watering trough after Shep attacked him defending me.

My mother's screams for Lance to stop brought me bolt upright in my blankets.

I awakened with tear-wet cheeks reliving my mother's burial in glorious spring sunshine, an event foreshadowed by her telling my ten-year-old ears her passing was okay since she had brought me into the world, a sentiment I was still trying to decipher. I experienced a dead heart the night I dreamed of the execution of my father in our dooryard by the Union militia that falsely accused him of being a Southern-leaning slaver. And looming over every torturous detail that intruded on my healing rest was the stark, hateful image of Lance's face as he murdered Shep.

I swear the Almighty blessed the seventh morning of my recovery. I came awake with a clear mind with bearable pain and hungrier than a bear fresh out of hibernation, having survived till then on meager sips of water and meat broth. Aunt Emma, God love her, was primed and ready with a bowl of soft-boiled eggs and crumbled bread, thin slices of fried ham, and coffee poured from a steaming pot. My stomach, never a stranger to anything that could be chewed and swallowed, shared my delight.

A pleased Aunt Emma observed, "I can swear to your uncle he needn't fear you'll be laid up till first frost. That man is a worrier, nephew. He thinks the future of his enterprises rests on your shoulders."

I ignored Aunt Emma's motherly concern that too much was being asked of me. I took considerable pride in Uncle Purse's belief and trust in me. From my deposit on his doorstep by Father's killers a week past my fourteenth birthday, I strove to make myself worthy of Uncle's support and care. No work was beneath me, whether that of the janitor, chambermaid, desk clerk, dining-hall potato peeler, stable hand, blacksmith, farrier, carpenter, or, in the last year, assistant bookkeeper. Whatever Uncle's combination hotel, public dining room, blacksmith forge, and public livery barn demanded of me, I provided, for a bountiful table, soft bed, and encouraging words are mighty scarce commodities for many of God's two-legged creatures.

Nor had I missed a weekly session with my hired tutor, Master Dominic Schofield. How could I? What other lad in Sedalia not born a lawyer's or merchant's son was privately schooled year round in the classics, mathematics, proper grammar, and history? To quote Sam Benson, Uncle's livery boss, I was the son the childless Purse and Emma Wainwright had surrendered any hope of having, and Uncle was determined to raise me proper without ever laying a belt or whip on me.

Aunt Emma spoke slowly, "I think you were too feverish to grasp what I said earlier. Sam and your uncle buried Shep in the far corner of the garden. Knowing how much you thought of that dog, Sam made a cross for the grave and painted his name on it. You best thank Sam first chance you have."

I calmly accepted her news regarding Shep's ultimate fate. I'd already shed sad tears over him in the dark of night, the sudden thud of his limp body atop my chest telling me he was gone from this earth.

Aunt Emma bit her lip and said, "I don't know how much you recall from being near shot to death, but U.S. Marshal Bannister is mighty anxious to talk at you. He has some crazy notion you might be able to identify the robber that killed Shep instead of you. I don't know how that could be true. Madge Wilson said he had a bandana tied across his face when he galloped past her. She claims all three robbers covered their faces. Madge might be Sedalia's chief gossip, but there's nothing wrong with her eyesight."

Madge Wilson's assertion aside, there was no mistaking what I'd seen. In all the excitement, Lance must have pulled down his bandana long enough for me to recognize him and then hid his face again as he made his escape. Somebody had witnessed him do so and that word had reached Marshal Bannister. Was I the only bystander who could identify any of the outlaws? Would I ever be free of Lance and his unbridled temper?

Aunt Emma's next words clarified how critical identifying the robbers was to Marshal Bannister, the last bastion of public law in the midst of the military and local civil war pitting soldier against soldier and neighbor against neighbor throughout the state of Missouri. "It isn't just the robbers making off with two thousand dollars that has the marshal riled up, it's their killing of Homer Spain, the clerk at Kellerman Mercantile. He wasn't even armed."

"When was Marshal Bannister here?"

"He's been by three times. Last time was yesterday afternoon.

You were sound asleep. I told him he could check back this morning, and if you were awake and not in too much pain, he could talk with you for a few minutes . . . no more. That's Dr. Gribble's standing orders for family and visitors."

I made no mention of what I could reveal to Marshal Bannister, and Aunt Emma, thankfully, didn't ask. Much as I disliked Lance, spreading the word he might be a murderer smelled of family betrayal, even when it concerned a bastard of a half brother. Marshal Bannister could break that news when he saw fit.

Aunt Emma left with her breakfast tray. The coffeepot was still warm when I heard voices in the hotel lobby. Measured footfalls preceded the sight of U.S. Marshal Forge Bannister's broad-shouldered, well-muscled body filling the doorway of my room. Bannister was dressed in black, as usual, and the pearl handle of the holstered revolver on his right hip protruded from beneath his suit coat. His tall boots were scuffed and worn down at the heel. However, his starched white shirt and collar, black string tie, ruddy features, neatly trimmed Vandyke beard and mustache, along with the deep tenor of his "Good morning, Owen," lent him the authoritative presence of a judge ascending the bench.

We weren't strangers. Forge Bannister stalled his bay gelding in our hotel livery whenever Federal business brought him to Pettis County from his office in Kansas City. The marshal preferred traveling on horseback to the bone-jarring ride of the Missouri Pacific Railroad's passenger cars. Rumor had it Bannister's half-blood Osage deputy he paid from his own pocket, John L. Whitefeather, actually dreaded mounting the smoking train. John L.'s seal-brown mare was, of course, also welcome to hotel oats, shoeing, and currying.

Whitefeather was two-thirds the size of his boss, but his fierce countenance, dark liquid eyes, and flintlock long rifle kept his fellow men, regardless of color, from teasing him about his mother having named him after John the Apostle in the Bible and adding a meaningless middle initial to give him as much of a white name as possible. I wondered what the fair-skinned lawman and half-blood man hunter discussed over nightly campfires other than the white, black, and red fugitives they were seeking.

I greeted my guest with a polite "Good morning, sir" and pointed at the plain wooden chair beside my bed. Marshal Bannister seated himself and perched his town hat, a black derby, on a knee. "How are the wounds healing?"

I was glad I knew Marshal Bannister well enough that I wasn't nervous around him. Had he been after me with an arrest warrant in hand, I would have been quaking. "Well enough. Dr. Gribble believes I'll make a complete recovery, sir."

"That's great news. I'd hate to lose a promising young man to complications after he's lucky enough to survive a close call with a bullet." From there, the Federal peace officer in Bannister came to the fore. "I'm interested in talking about your confrontation with the robber that shot your dog. Tell me exactly what you remember."

I saw no need to expose the youthful chivalry that had prompted me to bolt from the hotel. "I heard gunfire and rushed out to have a look-see, like everyone else. I caught a bullet alongside the head and landed on my rump in the street. Next thing, there was a horse towering over me and I was staring down the barrel of a pistol. Then the robber shot my dog and rode off."

Forge Bannister shifted his weight in the chair. Steel-gray eyes bored into me. "That pretty much matches what the other witnesses said, leastways those that weren't frightened half out of their wits. Now, allowing as how that blow to the head might have messed with your memory some, listen close and tell me if there's any smidgen of truth to what old Twig Logan claims he saw."

I once heard Sam Benson say that if Marshal Forge Bannister ever beat around the bush when it came to pursuing his official duties, it would be a damn short hike. He certainly hadn't raised much dust so far.

"Old Twig was headed for his morning breakfast at Stone's Café. He was on the far side of the hotel's front porch when all hell broke loose. He made himself as small as he could, but never looked away from the street. He says the robber pulled his red bandana down, called out to you, and leaned from the saddle so you could see his face, then said something to you after he shot your dog . . . something personal like. Is Twig embellishing things or telling the truth?"

Those eyes shone in the light pouring through the window above my bed. It was like being staked to the ground. Truth was, much as it surprised me at first, I feared Bannister's wrath if he learned later I had lied to him more than I did what grief Lance might heap on me if he learned I'd sicced the law on him. Maybe I had grown as much in smarts as I had in height and strength since moving under Uncle Purse's roof.

I swallowed to steady my voice and said, "Twig's telling it straight. That's what happened." I averted my eyes and confessed. "The robber that killed Shep was Lance Wainwright, my half brother."

A brief silence made a tomb of my room. "No need to be ashamed," Bannister finally said. "Lance isn't exactly a candidate for sainthood."

Lance's life after he had run off to escape Father's waspish tongue and the lash of his whip was a blank slate to me. Bannister's iron gaze seemed to have softened somewhat with my open support of Twig's testimony, and, goaded by curiosity, I summoned the courage to say, "Lance left our home place seven years ago. Has he been in trouble with the law before this robbery?"

"Never pursued him personally, but I heard of his doings from two prisoners hoping to escape the hanging noose. He's become a secesh bushwhacker. Those murdering bastards aren't hard to spot. At least two dozen witnesses, mostly family members of those they've shot, often as not in cold blood, have described them to me. They like to pin up one side of their hat brims with silver crescents decorated with either feathers or squirrel tails. They favor loose-fitting hunting shirts, with garlands of red and blue flowers embroidered across the front and around the cuffs, and knee-high boots sporting big Mexican spurs. They wear a pistol belt with two holstered revolvers, often carry two more revolvers thrust behind the belt or stashed in saddle holsters, and pack spare cylinders for their revolvers in the big pockets of their hunting shirts."

Bannister let me soak that much in, sucked air through his teeth, and continued, saying, "Lee Caswell, the gunsmith, was in the mercantile at the time of the robbery. He informed me the bushwhackers' handguns were Colt Navy revolvers. Missouri bushwhackers prefer rapid-fire weapons instead of a soldier's slower-loading long gun, and they've learned the Colt Navy is the most reliable and accurate pistol available. Hell's bells, I carry one myself. Does any of this general description fit your half brother?"

"The hat and shirt do. The only thing I remember about his revolver was the muzzle looked bigger than the mouth of a cannon. Everything happened so fast, the rest is a blur. I didn't recall the red bandana round Lance's neck till you mentioned it."

Bannister loosed a big sigh. "How well you got along with your half brother is a family issue, but killing an unarmed civilian during a robbery wearing civilian clothes won't be construed as an act of war by the Union Army. It's plain murder, and, unfortunately for him, Lance was also the sole robber who had flame-red hair like you. Once I report your firsthand identification of Lance to Judge Hiram Appleby in Kansas City, a warrant will be issued for his arrest. Whether we catch him now or after the war ends, he'll be hung."

Lance and I hadn't shared much in common besides family blood and the infamous red hair common to Wainwright males. His height exceeded six feet by three inches, while mine fell three inches short. Though my shoulders, chest, and arms weren't those of the "shitty, runty" ten-year-old lad he'd remembered, a lad yet to wield a hammer in the Wainwright Hotel blacksmithing shop, Lance still outsized me in mass and muscle. This made him a formidable foe in a physical confrontation. I was certain his confidence he could best me with fist or weapon of his choice at his whim had sparked his decision to scare me half to death rather than kill me when he had me helpless at the point of a gun. Same as Father, Lance bore hatred for those he deemed enemies with the passion of a sacred vow and wouldn't hesitate to destroy a blood relative responsible for a murder warrant bearing his name.

"Do you think you can catch him?"

Marshal Bannister stroked his bearded chin. "It won't be an easy chase. The bushwhackers he rides with roam at will. They claim they stand behind the Confederacy, avenging the killings of secesh sympathizers by Kansas Jayhawkers and Union militias. That's hogwash. Lance's crowd is no different than Bloody Bill Anderson's bunch. They kill and rob in the name of the South for personal gain. I suspect they murder blue coats and Lincoln lovers with equal joy. Bushwhackers travel lightning fast and they have sympathizers in every corner of Missouri that hide and feed them. That's what will make it hard to track down your half brother."

Bannister smiled and laughed softly. "But all the odds aren't on his side of the ledger. Mr. Kellerman has tendered a five-hundred-dollar reward to anyone providing information resulting in the arrest of the robber who murdered his store clerk, and the public will know who that man is, once the newspapers get wind of our warrant. We have more Union patrols than ever scouring the rough hill country that bushwhackers prefer for their camps, wearing down their horses and making it harder for their sympathizers to assist them. And Whitefeather tracks for me, thank God. Any word of Lance's whereabouts and he'll be on the scent. Old John L. knows how to use the telegraph, when it's working, and messages via train conductors, when it's not, to stay in touch with my office."

Marshal Bannister palmed his derby hat from his knee and stood. "I'll not tax you further. I don't need another reminder from the lady in charge how important your rest is, and I have important news for Mr. Kellerman regarding his reward money. You may have to identify Lance in a courtroom in the future, but we'll cross that bridge when we come to it. Thanks for your honesty, Owen. I find it quite admirable in these years of misplaced and misguided loyalties."

U.S. Marshal Forge Bannister's broad frame filled my doorway a second time and he was gone down the hallway. Much as I found the lawman's confidence regarding Lance's capture credible, it didn't come close to allaying my fear of my half brother. If Lance truly wanted my scalp, he would come for it alone, in the dark or in broad daylight when I least expected it. I had every intention of talking with my uncle yet that day. With me fast approaching the Union draft age of eighteen, he'd had Sam Benson teach me to shoot and it was high time I kept a loaded weapon handy.

The wrath and danger of Missouri's long, bloody guerilla war had barged within a step of the Wainwright threshold.

I fell into an exhausted sleep wondering how long we could keep it at bay.

# CHAPTER 2

My second visitor showed on the tenth day of my recovery. By then, I was using the outhouse with the help of Sam Benson as protection against a fall instead of the thunder jug under my bed. Aunt Emma was comfortable I was beyond blurting a cutting remark more genteel souls might not attribute to the blow on the head I'd suffered.

Without my bidding, Aunt Emma prepared for my second caller by dusting the exposed surfaces of my room with a damp cloth, having Sam Benson mop the floor, opening the windows to freshen the air, changing the bedclothes, dressing me in a laundered nightshirt, shaving me for the first time ever, and placing a vase of cut flowers on the book stand flanking my bed. I was certain less labor had been devoted to the mating of kings and queens in overseas kingdoms, but personal embarrassment was Aunt Emma's perpetual enemy.

The squeaky opening of the alley door at the rear of the hotel and a sharp rap on my bedroom door had me believing Sam Benson was returning from the livery for some unknown reason, as I was expecting my female guest to arrive via the lobby out front with Aunt Emma escorting her. The door opened before I could speak.

Not a trace of surprise showed on the face of Laura Kellerman. Her sparkling blue eyes surveyed my room with a swift roundabout gaze and settled on me, not noticing, I hoped, the blush warming my cheeks and neck. I cursed under my breath; so much for welcoming the first young female to visit my private quarters with more maturity than that of a ten-year-old.

She twirled the handle of her lavender parasol in her hands, smiled, and said a little breathlessly, "Good morning, Owen. You don't know how happy I am that you are well enough to see me. I sincerely feared for your life."

Lavender flowers dotted her white, high-collared, full-skirted dress. Her black hair was piled atop her head. She was a young female whose features—smooth forehead, prominent cheekbones, slightly aquiline nose, full-lipped mouth, white teeth, and firm chin—complemented each other with a perfection that gifted her with a startling beauty that made a man feel he was staring every time he looked at her.

Like you would expect from a male awed by her mere presence, my jaw locked. That wasn't the worst thing that could have happened to me, for in those seemingly long seconds of silence, I noticed her face shared a smidgen of my blush and her ample breasts were lifting and falling from what had to be nervous excitement on our part. She wasn't as calm and collected visiting me in blanket-covered bedclothes alone in my room as I'd first thought.

I started with what I was least likely to mumble. "Dr. Gribble believes I'll make a full recovery."

Wanting her to linger, I pointed to my guest chair. She nodded and seated herself. "Believe me, that's the only good news anyone has heard since the murder of poor Mr. Spain. We miss him terribly at the mercantile. He had no family here and never missed a day of work. He kept the inventory for the general store and my millinery shop. He taught me the hardware trade to keep me busy when female customers were scarce, which happens, since the ladies buy with the seasons. He made the freighters aware of me. He demanded they mind their manners with me about."

The Kellerman Mercantile was next door to the Buckhorn Brothers Warehouse that supplied freighting companies with bulk goods for the overland haul to the far Southwest and Santa Fe. I had observed bushy-bearded, hard-fatted bullwhackers in their wide-brimmed slouch hats shopping at Kellermans while they waited for their enormous six-yoke wagons to be loaded. The respect that rough lot showed Laura Kellerman was indeed quite extraordinary. Had she visited their campgrounds on Flat Creek, south of town, I had no doubt for the price of a sweet smile they would have knelt on a knee and offered her a mug of their habitual brew, a mixture of whiskey and New Orleans molasses, and a plate of their steady diet, bread and bacon.

Hesitation and shyness behind me, there were questions I wanted to ask her and I seized the opportunity. "Where were you when Mr. Spain was killed? Were you in the mercantile?"

"No, at the first shots, Mr. Parker grabbed hold of me and practically carried me into his butcher shop and guarded the door with a shotgun. He let me go to you, once the last robber was out of sight up the street. The side of your head was covered with blood."

Her lip trembled as she recalled what had to have been a shocking scene for her. "I was certain you were dead, till you moaned. Lucky for you, Dr. Gribble was in his office above Harmon's Grocery. He had you brought straight here to your room. Your aunt stopped me in the lobby. She promised she'd send word about you, and she did later that day, and every day since, God bless her."

I was impressed by her sincere interest in my condition. Maybe her feelings for me went deeper than I had dared imagine. I'd never had an opportunity to properly court her. I'd managed snatches of conversation with her while I shopped at Kellerman's for the hotel, saddling and unsaddling the riding horse her father stabled at the hotel livery, and on those occasions her widowed father treated her to dinner at the hotel dining room. Truth be known, given how little time I'd spent with her, and her being two years older, what she felt for me might be nothing more than brotherly love, if not mere affection, which I dreaded and refused to countenance.

Wanting to prolong her visit, I asked, "Exactly what happened inside the mercantile? Was your father with Mr. Spain when the robbers appeared?"

"Yes, he was in his office in the rear. Mr. Spain had just opened for the day. The bandits confronted Mr. Spain, and Father heard them demand he open the safe in the corner behind the counter. Mr. Spain must have hesitated, because they shot him. Just killed him like you'd stomp on a bug."

A tear ran from the corner of her eye and she wiped her cheek with the side of her hand. "Before Father had a chance to pull the revolver he hides in his desk, one of the robbers barged into his office, trained his gun on him, and warned if he didn't want to join the old geezer out front in the grave, he better open the safe. Father always says no amount of money is worth your life. He opened the safe and put all the money in the stolen mailbags they handed him. Marshal Bannister claims the robbers had to know in advance Father and Mr. Spain would likely be alone in the store at opening hour and where the safe was. He said killing Mr. Spain spurred Father to act quickly, and they were back in the saddle and gone before the men in town realized what was happening and armed themselves. He called the robbery slick, professional thievery."

I broached the subject I hated to introduce. "And it was my half brother that murdered Mr. Spain."

Her head dipped and she fiddled with the handle of her parasol. She looked up, her eyes misty, and said, "And that presents a problem we have to deal with."

"How's that?"

"Father is so angry and upset, he doesn't even want me speaking to you. I believe he worries you might carry the same bad blood as your half brother. I reminded him that you were the one that identified Lance, but that didn't seem to matter to him. I wouldn't be surprised if he moved my riding horse to a different stable. You have to understand how protective Father is of me. He has accounted for every minute of my time since Mother died while he was away on business. He claims my happiness is his paramount goal."

Her sincere concern about our possibly losing touch with one another offset her father's unfair judgment of me enough that I was able to keep my temper in check. I needed to avoid hot, rash words that would confirm Stuart Kellerman's sudden decision that Owen Wainwright's company was no longer in the best interest of his daughter.

"Is that why you came to the back door?"

"Yes, I told Father I was picking up a new bridle for Jasper at Walker's Harness Shop. I went around the block to make sure he wouldn't hear of my visiting the hotel. There are a lot of curious eyes and loose tongues in Sedalia."

I hated her having to sneak about, but it might prove nigh impossible for us to meet otherwise if her father moved her horse to a different stable, forbade her to wait on me at his mercantile, and ceased dining at the hotel with her.

She shot to her feet. "I best move along. I haven't picked up Jasper's bridle yet, and Father will get suspicious if I'm gone overly long."

Imagine my surprise when Laura Kellerman, the proper young lady, stepped to the side of my bed, leaned over, and kissed me flush on the mouth. It was the first time we'd ever touched each other. I mean, we'd never so much as shaken hands before.

I will confess to the following: the softness of her lips, the smell of her, the brush of her breast against my arm, and the length of her kiss convinced me in a flash that I wanted more of all of that, and sooner rather than later. She ignited a rapturous physical hunger that jarred every nerve in my body. My dreams had not been wild imaginings. The real thing was much better by a whopping margin.

Somehow in my stunned blissful state, I let her depart, in a rustle of her skirts, without saying good-bye, but the slight sniffle I heard as she closed the door to my room told me social amenities weren't foremost in her mind either.

My excitement flagged as my thoughts turned to her father again. Stuart Kellerman was now a major obstacle in any attempt to romance his daughter. He could readily point out that I was a young man with limited-to-no prospects. I resided with an uncle and aunt who allowed me to work for my room and board. I had no savings or any form of legitimate inheritance awaiting me. My personal property amounted to my clothes, boots, a few books, a pocketknife, and two fishing poles. I possessed a good mind, strong body, and willingness to undertake whatever task needed doing, but so did many other young males with more promising futures.

Looking down the road, had I the sense God gave rabbits, I had better jump at Master Schofield's offer to train me to read for the law. My hired tutor believed I had the brains and common sense required of a lawyer, and I wasn't afraid of book learning. He stressed that in any of the many towns he'd visited in his teaching career, if there was but one brick house, a learned man who practiced law owned it.

Vowing to discuss a legal career with Master Schofield on the morrow, I endured a restless night early on, the warmth of Laura Kellerman's kiss vying with anger over Lance's latest intrusion into my affairs. I finally slept after reminding myself that no man can predict whether the road the Lord has laid out for him will be smooth . . . or filled with ruts.

He could only pray he was up to the challenge.

And I did.

# CHAPTER 3

*I*N ANOTHER WEEK I WAS OUT AND ABOUT, SLOWLY RESUMING MY chores. I wore a cap to hide the stitches in my scalp till the hair grew back, a concession to male vanity I freely acknowledge. The number of people who insisted on expressing their condolences for my loss of Shep at the hands of a bushwhacking robber and murderer—without any mention of the guilty party's name—shocked and pleased me. The sympathizers did not include Stuart Kellerman on the one night he dined alone at the hotel. His bare "hello" was as frigid as a frozen lake frog's ass.

One of the two occasions on which I spent time in the presence of Laura Kellerman after her visit to my room occurred accidently during the temporary encampment of Colonel Nugent's Kansas Regiment on the rising ground just west of town. Nugent's Union officers and a group of local fun-seekers arranged for a civilian concert at the Kansas Regiment's campsite. Banding together, male townsmen devoid of pride created what they charitably dubbed the "concert troupe of trained birds and beasts." With each member impersonating a domestic animal or fowl, the "troupe" formed a line and performed an overture never before heard by a single watcher. I mean, the donkey brayed, the bull bellowed, the horse whickered, the pig squealed, the calf bawled, the goose honked, the hen clucked, the rooster crowed, the turkey gobbled, the duck quacked, the hound howled, and the peacock shrieked. The upshot was amateur mimicry that had tears of merriment streaming down nearly every cheek and the audience members' sides aching from laughter.

Uncle Purse and I arrived a few minutes late that evening and he boldly made a place for us among the spectators beside Laura Kellerman and her surprise-to-me escort, Captain Nathaniel Crockett. I knew of Captain Crockett. He was twenty-three years old, six feet tall in his riding boots, yellow-haired, pale-eyed, cleft-chinned, clean-shaven, damnably handsome, according to Aunt Emma's dining-room observations, and his father was perhaps the wealthiest farmer in southern Missouri. Crockett's father had played a major role in recruiting, outfitting, and arming his son's Sedalia-based company in the 40th Regiment, Enrolled Missouri Militia. In his tailored blue uniform and cloak, Crockett was quite a sight atop his black stallion whenever he traveled local streets.

My mind ran a singular course when Laura Kellerman introduced Captain Nathaniel Crockett of the EMM. Did I have a serious, older rival for her affection from a substantial family? If Captain Crockett knew me at all, I was the underage nephew of hotel owner Purse Wainwright. My guard went up against saying or doing anything that might pinpoint my youth and paint me a buffoon of no consequence. I needn't have worried. The "troupe of trained birds and beasts" held the attention of everyone present, and at the close of its performance, Nathaniel Crockett, Laura Kellerman, Uncle Purse, and I went our own ways in separate buggies after quick good nights. I went to bed with mixed, concerned feelings, but understood that, despite our kiss, Stuart Kellerman's daughter was freer than a wild bird.

Yet another week passed and then Captain Crockett called at the hotel for Laura Kellerman's riding horse. Sam Benson handled the saddling of her bay mare with three white stockings. I caught a glimpse of Captain Crockett leading the saddled mare up the side alley, exiting the rear door of the hotel. My face was still knotted in disappointment as I entered the livery barn, where I encountered Sam Benson. "Something wrong, young pup?"

Given my worried mood, I might have taken offense at such a casual inquiry reflecting my age, had the speaker not been Sam Benson. Grizzled of jowl, frosty white of hair and brow, cheekbones deep lined by harsh weather, and nose oft broken, Sam Benson, a month short of his sixtieth birthday, was like a second stepfather to me. His past—before Uncle Purse hired him upon the opening of the hotel and livery stable three years ago—was a vast mystery that fascinated a naive ex–farm boy. I'd managed to piece together via snippets of overheard conversation that bent-backed Sam Benson had been a soldier with Grandfather Silas Wainwright in the Mexican War, and achieved the rank of sergeant major with the United States Cavalry after that conflict. He tracked the killer of his wife from Missouri, clean across Texas to beyond the Rio Grande, and hung him with his own hands. I once spied a volume of Shakespeare's plays with a cracked leather cover on a night table in his livery stable quarters. I never mentioned that sighting, for fear he would think I'd been snooping where I didn't belong. I swear, there wasn't a question pertaining to horses, war, guns, and hunting hounds Sam Benson couldn't answer. I often felt the Lord had sent Sam Benson and Uncle Purse my way to fill an ignorant void as to what manhood was all about.

Mr. Benson's response when I didn't answer him was soft-toned. "Don't fret too much about that gal of yours. It ain't worth your time."

I halted in midstride. "What's that mean?" I shot back, my meaning pointed, but my tone matching his.

One corner of his mouth slanted upward in a crooked grin. "Like I said afore, some men aren't what they seem."

"Captain Nathaniel Crockett seems awfully cocksure of himself to me," I insisted.

"Crockett is a lily-livered officer with the morals of a bushwhacker."

That contention grabbed my attention whole hog and I waited for him to continue.

"Crockett craves the attention and the chance to kill that war affords the military officer. It's not the cause that excites him, but the glory. That Kellerman gal will discern his heart is hollow of her own accord. I suspect her father is pushing her to nab what he deems a great catch for her . . . and him."

I hoped someday I would have Sam Benson's talent for reading our fellow men. His intriguing assessment of Nathaniel Crockett brightened the morning by a heap. He set me to mucking out the stalls of the livery barn, and the horse apples had no chance against my flying pitchfork. I stayed out of sight when Captain Crockett returned the Kellerman mare, tossing the reins to Mr. Benson after hailing him from outside the barn door, and rode away with chin in the air and no semblance of a thank-you for services rendered. His behavior was testament to Mr. Benson's discerning wisdom, and it lent extra pounds of *whap* to my hammer during the afternoon's shaping of a metal tire for a freight wagon at the forge with Uncle Purse's smithy, Titus Culver, a giant-armed black man.

The mental hullabaloo I'd fostered in my head over the unattached affection of Laura Kellerman faded into background noise with the appearance during the dinner hour of Billy Bower, son of Philo Bower, station telegraph operator for the Missouri Pacific Railroad. Billy was clutching a sheet of folded white paper. Uncle Purse had arranged for Philo to inform him of messages he received or transmitted pertaining to the war within Missouri's boundaries. For news of the larger national conflict outside the state, mainly General Grant's siege of Petersburg, Uncle relied on St. Louis newspapers fetched by train. He also garnered both local and national military news courting whatever officer was currently commanding the regular Union forces assigned to garrison Sedalia, often in the company of former Union general George R. Smith, Sedalia's founder.

We were just finishing Uncle's favorite meal—pot-roasted beef, with boiled, skin-on smashed potatoes and drippings gravy—in a hotel dining room deserted except for family members. Uncle thanked Billy and, with wire-rimmed glasses glinting in whale oil lamplight, opened Philo's latest submission. His features sober and eyes somber, Uncle finished reading and turned to me. "Owen, would you please ask Sam Benson to join us. Emma, please bring me two squat glasses and a bottle of our best corn whiskey. We'll need a little libation digesting what Philo has kindly forwarded."

Uncle caught me half out of my chair. "Owen, you can stay and listen, once you return with Sam. You'll be old enough to soldier right soon."

* * *

Sam Benson sat in the chair next to me and accepted a glass of whiskey. "Has to be momentous news to warrant a parley at this late hour, Purse. Something to do with the war most likely."

Hand waving Philo's message, Uncle Purse chuckled and said, "Emma's right. You must hear the katydids before they hatch. Philo Bower confirmed General Sterling Price's invading Confederate Army couldn't dent the defenses of St. Louis, and the Rebels are now trekking to the west, intending to continue their raid into the center of the state. General Price has had his nose bloodied and he hopes large numbers of secesh-leaning Missourians will join his depleted forces. His troops will be seeking food and plunder, in addition to replacement soldiers, no matter which direction they march."

The prior word reaching Sedalia about General Sterling Price's last-ditch attempt to secure Missouri for the Confederacy had been sketchy, smelling of few facts and much exaggeration. "Does Philo have new information we can trust?" Sam Benson inquired between measured sips of his whiskey.

Uncle Purse nodded. "All regular Union troops manning our local fort are being withdrawn today. They're needed at Jefferson City to our east. The Federal high command is worried Price's advance will embolden straggling gangs of bushwhackers and other irregulars and they'll swoop down on unprotected towns with abandoned posts. General Rosecrans has asked Colonel Crawford of our Fortieth Regiment, Enrolled Missouri Militia, to raise a local force to defend Sedalia in their absence. I take that to mean every man, uniformed or not."

Sam Benson snorted. "Interesting that the Union boys have been hell-bent to protect their corral full of cattle and mules at the south edge of town and their supply depot at the railhead. Now they plan to bust off and foist their guard duty on what extra homebodies we can muster."

Uncle Purse swished whiskey in his mouth and drummed fingers on the table, calculating in his head. "Sam, I figure we can pull together six hundred men. You're the veteran soldier at the table. How would we stand then?"

A chronically gimpy knee from a barrel of salt rolling over his leg had kept Uncle Purse from wearing a military uniform and he deferred to veteran Sam Benson on military questions pertaining to strategy and tactics. "If we have enough time, we can throw up shallow barricades and maybe put up a pretty stiff fight against bushwhackers and the irregulars. It will depend on the number of men we recruit and what kind of weapons they have. We won't have cannons, and if Rebel forces with cannons show up, they will prevail in the end, lest Rosecrans somehow sends reinforcements in time, which is like betting a barn cat will whip a mountain lion."

It was then my tongue jumped off its leash. "I'll really get to see a Confederate Army?"

Sam Benson's crooked grin offset the frown I drew from Uncle Purse for interrupting adult conversation. "Any army on the march short of food and riding animals can't afford to pass over what Sedalia has to offer. There's not another corral within a hundred miles holding two thousand cows and mules."

Sam Benson's brown eyes softened. "Owen, maybe you'll have a chance to be a soldier other than dreaming about it. Like your uncle said, General Rosecrans's orders surely meant every male that can stand upright and fire a gun."

My tongue refused to obey me. "But I don't even own a gun."

Mr. Benson and Uncle Purse were fully aware I devoured the war news contained in the St. Louis newspapers, and both men knew how anxious I was to serve the Union cause under arms. To date, my age had provided a ready excuse for discouraging my enlistment in the Enrolled Missouri Militia, the state-mandated local home guard composed of all males eighteen to fifty, or a regular full-time uniformed Union military force, like the Seventh Cavalry, Missouri State Militia. The old excuse was about to lose its credence with my eighteenth birthday just a week away.

A sad expression gone in an instant flitted across Uncle's finely wrought countenance. Purse Wainwright was known for his forthrightness, his dislike for shallow thinking and any attempt to pull wool over his eyes. "Sam, it is time we rectified Owen's situation, and this evening is as good a time as any. Please follow through as we discussed while he was on the mend after we finish here."

Sam Benson's simple nod excited me to no end. I somehow kept from bouncing in my chair while Uncle Purse announced the three of us would attend Colonel Crawford's public meeting scheduled for noon tomorrow at the Missouri Pacific Railroad station.

"We'll learn Crawford's strategy for defending the town and what the public thinks of it, I'm sure. Now, go along, the two of you."

With a firm "Good night, and thank you, Purse," Sam Benson finished his whiskey and led me to his quarters in the livery barn. The single room's furnishings consisted of a canvas cot with wooden legs, a folding wall desk and stool, a three-drawer dresser, a night table with a whale oil lamp, a small cast-iron stove for heat, and wall pegs for clothing. In extremely cold weather, Aunt Emma assigned him a hotel room. He and blacksmith Titus Culver took their meals supplied by the hotel kitchen at a table in the forge in warm weather and at the kitchen table during winter months. Titus boarded uptown with his woman in one of the shanties adjoining the army's huge corral year-round.

He ignited a match with a flick of his thumbnail, lit the whale oil lamp, and set it atop the dresser. Without undue ceremony, he lifted a holstered revolver from a wall peg and presented the belt and weapon to me. "Buckle it around your waist. It's a thirty-six-caliber six-shot 1851 Colt Navy. It was brand-spanking-new and freshly stolen from the U.S. Cavalry the dawn I hung Felipe Russell, the half-breed Mex that murdered my wife. I figured Felipe had no need for a Colt Navy, burning in hell like he is."

I fastened the belt about my waist with the pistol's butt pointed forward on my left hip, as Sam Benson had with a different weapon during our target practice. I drew Felipe Russell's Colt Navy, and found it was lighter than I anticipated.

Noticing my raised brow, he explained, "It isn't loaded. I never store a loaded gun long-term."

He reached to a second wall peg for a leather bag equipped with shoulder straps. "I packed the bag with a powder flask, lead balls, a can of oil, wrench, reamer, and cleaning rags. You're armed and equipped like them bushwhackers. Might rile some folks' tender sentiments, but there's nothing wrong with aping the means of professional killers if you intend to take up their trade and kill them in turn. War tends to reward those that forget their manners and mind their business."

I appreciated Sam Benson not citing Lance by name as an example of those he declared "professional killers" or reminding me my half brother carried the same make of revolver. It was further proof that he thought of me as a friend, beyond my being the boss's son.

I must have thanked him a hundred times for his gift before he succeeded in shooing me off to bed. I remember how fondly I caressed Felipe Russell's Colt Navy half the night. I couldn't lay it aside. Silly or not, I daydreamed like a child, concocting imaginary military actions featuring blazing guns that won me the admiration of Union military authorities, the public press, and the lovely lass Laura Kellerman. I was acclaimed "the Savior of Sedalia" and adorned with medals that resembled hanging fruit on my chest, while a disgraced Captain Nathanial Crockett stood by with his uniform bare of ribbons, reduced in rank to that of a lowly horse holder.

When a crowing rooster awakened me the next morning, my new revolver was buried beneath me. The hammer wasn't cocked like before, and my finger was locked on a pulled trigger. Had it been loaded, I might have blown off body parts vital for romantic pursuits or done myself in for good.

It was a lesson sincerely learned.

In the future, it was sleep alone or only with a willing female.

# CHAPTER 4

THE MORNING I AWAKENED WITH SAM BENSON'S GIFT REVOLVER BEneath me, September 14, 1864, sticks in my mind like a date chiseled on a family gravestone, for it was the first day I was a soldier for real, carrying a real weapon. My chores that morning seemed to last forever and high noon was a magical hour beyond the clock's reach. Finally, before growing impatience had me shuffling my feet and rattling tools, Sam Benson called out, "Fetch your Navy. Time to saddle your horse."

Colonel Crawford's meeting announcement had asked potential soldiers to provide their own gun and horse. Given Uncle's gimpy knee and Sam Benson's bad back, the two of them decided to offer armed service to Colonel Crawford afoot. I would offer mounted service on Badboy, a seven-year-old hammer-headed roan in excellent riding shape and broken to gunfire, the animal beneath Sam Benson the afternoon he appeared on our doorstep seeking employment. The first time Mr. Benson helped me aboard Badboy, he assured me that the horse's name stemmed from misbehavior before he was castrated and broken to the saddle. The gelding's left hip bore the letters *WL*, the registered brand of the Wainwright Livery.

Feeling like a soldier before the fact excited me during our march to the Missouri Pacific station, adding to the usual thrill a new-to-the-city farm boy like me experienced whenever I was out and about in wartime Sedalia. From the town's founding through its first three years, the railroad, the Union military, and the freighting business ruled the roost. The fortuitous arrival of the first passenger train on January 17, 1861, coincided with the outbreak of the War of the Rebellion and stoked the fortunes of Sedalia by stalling the western advance of the Missouri Pacific for the conflict's duration. Sedalia became a Union military post manned monthly by hundreds of blue-clad soldiers from various cavalry and infantry regiments with their subsistence and equipment supplied by rail and their Federal pay pouring into the coffers of local merchants. The Union Army wasted no time building a huge corral and purchasing droves of cattle and ponies from as far away as the Indian Territory.

Being the western terminus of the Missouri Pacific made Sedalia the headquarters for the great Southwest wagon trade feeding Santa Fe and El Paso and the eastern headquarters of the Overland Stage Line. Main Street was filled day to day with covered wagons filled with goods. The prairie around the city was dotted with campfires and wagons of freighters, except in the winter months, with the greatest concentration favoring the fords and large pools on Salt Creek to the south of town. Over a hotel dinner one evening, Mr. Kellerman had pointed out that a thorough appreciation of the scope of the freighting business, and its critical importance to Sedalia, accounted for the wagon trains that traveled there. These convoys came from south and southwest Missouri, southeastern Kansas, Arkansas, the Indian Territory, and even Texas, carrying hides, pelts, and furs to be exchanged for supplies or shipped to the East. Mr. Kellerman's astute observation led Uncle Purse to comment later, "Stuart has a keen hound's nose for dollars."

For a young man my age, the lure of Sedalia's surrounding countryside augmented the throbbing excitement of the town's activities. Stretches of the Pearl River beyond city limits abounded with fish. The Big Muddy stream three miles to the north, Flat Creek two miles and a half south, and Brushy Creek two miles and a half west offered both fishing holes and expanses of woods for hunting. Sam Benson and I were familiar with the best wild spots to ply bait and bullet in Pettis County, and our take of gilled and furred animals had graced the menu of the Wainwright Hotel dining room on many occasions.

Our march to the depot took us down Main Street through the heart of Sedalia. The newly built town didn't warm Aunt Emma's heart. To a thirty-year resident of Lexington, Kentucky, with its elegant brick homes and public buildings and cobblestoned boulevards, Sedalia mere step beyond a howling wilderness. Weather had worn every surface of Sedalia's wooden cottages, warehouses, and businesses a dull gray, a clear warning to Aunt Emma that Sedalia's population of 1,000 souls resided in a raw town one big fire from being scorched earth. She often voiced the opinion that the initial trainload of bricks unloaded at the Missouri Pacific yards would be the first sign Sedalia had hope of being more than a railroad boomtown. A second would be the elimination of the small, hand-forged shovel we supplied at the front and rear doors of the hotel for guests and family members to clean mud from their footgear before entering the premises.

I couldn't complain about the weather on my first day of soldiering. A late-summer sun brightened a clear sky and a slight breeze dried sweat on my skin. I must admit Uncle Purse and Sam Benson were an oddity that drew curious stares from more mobile citizens, since they rode to Colonel Crawford's public meeting in the livery buggy. They had explained before departing the hotel that, given their age and limitations, their potential military value amounted to manning a defensive line, not traipsing across country after the enemy. Mr. Benson joked they would most assuredly be the first prisoners taken if the enemy prevailed.

Colonel Crawford's summons drew a crowd in the hundreds to the Missouri Pacific station. Every man present sensed a new chapter of the war was about to unfold for us. From the outset of the conflict, Federal military regiments and locally recruited militia companies loyal to the Union had garrisoned Sedalia, protecting the town against organized assaults. The removal of Federal soldiers exposed a much-weakened town to an attack by General Price's invading Confederate force of twelve thousand men, a far deadlier threat than that posed in the past by mounted bands of bushwhackers and guerillas riding under black flags.

From atop Badboy, I saw veteran militiamen in blue uniform and male citizens in everyday garb to be present in roughly equal numbers. I had no trouble identifying a cluster of uniformed soldiers gathered on horseback at the western edge of the platform. They were B Company of the Enrolled Missouri Militia, the mounted unit financed by ardent Unionist Mr. Clay Crockett. Nathaniel Crockett, his son, sat before B Company on his black stallion. Taken together, was I to hazard a guess, Colonel Crawford's summons had drawn roughly six hundred men, the number predicted by Uncle Purse.

John D. Crawford was already a local legend. Just twenty-six years of age, he was commissioned as colonel of the 40th Regiment, Enrolled Missouri Militia, the previous June. The promotion carried with it command of the Federal post at Sedalia, which made him the most powerful person in town, since the whole state of Missouri had been under martial law administered by the Union Army for three solid years. Spare of build, ginger of beard and mustache, blue eyes snapping with excitement, baritone voice carrying to the outer fringes of his assembled listeners, Crawford, blue uniform bearing a minimum of gold braid, held sway from the center of the depot's platform. He scanned the crowd front to back, left to right, as he spoke.

"Time is critical to the preparation of our defenses. We must construct redoubts, where appropriate, and assign men to them according to their arms. Smaller units must fortify various points throughout the town to protect the civilian population. We need mobile units to scout beyond the city limits and provide us proper warning of the approaching enemy. Every single man of you is critical to our cause when the need for you arises. Under no circumstances can we count upon the Confederates bypassing our town. We must be vigilant day and night."

Young Colonel Crawford made a mighty hefty impression on men willing to bear arms for the Union, regardless of their age, though some weren't entirely sold on the idea. A loud question reflecting the concern of its wavering owner interrupted his presentation. "What about guns and ammunition? Will you supply those who came empty-handed?"

Colonel Crawford upheld his reputation for absolute honesty with a quick response. "We must make do with the arms and ammunition in our possession. Men without weapons will help with the digging and construction of the redoubts and stand by as fillers on the firing line for those killed or wounded."

The last fetched a knowing chuckle from Sam Benson. "Every bullet counts when the fighting gets the thickest."

Colonel Crawford moved ahead, out pacing more questions. "Any man with a horse and a weapon will report to Captain Crockett on my right. Those with weapons will report to Captain Larson to my front. Those without weapons will report to Lieutenant Atherton on my left. All others are dismissed."

As I went forward to report as ordered, I passed through a large number of local citizens departing in the opposite direction. I heard them say they were declining military duty because they were worried enough guns and ammunition weren't available to arm them effectively. The ease with which they chose to turn their backs on the responsibility Uncle Purse claimed townsmen shared—to assist with the defense of their families and their property—would have embarrassed me to the quick.

I hadn't anticipated a situation where I would be in the charge of Captain Nathaniel Crockett. Four other dismounted riders had already formed a line abreast facing him. I dismounted and filled in at the end of the line with Badboy.

Captain Crockett sat mute on his stallion till it was apparent no additional armed and mounted recruits were to be had. He then worked his way down the line afoot, asking our names and examining our horses and weapons. When he came to me, he said, "Owen Wainwright, correct?"

At my nod, he stroked Badboy's neck. "Not the handsomest of horses," Crockett proclaimed. "Is he sound of leg and bottom?"

"Yes, sir, he can stay up with the pretty boys long as they want to run," I said, glad Crockett hadn't asked me Badboy's name, as he had the others.

"That's an old-style U.S. military saddle he's wearing. You're too young to have served in the Union Cavalry. Does it belong to a relative?"

"No, sir, to Mr. Benson, the livery man at the Wainwright stable."

Crockett snorted, said, "Interesting. I had no clue that broken-down old codger was ever a cavalryman." He then straightened his shoulders and declared, "See that you don't bring disgrace to it."

His ignorant, unnecessary insult of Sam Benson lit my fuse, but I swallowed hard, buying time to avoid an unwise retort. Temper checked, I responded with a respectful "I won't, sir."

An obviously impatient Crockett said, "Revolver, please."

I tugged the Russell Colt Navy from its holster, rolled it forward on my trigger finger, flipped it in my hand, and presented it to him butt first, a maneuver Sam Benson had shown me.

Crockett's brow lifted in surprise. He said nothing, however, till he'd inspected the revolver, spinning the empty cylinder and checking the barrel. "This weapon is clean and in excellent shape. Shows hardly any sign of wear. Do you always carry it butt forward on your left hip?"

I risked venturing on shaky ground by responding, "That's how Mr. Benson prefers to carry a belt gun on the ground and on horseback."

Crockett's grimace was fleeting, but noticeable. "Since we're not undertaking any formal training on such short notice, I'll permit that kind of carry for now. Hear me, *for now.*"

Crockett returned the Russell Colt Navy to me and mounted his stallion. He had wanted to correct how I was carrying my weapon by ordering me to switch it to the proper U.S. Cavalry position on my right hip, which Sam Benson had rejected earlier in private. But he'd hesitated, a strange twist when he possessed the authority of a god by militia law. Had Laura Kellerman's father, or Laura herself, said something that painted me as a rival and Crockett didn't want to risk publicly ruffling my feathers and possibly hurt his chances with her? Of one thing I was certain, Captain Nathaniel Crockett had the makings of what Aunt Emma called "a horse's ass," a man too concerned with himself to be trusted.

We five recruits were anxiously wondering what would come next in our budding military careers. Captain Crockett didn't disappoint us. He looked us over a final time and said, "We're establishing a camp east of town, out on Washington Avenue. 'Reveille' is seven a.m. Lieutenant Kendrick will place you on the company roster at that time and issue further orders. Be late at your peril. Password is grindstone."

Lifting his reins, Crockett turned the black stallion, shouted,

"Troop, left by twos . . . March," then led the column off, a rigid statue in the saddle, eyes straight ahead.

The recruit next to me, whose name was Joey Barnes, clucked his tongue and quipped, "Captain Crockett reminds me of a picture of Napoleon I seen. Serious as he is about soldiering, let's pray he ain't full of hot air."

Sam Benson made sure the long, boring afternoon and evening I feared passed swiftly. He taught me to salute properly, showed me how to take the Russell Colt Navy apart for cleaning and oiling, made me practice replacing the revolver's cylinder without a wasted moment for situations when rapid fire was ordered. He lectured me how the horse was a cavalryman's most important tool and must receive proper care in camp and in the field before all other duties. He cited Shakespeare's tale of how the loss of a horseshoe nail caused the defeat of a great kingdom's army. I hid my surprise at the mere mention of Shakespeare's name, something Mr. Benson had never done before. True friends respect their friend's privacy.

Aunt Emma called me to breakfast at 4:45 a.m., and Joey Barnes, Hank Little, Joshua Best, and Liam Northcut drew rein in front of the livery barn a half hour later, at five-fifteen. We had agreed it was best if we recruits arrived at the B Company campsite together. Despite our excitement, we laughed that none of us had forgotten Captain Crockett's password.

The night's full moon was down and dawn a growing band of white along the eastern horizon at the intersection of Ohio Avenue and South Main Street. Not a soul was in sight. The only sounds were the clopping of our horses' hoofs. Our passage roused but one dog that barked twice and went back to sleep. We rode South Main across Lamine and Massachusetts Avenues and turned north on Washington Avenue.

The rat-a-tat of shod hoofs on the wooden planks of the bridge spanning the deep cut of the Missouri Pacific roadbed echoed like gunshots in the silence. A mile beyond the railroad, B Company's white-canopied supply wagon stood out in the full flush of dawn light among the tall brown grasses of the open prairie surrounding the whole of Sedalia. We angled to the northeast in that direction, alert for the challenge of sentries.

"Halt and be recognized!"

The command hung in the air. Three bodies rose from the ground. Rifle barrels leveled at shoulder height and the same bass voice boomed, "Password?"

The five of us chimed together, "Grindstone."

The corporal in charge of the sentries stepped forward. "You greenhorns are mighty welcome. Starkey, take them to the sergeant. These boys are too valuable to chance anything happening to them."

That statement had me exchanging frowns with Joey Barnes. Exactly what made five inexperienced cavalrymen so valuable beyond a slight increase in numbers and weapons? I'd counted forty-seven riders, including Captain Crockett, as B Company departed the MP station at noon yesterday. Maybe there were dull, dirty, tiresome duties the veterans were looking for a chance to foist on newcomers? Or was a horse-holding assignment, while the veterans did the fighting, to be our introduction to B Company?

The sentries were standing guard afoot. Nonetheless, Starkey marched at a brisk pace and the distance to our destination shrank rapidly. Flames flared and leaped skyward in different locations. Company cooks were at their task. Shadowy soldiers idled between two double rows of picketed horses. Starkey led us straight to the supply wagon, smack in the center of the horse rows, and motioned for us to dismount.

I attributed the smile on the unshaven, pug-nosed, square-chinned officer of my height who answered when Starkey called out, "Sergeant Butler, recruits on board," to our having arrived before the blowing of "Reveille." The first words from the responder's bulldog pipes didn't disappoint me.

"Damn good thing they're here early. The Lord can't afford to be late in this outfit." A clearing of Sergeant Butler's throat and a sideways spit preceded his orders: "Secure their horses, Starkey. We don't need a spooked horse on the loose during breakfast."

Starkey collected our reins, and Butler peered over his shoulder and yelled, "Lieutenant Kendrick, our recruits have arrived!"

A bugler blew "Reveille" as an officer, with tawny hair and mustache, kind brown eyes, narrow shoulders, slim hips, and the bowed legs common to a true horseman, rounded the front corner of the supply wagon and stepped forth, holding a bound ledger in dainty-appearing hands. Lieutenant Kendrick halted, tilted his head to catch the soaring notes of the bugle, came to attention, and saluted. Sergeant Butler matched Kendrick's formal recognition of the day's start, and at my urging nod, my fellow recruits and I did likewise.

Lieutenant Kendrick then administered an oath of allegiance to the state of Missouri and the Union and added our names to the B Company muster roll. "Gentlemen, you are now officially members of the Fortieth Regiment, Enrolled Missouri Militia, subject to the orders of its officers and bound by the duties assigned to you. Be aware, any breach of those orders and duties will not go unpunished."

Satisfied his point regarding discipline had registered with us, Kendrick asked Sergeant Butler, "How can we outfit these gentlemen?"

Butler lowered the tailgate of the supply wagon and laid out a selection of blue shell jackets and forage caps of the same color. "I figured shirts and hats for now, Lieutenant, pants and boots later, given our low supply. Step up, privates, and make your pick."

I didn't miss the bullet hole in the chest of the plain shell jacket that fit me best. Apparently, frugality wasn't a stranger to the $40^{th}$ Regiment's supplier, be it Clayton Crockett, the state of Missouri, or the Federal government.

Once we were more properly uniformed, Lieutenant Kendrick inspected us back and front while we stood at attention and said, "Weapons, Sergeant?"

My four companions were farm boys by their sackcloth coats, cotton trousers, and brogan shoes, armed with three dull metal shotguns and a flintlock rifle. All had powder horns looped over a shoulder. None carried a shot bag, meaning what minimal number of balls, nipples, and patches they toted were stuffed in their pants pockets. The most modern gun we carried was my 1851 Russell Colt Navy.

"None to be had, Lieutenant, not since the bushwhackers robbed the train carrying the last shipment of revolvers, carbines, and ammunition Colonel Crawford ordered out of Mr. Crockett's purse. These lads must make do with their long guns, Private Wainwright's pistol, and what ammunition they have till the lost shipment is replaced."

A knot of doubt and fear tightened my gut string. The civilian volunteers answering Colonel Crawford's summons at the MP depot had paraded a motley array of firearms with a limited supply of ammunition, the same as my companions and me. And though I had some confidence in my ability to hit what I was aiming at, thanks to Sam Benson's training, how accurately did any of Colonel Crawford's hastily assembled civilian force shoot? Indeed, like me, how many of Sedalia's defenders, beyond the veterans of Crawford's 40th Regiment, had ever shot at a fellow human being?

Right then, Sam Benson's axiom for iffy military situations came to mind. Sam and Uncle Purse were enjoying a late-evening glass of whiskey at the kitchen table one night, talking loud enough for me to overhear them from my bedroom. Uncle Purse's "Surrounded by a slew of Mexican guerillas, and low on ammunition, sounds pretty desperate to me" had prompted Sam Benson to respond, "No matter how great the odds against you, you ply the sword the best you can, praying the Lord has chosen to side with you and not the enemy that particular day. Grit and prayer have spared many a trooper."

The question looming over Sedalia that September was apparent to every adult citizen drawing breath: Would our makeshift home guard and single regiment of veteran militia numbering in mere hundreds have enough grit and answered prayers to withstand an army of thousands?

B Company and the other units of the 40th Regiment, EMM, were about to be made aware that our officers, led by Colonel Crawford, were serious when it came to not being caught off guard and unprepared by General Price's Confederate Army. This meant we newcomers were soon to learn there was a heap more to being a cavalryman than mounting a four-legged animal and the glory of fighting from the saddle.

# CHAPTER 5

THE START OF MY FIRST DAY IN THE MOUNTED MILITIA FOLLOWED SAM Benson's depiction. After the calling of the roll and the standard "Stables" call for the feeding of our horses, B Troop settled around four fires for breakfast. Having already eaten, I passed on the army fare offered me, but Joey Barnes, Hank Little, Joshua Best, and Liam Northcut had gone hungry, except for a few wedges of corn bread for their evening meal, and slept overnight on bare ground without blankets at the edge of town. The four farm sons ate their share of bread and bacon, both fried in a pan, washed down with scalding-hot black coffee laced with sugar. I did partake of the coffee and a carelessly large first sip gave me a burned lip I regretted. My new messmates enjoyed a hearty chuckle at my expense.

The morning meal was followed by the water call. We led our horses by squads to the nearest source of water, a fair stream running parallel to our camp, and let them tank up. At that point, we recruits were primed for drill and target practice. It was then our day veered from the ordinary.

Sergeant Butler formed his mounted First Platoon and its five new members to hear an address by Captain Crockett from his stallion. "The construction of trenching around Sedalia to help thwart the attack of the Confederates is scheduled to begin this morning. B Company will assist with that construction by platoon in four-hour shifts each day, beginning with the First Platoon."

Crockett ignored the groans of Butler's veterans, though his tone conveyed his own displeasure with Crawford's decision. "The

Second Platoon will patrol the surrounding country in small details in the meantime. Colonel Crawford believes no soldier of the Fortieth Regiment should be spared the shovel and the pickax because he serves on horseback. Lieutenant Kendrick, the platoon is yours."

At least we weren't made to walk to what Sergeant Butler deemed "the devil's work every soldier comes to love, once the shooting starts." Expressions are revealing and I can tell you that digging and shoveling under a blazing September sun resulted in numerous locked jaws to mute the endless swearing officers loathe. We toiled bare-chested and sluiced off with buckets of water from town wells or washed in the stream above our campsite. Gradually, over a period of twelve monotonous morning and afternoon shifts, the eastern portion of the defensive works, three city blocks long, was staked out by Colonel Crawford. North of the Missouri Pacific Railroad track, it arose like the leavings of a burrowing worm. Elongated six-foot-deep pits were backed by a six-foot-high embankment, built by one hundred shovels, compliments of Kellerman Mercantile and Federal military warehouses, working simultaneously. We then topped the embankment of each rifle pit with two layers of railroad ties separated by wooden blocks to create a safe firing port for its defenders. The finishing touch for our defensive line was a small earthen fort near Washington Avenue with a flagstaff at its center flying the Union flag.

The carping and moaning and sweating we'd done with each shovel of dirt shamed us when news of the September 27 massacre at Centralia, Missouri, ninety miles to the northeast of Sedalia, reached us. It arrived piecemeal by wire and military courier across three days, a tale of blood loss and death Colonel Crawford shared with us in great detail, I'm certain, to harden our resolve.

William "Bloody Bill" Anderson and eighty of his men, some dressed in stolen Union Army uniforms, had swept in on a defenseless town half our size to cut the Northern Missouri Railroad. They initiated a brief reign of terror by brazenly robbing and plundering Centralia's citizens and businesses and consuming large quantities of that warm friend alcohol from vessels ranging from bar glasses to new boots. Anderson's men had enough wits remaining to block the railroad.

A plume of smoke to the east announced the pending arrival of the 11:35 train from Mexico, Missouri. Anderson's men lined the platform at Centralia's big new station in eager anticipation. The Northern Missouri engineer realized too late he had mistaken the disguised bushwhackers for friendly troops, and his train was quickly swarmed by pistol-wielding enemies. Delighted guerillas robbed 125 passengers of money, watches, and anything they thought valuable.

The joyful, drunken mood of Anderson's men soured with the discovery that one of the train cars held twenty-four Union soldiers on leave after the Battle of Atlanta, bound for homes farther west in Missouri and Kansas. Screaming their desire to avenge six of their kind the Union Army had taken prisoner, shot, mutilated, and scalped weeks before, the guerillas segregated the blue-coated soldiers on the opposite side of the train from the fleeced passengers. There, the captives were ordered to strip off their uniforms and summarily shot, mutilated, and scalped. In a final expression of hate and vengeance seeking, the train was set afire and sent running down the tracks toward Sturgeon, Missouri, and the last departing raiders torched the Northern Missouri station.

The murder of twenty-four of our unarmed Union boys was a bitter pill to swallow, but the absence of any means of resistance on the part of the Centralia victims lessened the dose at first. We would have organized lines and earthworks and present a united front. That spasm of optimism and hope was nearly extinguished by what transpired that same September 27 afternoon outside of Centralia. At midafternoon, Major A.V.E. Johnston led 146 men of the newly recruited 39th Missouri Infantry into Centralia. Townsmen warned Johnston that Anderson's bushwhackers numbered at least eighty well-armed men. The determined Union major decided to pursue the killers. Once beyond Centralia, the advance guard of the 39th Missouri spotted a band of ten guerillas up ahead. They retreated southward. The advance guard pursued, with Major Johnston and the main body of the mounted 39th Missouri following at a brisk walk. Two miles farther along, the guerilla band swung to the east and disappeared over a ridge.

From the crest of the ridge, an open plain stretched for a quarter mile to a wide belt of trees bordering Young's Creek. Rows of mounted bushwhackers emerged from the trees at a slow walk. To the puzzlement of Johnston and his officers, Anderson's men halted their horses a few strides into the open and dismounted. The eighty-odd guerillas, by Johnston's count, removed their stolen Union jackets, checked weapons and saddle girths, remounted their horses, and reformed their multiple lines into a single rank. Per Colonel Crawford's personal report to our ranks at our Sedalia campsite, they were obviously intending to mount a charge.

Colonel Crawford's voice cracked slightly with excitement as he related how Major Johnston, per an action report from a surviving member of the advance guard, then ordered his ninety-odd troops to dismount and deploy in a double row roughly 150 yards long with fixed bayonets. The motionless opposing forces stared at each other while a single rider clothed in black rode along behind the bushwhacker line. The survivor claimed the rider in black had to be Bloody Bill Anderson himself. The rider came to the front, raised and lowered his hat three separate times, and started his followers forward at a slow walk. At the same time, a second line of raiders, twice the size of the first, emerged from the woods, and still more of them popped from the brush-choked ravines on both Union flanks. The walking of the raiders' horses exploded into a gallop at the verbal scream of "Charge" by its point rider.

The advanced guard survivor was knocked from his feet by the shoulder of a raider's horse and thrown into a clump of brush. Weapon lost to him, he hid there for the balance of the Battle of Centralia, witnessing how slow volleys of single-shot Enfield rifles with their .577-caliber slugs, which ripped guts to pieces and shattered arm and leg bones to where amputation was mandatory, were no match for bushwhackers with a rapid-fire Colt Navy in either hand. The raiders' lethal charge overwhelmed the double line of the 39th and the horses and thirty horse holders behind it, at a cost to the Union of at least 126 men killed in action, among them Major Johnston.

We listeners had no way of knowing how much to that point Colonel Crawford had embellished the survivor's tale. He left to our imagination how the bushwhackers surely abused those that initially survived the raider assault and the corpses of our dead.

It was a wise choice. The silence of his audience and the soft curses that accompanied his soft-spoken portrayal of the disastrous execution of the Centralia captives and the annihilation of the 39th Missouri had to assure Crawford he had scared the bejesus out of us. He had us questioning, could we stand firm with a thousand pounding hoofs and banging revolvers galloping toward our earthen line? Much more detail about the rout at Centralia might have sent the least experienced among us running for home and a locked door.

Fearsome images of the Centralia debacle lingered in our heads and kept us sharp-eyed and keen of ear on our daily patrols. The slightest sign of movement or a solid shape that didn't seem to belong to the sweeping grassland of the prairie and the tall trees of the woods beyond it drew minute attention till we determined if what we were seeing was a danger to us. Had I been less alert the following week, I would have been at the worst a captive of the very enemy we feared.

Joey Barnes, veteran trooper Theo Corson, and I were dispatched on a scout to the north toward the Big Muddy under the command of Sergeant Butler. We saw nothing untoward through a sunny morning devoid of wind. Just past noon, we rounded a wooded hill that shouldered against the narrow road we were riding. Soon as we were well past the protruding point of land, to where the woods shielded it from our view, Sergeant Butler angled his bay gelding into the trees on that side of the road and stepped down in a clearing large enough to hold our horses.

"Dismount and check your weapons. I want them loaded, but not cocked. I caught winks of light near the middle of that hill back yonder. I'm certain it was sunlight bouncing off metal, most likely a rifle barrel. An enemy spy might have information useful to Colonel Crawford. We're going to chance he's alone. Barnes, your cousin says you move quiet enough to hunt deer in the open. You and I will circle uphill and get behind him. Corson, you have your pocket watch. Give us fifteen minutes. Then you and Wainwright sneak back up the road and take a position in the trees where the bottom of the hill is closest to the road. If we spook him, he'll head downhill. Keep in mind, he's more valuable alive, but not worth getting one of us killed."

Private Theo Corson pulled a stem-winding watch from his

jacket pocket and squatted by his horse. I did likewise. Sergeant Butler and Joey Barnes tree-tied their horses and moved off. Corson's aged, bearded face was bland, dark eyes steady, body slack and relaxed. After three years of service in B Company, he appeared calm enough to be hunting a four-legged creature that couldn't shoot back. His confidence settled my jittery nerves.

I swear the minutes flew by. Corson rose to his feet and pocketed his watch. He was armed with a Colt Navy, same as me. "Keep a solid hold on that pistol and be ready. Don't spook and plug a tree. He comes our way, then we give him a chance to surrender if we can. He puts up a fight, remember what happened at Centralia. I'm not in the mood to dig your grave or occupy one my own self."

We tree-tied our horses and my first manhunt started. Within a few yards, it was apparent Corson was at home in the woods. I'd never had the pleasure of hunting with Joey Barnes, but Corson matched my half brother Lance's knack for slipping through brush and ground cover with the least disturbance. His footfalls were those of a ghost, and he mapped the clearest path in his head on the move. I was quiet enough traipsing on his heels to avoid the cold, over-the-shoulder stares I'd drawn from Lance the few times he'd let me accompany him to help pack home the game he killed, since he never trusted me with a gun.

Corson's raised hand signaled a halt. He touched a tree in front of me with his free hand, leaned toward me, and whispered in my ear, "Keep cover behind this oak and keep a lookout uphill. I'll be over to your left about twenty yards or so. If he hears Sarge or Barnes, he'll think the danger is behind him and we may be able to take him by surprise. Just remember, I'm on your left—and don't forget, it's him or us."

Next thing, I was by myself fighting the urge to hug that oak tree with both arms. In the absolute quiet after Corson left me, my breathing sounded louder than a raging tornado. I shrugged off that silly notion, blinked my eyes to clear them, and studied the hillside to the outer limit of my vision through the trees.

I stayed motionless on one knee long enough that the muscles behind my leg began to cramp. About the moment I began wondering if we weren't hunting a phantom, a rustling of brush off to my right made enough noise to register with my ears. I waited, jaw hung open to better my hearing, Russell Colt Navy aimed in that direction.

Nothing. A full minute passed. Nothing.

The old Wainwright family curse of abject, unexplainable stubbornness gripped me. With not a whisper of breeze stirring the air, I was certain I'd heard something foreign to my surroundings. I had to have a closer look. Nothing else would satisfy me. Corson had not ordered me to hold fast, no matter what happened. What if I stayed put and the spy escaped our trap?

Before I could entertain any second thoughts, I came upright in a crouch. Left hand bracing a now-cocked revolver in the grip of my right hand at the end of extended arms, I carefully placed each step on the mossy loam beneath my boots. A wall of brush rose between widely spaced trees, where sunlight touched the ground. I stood still, listening hard again.

Frustrated and feeling like the fool who imagined something that didn't exist, I parted leafy branches with my left hand, lowered my head, pushed through the obstructing bushes, and found myself looking down the barrel of a shotgun pointing up at me from the ground. Though it was too late, my arm instinctively trained the cocked Russell Colt Navy on the shotgun's owner with all possible speed. I winced, anticipating the blast that would tear off half my stupid head.

The menacing shotgun did not fire. The owner's hesitation, in turn, froze my trigger finger an ounce short of the pressure needed to fire my weapon. Like two forest creatures poised to strike, we stared at each other, panting hard. The tanned skin of the face hovering over the stock of the shotgun was as blemish free as that of Laura Kellerman and too baby smooth to sprout whiskers. Cobalt blue eyes neither wavered nor blinked. Wisps of black hair peeked from beneath the red bandana wrapping the shotgun owner's head. His body appeared lost in his loose-fitting shirt with huge front and side pockets. Far as I could tell, I was confronting a twelve- or thirteen-year-old male, not a grown man.

The unmistakable bulldog voice of Sergeant Frank Butler roared from the hillside above us, interrupting our standoff. "Freeze . . . or you're a dead man!" A second or two later, Butler's voice called with much glee, "We've got him, Corson! Meet us at the horses."

We had the prisoner we wanted—probably a soldier much older than my adversary, and more knowledgeable regarding the location and distribution of General Price's Confederate Army. I saw no reason for me to lose my life trying to corral a second prisoner of questionable value.

I slowly raised my open-palmed left hand. "I'm going to lower the hammer of my revolver and back away. No point in our killing each other. They'll never know you were here. Understood?"

I was pleased the shotgun owner took me at my word and nodded without hesitation. He wasn't ready to die today either. What I didn't need right then was for Theo Corson to come searching for me. I backed through the screening bushes, turned, and yelled, "Mr. Corson, I'll meet you in the road!"

I sighed loudly when Corson responded, "Fine with me."

It was disappointing that I didn't dare share with my comrades the details of surviving my first brow-to-brow meeting with an armed enemy. First off, I hadn't exactly conducted myself in the disciplined manner bespeaking the maturity and common sense expected of a soldier, and could easily have been killed. Secondly, though he was armed, my bunkmates would rag on me without mercy for backing away from a mere child. Thirdly, I wasn't sure how our company commander might react to my not attempting to talk an enemy into surrendering, not when I had the support of my fellow scouts available. Sealed lips, dear reader, are the best defense for soldiers guilty of questionable conduct out of the sight of their superior officers.

I fell asleep that night thinking war was so cold and impersonal I would never know the name of the boyish owner of that big-bored shotgun.

In another time, he might have made a good friend.

"Wainwright, Captain Crockett wants to speak with you."

Caught by surprise, I glanced at my messmates seated around our evening fire. "Do you know what about, Sarge?"

"No, but you better put the shag on. He sounded downright impatient to complete his business for today. Leave your sidearm behind, nothing needs shooting in the captain's tent."

Joey Barnes's quip that Captain Crockett's feisty stallion must have stepped on his horse holder's foot again, and Hank Little's assertion that most likely the stallion needed his arse wiped, ignited a wave of chuckling. Theo Corson kept the laughter going with a weightier remark after Sergeant Butler's departure that maybe I should take my revolver and do everyone a favor and shoot the captain.

Those comments portrayed B Company's distrust of Crockett's imperial attitude. His aloofness caused the unit's veterans to question his concern for their well-being. In their opinion, he had been bold in previous actions to the point of recklessness. The captain pursued what they deemed a quick victory and personal recognition, with little regard for the cost in friendly casualties. From telegraphic messages and rumor, we knew to the man that whatever elements of General Price's Confederate Army we might face contesting the possession of Sedalia, the odds were the enemy would be vastly superior in numbers and guns. This made a glory hound of an officer doubly dangerous.

Whereas the rank and file, and the noncommissioned officers of B Company, slept on bare ground in the open with saddles for pillows, Captain Crockett and his commissioned officers occupied conical Sibley tents at the head of our dual picket line. I marched between those picket lines, aware my passage attracted the stares of my fellow enlistees despite the fading twilight.

The sentry at the door of Crockett's Sibley was nodding off on his feet. I hissed at him and he came to attention. "Private Wainwright to see Captain Crockett."

The thankful sentry hastened to announce me. Crockett yelled, "You may enter," and I stepped inside. Our company commander was seated at a desk fashioned from an empty cartridge case. A globed oil lamp hung from a wire crisscrossing the Sibley tent above his head. His pale, feral eyes matched the yellow glow of the lantern.

I saluted and said, "Reporting as ordered, sir."

He let me stand at attention, forage cap in hand, while he studied me from crown to boots for at least two solid minutes, as if he had never seen me before. Seemingly satisfied with what he saw physically, he asked, "What kind of rider are you?"

"Sir, I've been riding since I was old enough to sit astride."

"On what kind of horse? A plow horse or a spirited animal?"

I realized conversing with Captain Nathaniel Crockett required quick thinking and precise, measured responses. He was in this instance interested in my riding ability solely from the standpoint of the cavalryman. "I can stay on any horse at any speed. I've ridden owners' horses in races a quarter mile and a full mile in length."

"How well do you shoot?"

I was also learning abrupt changes of topic were commonplace with my captain. "Mr. Benson trained me at various distances with revolver and rifle," I answered. "I have never shot at another man from the ground or from the back of a horse. Mr. Benson believes I shoot accurately and could be an excellent marksman with more practice."

"Private Wainwright, I have need of a courier and a handler for my stallion, Sahib. I will be straightforward with you. You have the recommendation of Colonel Crawford. The colonel is acquainted with your uncle, whose friendship he prizes and opinion he respects. I must have a courier I can trust in any circumstance. I'm prepared to offer you the duties I just enumerated. Do you want to serve as my courier and tend to Sahib?"

He'd put forward a lot for me to swallow all at once. Did I want to be seen and known as Captain Crockett's errand boy and horse groomer? Did I want to be tied to a rival openly courting Laura Kellerman? How would she feel about that? Would I appear a lesser man in her eyes? Would I open the gate to constant teasing by my messmates and perhaps others in the rank and file?

From the other end of the stick, the duties being offered me were the opposite of building fortifications, digging slit trenches, and fatigue chores. I loved horses and the prospect of duty close to where regimental and company command decisions were made sounded exciting. And even finer was the outside chance I might somehow get to exchange a few words with Laura Kellerman.

Careful to keep my voice calm and sounding what I hoped was halfway mature, I answered, "I will gladly serve as your courier and tend to your mount, sir."

Crockett's smile exuded warmth that contrasted sharply with his usual cold, professional manner. "That's the most respectful response I've received to a proposal from a company member in weeks."

The fleeting impression of warmth melted with Crockett's smile. "The telegraph to the East connecting us with Jefferson City was cut yesterday just after Colonel Crawford received a telegram from General Brown, district commander at Jefferson City, informing Crawford he had word the Confederates were planning to burn the Otterville Bridge. With the bridge burned and the telegraph down, we are cut off from all communications with headquarters and from all outside aid. General Brown's telegram, therefore, ordered Colonel Crawford to collect his horses and arms and leave Sedalia to its own fate, as we would be at the mercy of the enemy."

My heart beat faster. This was momentous news. Who else knew of Sedalia's desperate condition?

Captain Crockett saw me squirming from foot to foot. "Colonel Crawford and the Fortieth Regiment's commissioned officers met with General Smith, your uncle, and the other members of the Sedalia council. The decision was made to hold Sedalia till we are driven out. Given our situation, it was imperative that we confirm the burning of the Otterville Bridge. Colonel Crawford hand-picked twenty-five men to travel by train to Otterville this morning for that purpose. He confirmed the burning of the bridge. Crawford's convinced Confederates are in the rough country east of Otterville in large numbers. He's making a second reconnoiter of the area by horseback in the morning. I am to accompany him. You are to report to me with your mount before breakfast."

Captain Nathaniel Crockett rose to his feet. "Wainwright, I want you armed at all times. Keep in mind that I'm determined no Confederate bushwhacker will ever mount Sahib. If the thought of possibly sacrificing your life for that of a horse disturbs you, I'll make other arrangements."

And so we reached the real nub of my new assignment. The added duty of horse guard didn't bother me. My attachment to Badboy equaled Crockett's deep feelings for his Sahib and I shared his protective instincts. Any horse captured or confiscated by Missouri bushwhackers faced a dismal future, for they rode them to death without hesitation to escape capture and the hanging rope.

"I'll do my best to keep him safely in our hands, sir."

My promise drew a second rare smile from Captain Crockett. "Then that concludes our business for this evening. I bid you good night."

His failure to thank me for sincerely committing my future to protecting his beloved stallion was not unexpected. The financial success of the Crockett family farms in southern Pettis County was driven by what Stuart Kellerman called a "total devotion to the task at hand, while always planning ahead." It was a working philosophy that carried them through good seasons, as well as bank failures, droughts, and other natural disasters. No time was wasted on social amenities. An agreement was an agreement. According to Mr. Kellerman, the telling toll of the bell for the Crockett family was the fact that no Crockett ever went back on his word. Nor did they forgive those who reneged on them for any reason.

Perhaps the dogged, persistent nature of his family explained Captain Crockett's iron-handed devotion to discipline and duty rather than personal ambition. But then hadn't Sam Benson claimed the same Captain Crockett was "hollow of heart"?

No matter what made him tick, I sensed Crockett would treat me fairly as a soldier, as he needed my services. How he would treat a rival lover was an open question I had best keep in mind for my own protection.

Not wanting to appear young and foolish, my greatest fear since coming to live with Uncle Purse, I resisted the urge to skip back to my mess fire. My transfer from mounted trooper to horse guard had occurred at an opportune time. I would be part of Colonel Crawford's morning expedition to Otterville, a mere seventeen miles from Sedalia.

The war was creeping ever closer.

And, danger or no danger, my craving for a taste of it was a growing lump of excitement in my chest.

# CHAPTER 6

COLONEL CRAWFORD'S ADJUTANT BROUGHT NEW ORDERS FOR CAPtain Crockett during breakfast. Word from one of our scouts claimed a sizable force of Union cavalry was passing near Georgetown, eight miles north of Sedalia. Captain Crockett was to form a ten-man detail and undertake an immediate patrol in that direction and learn the truth of the rumor.

Pouring the dregs of his morning coffee on the fire before his tent, Crockett turned to Lieutenant Kendrick. "Niles, you will accompany Colonel Crawford to Otterville in my place. Have Sergeant Butler pick eight men and make sure they have ample ammunition and water. Tell Butler they are to report to me in twenty minutes. Wainwright, saddle our horses and see that our canteens are full. Higgins, stand firm. I will have a written communication for Colonel Crawford in your hands shortly."

My disappointment over missing Colonel Crawford's reconnoitering of Otterville died a quick death. Action of any kind beat drill and daily fatigue duties. And who knew with the telegraph out, was there perhaps a chance the rumored Union force, or a part of it, was intended to reinforce Sedalia's defenses?

We rode in a double-file column with Captain Crockett and Sergeant Butler at the point, then Theo Corson and me, followed by the rest of the detail. A few clumps of white cloud tracked across an otherwise clear sky, continuing a dry-weather summer, long on heat and dust. We alternated between a walk and trot, a pace that ate the miles in a hurry. Beyond the open Sedalia prairie, the wagon road wound through oak and hickory woodlands scored by ridges and gullies.

We passed the hill where Theo and Joey Barnes captured the Rebel bushwhacker, who later refused to reveal what, if anything, he knew about General Price's Confederate Army. We splashed across the Big Muddy, and five miles later, we approached Georgetown at a brisk walk.

By chance, I slept at night next to the much older Theo Corson. He had taken a liking to me and shared his thoughts whenever the mood struck him. "Stay alert, pup. Those favoring the Union cause hold sway in Sedalia. The secessionist fever rules Georgetown. I drove freight from the railhead to Georgetown for the Wicker brothers. I was there the night the public mob burned alive a slave accused of murder. He had no more chance than a fly buzzing a horse's ass becoming the king of England."

I was aware the founding of Georgetown had preceded that of Sedalia by some years. The town's growth was permanently stunted by the refusal of its leading citizens to support General George Smith's crusade to entice the Missouri Pacific Railroad to a central path across Missouri, instead of following the bank of the Missouri River in the state's northern tier. General Smith proceeded to purchase 350 acres in Pettis County, acquired the necessary political and financial backing, began selling lots, and Sedalia was founded in the middle of his farm, smack on the newly built east-west tracks of the Missouri Pacific. Per Aunt Emma, Uncle Purse abandoned his plans to build in Georgetown and was present with money in hand the day the first Sedalia lots went on sale. While nobody asked for my opinion, I firmly believed Uncle Purse's nose as to where a dollar could be gained matched that of Stuart Kellerman.

Our arrival in Georgetown was most opportune, for a sizable force of Union cavalry led by Brigadier General John Sanborn, totaling three brigades of twenty-five hundred men and eight pieces of artillery, was indeed passing through it. The marching column's hoofs churned up a billowing cloud of dust that filled Main Street, sidewalk to sidewalk, and drifted against the doors and windows of Georgetown's houses, two-story courthouse, businesses, and churches. All but a few bystanders moved indoors to escape the eye-clogging, throat-plugging air.

The single spot of suitable open ground was the lawn beside the courthouse and Captain Crockett led us there. We dismounted, cleansed our mouths with water from our canteens, and squatted with reins in hand to watch the parade of Federal regulars pound through at a steady clip, their alert officers poised to prevent any looting or harassment of townsfolk. It was the largest number of uniformly outfitted and armed soldiers I'd ever seen at one time and I was duly impressed, the sight sending shivers up and down my spine.

Never an officer to suffer from delay, Captain Crockett confronted a brigade colonel and confirmed General Sanborn was stationed at the head of the column. "Mount up! Sarge, lead us to the south around town. We need to catch the head of the column without delay."

Sergeant Frank Butler shared certain qualities with Captain Crockett, one being a single-purpose bent of mind. Barely clear of Georgetown's southernmost dwelling, we swung off the Sedalia Road and headed west at a trot, disdaining the need for a street if none were in the offing. We skirted backyard outhouses, woodpiles, storage sheds, barns, clotheslines, and small orchards. We went straight through a half-acre garden, melons squashing under hoofs, red fruit flying from vines, the pitchfork of the female owner launched like a lance barely missing the backside of the hindmost rider of our detail. Wild laughter had my belly hurting before Sarge had us clear of Georgetown. I wasn't alone in that regard.

Captain Crockett took the lead again. We trotted alongside the Federal column, the Captain's oft-repeated "Coming through" clearing a single-line path for us. We raised some Yankee eyebrows and garnered a few demeaning curses, but we gained our objective without provoking any physical retaliation. Soldierly pride had to be accounted for, day and night, no matter the endeavor.

John Sanborn was the first brigadier general I had the privilege of meeting and observing in person. He was of medium build and had a tall forehead bespeaking a growing baldness. His cheeks were cleanly shaven, his mustache and short beard coal black, and his dark eyes deep set beneath his forage cap. He rode a gray horse, with his back straight, but his body relaxed, indicating he was no stranger to the saddle. His resolute expression didn't falter when Captain Crockett intruded upon his morning travel with no warning.

Voice high pitched to ensure he would be heard, Crockett eased Sahib parallel to the troopers riding directly behind General Sanborn and shouted, "General, a word if you please?"

Given the Missouri bushwhackers' skill at dressing as Union soldiers in stolen uniforms, I frankly didn't fathom how General Sanborn's staff had allowed us to get so close to him without challenging who we were. Too late, an officer wearing lieutenant bars realized the strange, unannounced officer on a black horse might be a threat to his superior officer. He whipped his revolver from its holster, cocked it, aimed it at Captain Crockett, and yelled, "Hold where you are!"

An instant later, I was totally surprised by the presence of the revolver in my hand, pointing at the lieutenant. One glance at our blue militia uniforms and mismatched weapons told a quick-thinking Brigadier General Sanborn what was transpiring. He halted his horse, and with it, the entire mile-long column. "Put up those revolvers. We don't make a habit of shooting our fellow Lincoln men."

I sheepishly lowered the hammer and holstered my revolver. Theo Corson leaned toward me in his saddle and spat. "No shame necessary. You were protecting a superior officer."

Captain Crockett regained the initiative. "General Sanborn, I have a message for you from Colonel Crawford at Sedalia. May we speak alone for a minute?"

Sanborn nodded and reined his horse to the side of the road. A long-jawed major with a harelip replaced him and pointed down the road with a sweep of his arm. "Column forward. March."

Peering my way, Captain Crockett said, "After me, Wainwright. You're my witness."

The captain's choosing me to hear his conversation with General Sanborn allayed my fear that, unlike Theo Corson, he might consider my pulling a revolver on the general's lieutenant without an order from him a serious breach of discipline.

General and captain rode a little distance from the road to ensure their privacy. The general offered no objection to my presence and opened the conversation. "Now, young man, first your name, then your business."

"Captain Nathaniel Crockett, B Company, Fortieth Regiment, Enrolled Missouri Militia. General, Colonel Crawford, commanding the Fortieth and the Sedalia Military District, is reconnoitering the vicinity of Otterville as we speak. He is convinced large numbers of General Price's Confederates are east of there intending an advance on Sedalia. We have at most three hundred fifty veteran militia and untrained citizens with minimal ammunition to secure and hold Sedalia. Crawford is inquiring, sir, if you are in a position to allocate reinforcements in any number, large or small, to aid our cause."

General Sanborn shifted his weight atop his horse and returned Captain Crockett's steady gaze. "Captain, General Rosecrans suspects General Price's army is concentrating at Lexington on the Missouri, fifty-some miles to the north of Georgetown. That is my destination per my most recent orders. I have no leeway to dilute my strength in the meantime. I understand your plight, but there's nothing I can do for you. If events unfold as we anticipate, Sedalia should be safe from a concentrated attack."

Captain Crockett had no quit in him. "General, Colonel Crawford believes the Confederates need meat for their army and can't afford to bypass the two thousand head of Union cattle in Sedalia's public corral."

"That possibility is known to my superiors, but that loss pales against our missing a chance to confront Price in sufficient numbers. We suspect that his failure to successfully besiege St. Louis and Jefferson City, and the losses he has suffered, leave him little choice but to retreat across northern Missouri through Lexington and Westport. I repeat, Captain, much as my heart inclines me to intervene on your behalf, I cannot alter my orders."

I watched a resigned Nathaniel Crockett stand in his stirrups and salute a superior officer. "I won't delay you further, sir. I understand your situation. In your boots, I, too, would obey my most recent orders."

General Sanborn's warm smile returning Crockett's salute was genuine. "I wish you the best of luck. Let's pray the threat of my column to Price's flank draws the enemy away from Sedalia."

We didn't wait for the remainder of General Sanborn's brigades to pass us by. Sarge again guided our detail cross-country, but well to the south of Georgetown, away from civilian backyards. Word had passed to those of us who hadn't witnessed the thrown pitchfork and we had no qualms about negotiating a short stretch of rough terrain to avoid a possible encounter with gardeners and property owners of secession sentiment who might have a gun handy.

Avoiding a touchy incident that threatened a life, however, wasn't in the cards dealt us that particular morning. We were blowing our horses in a shady glen just short of the Sedalia Road. I was standing next to Sarge and Captain Crockett when a sound that resembled the buzzing flight of a hornet zipped past. It was so close to my ear, I ducked, out of fear of being stung, in coordination with the crack of a firing rifle echoing through the woods.

Sarge bawled, "Sniper. Take cover."

The next bullet sound I heard accompanied my nose-first dive into the mossy loam next to Badboy's front hoofs. A final shot rang out and then the glen was silent as a tomb, except for leafed branches stirred by an afternoon breeze and a faint crackling of brush on the hillside behind the detail.

I looked up, straight into the pale eyes of a prone Captain Crockett. We were lucky we hadn't banged heads seeking whatever meager protection bare ground had to offer. The way our bodies were aligned, and the fact the errant bullets had come from behind me, had me guessing without ever knowing for certain that the sniper or snipers hadn't been targeting me in my faded blue shell jacket and forage cap riding a hammer-headed roan horse. They were shooting at the taller officer wearing the tailored frock coat trimmed in gold and feathered campaign hat riding a magnificent black stallion. The old hunter's saw that the colorful male cock bird draws the hunter's attention instead of the dull hen was never truer.

Sergeant Butler was the first trooper on his feet. "They're gone, the cowardly bastards. Anyone hit? . . . Captain . . . Wainwright . . . Corson . . . Higgins . . . Shaw . . . speak up, damn it. Barnes . . . Leslie . . . Kittle?"

All answered, "No." We had somehow escaped the ambush unscathed. Nothing thrilled me more, however, than the selfish realization I'd survived the sniper's bullets without crapping my drawers. Let no veteran soldier tell you otherwise, dear reader. A man doesn't know till he lives through it how his bowels will react to the fright of a killing bullet missing him by a hair's width.

Our return ride to Sedalia was uneventful but for an observation Theo Corson shared with me from our station at the rear of the detail, which I long remembered. "This Missouri war is wilder than a booby hatch crammed with armed lunatics. It's not two armies marching to meet each other and do battle and then resting in camp before doing battle again till one side strikes its flag. This fight is an 'everywhere, all the time, never stop war.' Usually, a man needn't worry about the family he left at home, lest they find themselves in the path of a marching army or the fighting takes place near his hearth. Missouri is a throwback to the dooryard Injun wars with the added threat that your once-friendly white neighbor might prove your worst enemy."

My brief association with Theo Corson reinforced what I'd learned from Sam Benson, namely, to never judge a man by his appearance, age, or what others said about him. You learned the essence of a man from what he knew, and he told you that by what he said and how he treated his fellow men. I was to never learn how much formal education Theo had acquired. But like Mr. Benson, he missed nothing that occurred around him and shared his knowledge freely with those who chose to listen.

Between shifts building earthworks and patrols in small details, Captain Crockett had scheduled target practice, limited to ten rounds per trooper. It was for new recruits under the tutelage of Sergeant Butler and Theo to teach us basic shooting commands and learn how each of us handled our weapon. After one such session, Theo took me aside and had me reload the Russell Colt Navy for him.

"Very good," he said, after I'd finished loading the first two chambers. "Sam Benson taught you well."

Theo smiled at the quick lift of my brow. "I play poker at Scanlon's Saloon with Sam, only when we play for matchsticks." Asking for the Russell Colt Navy and my powder flask, he said, "I wasn't always a lawful citizen. I beat a different drum after meeting Forge Bannister, with his gun drawn and cuffs in hand, and spending a stretch in prison. I learned a trick on the run from Alton Bragg, a man more dangerous than Bloody Bill Anderson and Quantrill together. He discovered trying to save scarce gunpowder that with a smaller charge the ball ranged just as far and penetrated nearly as deep. The smaller charge reduced the recoil and the bounce of the barrel when the revolver fires, making the second and third and fourth shots quicker and more accurate when you rapid-fire your weapon. That's how the bushwhackers and guerillas with a gun in each hand terrorize whole towns. Let me show you what I'm talking about."

With my second reloading, a patient Theo nodded and said, "You have the hang of it. I can tell watching you shoot that Sam taught you aiming a revolver is the same as pointing your finger. Too many beginners waste time worrying about making certain the front and rear sights are properly aligned, or they just jab the gun at the target and pull the trigger. It's the long second you take to 'point your finger' that separates the living from the dead when the smoke clears."

Remembering the reloading lesson with Theo had me thinking back over my twenty days under oath with the 40th Regiment, EMM. My fervent hope and prayer was that I had acquired enough basic knowledge and training during regimental and company drill and limited target practice to acquit myself under fire with the courage and steadfastness expected of me.

The challenges of bearing arms in a war flew to the nether reaches of my head when I spied the Kellerman bay mare with white stockings tied to the post before Captain Crockett's tent. My first thought was it had to be Stuart Kellerman calling on Captain Crockett, for I had not to date seen a woman—wife, daughter, or otherwise—visit our camp. Then I caught a splash of red upstream from Crockett's quarters and recognized Laura strolling leisurely along on the arm of Lieutenant Anders. Though she was wearing a leather jacket with fringe on the sleeves, a red cotton shirt, a leather riding skirt, and tall boots with two-inch heels, there was nothing manly about any part of her.

With her mare tied where it was, she had obviously asked for Crockett and not me upon her arrival. Captain Crockett saw her, too, and touched spurs to his stallion. I followed on Badboy at a walk, trying to determine how I should conduct myself.

I watched Captain Nathaniel Crockett dismount before his stallion came to a halt, land on his feet nimble as a bird on a swaying limb, and bow at the waist. The man had a flair for the dramatic. By damned, if he didn't.

To my surprise, Crockett's bold move to impress Laura Kellerman didn't upset me. Either I trusted her or I didn't. The warmth and frankness of her kiss on her visit to my room during my recovery led me to believe she would not intentionally embarrass me in public. I dismounted and led Badboy forward. A crowd of soldiers who appreciated feminine beauty, heretofore watching from afar, began to collect around their commanding officer and our female camp guest.

I drew close enough to hear Captain Crockett say, "And to what do we owe your visit, Miss Kellerman?"

Laura held out a thin package, a foot square, wrapped in brown paper. "I have a gift for Private Wainwright."

I saw Captain Crockett's head cock sideways. "You don't say." Then, with his gaze never leaving Laura, he called, "Private Wainwright, front and center, please."

My fellow troopers cleared a path. Lord, she was radiant in the bright sunshine. She stepped toward me, offered me her package, and, with a pronounced wink, said, "Private, this is from your aunt Emma. She felt twenty days was long enough for any man to wear a single pair of drawers. She liked the silk ones I showed her. She couldn't come herself, so I promised her I would deliver them on my afternoon ride."

I accepted the wrapped underwear. Her wink made the giggles and guffaws of the listening troopers bearable. My lack of embarrassment astounded me. She had trusted me to have enough of a sense of humor to play along with her and Aunt Emma. They had contrived a slick means by which she could visit me and not upset the camp's officers and my comrades, for every man present, sure as summer follows spring, was sorry he wasn't filling my boots.

Captain Crockett stood mute, fascinated by the magnetism of Laura Kellerman, and she kept all eyes on her by asking, "Captain, would I be too forward if I asked your permission for Private Wainwright to escort me back to town?"

What choice did he have? Refusal of such a request from a beautiful woman would brand him a cad, the opposite of the officer who had made a gallant, show-off dismount trying to impress her. Crockett's mouth tightened. It went against his dogged, never-fail nature, but he managed what passed for a smile, then said, "Private Wainwright will gladly see you safely back to town. In the future, it might be best if you did not ride the countryside alone in these perilous times. Private, see that you don't tarry. Perhaps a creek bath yet today is in order after the ladies have gone to so much trouble on your behalf. Always a pleasure to share your company, Miss Kellerman."

Extending her hand and flashing a sun-shaming smile, Laura Kellerman said, "The same here, my dear captain."

Captain Nathaniel Crockett kissed the proffered hand, nodded, gathered the reins of his stallion, bounced on his left foot, and swung into the saddle with the grace and athleticism of an expert horseman. His romantic intentions had been blunted, but that didn't keep him from making what was, in his opinion, a grand exit.

We walked to Laura's mare. The cheers of her newly acquired admirers, undoubtedly orchestrated by the sheer orneriness and enthusiasm of Joey Barnes, made conversation nigh impossible. I was happy the package of silk drawers hadn't been opened. That might have fostered a riot. I shook my head. What awaited me upon my return might be another story altogether.

Laura was riding sidesaddle that afternoon. I cupped my hands, boosted her aboard the mare, and passed the brown paper package to her while I mounted Badboy. It was quickly evident she had no interest in a leisurely ride to Sedalia. She urged the mare into a trot and we maintained that pace till we turned west on South Main Street, where wagon and pedestrian traffic slowed us to a walk.

She slipped from the saddle without assistance before her father's mercantile, hurried across the sidewalk, fetched a key from a jacket pocket, unlocked the front door, and beckoned for me to follow her. I dismounted, tied the horses to the store's hitching post, and did as she wished.

Inside, she walked a straight-as-an-arrow path through a large room with wall shelves and freestanding displays containing all the merchandise made of wood, glass, chinaware, cloth, wax, iron, tin, steel, pillow feathers, and linen required to furnish a home. From living room to dining room, bedroom to kitchen, everything was there, and then through a second sizable room filled with farm implements—plows, harrows, and reapers. Beyond the two oversized rooms were two smaller rooms and Stuart Kellerman's office. A hardware store occupied the largest of the smaller rooms, and Laura's millinery and ladies' specialty shop filled the other.

Laura went directly into her place of business. Being a young man unfamiliar with the smell of perfume and the shop's treasure trove of ladies' hats, garments, and accessories, particularly the underthings of silk and lace that fire the male imagination to unknown heights, I was always uncomfortable visiting her there. Never had I entered when another woman was present, for fear of blushing.

She laid the silk drawers aside, turned to face me, and, with a sly grin, pulled a velvet pouch with a golden drawstring from a pocket of her leather jacket. "I have a personal gift for you, just from me."

"You could have given it to me at camp," I blurted, instantly hating my loose tongue. *She's holding the reins, dimwit; don't spoil the race before the starting gun is fired.*

With a deep sigh, she said, "Father went to Smithton in your livery buggy. He's insisting Aunt Claire stay here in Sedalia with us till the war ends. It may sound selfish of me and very brazen, but I wanted a few minutes alone with you."

She paused, swallowed hard, and said, "I wanted to give you something to remind you I'll be praying that nothing happens to you."

She handed me the velvet pouch. I tugged the drawstring open and dumped the contents into my palm. Her gift was a Waltham pocket watch with a silver case and a silver winding key.

"Open it," she urged.

I did, and she said, "Read the inscription."

I was flat taken aback by what I read: *Love, L.K.*

I stammered, saying, "You . . . you didn't waste any words. I . . . I don't know how to thank you."

"Here, I'll show you," she answered while stepping against my chest and putting her arms around my neck.

I was lost so quickly in soft lips and pressing female flesh, to this day, I don't know how I held on to her watch and the velvet pouch. I swear that woman had my lungs nigh onto bursting before she gulped just enough air to keep a small bird alive and came back for more.

In my mounting excitement, I lifted her off the floor. She finally broke off our kiss and, chest heaving, rested her forehead on my chin. I lowered her gently and she murmured, "I've wanted that with you forever."

She stepped back, reached for her original gift, and said, "Come along. Too many nosy people that know Father is out of town saw us enter the store together. I don't want to start rumors that will have his ears burning. It's easier if he keeps believing dear Captain Crockett is a suitable match for his daughter."

Those words diminished my disappointment at being shown the door with my blood still pounding. Had we been in her home, I would have been tempted to carry her to her bed and have my way with her; and given the passion of her kisses, I was almost dead certain she would have offered little resistance. It wasn't lost on me that this was perhaps why she had chosen the store for a romantic rendezvous.

We parted at the door with a simple good-bye, and I was halfway back to camp, unable to stop daydreaming of what might have been, before I realized I hadn't said a thing about returning her love. On further thought, that didn't seem a major oversight on my part, not in light of how I'd matched the depth of her passion, and it was obvious we would meet again in the future.

I chuckled. She'd certainly revealed her true feelings for one Captain Nathaniel Crockett. I admired her skill at using him as a foil to thwart any concerns on her father's part about one Owen Wainwright making off with his precious daughter.

The sight of armed sentries suffocated my romantic rumination. The brown-wrapped silk drawers felt bigger than a bale of hay under my arm. It was just my luck B Company had finished their duties for the day. At this moment, they were enjoying some leisurely minutes, sipping coffee and smoking and chewing tobacco, while the cooks finished preparing a supper of freshly butchered beef boiled with desiccated vegetables.

The greeting of eagle-eyed Joey Barnes was a clear sign something was afoot. "Hey, boys, Silk is back."

Silk?

I dismounted at our mess fire. Sergeant Butler handed Badboy's reins to Hank Kittle, a second not-so-good sign. Whatever was now about to unfold had Sarge's approval, and it opened Joey Barnes's imaginative mind, which was home to pranks and discomforting carryings-on unknown to us common souls.

I had an inkling of what to expect when Joey held forth a large towel and a bar of soap as big as my fist. "Captain Crockett was the one who suggested a creek bath and he supplied the towel. Wagner provided the soap his mother insisted he bring to camp with him. Bring him along, boys. Don't hurt him. Just bring him."

The whole mess marched to the creek with me in the middle. Troopers from other mess fires who had caught a hint of the forthcoming aftermath of Laura Kellerman's boredom-busting visit massed behind us. I gave not a hint of resistance. I even relinquished the possession of the now-infamous, but as yet unseen, silk drawers to Sarge. I was going into the creek, no matter what. The only question was in what stage of dress would I enter the water.

I decided before we reached the creek that it was in my best interest to put on a show that would satisfy the crowd to the extent they would be on my side if Joey and my messmates continued to make fun of me over a singular event. The nickname of Silk, like it or not, was unshakable. It was my dog leash for the duration of my career in the militia.

The procession moved upstream till we encountered a large pool of water overhung by tall trees whose depth suited Sarge. I grabbed the bull by the horns, shooed everybody back a few strides, and undressed a piece of clothing and a boot at a time, twirling each on the end of my fingers and then flinging it aside. They came for me when I was completely naked; the four heftiest members of B Company each grabbed an arm or leg, swung me to and fro, till I feared the loss of a limb. They then cast me a considerable distance out over the stream as the howling of my audience reached a crescendo.

I had no intention of disappointing them. I planned on matching their howls, and when the unexpected chill of the water shriveled my stones to the size of teardrops, I exceeded my goal by several octaves. I nearly wore out that bar of soap in record time.

The minute the howling tapered off, Sarge ripped the wrapping off the silk drawers and held them above his head for all to see. The caterwauling resumed and reached new heights. My dear God, they were, of all things, robin egg blue in color. I did blush then, from crown to heel.

I padded up the bank. Joey Barnes flipped me Captain Crockett's towel. They waited patiently while I dried off. Sarge offered me the silk drawers with a fully extended arm, holding them between a forefinger and thumb like it was beneath him to even be touching them.

I saw my chance to end the whole affair on a note of my choosing. I snatched the drawers from Sarge's hand, stepped into them, and then pulled them on slowly with wriggles of my hips, provoking feigned leers here and there and wild hooting everywhere. I literally brought the house down by snapping the waistband, once I had the drawers fully on, an invention of my own. Then, cocking a knee provocatively, I placed a hand, with the thumb and fingers imitating a fan, behind my ear, gestures I'd seen an older Kate Hackett employ teasing younger boys behind the church stable during an evening social. Honest to gosh, the hooting turned to cheers when Joey shouted, "Let's hear it for Silk!"

The exhausted, hungry crowd broke up. Sarge and Joey stayed with me while I finished dressing. Sarge tendered me a rare compliment. "Silk, I believe you'll make one fine horse guard."

"If you don't," Joey said, "there's always a female wig and the stage."

That quip kept us laughing till the evening meal was served. Sergeant Butler came to our fire as we chewed our final bites. "Wainwright, Captain Crockett has need of your services. Report immediately with your horse and saddle Sahib for him. Colonel Crawford has called a council of war at his Sedalia headquarters."

I didn't save any breath. I strapped on the Russell Colt Navy, jogged to the captain's tent leading Badboy, and, without first reporting, saddled his stallion. The big black was becoming accustomed to the sight and smell of me, the sound of my voice, and my patient approach. I treated Sahib in accordance with Sam Benson's dictum that horses don't like abrupt moves and noises and loved treats, which had never failed me.

The sentry in front of the captain's tent was holding the reins of the blaze-faced horse normally ridden by Lieutenant Kendrick, so it was no surprise when Kendrick emerged from Crockett's tent with our company commander. I passed Sahib's reins to Captain Crockett, waited while the two officers mounted, then swung aboard Badboy.

The evening ride to Sedalia was without conversation. I sensed my two companions had much on their minds. Kendrick had accompanied Colonel Crawford's cavalry reconnaissance to Otterville that morning. I was sincerely interested in what had been learned in Otterville and what, if anything, was new regarding the colonel's planned defense of Sedalia, but feared I would be left outside with the sentries and the horses.

Colonel Crawford's council of war took place in the large dwelling on South Main Street housing his headquarters and most attendees had arrived on foot. There was empty hitch-rack space at the grocery store next door. Once we had dismounted and tied our horses, I turned to Captain Crockett for orders I fully expected would leave me in charge of the horses.

"If you're to be my courier, you need to recognize commanding officers by sight. Find a place where you can watch everyone and pay attention. An extra pair of keen eyes and ears can be quite helpful," he said.

I felt a foot taller following Crockett and Kendrick past the sentries at the front door. Apparently, Crockett bore me no ill feelings over the outcome of Laura's visit, or his duty-first nature had put any disappointment on his part toward the back of his mind, to be dealt with later. Either way, I took my new assignment as an indication that he would give me every opportunity to fail or succeed in my comrades' eyes, Colonel Crawford's, and, in turn, Laura's.

Colonel Crawford's headquarters was located in a former parlor furnished with two desks and a dozen ladder-back chairs lit by wall lamps and glass-globed desk lanterns; their wicks flickered in a cross breeze sifting between open windows on the street and alley sides of the room. Tobacco smoke and the dried sweat smell of unwashed bodies assailed my nose. Fresh from a creek bath with soap harsh enough to peel the hide from a stud hog, I had to be the sweetest-smelling thing in miles.

I slid forward along the nearest sidewall till I had a clear view of those seated at the desks and chairs. A standing Colonel Crawford was holding sway at that moment. "We engaged an enemy squad near the Otterville mill and blacksmith shop. The exchange of fire resulted in a single Rebel casualty and a rapid retreat on their part. We ventured down the Missouri Pacific right-of-way to the edge of the stone bluff overlooking the Lamine River Bridge. Last year's rebuilt bridge, a flimsy single-track structure with no guardrail, was mere kindling for the Rebel torch. We observed enemy troop movement beyond the Lamine exceeding our strength and I deemed it appropriate to withdraw at the juncture."

The slight slouch in Colonel Crawford's familiar upright figure I attributed to the physical strain of his tiresome efforts to organize home defense forces from scratch in Sedalia, Warrensburg, and Clinton, perhaps to no avail given the odds arrayed against him. Fortunately, his voice and the determination and will behind it had not diminished. Crawford's gaze settled on the newly arrived Captain Crockett. "Nathaniel, please report on your Georgetown reconnaissance. Any hope of reinforcements from that quarter?"

"To be blunt, no, sir, there isn't. We encountered Brigadier General Sanborn and three brigades of our regular cavalry passing through the town. His strict order from General Rosecrans is to advance on Lexington, the presumed converging point of General Price's remaining forces. I conveyed your conviction that the Confederates can't afford to ignore the beef cattle in our corral. He shares your concern, but he could only offer the likelihood of his advance drawing the whole attention of the enemy."

Neither Colonel Crawford's demeanor nor his tone changed with the disappointing news. "Gentlemen, we are still on our own.

Based on our latest scouting reports, I'm anticipating an enemy attack tomorrow. Captain Donohue's C Company will take a position behind the companies manning the eastern sector of our trenches in the area of Washington Avenue. Captain Crockett's B Company will take a similar position at the center of our lines behind the MP station. Captain Parker's A Company will support the western sector in the area of Moniteau Avenue. Gentlemen, please move your men into proper position between roll call and breakfast."

Though I had observed each of the company captains previously, I confirmed their identities for future reference by their responding nods. Both Donohue and Parker were my height and build and sported luxuriant brown beards, one trimmed and the other shaggy. The next officer to receive orders from Crawford was startlingly different in appearance. To the best of my knowledge, Captain Keen Doyle was a head taller than any man in Pettis County. And, if my hair was flame red, his beard was redder than hell's perpetual inferno. He had formed a mounted home guard rifle company at the outbreak of the war and played a key role, per Uncle Purse, in keeping Pettis County under the Union flag. After recovering from a leg wound, he had resuscitated his home guard company the previous spring and made it available to Colonel Crawford on his promotion to district commander. No duty or mission was beneath Keen Doyle and his twenty-odd men.

"Captain Doyle, your company will serve as a reserve attached to my headquarters. Captain Donohue, at daylight, you will send a scouting party due east, Crockett due north, and Parker due west. Limit your parties to ten men. Report any enemy contact by courier to my headquarters immediately."

Colonel Crawford's steady, unflinching gaze lingered on each of the remaining officers. "You men manning the trenches afoot must be on full alert and ready to fight round the clock. Every man who can stand and aim a weapon will stay within easy access of the line. No personal leave. No home visits. No sick leave, lest a man is bedridden. Gentlemen, our town, our homes, our families, may soon be under attack. There is no one else to defend them. Any questions?"

Crawford's crisp, straightforward instructions left little room for any misunderstanding.

"May the Lord watch after you and your charges. You're dismissed."

Our ride back to camp was as silent as our ride to Colonel Crawford's council of war. We had spent days preparing for what Sedalia's citizens and defenders were likely to face on the morrow. Quantrill's killing of 150 adult males and boys, and his subsequent burning of Lawrence, Kansas, as well as Bloody Bill Anderson's brazen slaughter of helpless Union soldiers at Centralia in our home state, haunted peace-seeking Missourians. The loss of civilian property, homes, and buildings to fire had compounded the horror of the war to where the sighting of any body of armed men, whether clad in blue, gray, or homespun, instilled fear in men, women, and children—the searing, gut-wrenching fear that scarred souls and fostered nightmares for years afterward.

I lay awake atop my blanket under a star-studded sky long after "Taps" had sounded, fixated not on the danger I might face come daylight, but the stunning kiss I'd shared with Laura Kellerman. I swear I could still feel the softness and warmth of her lips and the press of her breasts against my chest. She hadn't held anything back, which only inflamed my imagination as to how hot a fire she could ignite in the man lucky enough to share a bed with her.

I experienced no shame thinking those thoughts. I meant her no disrespect. I was an honest man with honest intentions. My goal was to survive the war I'd so willingly gotten myself into, and pursue her hand, no matter how high a mountain I might have to climb to win it.

I dozed off dreaming, not of bed mating so hot my palms smoked, but rather a public gathering at which my would-be love and I were introduced as "Mr. Owen Wainwright, attorney-at-law, and his wife, Laura."

My fanciful dream pointed to the distant future, not the next morning, the morning the Confederate Army appeared and unleashed another hell-bending event of the most memorable months of my young life.

# PART II

# THE SIEGE OF SEDALIA

# CHAPTER 7

THE LARGE ENEMY PARTY FILLED THE MEADOW BELOW US. THE DRESS of two-thirds of them was the gray uniform and slouch hats of Confederate regulars and they were armed with the long Enfield rifles common to Rebel regiments. The balance of the resting horsemen straddling the Georgetown Road, those closest to our scouting detail, toted numerous revolvers to the man. Their pinned-up hat brims, large-pocketed shirts, tall boots and spurs, and Texas saddle gear screamed the word that shortened my breath and held me spellbound: *bushwhackers.*

I couldn't help myself. My eyes were glued to them. Lieutenant Kendrick's grandfather, an officer in the British Navy, deserted his post during the American Revolution and bequeathed his American-born grandson a dual-power Dollond pocket telescope. After studying the Confederate force for a full minute, Kendrick passed me his prized possession.

The revolver-armed marauders appeared at arm's length in the lens of the Dollond.

What drew my attention immediately was a bobbing dab of red in a sea of gray cloth and brown horsehair. The red daub was the head garb of one of the bushwhackers. Was he the one who had threatened my life with a shotgun just a few days ago?

Taking advantage of the daylight, I sought a tighter view of the owner of what had to be a red scarf worn in lieu of a hat. Whoever he was had narrow hips and shoulders and mainly kept his backside to me. The bobbing motion resulted from his pouring liquid of some kind from a jug into tin cups presented by his fellow riders as he moved among them. Was he healing from a head wound? If not, he was acting like a servant with less statute than his companions, providing the service men would expect from a tavern maid. But I couldn't imagine any female riding with death-dealing bushwhackers, particularly in the bloodstained counties of Missouri.

Cup filling completed, Red Scarf plopped down next to an undersized bay horse, rested the jug between his knees, and sat with his head lowered as if exhausted. My Waltham watch had read quarter after nine, fifteen minutes ago. The Confederates had been doing some hard riding, closing on Sedalia. The credibility of Colonel Crawford's warning was increasing by the hour.

Lieutenant Kendrick held out his hand and I returned his Dollond. "Wainwright, drop back down the hill to the horses. Cut through the woods and hightail it to Crockett's headquarters. Tell him we spotted a force of approximately forty Confederate cavalry, in the company of twenty irregulars, six miles from town on the Georgetown Road. Those numbers match your count?"

Fortunately, Kendrick forged ahead, sparing me the embarrassment of admitting I'd been studying Red Scarf and neglected to make the count he'd requested with the loan of his pocket telescope. "Don't forget. Crockett has relocated the company behind our trenches near the railroad station. We'll be along directly, but Colonel Crawford needs this word fast as we can get it to him."

I scooted backward till I was well below the brow of the hill before coming to my feet, disappointed I hadn't caught a glimpse of Red Scarf's face. Badboy's head popped up at my approach. I patted his neck and swung aboard. I cleared my head of other thoughts and found the game trail wide enough to accommodate horses single file that we'd traveled to flank the Confederates on the Georgetown Road.

Low-hanging branches didn't bother Badboy. He pushed ahead, trusting the touch of the reins on his neck and the occasional tap of a boot toe. At what I estimated to be half of a mile, I quartered to my left and followed the drought-dried bed of a stony hillside trough to the Georgetown Road, checking for riders in both directions before exiting the cover of the woods. A touch of my spurs lifted Badboy into a gallop. I alternated between a fast walk and a gallop, allowing for the impact the morning's growing heat and the physical demand placed on the fine animal beneath me.

Passing from the forest to the prairie surrounding Sedalia was akin to emerging from a dark room into full sunshine. Open prairie was extremely deceptive terrain. What appeared a level surface covered with knee-high grasses was instead undulating ground scored with shallow rills and rifts dug by rainwater seeking the nearest low point. Lest he take care, a rider could fall prey to buffalo wallows formed by the collection of the same rain in depressions large enough to ensnare him and his horse.

I clung to the packed surface of Georgetown Road to its termination at Washington Avenue, which put me on the eastern fringe of Sedalia, and then turned west, crossing in front of the town's defensive works. Badboy's speed and the sense of urgency conveyed by the sweaty foam on his chest and shoulders roused questioning barks from bored Yankees manning the rifle ports of the embankment. The bulky three-story slope-roofed Missouri Pacific station loomed ahead of us. I spied the B Company battle flag flying on its embedded staff and reined Badboy across the first available dirt walkway spanning the six-foot-deep ditch my willing back had helped dig.

A strange sight, seen out of the corner of my eye from atop the dirt bridge, turned my head. At the extreme western end of the Sedalia defensive works, a gang of nine black men was hard at work, with pick, shovel, and wheelbarrow, extending the town's defenses. Freed or not, black males observed aiding those supporting the Northern military cause had been subjected to cruel measures, ranging from burning alive and hanging to hasty execution at the hands of Confederate soldiers and bushwhackers. It was a high price to pay for a loyalty seldom gainfully rewarded, which was why Uncle Purse went to great lengths to protect Titus Culver, the Wainwright blacksmith, from such treatment. Uncle Purse declared Titus "slave" or "free" depending on his audience, accounting for both Missourians who supported the Union, but not the abolition of slavery, and those favoring outright abolition.

Joey Barnes spied me and reached for Badboy's reins. "I'll get him to water and cool him down while you report to Captain Crockett."

An anxious Captain Nathaniel Crockett was beside me with Joey's last word hanging in the air. He accepted my brief report with a nodding head. "Well enough. Take Barnes's horse and inform Colonel Crawford. Pay due attention to any new orders that might be forthcoming for B Company."

Skirting the Missouri Pacific station, Colonel Crawford's strategy was apparent even to a military neophyte like me. His mounted forces were positioned in the open space between the line of the railroad and his fixed trenches with their rifle ports. His primary objective was to defend the town with no real concern for pursuing the enemy, should he be turned away. Rather, his mounted forces reinforced his main line of resistance and could be dispatched to any part of town in which the Confederates achieved a breakthrough.

When I reached South Main Street, it was nearly deserted except the area of Colonel Crawford's headquarters. Horses lined hitch racks, and the bulk of the dismounted horsemen idling on sidewalk benches on both sides of the roadway had bands of yellow ribbon around the crowns of their hats and upper arms. They wore black frock coats and toted breech-loading Sharps carbines issued regular Union cavalry. They were members of Captain Keen Doyle's famed mounted rifle company.

What captured my eye, first and foremost, was the buggy standing in the middle of the street with its team ground hitched, as if an explosion under their hoofs wouldn't spook them. The gold letters on the front of the buggy's blue dashboard read WAINWRIGHT HOTEL and its two matching sorrel horses would indeed stand stone solid except for an occasional swishing of their tails till their driver returned. I hadn't seen Uncle Purse since reporting to B Company's camp, and in my excitement, I almost embarrassed myself to tears by forgetting that Joey Barnes's horse liked to sidestep slightly during his rider's mounting and dismounting. Luckily, I caught the shifting of the gelding's weight early enough to cling to the saddle horn and maintain my balance standing one-footed in the near stirrup and not go sprawling into the dust of the street before Captain Keen Doyle's veteran riflemen.

Colonel Crawford's headquarters was crowded. The regimental

clerk Fellows was stationed at the door with his familiar clipboard. "Your business, Private?"

"I bear a sighting of the enemy report from Captain Crockett."

"Follow me. I'll take you directly to the colonel. Wainwright, isn't it?"

We wound through a host of seated and standing observers. Uncle Purse, apparently representing the town council, was seated to the left of Colonel Crawford and Captain Keen Doyle to his right. Without hesitation, Fellows lifted his clipboard, signaling Colonel Crawford that he needed to intercede. Crawford silenced the speaker addressing him with a raised hand.

Fellows's announcement of my name and business provoked intense stares my way among the headquarters occupants.

"Step forward, Private Wainwright," Crawford ordered. "Where did this sighting take place and by whom?"

I had never before been asked to address a gathering of adult men, particularly one with power over life and death. Had it not been for the fiasco surrounding my blue silk drawers, I believe I would have stammered around and let fear steal my voice. Somehow, cavorting in front of grown men, naked and drawing cheers, made speaking to them fully clothed less challenging than baiting a fishhook.

"Lieutenant Kendrick observed approximately forty mounted Confederate cavalry and twenty mounted irregulars on the Georgetown Road six miles from town, about nine-fifteen this morning."

"Were you present, Private?"

"Yes, sir."

"How did Kendrick know the irregulars from Confederate cavalry?"

"The irregulars wore fancy felt hats and shirts, boots with big spurs, and were armed with pistols. The cavalry wore gray uniforms and were armed mostly with muzzle-loading rifles."

"Were the bushwhackers in the lead?"

"Yes, sir."

Colonel Crawford sighed and turned his attention to our audience. "Just what I feared. The bushwhackers are aiding General Price's army to further their killing and looting. They'll take the lead in burning our town. I want word sent up and down our lines. We'll fight them out in the open. I don't want any shooting from within buildings that gives them a ready-made excuse to torch them unless lives are at stake. Is that understood?"

Heads nodded throughout Crawford's headquarters. "Captain Doyle, your rifle company will proceed out the Georgetown Road and escort Lieutenant Kendrick's scouting party back to town. We need not chance the loss of good men to a larger force. Private Wainwright knows their last location. He will accompany you. You are dismissed, gentlemen."

I was disappointed I could only nod at Uncle Purse as we exited. He smiled in return, the same satisfied smile he'd flashed when I completed my first horseshoeing from the heating and shaping and cooling of the shoes to the last rap of the hammer with no adult assistance.

I felt small, like everyone else in creation following the giant Keen Doyle from the room. Outside, in the bright sunshine, his red hair and beard seemed to catch fire. The freckles covering his cheekbones resembled burning embers. The red hair of the Wainwright family was an insult to the color compared to that of Doyle's.

His booming voice matched Doyle's oversized physique. Looking neither right nor left, he bellowed, "Mount up," and black-uniformed bodies responded like stage horses to the lash of the whip. I mean, men ignored the stirrup and vaulted into the saddle.

I squelched the urge to imitate them without the requisite skill and mounted Joey Barnes's gelding, per Sam Benson's methodical training, turning him first before climbing aboard, and allowing for his habitual sidestep. By then, Doyle's riflemen had formed up two abreast. Their leader beckoned for me to join him at the head of the column and we went east on South Main Street at a gallop. The few pedestrians, two mounted riders, and three wagons in our way briskly opened a path for us with a curse or two.

Given the length of Keen Doyle's lower limbs, I swore he could have extended his legs and run afoot while his horse was galloping beneath him. It was a comic image that had to have occurred to others, but I doubted anyone, military or civilian, had ever dared share it with him.

We reined left two blocks short of Washington Avenue and

headed north on Lamine Avenue, which meant Doyle intended to take a shortcut across open prairie to the Georgetown Road. Any childish concern I harbored about missing out on the day's action went up in smoke as I rode beside Keen Doyle, a man who feared nothing and was known for both seeking a fight when an issue needed settling and never failing to join a fight already under way. We were bound for a situation where the enemy outnumbered Lieutenant Kendrick's scouting party and Doyle's rifle company by three to one.

We crossed the stretch of open prairie separating us from the Georgetown Road at a trot without incident, me holding my breath every stride of our horses, Keen Doyle picking our route with total confidence. We were nearly past the only buffalo wallow of note before I realized it was there. We rested our horses for all of ten minutes by my watch, listening for the sound of hoofbeats and the echo of gunfire at Doyle's request, and then, hearing neither, set off again at a gallop.

How he heard it over the pounding of hoofs was forever a mystery, but a mile into the enveloping woods, by my calculation, Doyle's closed fist shot into the air and the column came to an abrupt halt. Doyle stood in his stirrups and cupped a palm behind his right ear. I did likewise, and a few breaths later, I caught the faint sound of running horses in the distance. It could only be Kendrick's party fleeing with the enemy in hot pursuit.

Still standing tall, Doyle turned his shoulder and called, "Split to each side of the road out of sight! We'll let our boys pass and give the bastards what for. Fire when I do. Follow me, Wainwright."

The beat of a fox's heart straining to reach his den ahead of baying hounds had nothing on mine. I followed Doyle's horse past the first line of trees, stepped down to the rear of his mount, and, not sure how to proceed, waited for orders with my pistol drawn but not cocked.

Doyle's deep chuckle and headshake seemed out of place in what to me were dangerous circumstances, but old hat to him. "Damn that Sam Benson, put a young chap around him and he'll have him soldiering jack quick. Never cock a pistol till you're ready to shoot. I can hear him saying that at the poker table while spreading a winning hand."

We eased toward the Georgetown Road with me hard on his heels. "Get a good view of the highway without exposing yourself. Pick a target and aim for his chest. Don't forget. Aim for his chest."

I sucked in a few deep breaths, settled on one knee behind an oak tree, wiped the sweaty palm of my gun hand dry on my thigh, and stared down the empty roadway, which suddenly looked no wider than a single-track game trail. The rat-a-tat of running horses and the pleading shouts of their riders for more speed drew ever closer.

Gunfire erupted.

With their commanding officer leading them, Lieutenant Kendrick's scouting party burst into view, leaning far forward in the saddle, quirts whipping their animals. Behind them came the pursuing enemy, a highway-clogging gang of bushwhackers. The foremost of them rode with their reins between their teeth, or looped around saddle horns, a smoking pistol in either hand, teeth bared by savage ferocity. It was a sight so frightful it threatened to flush a man's bowel clean if he lost control of his vitals. I didn't, maybe because, as crazy as it sounds, I was too busy following Doyle's orders to acknowledge the urge.

I pinned the front sight of the Russell Colt Navy on the chest of an embroidered shirt topping a paint pony. I remembered to adjust my aim as the target bore down on my position, a principle of mounted warfare conveyed by Theo Corson, though I'd never had occasion to practice it. Just when I thought Keen Doyle would never open fire and the enemy would swoop past unscathed, he did.

Coupled with the bang of Bushwhacker revolvers, the simultaneous discharge by Doyle's men of their breech-loading Sharps carbines overwhelmed my ears for an instant. I didn't waver at the surprise of it and, with aim certain, gently squeezed the trigger. The bushwhacker on the paint pony tumbled backward from the saddle with the recoil of the Russell Colt Navy. The realization I had undoubtedly killed my first fellow human didn't register until later, for unseated bushwhackers littered the Georgetown Road, and horses were screaming in pain. Before the remaining enemy could react to the scourge of death that had descended on them like a lightning bolt from a clear sky, the second volley of Doyle's riflemen tore into them. The fatalities and wounds already inflicted were doubled, instilling a common awareness that, in such tight quarters, flight, not resistance, was their sole chance to survive. The bushwhackers' pell-mell retreat saved a dozen of them; the balance still astride their mounts fell to the third and fourth volleys of the relentless breech-loading carbines, a weapon capable of firing eight to ten rounds per minute. To my surprise, I discovered I had been so immersed in the slaughtering ambush that my Russell Colt Navy clicked on a spent cartridge with the last squeeze of the trigger.

We had spared Lieutenant Kendrick's scouting party, per Colonel Crawford's orders, but the enemy not yet engaged still outnumbered us two to one, and the pound of hoofbeats in the distance indicated the remaining enemy combatants were advancing to the aid of their fallen comrades. Captain Keen Doyle, who loved a fight, was officer enough to know when to stand firm and when to flee and fight at another hour of his choosing. His deep voice matched the boom of a cannon.

"Mount up! After me, by twos! March!"

Except for one bloody arm wound and a member of Lieutenant Kendrick's scouting party needing the support of a comrade to stay in the saddle, I didn't spy a downed combatant wearing a black or blue uniform. That was most heartening, for Missouri bushwhackers and Kansas Jayhawkers were known for scalping, mutilating, and collecting the ears, noses, and fingers of their slain enemies. I swear our horses sensed our fear and lengthened their stride. We were out of the woods and speeding across open prairie in a time that would have had the breeders of fast horses cheering like mad.

Our pursuers gave up the chase and Captain Doyle slowed his mixed column to a trot, and then a walk within sight of Sedalia. Doyle and Lieutenant Kendrick, riding beside him, spoke loud enough I overheard their conversation.

"Damn clever ambush, Keen. Rare to best bushwhackers at a tactic they've honed to perfection."

"This would be a different war if every Union soldier toted a breechloader," Keen Doyle said. "You can't hold firm against a man with a pistol in either hand whether he's mounted or afoot if you're armed with a muzzleloader that fires but four shots per minute."

"I'm praying we'll face more Rebel regulars than bushwhackers the balance of the day. The good folks of Sedalia don't deserve what Quantrill and his men did to Lawrence."

Our approach to Sedalia's defensive earthworks was closely observed. The tension of those manning that line was obvious in their alert, curious stares and stiff limbs. Captain Doyle's riflemen proceeded to Colonel Crawford's headquarters. I naturally accompanied Lieutenant Kendrick to Captain Crockett's tent. Crockett's first words explained the posture of the town's defenders: "We have reports of sizable enemy forces approaching from the east and west."

"And from the north now," Lieutenant Kendrick reported.

The postnoon sun was high overhead, its heat a bright steady beam. Crockett saw me remove my kepi and swipe sweat from my forehead with the back of my hand. "Get down. The horse handlers will water your horses. Grab a bite at my fire. I have a notion there won't be time for that shortly."

Being the son of a father that financed a mounted militia company for his son to command, Captain Nathaniel Crockett enjoyed the services of a private cook. Two generous ladles of Padre Smith's beef and beans, seasoned with dried peppers and onions, after a hasty predawn breakfast of a piece of hardtack, soaked in sugar-laced coffee, and a slice of blackened bacon filled a ravenously hungry stomach quite nicely. I gulped down the first ladle, and feeling less starved, I did better at chewing the contents of the second.

Lieutenant Kendrick managed to eat his single ladle of Padre Smith's specialty while reporting the details of his morning scout and subsequent flight from the enemy. When Kendrick reached the point where Captain Doyle's ambush interrupted the pursuit of the enemy, Captain Crockett's intent gaze fixed on me as he swallowed the last of his coffee. "That was a longer ride to and from headquarters than we anticipated, was it not?"

"Yes, sir, Captain Doyle gave me no say in the matter. I was to lead him to Lieutenant Kendrick's detail straightaway."

"I understand. Doyle isn't inclined to brook the slightest hesitation in a subordinate, the same as me. Did you participate in the ambush?"

"Yes, sir, I was hidden next to Captain Doyle. I believe one of my shots unhorsed a bushwhacker."

"Any qualms about killing a man from ambush?"

My quick answer came from the heart. "No, sir, they were catching up to Lieutenant Kendrick's men, and by the looks on their faces, they weren't interested in taking prisoners."

"In all that excitement, did you remember to reload your weapon?"

"Yes, sir, but not having much practice on horseback, I waited till we slowed our horses to a walk."

Stern Captain Crockett granted me an unexpected smile. "Smart move, lad. You have a penchant for thinking like an officer."

An excited hue and cry escaped many throats behind us.

"Here they come! Here come the Rebels!"

# CHAPTER 8

WITHOUT SPEAKING, LIEUTENANT KENDRICK OFFERED ME HIS DOLlond telescope. The mounted Confederate force attacking, at full gallop, the flag-flying dirt fort near Washington Avenue totaled a hundred-plus regular gray-uniformed cavalry. The attackers' keening Rebel yell welled above the pound of hoofs and the crack of short- and long-barreled weapons. Other than a shudder or two, my nerve didn't desert me and I stood in my stirrups, ears straining, awaiting a bugle call to action.

At a range of forty yards, the scream of "Fire" from the Union officers and sergeants manning Sedalia's rifle pits coursed along our defensive line, lacing the onrushing Rebels with a volley whose rippling discharge resembled one continuous explosion. Though a few riders swayed in the saddle, and I counted five horses down, the Confederate charge didn't falter. If anything, their Rebel yell rose to a higher pitch.

Lieutenant Kendrick declined the return of the Dollond and I stuffed the telescope in a jacket pocket for safekeeping. At a range of ten yards, we managed a ragged second volley from the rifle pits as the first mounted Rebels passed between them and confronted elements of the 40th Regiment, EMM. We were waiting for them, weapons drawn, and searching for targets.

Near Washington Avenue, the focal point of the Rebel assault, a few occupants of our rifle pits broke and ran. Captain Crockett and his fellow officers shouted orders to fire. We unleashed a volley from horseback and the next moment our buglers blew the "Charge."

B Company was far enough to the west of Washington Avenue that we struck the Confederate right flank, while A Company met the enemy, brow to brow. Our united effort stunted the Rebel assault. Riders and horses met in a wild, confused melee, which went in mere minutes from a close-order fight with guns to a slugfest utilizing emptied weapons, knives, and fists. The will of the Confederates shattered when they realized they were in danger of being surrounded and taken prisoner by the 40th. An astute Rebel officer instigated the blowing of "Recall" and we were suddenly looking at the hindquarters of departing grayback horses.

My vivid memory of my first battle with the enemy atop a horse was the backhanded slash of a Bowie knife wielded by a bushwhacker that narrowly missed gutting me like a helpless hooked fish. I cheered our victory with my fellows, cheers that dissipated with the abruptness of a hand clap when reverberating booms north of town signified the firing of the weapons we dreaded the most—Confederate artillery.

Fingers pointed skyward and there was no difficulty tracking the arcing black balls descending on the town behind us from beyond the city cemetery.

"Damn it to hell and all," Captain Crockett lamented. "General Smith repaired the telegraph from Otterville long enough to inform Colonel Crawford he can reinforce us by late evening today. That may be too late."

Colonel Crawford had contended we could hold against a force of equal size if our nerve didn't falter and our ammunition was adequate, providing the Confederates didn't swing the odds in their favor by bringing artillery and superior manpower into play. This observation echoed Sam Benson's rationale the evening before I became a soldier for real.

Lieutenant Kendrick inquired, "Captain, you mentioned earlier, enemy forces are approaching from east and west. Do we know in what numbers?"

"If our scouts can count, over a thousand men between them," Crockett answered.

"The Rebs must be in dire need of the eight hundred steers and the mules in the south corral to send over a thousand men and an artillery battery to fetch them," Kendrick conjectured.

What popped into my mind weren't live steers and mules, but dead soldiers and civilians, along with burning buildings, a repeat of the Lawrence and Centralia debacles. The image of the Wainwright Hotel and Livery reduced to a pile of smoldering ashes chilled my very soul.

Niles Kendrick then posed a vital question, what with the future of Sedalia at stake. "Did General Smith have specific orders for Colonel Crawford in the event we can't hold the Rebs at bay till he arrives?"

Crockett nodded. "If the situation becomes untenable, Crawford has orders to withdraw his regular forces, horses, and guns, and let the locals fend for themselves."

Harsh and devastating as the deliberate abandonment of Sedalia's civilian population sounded, I understood that defeating the remaining forces of General Price's Confederate Army required the preservation of the Union's organized military resources in their entirety if Missouri was ever to know peace, and law and order, again. Four long years of fighting had taught Missourians young and old, white or black, that the waging of war penetrates the sinews of those caught in its throes, whether they bear a weapon or not, and dispenses worry and woe at its whim.

Within forty minutes of B Company returning to its assigned post, Confederate cavalry, supported by three pieces of artillery, was attacking the entire length of our northern defensive line, from west to east, and attempting to skirt our left flank and gain access to the cattle corral in Sedalia's southwestern quarter. The bang of pistol and crack of rifle was a deadly chatter punctuated by the steady boom of cannon. Bullets zinged past kepi and slouch-hatted heads like angry hornets. Wounded men screamed with pain and begged for water beneath a frying-pan hot sun. Pockmarked bullet holes riddled the exterior walls of our rifle pits. The carcasses of slain Confederate horses became fortresses for Rebels trapped in the open before the same rifle pits.

By my pocket watch, ninety minutes had lapsed when the scales of the fight tipped in the Confederates' favor. Beyond their decided numerical superiority, every mounted Confederate was a moving target. I spied rifle pit defenders with empty guns and little or no ammunition inching backward toward the railroad at their rear, the big Missouri Pacific station looming directly behind me, an inviting source of refuge. The rifle pit abandonment intensified, and the Union cavalry supporting them on the ground and from the saddle, now stretched too thin, had no choice but to follow suit. Equally troubling, the bark of small-arms fire could be heard within Sedalia. Had the graybacks turned our left flank?

In the midst of our general retreat, Lieutenant Kendrick pointed toward the eastern end of our earthworks, where armed men in the area of the dirt fort, so prized by the Confederates, were advancing from our ranks, not giving way. I snatched the Dollond telescope from my jacket pocket and trained its lens on the circular wall of the fort and the Union flag flying defiantly above it. The twenty-man reinforcing party, clad in both militia black and civilian dress, hustled into the dirt fort whose rifle ports soon bristled with weapons.

"Our men, right?" Kendrick inquired.

"Yes, sir," I answered. "Bold as polished brass and twice as stout."

"Till they're overrun and cut off," Captain Crockett warned.

A panting courier, with apple-red cheeks and spittle in the corners of his mouth, sawed on his horse's reins and avoided a collision with Captain Crockett's horse. "Colonel Crawford wishes to inform you, we are withdrawing, sir. You are to fall back on his headquarters on South Main Street in good order."

Orders delivered, the courier spurred his horse and departed bent low over his horse's neck. Captain Crockett snorted, said, "That lad is right serious about doing his duty," turned in his saddle, then yelled, "Sergeant Butler, after me by fours, if you please."

Butler's shouted command rang out above the diminishing gunfire. Bugle calls followed and B Company withdrew in the stipulated good order, circled the Missouri Pacific station to the west, crossed the MP tracks, trotted a block south on Osage Avenue, and reined east on South Main Street. Sporadic rifle fire continued behind the buildings shielding us from Union militia making a final stand. Their stubborn courage warmed my heart.

A cannonball smashed into the upper facade of a building on my right and splinters of wood rained down as we drew rein in front of Colonel Crawford's headquarters. Company C of the 40$^{th}$ Regiment could be seen turning from South Main onto Lamine Avenue, two blocks beyond Crawford's headquarters, indicating our withdrawal would take us to the south away from the core strength of our Rebel foes.

Captain Keen Doyle's riflemen were idling two abreast on their horses on the far side of South Main. Doyle led Colonel Crawford and his regimental staff from the colonel's headquarters. Crawford halted before Captain Crockett's stallion. "Time is of the essence. Captain McCord is commanding the band of men defending the fort at Washington Avenue on their own initiative. You are well acquainted with Jack. He chased my courier off before he could speak. I want you to personally convey to Jack that the Fortieth is withdrawing. Jack might be a hardheaded cuss, but he'd fight the devil himself with a shoehorn, and I owe him and his followers a chance to avoid capture. Captain Doyle, detail two of your boys to escort Captain Crockett."

Keen Doyle's bull voice boomed forth instantly. "Jacobs and Harmon, front and center, if you please."

Two black-coated riflemen, Sharps breechloaders resting in the crook of an elbow, hupped their mounts across South Main, halted before their captain, and saluted. Keen Doyle's orders were short and blunt. "Until he dismisses you, you will accompany Captain Crockett and safeguard him against all harm. Understood?" As they nodded their assent, the sober cast of the bearded riflemen's features signaled they were prepared to offer up their own lives for that of Captain Crockett's if necessary.

My shock at what happened next was genuine. "Wainwright, stay close on our heels," Crockett ordered without even a glance in my direction. "Lieutenant Kendrick, take command in my absence, if you please."

We proceeded down South Main Street at a gallop, with Doyle's riflemen flanking Captain Crockett and me. The three-block ride to Washington Avenue seemed to last forever. Soon as we entered the intersection, the sounds of battle washed over us. Captain McCord's party was holding fast against repeated Confederate charges. We had just cleared the last house on Washington Avenue, gaining a clear view of the fort, when a familiar buggy pulled by a team of galloping sorrel horses closed on us. My heart raced. Had

Sam Benson and Uncle Purse joined the fight with Captain McCord?

As the buggy raced past us, a lump of fear knotted my innards. Sam Benson was at the reins, whipping the sorrels to greater speed, if that were possible. Uncle Purse was sprawled next to him, head lolling backward, left shoulder and arm coated with bright red blood.

Before I realized what I was doing, I'd brought Badboy to a skidding halt. My head automatically snapped around and I stared after the racing buggy. My impulse was to chase after it. But I had become enough of a soldier that my sense of duty froze me in place.

Then Captain Crockett was addressing me. "Mark my words. I'm giving you permission to look after your uncle and your family. Ditch your blue jacket and kepi. The Confederates don't have time to waste on prisoners. They have executed regular soldiers they've captured. I want a report on the Rebel occupation and withdrawal from Sedalia, which will likely be late this evening, as they'll be anxious to get beef moving to Price's hungry army. Are you up to it? Can I trust you?"

Crockett didn't wait for an answer. Tugging on his impatient stallion's reins to keep him calm, he continued, "One more chore for you. If the opportunity arises, search out Laura Kellerman. Provide her and her father any assistance possible."

The surprise on my face must have been as obvious as a wart on a pretty girl's cheek. "She's in love with you, Private, not me," Crockett conceded with a meager grin, "and like a good hound, I don't cling to a cold trail for long. Stuff that jacket and kepi in your saddle wallet and have at it before the damn Rebels overrun the town."

With that, Crockett spun his stallion, and he and his escort sped for the fort. In a few short breaths, I stashed my blue shell jacket and kepi in one of my saddlebags; and to appear even less of a soldier, I stashed the holstered Russell Colt Navy in the other. I couldn't part with the Dollond telescope, which fit neck-first into a pants pocket quite nicely.

I laid spurs to Badboy, marveling at the forthrightness, generosity, and honesty of Captain Nathaniel Crockett, for he'd proven himself on this occasion a bigger and better man than the narrow-minded, arrogant, glory-seeking officer he appeared on first impression.

He had, in turn, given me a heavy responsibility to bear.

Much had changed on South Main Street in my brief absence. While the sound of gunfire roared around the fort in the northeast sector of town, the fight elsewhere had slackened to an occasional gunshot and the Confederate cannon had ceased firing. I could see armed citizens flushed from our earthen rifle pits, with arms up and weapons resting in the dirt at their feet, surrendering the length of South Main Street to Confederate Rebels.

The Wainwright Hotel was situated on the corner of Ohio Avenue and Sixth Street, two blocks below South Main, three blocks to the west of me. I put spurs to Badboy and continued south on Washington Avenue, across Lyon Street to Sixth. I found Sixth empty of armed combatants and spied neither human nor beast till I reached my destination. Colonel Crawford's quick withdrawal had apparently succeeded.

A dozen horses were tied to the porch posts and hitch rail of the Wainwright. A fancy-hatted, big-shirted bushwhacker, bristling with pistols in belt holsters, lounged against a porch post. He came to attention. Glad I had stashed the Russell Colt Navy in my saddlebags, I lifted my hands, and before he could challenge me, I said, "I'm unarmed. I live here."

He studied me from bare head, cotton shirt, and cord trousers to half boots, and grunted, "Livery's in the rear. Tie off there."

I dismounted and led Badboy down the alley beside the hotel. The livery barn was deserted. The Wainwright buggy, sorrels ground hitched, stood in the bay of the barn. I tied Badboy in a stall, loosened the cinch on his saddle, and supplied him a nosebag baited with grain. Following Sam Benson's dictum that except in a dire emergency, a true liveryman and horse wrangler never neglected an animal in need of tending, I stripped the harness from the sorrels and turned them loose in the livery corral, where hay and water were available. Finally, in light of not knowing who occupied the Wainwright bar and dining room, being prudent, I hid my saddlebags beneath Sam Benson's bed, surprised how much a natural sense of caution had seeped into my behavior.

Familiar with the smell of blood from my earlier head wound, I sniffed it as I stepped from the alley into the hotel. The door of my room was ajar. I gently shoved it open. Uncle Purse was prone in my bed, left shoulder swathed in white bandages. Dr. Franklin Gribble was hovering over him. Sam Benson was seated in a ladder-back chair at the head of the bed.

Uncle's eyes were open. He appeared to be resting pain free. Dr. Gribble was saying, "That's what you get for thinking two old goats shooting from a buggy could make a difference in a cavalry fight. You're lucky that bullet went clean through your shoulder without hitting bone. Lucky, too, the both of you weren't killed. When the laudanum wears off, you'll have regrets you can't ignore. Serve you right."

"Pshaw, Frank, a man can't stand aside and let others do for him, no matter his age. What was all that commotion out front while you were tending to me? I was pretty woozy at the time."

"We have some well-armed guests from the Rebel side who look to be a rowdy bunch if they're crossed any which way," Sam Benson said. "Emma is preparing to feed them."

Sam Benson's depiction of the dining room's occupants confirmed my suspicion. "They're bushwhackers. I best help Aunt Emma," I blurted without announcing myself.

Three pairs of eyes found me at once. "What are you doing home out of uniform?" Uncle Purse demanded.

"You galloped past us in the hotel buggy. I'm under orders from Captain Crockett to provide my family what assistance I can and then report back to him."

"Damn generous of such a coldhearted bastard," Sam Benson persisted. "You sure that's all he intended?"

I might have blushed, but I didn't stammer. "He said, time allowing, to check on Laura Kellerman too."

Sam Benson's smile was that of a delighted kitten with whiskers dripping fresh cream. I made no attempt to correct his assessment of Nathaniel Crockett. Battles too hard to win in short minutes are best left alone.

"Since you're here out of uniform and unarmed," Uncle Purse decided, "run along with you. Don't fret about me."

Fresh surprises awaited me in the kitchen. First was the longest, leanest, blackest hound I'd ever seen. He was curled up on the floor next to the kitchen's rear door, huge paws flanking his muzzle. The soft thump of my approaching boots lifted the hound's head. He growled low in his throat and flashed fangs that seemed as long as my thumbs. His eyes gleamed like a catamount's. Had a lantern caught the yellow gleam of those eyes at night in dark woods, I would've wet my drawers. I came close to that, a step into the kitchen.

"Jacks."

The single word of command lowered the hound's head, and he licked his lips and nose with a tongue as long as my arm and fell asleep again. My second surprise was the source of the command. He was at the large block table in the center of the kitchen, slicing roasted pork shoulder on a wooden cutting board with a long-bladed knife. There was no mistaking the black wisps of hair dangling from beneath the red bandana wound about his head. His tanned skin was still blemish free and too smooth to sprout whiskers. His cobalt blue eyes were unblinking, blazing stones. His large-bore shotgun, butt resting on the floor, was leaning against the lip of the table within easy reach. The same loose-fitting shirt with huge front and side pockets dwarfed a slim frame that stood about five feet two inches. The smallish bay horse tied to the hotel's hitch rack registered with me just then.

I marveled at the coincidence of my confrontation with this same young boy in the brush alongside the Georgetown Road, my observing of him from afar through Kendrick's binoculars while he served his comrades in the middle of the same road, my participation in the ambushing of his comrades with Keen Doyle's riflemen, and our coming together in Aunt Emma's kitchen. Had sheer fate chosen to intertwine our lives? The odds against our chance meetings defied calculation.

The cobalt blue eyes staring back at me narrowed for an instant, enough to let me know the young bushwhacker was searching his memory for when and where he might have met me before. Aunt

Emma entered from the dining room, interrupting the youth's stare.

She spied me, gasped aloud, set the pitcher she was holding on the table, rushed to me, and clasped me in a bear hug. Let me tell you, Emma Bowels Wainwright was no small female. She could put the squeeze on you something fierce when she was het up emotionally, and I was running out of sustainable air fast when she finally let go of me and held me at arm's length. "It's good to lay eyes on you, nephew."

But het up as she was, responsibility for boarder and diner shoved its way to the forefront in Aunt Emma's mind. She kissed my cheek and returned to her work without bothering to ask how I came to be in her kitchen.

It was Saturday, and anticipating a show of diners at some point, war or no war, Aunt Emma and Megan Evans, orphaned daughter of a slave-owning family massacred by Kansas Red Legs, had been cooking and baking since daylight. They created fare that would quite handsomely feed her unexpected Confederate guests with soldierly appetites that hadn't known true appeasement for who knew how long. Besides the sliced pork, steaming bowls of boiled greens, potatoes, black-eyed peas, cream gravy, baskets of oven-hot biscuits, and pies fashioned from cherries, rhubarb, and apples filled the balance of the large block table. It was a veritable feast and Aunt Emma, a true lover of tasty food, was anxious to serve it to her patrons, no matter how slim the prospects of moneyed payment for her endeavor.

"Our guests have had enough liquid libation. We best fill their bellies. Keep slicing, Morgan. Megan, help me fill a few plates and Owen and I will start serving while you fill the rest."

The hotel kitchen was supplied with metal trays that held three plates each. I had much practice balancing a tray on a forearm, carrying a basket of biscuits with my free hand, and backing through the swinging door of the dining room. I was in the middle of the doorway when Aunt Emma warned, "I've not seen him, but I heard one of our imbibers bragging on your half brother by name."

My aunt adhered to an unbending faith in a protective Creator, and though her guests could yet damage her property or perhaps burn it to the ground, no anxiety or concern for the rough character and reputation of the armed enemy presently cavorting in her dining room marred her features. None ever would, not even if Lance Wainwright, the family outcast, suddenly appeared.

Aunt Emma took the lead and sang out brightly, "Dinner is served, gentlemen."

Six of our pistol-toting Rebel guests were sitting at tables. With the creaking of the dining room's wooden floor and the clinking of spur rowels, an additional three were table bound with Aunt Emma's call to dinner. Every man jack matched the garb and weapons of the bushwhackers we'd ambushed on the Georgetown Road. All were poised with knife and fork at the ready when a new figure emerged from the hotel lobby.

"Hats off, buckos. Gentlemen are expected to dine with heads uncovered at fine establishments like the Wainwright."

The speaker's dress and weapons were a stark contrast to those already seated. He wore a suit of tan broadcloth, a white shirt in need of washing, a black string tie, buckskin trousers, and knee-high black riding boots polished to a high gloss. He sported a finely trimmed dark brown mustache and short beard. He carried a broad-brimmed white hat with a band of red silk in his left hand. The carved butt of a single pistol protruded from a holster on his right hip. Like Captain Nathaniel Crockett, here was a man who dressed to command attention.

Hooded brown eyes, difficult to read, fixed on my aunt. "Mrs. Wainwright, my men and I are thankful for your offer to provide us sustenance. It has been a mean day for us soldiers."

"Captain Logan, an enemy that leaves the fighting at my doorstep is welcome at my table. My helper here is Owen Wainwright, my nephew."

In two trips, Aunt Emma and I had everyone served. Megan Evans carried a plate and a pot of coffee to the horse guard on the front porch. I assumed she also fed Uncle Purse and Sam Benson. Morgan and his long-fanged black hound ate in the kitchen. I can swear that bunch of Rebels did themselves proud when it came to satisfying their hunger. They nearly wore through the bottom of Aunt Emma's porcelain dishes scraping them bare.

The complete absence of rifle fire and exploding cannon toward the end of the meal indicated the attacking Confederates had taken complete control of Sedalia. Every remaining resident now faced the same dilemma: how would the Rebels celebrate their victory?

I had to admire Captain Logan's audacity in arranging a celebratory dinner for his detail before the last round was fired. The front door of the hotel opened and the horse guard from the hotel's porch strode through the lobby and addressed Captain Logan. "Sir, a messenger brought word you and the detail are to report to Colonel Lawton at the railroad depot immediately. Something to do with burning and looting."

Captain Logan stood, wiped his mouth with a cloth napkin, and said, "Ma'am, I searched the back hallway while you were in the kitchen. I'm aware of your husband's wound and the presence of Mr. Benson. Long as they stay put, things will remain peaceful. If you'll excuse us, we have business elsewhere. Sergeant Holloway, you, your son, that damn hound of his, and Private Westwood, hang tight. We've enjoyed Mrs. Wainwright's hospitality and I'll not have anything untoward happen to her, her family, or her business. Understand?"

Sergeant Micah Holloway's rapid, firm "Yes, sir" made it clear he understood his orders.

Captain Logan's attention settled on me. "Young man, you're Lance Wainwright's half brother, are you not?"

That inquiry gave me a clue as to how Captain Logan and his detail had learned of the Wainwright Hotel and its reputation for fine fare. "Follow me, Owen. I have some questions for you."

I had no druthers.

But I, too, had questions:

Where was my half brother?

Was he about to upend my life yet again?

# CHAPTER 9

"I'M HOPING WE HAVE BLACK-UNIFORMED PRISONERS WITH YELLOW armbands toting Sharps rifles. We'll execute every one of those bastards in the blink of an eye."

That pledge from a rider behind Captain Logan and me reeked of venom and lifted the hair on the back of my neck. As we neared the commercial center of Sedalia, we encountered a significant number of civilian prisoners guarded by Confederate soldiers. The prisoners' confiscated weapons were being shattered on hitch racks, porch posts, and building corners and their owners pushed northward on Ohio Avenue. I saw altercations between captor and prisoner that resulted in a hard shove or the application of a Rebel rifle butt, but in the main, civilians were humanely treated if they kept their feet moving. To the southwest, a dark boiling cloud rose above intervening buildings. The victors were rounding up cattle and mules at the public corral.

Captain Logan led his detail across South Main Street. A quick glance west and east revealed the loading of the contents of the large government storehouse at South Main and Kentucky Avenue onto stolen wagons and the rampant pillaging of businesses offering clothing and foodstuffs. We passed between buildings on the opposite berm of South Main, bringing us before the platform of the Missouri Pacific station, where civilian prisoners were being massed for final disposition. Faces inside the depot, some of them female, were pressed against first-floor windows. Stock-broken Yankee rifles and shotguns were stacked alongside the MP right-of-way. The victors in gray had confiscated every weapon.

A stovepipe-thin male dressed in a ragged, threadbare black suit and broad-brimmed planter's hat, riding a common-variety brown horse with no distinguishing features, approached the western edge of the crowd from the direction of Osage Avenue at the head of a contingent of Confederate officers. The brown horse's rider resembled the starving Bible-thumping preacher in poor straits that had visited our homestead on my eighth birthday. A piercing voice yelled, "It's General Thompson!"

In the ensuing hush, Captain Logan glanced my way. "Sedalia folks better pray our boys listen to our top dog. Might be the end of your town if they don't."

General M. Jeff Thompson positioned his horse at the front and center of his civilian captives, who looked much tamer minus their weapons. "Citizens of Sedalia, I am not in possession of printed paroles and haven't the time to write them. I am, therefore, compelled to grant verbal paroles to your home guards and militia companies on the condition peace prevails till my forces have withdrawn."

Two hundred captives heaved a relieved sigh, while murmurs of discontent and muffled curses rippled through the ranks of the victorious Confederates. Thompson's voice lifted, stiffened by anger, "I repeat, all enemy combatants that have surrendered are paroled, providing peace prevails till our withdrawal is complete. Officers, arrest any soldier who chooses to disobey my orders."

General Thompson lifted a hand to squelch further unrest among his fellow Confederates, his gaze never leaving his civilian audience. "I have done what I can to protect your businesses and homes from the torch. We are working to stop the looting of nonmilitary stores that was under way upon my arrival. I can't forebear removal of supplies necessary to the sustenance of my army. Unfortunately, we have no means of reimbursing you for your losses. All prisoners will hold in place for now." Thompson's final words were a welcome humanitarian gesture. "You may have access to the station's wells for water in the meantime."

"Captain Logan."

The call, that of a skeletal, middle-aged Rebel colonel, snaked over my shoulder. Captain Logan's brow lifted with his recognition of the speaker. "Colonel Lawton, I was about to seek you out."

Colonel Lawton straightened his narrow shoulders, as if heightening his authority. "Good, I bear orders for you from General Thompson. Your detail will be the last to depart the field. Specifically, you are to prevent the burning of the town."

Anger knotted the corners of Logan's mouth. "The whole damn town, sir? My detail has only fourteen men reporting for duty, one of them a mere kid."

Lawton leaned forward in his saddle, head cocked sideways. "You heard General Thompson. No burning of buildings. We officers can clear the bulk of our brigades from the town. It's the stragglers who like to hide and linger behind, till they can loot and burn, that concern him. Brett, you and your detail don't take squat from anybody, and you and your boys, being General Thompson's handpicked scouts, the boys in gray are fully aware of your reputation. Ten of your men are worth two dozen of any other unit in Price's army, maybe more."

The naked compliment gave me insight into the stature of Captain Brett Logan and his detail in the eyes of their superior officers and explained why Logan had assumed he could break off from the action at hand and treat his fellow scouts to a private dinner at the Wainwright Hotel without fear of reprimand.

"Frank, you ever talk a man into kissing a running hog's ass from the back of a horse?" Logan asked, chuckling.

"Naw," Lawton admitted, "but I did win fifty dollars talking a mule into shitting on command."

A grinning Captain Logan allowed the laughter Lawton's tall tale evoked among his detail to slacken before saying, "I apologize for my temper, Frank. We will, of course, abide by Thompson's orders."

"I'll so inform him," Lawton responded, and started to turn his horse, only to drop back into the saddle. "Pay particular attention to the railroad depot, Captain. General Thompson fears, were the wind blowing right tonight, a fire in a building that large might ignite the whole town."

I impulsively pulled out my pocket watch. It was 6:15. One of Logan's men saw me holding Laura's gift and reached to snatch it from my hand. With Brett Logan's curt "Let it be," the hand withdrew at equal speed. It was a lesson I wouldn't forget. I was not considered an ally with the right to personal property by Logan's detail.

After asking me the time, Captain Logan studied the westward arc of the sun and issued his first orders of the early evening. "Corporal Tate, fetch Holloway, his son, and Westwood from the hotel. Wainwright, you're riding Westwood's horse. Do you have a horse of your own?"

"Yes, sir, a hammer-headed roan gelding. He's saddled and tied in the hotel's livery barn."

Curiosity aroused, Logan's head perked up. "Where were you earlier today? Were you bearing arms against us, by damned?"

Had I been a day younger, a straight face would have been too much of a challenge. I stared back at Brett Logan with leveled eyes and pretended the freshly anointed Silk was on that creek bank once more. "No, sir, I snuck away from my uncle's hotel and watched the fight from between two buildings on the north side of South Main Street. When our men began to give way, I made for home. I didn't expect you and your men to be there."

Logan thought a moment and nodded, buying my lies. "Tate, bring Wainwright's roan with you too. He needn't walk home, not after the meal his aunt fed us. Holmes, you and Lake rustle some wood and build us a fire. A cup of coffee would taste real fine. The rest of you, step down and rest easy. Wainwright, after me."

I took some comfort from Logan's orders. It appeared he expected to release me. What did he want in the meantime?

Logan led me beyond earshot and motioned for me to dismount. He dropped to a knee and plucked a long blade from a cluster of prairie grass to chew on. "We need to talk about your brother, Lance. He's been riding with us for two years. He's a jewel of a soldier. I've never witnessed a braver man under fire. Men follow him into battle like moths chasing lantern light. On the other hand, he can be nastier than an infected bull testicle. He had no trouble early on tolerating unarmed civilians caught in the middle of a fight, often not of their making or choosing. The last two months, though, any man he suspects isn't blindly loyal to the Confederacy is worthy only of execution and their property subject to confiscation or the torch. I'm no lawless bushwhacker who makes war on defenseless citizens, and I won't command those that do."

Brett Logan chewed on his grass blade. "I was laid up the first of August, recovering from a leg wound. General Price's campaign was still organizing its departure from Arkansas, so I set a rendezvous date for the fifteenth of August and gave my detail leave till then, with General Thompson's permission. When we rendezvoused, Lance, Pat Shannon, and Tom Boyd had a heap of money on them. I was curious where the money came from, but the three of them were tight-lipped as a stone statue, and we'd a war to fight and I didn't pursue the subject. I did hear Lance bragging one evening about how easy the pickings had been at Sedalia. Then Pat Shannon, the most superstitious soul on God's green earth, didn't realize I was close by, making a last check of our horses, and blurted louder than he intended how queasy he was about returning to where they'd killed an old, unarmed clerk during a robbery. Lance threatened to shoot Shannon if he said another word and, needless to say, Pat clammed up like he'd been shot dead for real."

Logan sighed and pitched his grass stem. "Was a clerk killed in Sedalia during a robbery last August?"

I hesitated but a couple of seconds. Logan could gain such information from any man among the prisoners crowding the front of the station. "The Kellerman Mercantile was robbed on the seventh. The three robbers coerced Mr. Kellerman into opening his safe by murdering his store clerk. They stole two thousand dollars."

Logan whistled softly in amazement. "Were they identified?"

"The shooter was. It was Lance. A stray bullet knocked me down in front of the Wainwright Hotel during the bandits' flight. Lance stopped his horse long enough to pull down his mask and shoot my dog so I'd have something to remember him by."

"Did anyone else see his face?"

"Not that I'm aware of."

"Were Lance's companions wearing masks?"

"Yes, sir."

Logan's next question showed a nimble, penetrating mind. "Then how do you know it was Lance that killed the clerk inside Kellerman's?"

"He was the only bandit with red hair like mine."

Logan scowled and stroked his beard. "It's Lance's rash decisions that concern me. I was at the rear of the column this morning, conferring with Colonel Lawton, when one of our flankers flushed a small Yankee party to the northeast. We'd already scouted Sedalia. We had nothing to gain chasing after a piddling bunch of Yankees. But Lance went busting after them with my whole detail like a glory-hunting schoolboy and led them straight into an ambush. We were up against Sharps breechloaders and lost ten fine men blown to hell and beyond."

I couldn't resist any longer and had to ask, "Where is Lance?"

"Colonel Lawton had word from a scout who rode his horse nigh onto death reaching our camp that bluebelly reinforcements are advancing along the Missouri Pacific line from Jefferson City. At General Thompson's request, I sent Lance, Pat Shannon, and Tom Boyd to confirm or deny what the messenger claimed. Frankly, I wanted Lance out of my sight for a spell. They have yet to return."

Spur rowels jingled. A lean arm extended a tin cup toward Brett Logan. "Coffee with a splash of brandy for the night chill, sir."

"Much appreciated, Upton."

I had one more question gnawing at me. "What brought you to the Wainwright Hotel this afternoon?"

"The Wainwright name. I knew Lance was from Pettis County, and Colonel Lawton had bragged the other evening how much he'd enjoyed your aunt's cooking on a visit to Sedalia before the war came calling. And, trust me, Frank knows his eats. I figured if I were lucky, I'd learn if Lance had indeed been involved in a lucrative robbery, and a good meal would take the boys' minds off their being ambushed so handily."

The cloud of hoof-stirred dust hovering above the cattle corral to the southwest swelled ever larger. Farmers with a distance to travel were the first prisoners paroled, per the shouted commands we overheard. There was no smudge of smoke or leap of flame suggesting a man-made fire. General Thompson's peace reigned for the moment.

A silent Logan sipped his brandy-laced coffee. I wondered what he was thinking. "He shot your dog?"

"Yes, sir, Lance ran off from our home place when I was ten. We weren't true brothers."

I considered how much of my family's history I wanted to share, suspecting Lance hadn't told much beyond how devoted to the whip our father had been, if that. However, before I could stay my tongue, the floodgate was open and I was confiding in a stranger I had known for a few hours, as if he wore a ministerial collar.

"Our father believed Lance and I owed him work equal to a hired hand soon as we could tote a bucket of water and toss a forkful of hay. Lance's mother died before I was born. My mother was twenty years younger than my father. When I was eight, he beat me with the same whip he used on Lance while Mother was sick in bed. She threatened to leave him if he ever beat me again. Father was twice as tough on Lance from then on and Lance came to resent Mother and me. One morning, Lance was just gone. A bit later, my mother felt a pain in her belly. She just faded away till she didn't have the strength to draw a breath."

As it always did, dwelling on Mother's passing threatened to bring me to tears. I paused and cleared my throat. Captain Logan seemed to understand and waited patiently while I composed myself. "With the loss of Lance and then Mother, Father was in a foul temper forever. I was fourteen and preparing to run off, like Lance, the night six home guard Union militia seized our farm. Father had given temporary shelter to a runaway slave in return for food and his help widening a ditch. The Union militia's officers, our neighbors the Strand brothers, were strict abolitionists. The Strands discounted Father's argument that the slave was free to leave, once the agreed-upon work was completed. They had the excuse they needed to hang the man who'd publicly called them 'Negro-loving sons of bitches' in a fit of anger during a court hearing to settle a property line dispute. Mother always said Father's titanic temper would be his undoing."

"Did they make you watch the hanging?"

"No, sir, they locked me in a feed bin. They made Anson, the runaway, and me dig Father's grave, while they burned the house and barn. They debated what to do with me, and Milo Strand ordered two militiamen to drop me on my uncle's doorstep. Neither one of the militiamen said a word the whole ride to Sedalia."

Logan finished the last of his coffee. "The war has been used as an excuse by murderers and revenge seekers on both sides for their own gain and I'm tired of it. Maybe I've been fighting this damnable conflict too long. Maybe I've witnessed too many dead bodies.

Seen too much blood spilled. Written too many letters notifying mothers their sons have perished in a great and noble conflict. My problem is the end of the war isn't in sight. There are a lot of rough, sharp edges to Lance and a streak of pure cruelty in him, perhaps tied to the whip scars on his backside. But he's a warrior and I need him to help hold the last of my detail together. We may be reduced as a fighting unit. That doesn't mean we can't scout and spy with the best of the advance units attached to Generals Thompson and Price."

Captain Logan's frankness in spelling out his dilemma in dealing with Lance's conduct under arms and his disdain for civilian rights led me to decide I had to tell him that U.S. Marshal Forge Bannister held a Federal warrant calling for Lance's arrest for murder, and it carried a reward of $500, dead or alive. I saw no surprise in his expression as he heard me out.

"The death toll of war forces an officer to accept the support of all those souls, misguided or not, who will bear arms and risk their lives for the cause they share together. For me, this war was defending the rights of the state against the tyranny of the Unionists. I've argued for those rights in the courts and fought for them on the battlefield. Not a single instigator of this war anticipated how the expected clash on the battlefield would spill over into town squares and farm dooryards, far and wide. General Sheridan's raping and burning of the Shenandoah Valley is no less savage and destructive than what unchecked guerillas, be they Jayhawker or bushwhacker, have wrought in Kansas and Missouri."

Brett Logan's pointed, lucid assessment of the impact of the war on noncombatants and reference to the courts branded him what I dreamed of becoming: a learned lawyer. He would be a formidable opponent before the bar.

Logan rose to his feet at the sound of approaching horsemen. "Makes no difference how tired or dissuaded I am, I took an oath and I've no option except to pursue victory for the Confederacy so long as I can mount a horse and have men to lead. That goal must temper every decision an officer makes, every order he gives. Remember that if you ever find yourself in my boots."

The three horsemen pulled rein before Captain Logan and me. Though Lance Wainwright spoke to Logan, my newly arrived half brother's stare was fixed on me. "Reporting as ordered, Captain. Union reinforcements are three hours behind us."

The fury in Lance's eyes would have melted steel. My sudden appearance beside Brett Logan had to warn him his commanding officer might have learned the truth regarding his participation in the Kellerman robbery, and if I had been totally forthcoming, his murdering of old Spain. I had a gut feeling my life was in danger despite Logan's presence. The odds against Lance being arrested in wartime, and my identifying him in a Federal court, were great, but that slim chance existed, and the cost of a single bullet erased it completely.

Did anyone else notice Lance's cross-draw grip on the butt of the revolver on his left hip? I fought the urge to hide behind Captain Logan. Damn if I'd give Lance the pleasure of watching me squirm.

I went forward alive and upright after that evening, never again doubting the ability of lawyer Brett Logan to think quickly in a tight situation that would have strangled the creativity of many a man. "We'll pass that information to Colonel Lawton straightaway. Lance, you haven't seen him for a long while, but I'm sure you remember your half brother, Owen, here. The boys and I had occasion to dine at the Wainwright Hotel earlier. Your aunt Emma, a fine woman and a fine cook, got to bragging on young Owen. Seems he is a fine blacksmith and horse wrangler, a good campfire cook, can hunt game without a hound, and possesses intelligence, schooling, and proper manners. Your aunt wasn't happy when I told her Owen would be accompanying our campaign henceforth as my aide-de-camp. I will say, though, Union dollars as pay for our meal did seem to lighten her loss."

Somehow I kept my jaw from dropping like a falling rock. Yes, Aunt Emma had bragged about me in the very terms Logan spelled out. And, yes, he had paid for his detail's meals with Union dollars. But there had been not one word regarding my accompanying his detail on their campaign. He had created that on the spur of the moment out of whole cloth.

Logan's ploy to defuse Lance's fiery temper before it could ignite succeeded. I saw Lance's hand slip free of the butt of his revolver and caught the relaxation of Logan's upper body a heartbeat later. I was safe, at least for now. For how long was as uncertain as my future tenure as a Confederate bushwhacker.

More hoofbeats announced the coming of Sergeant Holloway, his son, and Private Westwood. The lashings of the canvas bags carried by the packhorse Morgan Holloway led were the workmanship of Sam Benson. Aunt Emma hadn't cheated on the foodstuffs Logan had included in the price of her meal. The long-legged, lean-bellied black hound brought up the rear. It gladdened me that Westwood was riding Badboy. I'd have one friend with me from the start.

The yard of the MP station was emptying of paroled captives. My watch told me it was five minutes before seven-thirty. Captain Logan split his detail into two squads, led by Lance and Sergeant Holloway, and sent them on a patrol of South Main Street looking for evidence of the fires forbidden by General Thompson. Logan, Morgan Holloway, and I edged closer to the most tempting target for the torch, the three-story depot.

Someone shouted at the top of their lungs within the depot as the last of the paroled captives drifted away to return to their homes. Tongues of flame backlit the building's front windows. A puff of smoke shot out the main doorway. Loud female caterwauling and equally loud cursing, obviously male in origin, erupted near that same entryway.

To our astonishment, four stumbling, lurching, drunken Confederate soldiers burst out onto the platform of the depot. The cause of their flight, with their torches still in hand, came directly behind them. I never again doubted the power of gray-haired females, for, with brooms raised, they screeched damnation to all creatures in long pants till kingdom come. I recognized the two women leading the pursuit. More gray-haired women surged from behind the depot. In both hands, these women were holding water buckets. Aunt Emma's Ladies' Reading Society had appointed themselves guardians of Sedalia's most valuable commercial structure and they were enjoying a right smart turn at it.

Lance and the returning fire seekers missed out on the fun and were left scratching chins at the sight of a dozen grandmothers making for Osage Avenue in perfect military formation, with brooms over their left shoulders. Personal laughter leaving him nearly breathless, Captain Logan inquired, "Lieutenant, what is the status of the town?"

"Quiet and well, sir. Little fire damage. No sign of fresh smoke or fire throughout."

The pointed brevity and clarity of Lance's report impressed me. But then, despite his bullish, unforgiving, hate-burdened manner, and the wearing of his emotions on his sleeve like Father, he had never shown a dearth where brains were concerned.

Captain Logan donned his riding gloves. "Gentlemen, Sedalia has survived its capture and release without major damage and unnecessary death, as General Thompson wished. We have the prized beef we sought. A bait of moonlight riding awaits us. Sergeant Holloway, column of twos, if you please."

And so we departed Sedalia, with me a willing captive. Behind us, the town was a collection of gray-shadowed buildings crowned by the MP station under a rapidly darkening sky.

Poled torches with low-burning cloth wicks cast a yellow glow over the ground between the tracks of the MP and the Warrensburg Road at the extreme northwestern end of the town's abandoned rifle pits. Nine black bodies dressed in loose-fitting cotton shirts and trousers, and wearing tall brogan shoes, resting side by side, lined the right-of-way with a shovel beside each of them.

"What the hell!" exclaimed Sergeant Holloway. "Detail halt."

Without waiting for orders, Holloway jumped from the saddle and strode hurriedly to the aligned bodies. He examined the first two and the last two, and, head shaking, marched to Captain Logan's stirrup. "Single shot to the back of the head, sir. Assassinated for helping defend the town."

The dead men were the black workers I had spied, from afar, digging away that very morning. Of the events I witnessed on a wild day that saw me shoot a man from ambush, the wanton assassination of nine unarmed, well-intentioned black men burdened me with a memory that burned white-hot in nightmares and brought me awake in a cold sweat many a night.

I had no inkling as we resumed our march that the callous slaying of nine unknown black men in the midst of war would later spawn an unquenchable thirst in me to defend the rights of all men under the law regardless of their skin color.

But they surely did.

# PART III

# LOGAN'S SCOUTS

# CHAPTER 10

WE RODE INTO A BLACK NIGHT ROOFED WITH BRIGHT STARS. A HEAVY tiredness beset me, the weight of the day's events pressing me to the brink of total exhaustion. I fought to keep my shoulders squared and my chin up. The possible consequences of those events struck home a few miles from Sedalia and conspired to keep me awake in the saddle.

What would Uncle Purse think of my riding off with the Confederate Army? At least a few of the townsmen paroled at the depot were patrons of the Wainwright dining room and had surely recognized me. They would report what they had seen out of courtesy and their respect for a community leader. I trusted Uncle Purse would assume I had been taken prisoner and wasn't offered a parole. I couldn't vouchsafe the same for Stuart Kellerman when word of my apparent rejection of the Union cause reached him. He would most likely jump to the conclusion I had turned down a parole, and thereby proven his suspicion that my half brother's bad blood flowed freely in my veins.

And, more important, what would his daughter think? Had I thrown her aside for a chance to play soldier and go adventure hunting? Would she cave to her father's convictions?

I fingered the gift watch in my pocket. I refused to countenance the thought Laura would turn her back on me without knowing more of what had transpired, not after inscribing her love on the watch's lid and sharing that magnificent kiss in her millinery shop. Somehow—the how, I must admit, was undefined and uncertain, and sooner, hopefully, rather than later—I would send her word of my situation.

In the meantime, I had to stay alive. I didn't doubt that my willingness to be held captive and serve as Captain Logan's aide-de-camp had spared me a quick death, for Lance hadn't dare kill his commander's new servant in cold blood before that officer's very eyes. But the sparing of my life carried a steep price: providing a potential target for Lance's family hatred around the clock. He would always know where to find me. And a flying bullet in the midst of battle or in the middle of the night didn't scream its owner's name for all present to hear before striking its intended target.

As for protecting myself, I didn't foresee Captain Logan allowing me to bear arms. Maybe he would find my services of little real value if I couldn't bear arms on demand and would send me home. On second thought, the enthusiasm in his voice when he described my duties to Lance had sounded genuine, and I had too much pride to play the buffoon on purpose and embarrass Aunt Emma. Like it or not, I'd been dealt a hand in an adult game where mere survival made you a winner.

The only hindrance to foul intentions on Lance's part was Captain Logan. Lance had to know Logan was unhappy with his brazen treatment of civilians and his rash charge into disaster with the whole squad just hours ago. Logan's power and opinion were thin layers of protection for me, given Lance's temper, but it would force him to seek that rare opportunity when his chances of doing me harm without being caught in the act were minimal. I vowed with as much earnestness as I could muster that I would bump into Captain Brett Logan's heels so often, he would swear he had a second shadow.

I was riding behind Captain Logan, Sergeant Holloway, and Lance. We were in the rear of General Thompson's entire brigade, passing through a constant dust cloud thrown up by the cattle and the five wagonloads of supplies General Thompson's brigade had pilfered from Sedalia's stores and warehouses. Captain Logan's sneeze lifted his bottom from the saddle. "That's it. We're not being followed. Lead us ahead, Sergeant. The cattle drovers are enough of a rear guard for tonight."

Startled exclamations and mild cursing rose from General Thompson's column of fours as we wedged by horse-drawn cannons and fifteen hundred mounted men along the berm of the road after clearing the cattle and supply wagons. Sergeant Holloway held us in place in a single line near the head of the column, while Captain Logan conferred with the general and Colonel Lawton. A half-moon was out now and cast a silvery light on headgear and shoulders. A trooper in the column recognized the pinned-up brims on the hats of Logan's scouts and mouthed, "You gussied-up pistol lovers enjoy being ambushed?"

Lance straightened in the saddle and snarled, "Ask that again and I'll have you squealing like a throat-cut pig."

I saw Sergeant Holloway's hand clasp Lance's forearm, staying the drawing of the large knife he carried in a leather sheath beneath his shirt, with the handle protruding between two buttons. The size of the handle and cross guard and the lump of the sheath bulging Lance's shirt equaled those of a knife belonging to Sam Benson; its blade was a foot long and three inches wide, honed top to bottom with a curving saber point, enabling it to cut both upward and downward. Sergeant Holloway carried a knife just as large in a similar fashion.

Captain Logan's return blunted Lance's temper and Holloway freed his arm. Logan's firm, precise orders forestalled further ribbing from General Thompson's troopers. "Sergeant, please fetch Private Upton. We will be taking the point, Lieutenant." Spinning his mount, Logan's right arm swept forward. "Detail, column of twos, forward march."

Escaping the eye-watering, throat-drying dust cloud revived the spirits of the scouts somewhat. I heard enough snatches from the verbal exchanges of Captain Logan, Lance, Sergeant Holloway, and Private Upton to learn Upton hailed from Lexington, our eventual destination. The plan was, we would soon desert the main road and take byroads and then camp on the far bank of Muddy Creek. With Upton serving as our guide, we passed through farmed acreage interspersed with wooded country. Whatever intact houses we saw were dark at the windows at that hour. Here and there, a house, a barn, and outbuildings were burned-out hulks, victims of a war in almost its fourth year.

We reached Muddy Creek twenty minutes past midnight by my pocket watch. Dead tired or not, troopers first had to water their horses along the far bank of the creek and then unsaddle them wherever graze was available. Private Upton told me about Sergeant Holloway's sentiments regarding the care of the scouts' horses. "He thinks these four-legged creatures are working tools designed by the Almighty Lord, special gifts not to be abused or taken advantage of. None of us want to hear that again. Be warned. His tongue can peel skin from a man's backside."

Captain Logan outlawed fires. We went to bed empty-bellied without blankets and tents on bare ground chilled by a late-night autumn breeze. Jacketless and hatless, I shivered through the few hours we rested.

The smell of bacon frying drifted on the moving air during the morning saddling and horse watering. I discovered upon reporting to Captain Logan that Private Morgan Holloway was assigned to cook breakfast for the captain, Lance, and his father. Private Holloway was quick and nimble with coffeepot, fry pan, and small baking oven. He provided tin cups and plates from a burlap bag. For some unknown reason, a hint of blush showed on his cheeks as I seated myself opposite his other diners and accepted a steaming cup. There was no sign of Jacks, his black hound with the long legs and fangs.

Lance greeted me with a hollow "Good morning" and stared into the breakfast fire. I simply nodded and sipped my coffee. I couldn't shake the sense I was in the presence of a lean wolf watching a herd of sheep, always ready to strike. I took a deep breath and cursed silently.

*Grow a backbone. Stop playing the wimp when you're* not *in danger of bodily harm. On top of that, words aren't anything to fret over.*

Sergeant Micah Holloway was the source of his son's black hair and cobalt blue eyes. The vibrant blackness of his mustache, short beard, and the hair overhanging his ears shone in the light of the breakfast fire. The broken knuckles on the hands holding his morning cup of coffee suggested he was no stranger to fisticuffs. When he spoke, his voice, while not deep, had the forceful undertone of men like Uncle Purse and Sam Benson, men confident of their mental and physical abilities. "Captain, you mentioned last evening that General Thompson intended to replace the men we lost in the ambush. Any more to say on that?"

Brett Logan finished reading a written message delivered by courier during the night and answered, shaking the message for emphasis. "Yes, Lieutenant Graham Donovan and ten troopers with skirmishing and scouting experience will be joining us shortly."

I saw Lance's gaze lock on Captain Logan as Holloway asked, "How will we absorb them, sir?"

"We'll split the command into two squads of ten reporting to Lance and Donovan, and promote one of Donovan's men to sergeant if none of his group hold that rank. Two squads fully staffed allows us to scout in more than one direction when the occasion demands."

Because I was studying Lance closely, I spied the brightness that flared in his eyes and the clenching of his jaw. Captain Logan's realignment made imminent sense from a tactical and flexibility standpoint. But it was a demotion for Lance, who heretofore had been the second-ranking officer in Logan's scouts and the commanding officer in Logan's absence. Some fast chewing and swallowing of the bacon and the warmed-over biscuits from Aunt Emma's oven, served by Private Holloway, gave Lance time to hide his disappointment. He didn't dare raise an objection to Logan's scheme. He was, after all, still an officer. Captain Logan could have demoted him to corporal, broken him to the rank of private, or had him court-martialed for a grievous error, had he wished.

The veteran Sergeant Holloway, who had seized Lance's arm to prevent the drawing of his knife while responding to a heckler in his own ranks, would continue to report to Lance. I suspected that was a move made to keep my half brother's wild eagerness to fight under a modicum of control. Brett Logan knew nothing about the knife incident, but he was proving to be an observant, resourceful, and clever commanding officer.

A pattern of open, unbridled conversation and comradeship obviously prevailed at Logan's breakfast fire, for Private Morgan Holloway, his voice possessing the uneven, froglike quality of a lad teetering between youth and adulthood, inquired, "What's our objective today, Captain?"

"Finding and joining with General Price's army before we're defeated piecemeal," Logan said, his frustration showing. "We by-passed St. Louis and Jefferson City because the enemy was too entrenched and too powerful. The taking of Boonville last week was a minor victory at best. General Thompson admitted a bunch of locals swarmed to Price's cause, but not like Price anticipated, and most had no weapons. His initial force is shrinking fast. We need to come to grips with the enemy in force before attrition is our ruination."

"Is General Price as iffy as rumor has it?" Lance queried.

I was taken aback a little by Lance's bluntness. He was asking a superior officer to render a potentially negative opinion about the commanding general of the entire Confederate campaign, a bold-as-brass undertaking to me, based on my reading of American history under the tutelage of Master Schofield.

Captain Logan's failure to chastise Lance for overstepping his bounds and the forthrightness of his response indicated he had not lost total confidence in Lance as a fellow officer and confidant. "General Price's poor health has too often confined him to a farmhouse bed or a tent. I look to the likes of our General Thompson for leadership. His talent for constantly attacking and frustrating the Yankees with an undermanned regiment in the early years of the war caused General Grant to nickname him the Swamp Fox. He spent the first seven months of this year in Yankee prison camps, including Johnson's Island on Lake Erie throughout the winter. And whom did General Shelby trust after his promotion to lead his famed Iron Brigade, our home division and best fighting unit in Missouri? Why, our Jeff Thompson."

Considering the subject closed, Logan sipped coffee and said, "Eat up. The clock is ticking."

Morgan Holloway had chosen a seat beside me. Other than a quick introduction, we had not exchanged another word. Not wanting to appear unfriendly, I said, "I haven't seen your dog since we camped last night."

"He's hunting for his breakfast," Morgan said.

"You don't feed him?"

"No, he's on his own. He's an independent cuss."

"Had him long?"

"He sought refuge in our barn during a January sleet storm. The bottom of his left front paw had been torn open somehow and was bleeding. Had he not been hurt, I would never have gotten near him. He was so weak and hungry, he finally gave in and let me tend to him. Three weeks later, I went to feed him and he was gone. I thought I'd never see him again, but a month later, he was back. He roams far and wide as he pleases. When he's around, he's very protective of me."

Glancing across the fire, Morgan continued, "Father contends Jacks has adopted me like a substitute mother, if that makes any sense."

Micah Holloway swallowed a bite of well-chewed biscuit and said, "Had a mare horse take to me in the same manner. Animals that can't talk can be more loyal than men I've fought beside."

Footfalls rustled brown grass behind me. "Good morning, gentlemen. Have I found the fire of Captain Logan?"

Rising to his feet, Logan responded, "That you have, and you are Lieutenant Donovan?"

"That I am," said a raw-boned, gray-haired, gray-bearded officer, with a head featuring a hedgerow of bushy brows never touched by scissors, a violently hooked nose, and ears big and round as dinner plates. The knuckles on the hand attached to an arm long enough to reach across our breakfast fire were the size of walnuts. The boots housing the feet standing next to me had to consume the hide of an entire cow in their making. Though no taller than me, Lieutenant Graham Donovan had the bodily appendages of a giant.

Morgan Holloway leaned against my shoulder, giggled softly, and whispered, "Wonder how big the other parts of him are?"

I stifled a laugh with a closed fist, thinking I smelled the faint fragrance of lilacs on Morgan Holloway, and then dismissed that notion as silly, since men didn't smell like flowers, lest they'd just stepped from the barber's chair after a shave. And there was no hint of a female in Morgan's slim figure.

Donovan's oversized paw engulfed Captain Logan's. "At your service, sir. My boys are happy to escape the ranks for a bit and see something smack in front of them besides the back end of a horse."

Captain Logan introduced us and Donovan insisted that he shake all our hands. "Pleasure to meet the man who led the charge at Langley's Hole," Micah Holloway said. "Not often a dozen skirmishers rout a Yankee company in the dark of the night."

Donovan's booming laugh roared from deep in his chest. "Hell's bells, Holloway, half of them boys in blue was so young, they didn't carry a razor, and our Rebel yell had them shittin' themselves straight off."

Everyone laughed heartily at Donovan's ribald recounting of the Yankee rout except Lance. I couldn't fathom how Lance could be jealous of a Missouri soldier of Graham Donovan's age. But then my half brother had never been the center of things growing up. Father had discounted the importance of even birthdays. Maybe Father had sat upon his feelings so long and hard, a grown-up Lance craved adult attention and recognition even if it meant killing his own kind.

A second "Eat up" from Captain Logan had us gulping the last of our breakfast, while he quickly explained the reorganization of his scouts to his new lieutenant. I assumed without being told, I was to help Morgan Holloway scrape and clean tin breakfast plates with sand and water at Muddy Creek and return plates and coffee cups to his burlap bag. A second bag sufficed for his skillet and baking oven. Sergeant Holloway kicked dirt over the dying embers of our breakfast fire.

Master Schofield would grade Morgan Holloway a "quick read," for with little help from me, he balanced and retied the load of the scouts' pack mule with nearly the exact lashings employed by Sam Benson. I admitted honestly, "I could never load a mule to Mr. Benson's satisfaction."

"Your Mr. Benson was a true gentleman," Morgan Holloway conceded. "Your blacksmith tools are beneath the vittles, everything you need but anvil and bellows."

So Captain Logan hadn't forgotten his plan for providing blacksmithing services to his charges on the move. I'd taken note of the spare horseshoes tied to leather thongs hanging from the scouts' saddle horns. Apparently, Logan's men paid more attention to the health of their animals than Bloody Bill Anderson's guerillas.

Logan's scouts were waiting, prepared to mount, when Iron Brigade buglers on the opposite bank of Muddy Creek blew the call "To Horse." We lined out in Captain Logan's prescribed order of march: column of twos, with the captain and Lance's squad at the point, with a trooper flanking them to either side at thirty yards; then Morgan and the pack mule and me were in the middle, with Lieutenant Donovan's squad bringing up the rear, wending toward Lexington on the Missouri River, per the previous night's orders.

The air was cool, the sky studded with white clouds; the grasses of the open prairie were turning autumn brown and purple, and patches of timber were blanketed with yellow, orange, and red leaves. It was perfect weather for a horseback ride, minus the threat of a bullet from ambush. Riding in the dark on our departure from Sedalia, the lack of a firearm hadn't bothered me. I found riding unarmed in the open in broad daylight, with soldiers armed thrice over, mighty unsettling. When the fighting resumed, and it got mean and close—and it was bound to, given the determination of my captors to engage the enemy—would my captors have any concern for my safety and well-being in the middle of a battle?

Being unarmed was half of the dilemma confronting me. If my captors did arm me, they would expect me to fight with them, a turnabout I wasn't prepared to make.

I felt like a two-headed coin.

Someone, most likely beyond my purview, would flip that coin. I could only stay alert, make full use of what soldierly skills Sam Benson, Sergeant Frank Butler, and Theo Corson had taught me, and pray I had a say in how that coin landed.

# CHAPTER 11

AT MIDMORNING, I WAS SERIOUSLY FEELING THE HEAT OF THE SUN ON the back of my neck. A trooper I recognized from Lance's squadron reined his horse alongside Badboy and passed me a slouch hat and the gray jacket worn by mounted Confederate cavalry. The jacket was a perfect fit and provided a handier pocket for the Dollond telescope. The slouch hat was two sizes bigger than my head and rested atop my ears, but the shade its floppy brim provided my neck was most welcome. "Captain Logan thought you should be properly outfitted," my supplier said before spurring ahead to rejoin his squadron.

Taking in my new appearance, Morgan Holloway, quaky young voice loud enough to carry over the soft plop of hoofs, creak of saddle leather, and jingle of bridal chains, said, "Seems the captain thinks highly of his prisoner."

"Don't know if I would stake my life on that yet," I answered.

"Might be he was thinking of the three boys his wife lost at birth when he kept that brother of yours from shooting you."

My interest in Morgan Holloway grew a heap with that assertion, not for revealing what he knew about the personal life of Captain Brett Logan, but the fact he had been sufficiently aware of what was happening in front of the Missouri Pacific station the previous evening to deduce my life was in danger. "I owe Captain Logan for interceding on my behalf. Now I'm trying to adjust to being his prisoner. It feels strange to be at the end of another man's leash with no say about anything."

"Probably every black man I've ever laid eyes on feels the same way."

That insightful sentiment told me Morgan Holloway was mature for his age, aware of his surroundings, and likely had a degree of education. I wondered if his father, fighting for the Southern cause, had ever viewed black slaves in the same light. With the sentiment regarding slavery in Sedalia often vacillating between freedom and the chain, I had overheard conversations in the Wainwright Hotel dining room that credited slaves with a strong back and strong loins and little else, to which those favoring abolition took violent exception. Uncle Purse finally forbade discussion of the subject on the premises and enforced his ban with a handy, double-barreled, sawed-off shotgun, the most sobering argument killer known to mankind.

Intrigued by Morgan Holloway's demeanor, I spat to rid my mouth of the grit stirred up by our horses and asked, "How long have you been riding with Captain Logan?"

"About a year. Paw has been with him for three years."

"You have family somewhere?"

Eyes looking straight ahead, Morgan answered, "None. Mother died of the pox and the war took my brother. The Union Army used General Ewing's evacuation order to burn our farm in Jackson County and seize our cattle and horse stock."

The pain of old memories saddened Morgan's features and I thought he might cry. General Thomas Ewing's August 25, 1863, General Order No. 11 had required *all* persons in Jackson, Cass, Bates, and northern Vernon Counties to leave within fifteen days. Anyone certified as loyal to the Union could stay, but they had to move to military posts within the area for protection so the Yankee army could watch over them. Ewing's Order No. 11 was the Yankee army's solution for its failure to subdue the bands of Southern-leaning guerillas and bushwhackers terrorizing western Missouri with the support of family, friends, and sympathizers. With the men of area households, like Sergeant Micah Holloway, off fighting the war, the St. Louis newspapers had heralded how thousands of women, old folks, and children had abandoned their properties and headed east. It was a forced migration Uncle Purse had deemed excessively cruel, and one that would diminish neither the strength nor the blatant crimes of the guerillas. The St. Louis papers had agreed with Uncle regarding the latter in the ensuing months.

Without any prompting from me, Morgan Holloway continued, "Paw had me put on the captain's muster roll so he could provide for me and not depend on the charity of strangers."

The column dipped into a shallow valley. Wanting to continue our conversation, I chose a brighter subject. "Captain Logan referred to General Shelby's Iron Brigade at breakfast with considerable pride. What distinguishes the Iron Brigade from other Confederate units?"

"Paw says General Shelby organized his cavalry brigade in '62 in Lafayette County. Shelby and his brigade fought at Cane Hill and Prairie Grove with General Marmaduke's cavalry division. Last fall, he led a cavalry raid that crisscrossed Missouri for fifteen hundred miles, killed and wounded hundreds of Yankees, and won him a promotion to brigadier general. In every battle and skirmish, his men have been lauded for their courage under fire and the newspapers dubbed them the Iron Brigade."

"How many men and units are in his Iron Brigade?"

Morgan said, "One thousand four hundred and fifty-six of us answered roll call two days ago, according to Paw." Then, checking the units off on his fingers, he recited, "There's Lieutenant Colonel Gordon's Lafayette County Regiment, Major Smith's Southwest Missouri Regiment, Lieutenant Colonel Erwin's Jackson County Regiment, two battalions commanded by Captains Elliott and Slayback, two battalions of recruits led by Colonel Crisp and Major Johnson, and Captain Collier's Missouri Artillery."

Impressed with Morgan's detailed reply, I asked, "With his promotion, who reports to General Shelby?"

"General Shelby commands a division composed of three brigades, the Iron Brigade and the two brigades led by Colonel Jackman and Colonel Tyler."

I couldn't resist asking after a name I hadn't heard. "You didn't mention Colonel Lawton, the older tobacco-chewing officer that passed General Thompson's orders to Captain Logan at the MP station. He seemed to have some authority."

"Colonel Lawton is General Thompson's intelligence officer. Father says he dispatches individual troopers and details to spy on

Union troop movements, camps, and towns. Captain Logan and Paw call him Gray Fox. Colonel Lawton has even spied on towns personally."

Slowed by the immense cattle herd trailing behind us, we traveled primarily at a walk the entire morning, trotting ahead and blowing the horses for brief periods on the odd hours. During one of our halts, Captain Logan sought me out. He dismounted, acknowledged Morgan Holloway, and said, "Wainwright, we scouts are a long way from the division's farriers. Lest we receive new orders from General Shelby, we should reach Waverly, where there's a sizable blacksmith shop, in late afternoon, day after tomorrow. I know the owner of that shop. It may take you the whole night, but if I can avoid it, we're not engaging the enemy in force with horses missing shoes or going lame. Hopefully, if he's available, the owner's smithy can work with you."

"Sir, if half of our horses need shoeing, that's more than two men can shoe in a single night, and the Waverly shop may not have enough shoe stock."

My disclaimer didn't derail Brett Logan's planning. "We'll follow the same pattern, day and night, whenever we camp near a town with a forge, till we've reshod both squads. There's no better service you can provide my boys."

Joseph O. Shelby's Iron Brigade marched the balance of the day without locating General Price's friendly forces or encountering a sign of the enemy. With Logan's scouts split into two squads, the enlisted men supped that evening with Sergeants Holloway and Whitman. Lieutenant Donovan and Lance dined with Captain Logan and his guest, Colonel Lawton. Private Morgan Holloway cooked for the officers, with me assisting him.

The fare that evening was freshly butchered cuts of beef, sprinkled with salt, fried in Morgan's skillet or strung on iron skewers propped over the open fire, a hasty preparation perfected by General Thompson's quick-striking battalion earlier in the war. Hungry as we were, there were no complaints about the lack of butter for Morgan's oven-baked biscuits. The coffee was black, and strong, tongue-scorching-hot, straight from the pot.

The chief topic of discussion among the officers was the whereabouts of General Sterling Price's Confederate Army, rumored to be scattered to the north in the direction of Lexington, sizable Union forces beyond Price, supposedly nearer to Lexington, and yet another Union Army coming from Jefferson City in the Iron Brigade's rear.

Perhaps the belief he was speaking with fellow officers he trusted to keep the opinions he expressed confidential was what loosened Colonel Lawton's tongue, while we enjoyed a final cup of coffee topped by a dollop of Captain Logan's brandy. "Sterling Price is a ballooned shell of a once-bright, opportunistic officer. His health is not good, his mind unsettled and indecisive. He has neither the iron will nor the physical stamina to curb the looting and straggling that slow his army on the march and distract from the task at hand. If he must pull together information regarding the location of enemy forces, account for terrain and topographical features, and direct an attack that reacts to the strengths and weaknesses of the enemy as the battle unfolds, I'm afraid we will find ourselves at a severe disadvantage."

"What, if anything, can be done to swing the tide in our favor?" Brett Logan inquired.

Colonel Lawton's gaunt countenance was so thin, it resembled that of a starving man with no memory of his last meal, but his gray eyes brimmed with alert intelligence. "We field officers must decipher what we can about the enemy's location and movement daily, then hourly, once we're in contact with him, and keep each other informed by messenger. Perhaps we can influence Price's strategic decisions or make enough of them in the field on the spur of the moment to drive the Yankees across the border into Kansas. A partial victory on our part isn't the same as seizing control of Missouri and forcing the Union to transfer soldiers to the western theater. It won't arouse the antiwar sentiment in the East that Jeff Davis hopes will keep Lincoln from a second term and make the Yankees talk peace, not after Grant's besieging of Petersburg. It would, however, forestall the obliteration of Price's army and spare the bunch of us a spell in a Yankee prison camp."

Colonel Lawton drained his cup. "The Missouri River will eventually pinch the Rebel and Yankee armies together. We're in for more than one battle involving numbers in the thousands before one of us gains the upper hand. Captain, General Thompson wants your scouts to advance in skirmish-line formation ten yards apart in the morning. He wants no surprises at this juncture. I'll ride with you during the forenoon."

Shortly afterward, Lance and Donovan departed to check on the status of nightly roll call and confirm pickets had indeed been posted. Colonel Lawton and Captain Logan continued to talk freely in front of Morgan and me.

"Frank, you still believe most of Shelby's men will follow him to Mexico if we lose this war?"

"Yes, I do. Defeat tastes worse to many a Southern male than cow piss. Young men like your Lieutenant Wainwright will not live under Yankee rule and they're determined to benefit from fighting the war monetarily. Older men who once owned slaves and prospered aren't inclined to return home and suffer the indignity of Yankee condemnation either. They'll ride south and hope Shelby can carve out some sort of settlement in Mexico in return for providing its government a security force."

It was the first mention I'd heard of General Shelby's postwar Mexican venture. I knew from rumor and the St. Louis newspapers that Quantrill and Bloody Bill Anderson's guerillas and bushwhackers wintered in East Texas. Mexico was a big step beyond that, but I had no trouble imagining Lance trailing after General Shelby, for he would be beyond the reach of a murder warrant issued by a U.S. court. And, despite the wild randomness Lance exhibited on occasion, I didn't doubt that he had a hunk of the money from the Sedalia robbery stashed on his person, in his saddlebags, or buried where he could access it later.

Captain Logan had chosen a campsite near a spring surrounded by woods. Preparations for a predawn breakfast—filling the coffeepot, mixing and rolling the dough for biscuit baking on a small sideboard, slicing of bacon, and the gathering of fire wood—consumed twenty-five minutes. We saw to our private needs in bushes fifty paces into the woods, with Morgan Holloway seeking a more secluded area. Captain Logan's final words were a reminder that we would be traveling in a skirmish line stretching a hundred yards to either side of the road. Morgan and I would ride close up behind Logan and Lawton in the center of the line.

My last visual memory of October 16, 1864, my first full day marching with Logan's scouts, was the sight of Captain Logan making the daily entries in his orderly book by candlelight at 10:50 p.m., calling to mind his earlier statement that such recordkeeping might soon fall within the scope of my duties.

I remember sleeping soundly, warmed by the Confederate cavalry jacket and dreams of Laura Kellerman's soft lips and tight embrace. I woke to the chirping of birds and a strange snuffling. I rose on an elbow and there, after being absent from view the whole previous day, was the tall black hound Jacks, snoring away at his master's feet.

"I'm Owen Wainwright, Captain Logan's aide-de-camp. You are?"

"I be Joseph Nighthawk."

The aproned man providing his name at my request was an inch or so taller than me, six inches wider in the chest, the curled mat on his head gray, his eyes lined with yellow, his seamed cheeks, upper lip, and chin clean shaven, and his skin blacker than midnight. He wore a sleeveless shirt cut off below his ribs, revealing ridges of muscle across a flat stomach. As I expected, his right forearm and biceps were oversized, the telltale sign the man standing before me with the straightened shoulders and stiff spine of a younger man was a veteran blacksmith.

"Is the boss here, Joseph?" I inquired.

"Mr. Hanford ain't here. He owns the shop, I does the work."

"Joseph, I have sixteen horses that need shoeing by tomorrow morning. Can you be of help to me?"

Nighthawk flinched at the mention of sixteen horses in need of shoes and my abbreviated completion time. "Mr. Wainwright, I'm an able smithy, but I don't have fifty hands and angel wings."

"Suppose I was to work with you, Joseph? Titus Culver from Sedalia trained me. He says I trim and nail right smartly for my age."

Joseph Nighthawk said, "I know of your Titus Culver. He be a fine soul and tell the truth. But even with the two of us at the forge, we've enough shoes for ten animals at best."

Cheering erupted along Waverly's Main Street behind me. Nighthawk peered over my shoulder and I swear his eyes bugged and he danced a two-step jig. "Why it be General Shelby his own self."

From half a city block away, Brigadier General Joseph O. Shelby made an immediate impression that marked him a leader and soldier of distinction. He sat his horse with the practiced grace of a veteran cavalry officer. A tall black plume soared from the band of his slouch hat. His beard was a tan wave. He appeared handsome from a distance despite a square and massive face, and his butternut uniform lacking gold braid concealed a solid, muscular, lean-hipped frame. He returned the greetings of the worshipers surrounding him in a calm, resounding voice. I was as awed as Nighthawk seeing firsthand the general who had had three horses killed beneath him at Cane Hill.

Stories about General Shelby circulated daily through the ranks of the Iron Brigade. He had migrated to Waverly, Missouri, from Lexington, Kentucky, in 1852. Riding up Main Street till I found the Hanford Blacksmith Shop, it appeared Waverly with its iron foundry, flouring mill, ropewalk, large warehouses, numerous stores, two churches, and clusters of sturdy dwellings, framed on the north by the south bank of the three-quarter-mile-wide Missouri River, must have looked much the same to General Shelby when he originally stepped off a docking steamboat.

With slave labor, General Shelby and his partner had prospered, raising wheat, hemp, cattle, corn, hogs, and blooded horses on a jointly owned seven-hundred-acre farm, also manufacturing rope to tie cotton bales, with their hemp crop at their in-town ropewalk, and shipping it to St. Louis on their company steamboat. His success in civilian life continued, once Shelby donned Confederate gray. By the end of his Great Raid in autumn 1863, both the Northern press and local Union news sheets were deeming him the unbeatable scourge of the Yankee cause in his adopted state, and he was probably most popular in a hometown dominated by true-blue Southerners.

General Shelby and his adoring entourage of staff officers and public citizens crept past the blacksmith shop and Joseph Nighthawk's attention returned to me. "Joseph, I believe Captain Logan informed your boss by courier that the horses of his Confederate scouts would be brought here for shoeing late this afternoon. Did he make mention of that to you?"

A disarming smile revealed Nighthawk's white teeth. "Yes, sir, but I was expecting a soldier in uniform."

I had to admit my slouch hat, plain gray cavalry jacket, and light blue trousers, all free of ribbons, chevrons, officer insignia, and regimental badges, coupled with the absence of weapons on my person, didn't exactly brand me a person of military significance.

Any further questions regarding my identity and authority died when a stubby individual, with a lame left foot and an iron hook for a left hand, broke away from the crowd fawning over General Shelby and approached the blacksmith shop in a shambling gait. Nighthawk said, "There comes Mr. Hanford."

In the fading daylight, the buildings along the west side of Waverly's Main Street cast dark shadows. Mounted Confederate troopers filed past me. Many were warmly greeted and cut loose from their files on their own, for the ranks of Shelby's Iron Brigade were filled with natives of Waverly and Lafayette County. A lively evening loomed for Waverly's populace in home and tavern. I dismounted, set the canvas bag holding my farrier equipment on the ground, and pondered the long night awaiting me.

Mr. Hanford's small, round face was almost without brows and capped by a pug nose, thin lips, and cleft chin. His eyes were hooded, small, and blue in color. He seemed a half-asleep child instead of a grown adult dressed in a white cotton suit, blue shirt, and handwoven string tie.

"Are you Captain Logan's representative?"

"Yes, sir, " I responded with equal crispness, extending my hand. "Aide-de-camp Owen Wainwright. Pleased to meet you, sir."

Looking up and down the street, Hanford asked, "Where are these ponies of yours?"

I pulled Laura's watch from my pants pocket, opened the lid, and said, "Half of them should be here within five minutes. Captain Logan wanted you to know our circumstances so the shoeing could begin without delay."

"That's Brett Logan for you," Hanford said, chuckling. "He leaves nothing to chance."

"No, sir, he doesn't. Our current horses are in solid riding shape and equal replacements are scarce at the moment."

The string of eight scout horses arrived on schedule, led by

Sergeant Holloway, with Morgan Holloway, shotgun resting on his left thigh, riding drag. *Damn lad didn't go anywhere without that unwieldy weapon.*

Joseph Nighthawk was a professional blacksmith in the class of Titus Culver. He began each shoeing with a search for broken feet and sore tendons that would impair the horse's future performance. He made certain each hoof was properly trimmed and prepared before shaping a shoe for it at the forge, always shaping the front shoes first. He avoided shoes too long in the heel, too pointed at the toe, and made sure the foot surface of the shoe was level. And he was most fussy ensuring the nail holes in the shoe were neither too large nor too small and that the nails he used penetrated only the outer wall of the hoof when hammered in place.

While our shoeing was under way by the light of beam-hung lanterns, the comely eighteen-year-old daughter of the widowed Gabriel Hanford prepared a supper of chopped ham and potato hash, corn pudding, pumpkin bread, and hard cider for us. Her father busied himself serving his daughter's meal, filling the drinking water bucket, feeding wood to the forge fire, and recording the materials we used. Sergeant Holloway handled the horse string before and after their shoeing, and his son stood guard in the wide doorway of the shop in case the noisy revelers inhabiting the local taverns drifted in our direction. Jacks ate a plate of hash and curled up in a corner of the shop for a long sleep.

Near midnight by my watch, Nighthawk was seating the rear shoes of the final horse of the initial lot when Captain Logan rode up a virtually deserted Main Street, leading the balance of our horses needing shoes. Behind him came Private Upton, leading Morgan's packhorse. I knew without having to ask that the wooden keg tied to the packhorse contained an assortment of horseshoes requisitioned from our division quartermaster.

Captain Logan stepped down and handed the lead rope of the newly arrived horses to Micah Holloway. "Seems like things are well in hand here."

Voice loud enough to carry to me, Holloway said, "Yes, sir, the pup has kept up with the old dog."

Joseph Nighthawk's soft chuckle indicated he agreed with Holloway's grading of my horseshoeing skills. Then Gabriel Hanford chimed in. "He definitely knows one end of the hammer from the other, Brett."

Captain Logan extended his hand to Gabriel Hanford. "Thanks for your help, old friend. These days, foul winds can threaten you in supposedly safe harbors."

It was the most portentous statement made in my presence in my young life. A thunderous explosion blew out the front windows of the building opposite the Hanford Blacksmith Shop. I saw the outward concussion of the blast knock the feet from under Captain Logan, Micah Holloway, Morgan Holloway, and Gabriel Hanford. It toppled Private Upton from his saddle, and panicked horses secured to hitch racks and tied together, leaving me and Nighthawk just a scant second to brace our legs, partially turn our heads, and lift a protective arm in front of our eyes. When I looked out from under my uplifted arm, a thick curl of black smoke was snaking skyward in a reddish shroud of exploded powder.

Joseph Nighthawk had dropped to a knee. I clasped his shoulder. "What building is across the street?"

His answer was faint but understandable. "Master Gabriel's bank."

The word "bank" registered in my befuddled mind, and in a moment of clarity, I understood Gabriel Hanford owned a bank and someone had blown it up!

Someone was *robbing* his bank.

Not a soul within my range of vision was moving. I lunged forward. Morgan Holloway was trying to stand. The bodies and animals between him and the blast had shielded him somewhat. Later, I couldn't account for what happened next on my part. Others told me what I did.

I yanked Morgan to his feet, grabbed up his shotgun from where it had fallen, and pressed it into his arms. "If it's loaded, follow me."

Captain Logan was flat on his chest, struggling to breathe. I pulled aside the lapel of his tan suit coat, yanked his Colt Navy from its holster, and started across the street in a running crouch, trusting Morgan to follow me if he could be of any help.

In the middle of the street, in the stunning silence that followed the explosion, I swore I heard shouting voices and the neighing of horses in the alley beside the bank. I altered course and broke into a dead run for the corner of the demolished building. Once there,

I cocked the captain's revolver and peeked down the alley separating the bank from a grocery store.

Before debris completely blocking the alley past the side door of the bank, three soldiers were desperately working to control three excited, prancing horses, one of whom showed the sheen of blood at the hip. That the three robbers were dressed in Confederate gray was no surprise. They had blended perfectly with Shelby's arriving forces. Given the blocked alley, I suspected the bandits had planned to flee away from Main Street, but the explosion had unexpectedly blocked that exit.

I stared at the moonlit alley, praying for reinforcing footsteps and shouts behind me.

Nothing!

Not a sound.

Two of the bandits, canvas bags of what had to be paper money in hand, got a foot in near stirrups and swung aboard their horses. They booted their mounts into a gallop and drew revolvers with their free hands, ready to resist any attempt to foil their plans. The third bandit, empty-handed except for a long gun, finally mastered his frightened horse.

Instead of attempting to ambush the robbers from cover, I followed Theo Corson's training. Stepping into the alley, I turned sideways, extended my arm, and pointed the captain's revolver at the lead bandit. He spied me and snapped off a wild shot. Innards cold as ice, I fired twice. The second shot drove him from the saddle.

The riderless horse raced past, exposing me to the bearded second bandit. A bullet tugged at the sleeve of my shirt. My first shot hit the second bandit dead center in the chest. He dropped his revolver to grab at his wound and stayed upright for a few strides of his horse before slowly sliding from the saddle. The third bandit spurred his mount, loosed a keening Rebel yell, and trained the muzzle of his long gun on me. I squeezed the trigger and the captain's revolver misfired. Realizing I was a dead man, lest Morgan Holloway was behind me backing me up, I screamed, "Shoot!"

The tight spread of five ought buckshot from Morgan's shotgun shredded the throat of the third bandit. Blood spurting from his horrible wound, the racing robber slumped forward in the saddle and landed in a heap at my feet, left hand bouncing off my knee.

I was suddenly shaking from head to toe, unsettled by the realization of how close I'd come to dying not once, but twice, and mystified at the same time as to the source of the courage that had goaded me into acting on my own.

I struggled to get a grip on my raging feelings, turned about, and, to my utter surprise, Morgan Holloway crashed into my chest and wrapped his arms around me. His sobbing had a girlish pitch, which I attributed to the shock of his having not only taken a life, but having done so in such a gruesome, blood-gushing manner.

Micah Holloway, the first man to reach us, consoled his son. "Relax, Morg. You likely saved Owen's life."

"He most certainly did," I confirmed, stepping back as Morgan let go of me and dried his eyes on the sleeve of his jacket. "The captain's revolver jammed."

Sergeant Holloway stared the length of the shadowy alley. He held out a hand and I relinquished Logan's Colt Navy. "Damn accurate shooting, Wainwright, particularly when you're being shot at."

Rock solid on my feet again, I admitted, "I'm lucky I'm alive."

Drawn by the explosion and gunshots, lantern-bearing townsfolk and Iron Brigade soldiers were quickly on the scene, rifling the dead robbers' pockets, retrieving the canvas bags of cash, and helping themselves to the bandits' weapons. The presence of Gabriel Hanford guaranteed his money would be returned. Micah Holloway, Morgan, and I returned to the blacksmith shop, drawing me away from the crowd's wild speculation and growing questions about how the death of three would-be bank robbers had evolved and who was responsible.

Though knocked about, Captain Logan and Private Upton had escaped serious injury. Joseph Nighthawk was working at the forge as if nothing had happened. Chin resting on his paws, Jacks was sound asleep again.

At his request, I described what had transpired in the alley for Captain Logan in minimal detail, emphasizing Morgan's life-sparing shotgun blast. He studied Morgan and me and said, "Sergeant, I believe a couple of young pup soldiers just proved themselves under fire."

We weren't finished with the confrontation in the alley for the evening. Minutes later, Colonel Lawton and Walt Farley, Lafayette

County sheriff, sought us out attempting to flesh out the whole story of an attempted robbery that had fortunately led to the deaths of only the three bandits. "Young men, that was the Kinkaid brothers you sent to an early grave," Farley concluded after Morgan and I answered his terse questions. "Those boys are known far and wide for deeds the devil would shun."

Sheriff Farley wasn't kidding. While I assumed the history of the major battles fought in Missouri and the misdeeds of Quantrill and Bloody Bill Anderson would completely overshadow a shooting of less than a minute's duration in the backwater of the war, an unwanted fame for uncanny nighttime shooting would affix itself to me tighter than the girth on a bucking horse and never loosen.

With the departure of Colonel Lawton and Sheriff Farley, Captain Logan addressed our current situation. "Gentlemen, fate occasionally allows the wind to blow in our favor. Enough troopers are off visiting friends and relatives that I doubt we'll get an early start in the morning. That should give us the hours we need to finish our shoeing. General Price is camped in the vicinity of the Keiser Bridge on the Salt Fork of Blackwater River on the road to Lexington. We will finally rendezvous with his Army of the Missouri tomorrow. General Blunt's Union forces are concentrating at Lexington. Battle is looming, men, and we best be prepared."

I hammered at the forge nearly the balance of the night and rode to the rendezvous with the Army of Missouri the next morning half asleep in the saddle and plagued by an inescapable dilemma:

How would I comport myself if circumstances forced me to reveal my Yankee leanings?

If I refused to accept a weapon and become a Rebel, how would my friendly captors treat me then?

# CHAPTER 12

THE LATE DAWN BREEZE WAS COLD, THE SKY DULL IRON GRAY WHEN WE rejoined Shelby's Iron Brigade at the rear of General Price's Army of Missouri. The brigade was soon ordered to take the advance. The passage of fourteen hundred horses at a trot through divisions forced off the road generated a groundswell of hooting, hollering, and swearing curses of damnation that would, according to Sergeant Holloway, "draw blushes from the most hardened maidens of the night trade."

There was an excited buzz in the air that morning, stirred by concrete intelligence that a concentrated force of the enemy under the command of General Blunt was dug in at before Lexington and spoiling for a fight. Logan's scouts moved to the point in support of General Shelby's skirmish line. Captain Logan ordered Morgan and me to stay hard on the heels of the scouts and to take cover once the shooting started.

We were crossing open, gently rolling farmland that allowed me a long view in all directions with the Dollond telescope. The Iron Brigade received orders to make a flanking move to the left to intercept any Federal cavalry bound for Lexington on the Salt Fork Road. With the completion of the maneuver, the brigade formed a line of battle with Gordon's Lafayette County Regiment, Smith's Southwest Missouri Regiment, and Erwin's Jackson County Regiment on the right and Elliott's and Slayback's battalions on the left, supported by two battalions of recruits led by Colonel Crisp and Major Johnson.

Shots rang out as advancing Iron Brigade skirmishers made first contact with General Blunt's pickets at two in the afternoon, four miles from Lexington. The Union pickets fell back on their own skirmish line and lances of flame bloomed from behind bumps in the ground and hedgerows. Whining bullets drove Morgan and me from the saddle. Morgan hugged the ground. My curiosity kept me on one knee studying the unfolding action with my Dollond.

A three-hour fight ensued, marked by both irregular and intense firing between the opposing skirmish lines and the boom of artillery. The battle-experienced Morgan said, "Union cannon are mountain howitzers." When grayback cannons returned fire from a much longer range behind us, he said, "That would be Captain Collins's Parrott rifles."

The brisk cannon fire from long range had a telling effect on the war afoot. The boys in blue had been giving ground, hotly contesting every foot surrendered for three miles, but the rain of accurate balls from Collins's rifled long guns and the stress of the never-quit, close-quarter contest slowly sapped the wind from them. Colonel Slayback's battalion on the left was the first to strike a line of Union skirmishers that broke and ran. Ignited by Slayback's charge, Elliott's battalion successfully assaulted the hedgerow fronting it and the entire enemy skirmish line began crumbling.

My heart lurched when through the lens of the Dollond, I caught a clean view of the first soldier to leap high over the assaulted hedgerow. There was no mistaking the red hair, red beard, and red bandana of my half brother, lips parted in a Rebel yell I couldn't hear, a smoking revolver in either hand. He was a magnet for death and destruction, the soldier every officer wanted on his side.

The Confederate thrust drove General Blunt's skirmishers back on his battle line and I was finally close enough to scan the entire ranks of the defending Yankees aligned in front of Lexington.

"At least two brigades," Morgan judged from his belly, chin resting on a body-shielding rock. "I count eight mountain howitzers. Too bad for the Yankees, their cannons don't have the range of Captain Collins's Parrott rifles."

Even a neophyte in military strategy could discern that General

Blunt's situation was perilous. Holes in the Union ranks attested to the damage wrought by Confederate cannon. Gunfire to the left and right of the Iron Brigade meant the other brigades of General Shelby's division were drawing ever closer to positions from which they could threaten both flanks of Blunt's force. And with the arrival of General Price's additional divisions, Blunt's army of two thousand cavalrymen would be hopelessly outnumbered.

The rear ranks of the Yankees came to their feet and marched westward behind their battle line. A visible road crossing the Salt Fork Road, short of Lexington, ran the same direction. I knew from campfire discussions that the bluebellies' most likely destination, if they didn't hold at Lexington, was Independence.

Observing the Federals were in full retreat, General Thompson moved the Iron Brigade "left in front." Elliott's and Gordon's commands, the closest brigade units to the Union line of retreat, were ordered to lead the pursuit of the withdrawing enemy, and Logan's scouts, joined now by Colonel Lawton, naturally followed after them.

It was a long chase into nighttime darkness. No Iron Brigade officer knew the name of the Union regiment covering Blunt's retreat, but Colonel Lawton allowed the commanding officer was an exceptional tactician. The Union leader halted his troops and four mountain howitzers on every piece of ground favorable for making a stand, the fourth such halt being atop a shallow ridge permitting him to employ his long guns to maximum advantage.

"I'd like to talk turkey with that bluebelly," Colonel Lawton remarked. "In an even contest, he'd likely lay a whipping on me, come what may."

The Iron Brigade's pursuit might have continued through the night, had it not been for an order from General Shelby to return to Lexington, now six miles to our rear. The cursing over that prospect was as vehement as that attending our morning ride through the entire Army of Missouri. The poor aide conveying the order to each company captain took the bulk of the verbal abuse.

Back we went at a slogging pace, dismounting and walking occasionally to stay awake and spare tiring horses. General Thompson's concern for the well-being of those same horses led us through a sleeping Lexington to the public wharf, where we patiently watered them in the Missouri River. We then walked them to the bottomland above the town and went into camp.

I was so tired I tripped over my own feet unsaddling Badboy, but heard not a snicker of derision from my comrades. Somehow Morgan Holloway collected enough wood to start a fire and brew a pot of coffee. Though we were tucked up and worn thin as sewing thread, enough excitement from a day of fighting lingered to keep us awake for a while.

Captain Logan accepted a cup of coffee from Morgan and saluted Lance with it. "Thought you were going to hit your head on a cloud jumping that hedgerow. I'm glad there wasn't a Yankee with a bayonet anywhere to be seen. Take care not to endanger yourself unnecessarily. Good officers are growing scarcer by the hour."

"Yes, sir, but I think you will agree that sometimes you have to jolt even the best men into action."

So passed an intriguing exchange in which Lance accepted a compliment he liked and criticism he habitually didn't without rancor, perhaps because it came from a man and an officer he liked, admired, and respected. I had to admire Captain Logan's sly approach in reminding Lance he needed him to think like an officer first—except in the most extreme of circumstances.

Logan pulled his leather-bound company journal, pen, and ink bottle from his saddlebags. "Lieutenants, confirm your casualties?"

"None, sir, for my squad," Graham Donovan reported. "I'm just happy this was a fight without footsloggers and their bayonets. Ain't a horse in the world won't shy from those blades."

"Except for the totally blind stallion we captured at Sedalia that the quartermaster handed over to General Thompson," Logan reminded everyone. "The sight of a general flying heels over head from the saddle was a sight I'm sorry I missed."

The subsequent laughter overrode our tiredness for a brief interlude. "Thompson never did identify the culprit, from what I hear," Lance said. "I would've had the bastard hung."

"I figure the only signature on the paperwork was from a quartermaster clerk and the assignment was made in the general's absence," Logan said. "Maybe none of our boys was the wiser till the general climbed aboard. Any casualties to report, Lieutenant?"

"Slight wound to the right forearm of a private, sir," Lance responded. "I think the lack of hand-to-hand fighting kept our losses at a minimum."

The last person to partake of Morgan's late-night coffee was Colonel Lawton. He rode into the fading light of our cooking fire with the freshness of a twenty-year-old private on leave and leaped from the saddle. Morgan Holloway had a cup of the black stuff ready and waiting.

"What's the word, Colonel?" Captain Logan said.

"Appears to me, Blunt is withdrawing to the Little Blue River. He'll give us a tussle there. He'll be reinforced significantly if the Kansas militia will cross the state line."

"Gentlemen, I suggest we call it a day," Captain Logan said.

Colonel Lawton said, "Agreed, a battle-happy soldier must always anticipate a longer day on the morrow."

Saddle serving as a pillow, I settled for the night without a blanket but appreciating General Thompson's claim his brigade led a spartan life unburdened by tents. The stress of hammering a single tent peg home would have been my undoing.

I slept not the sleep of the recent dead, but the ancient dead of the Egyptian pharaohs.

Price's main army had camped three miles south of Lexington. Once under way on October 20, the Army of Missouri marched twenty-two miles without engaging the enemy and camped for the night above the village of Wellington at Fire Creek Prairie, near the line between Lafayette and Jackson Counties. Shelby's Iron Brigade had no problem marching within the main column. It was a rare calm day for skirmish-line veterans and I watched and overheard much ribbing and laughter during that long ride. I observed how closely Lieutenant Donovan's newly assigned squad fit together with Captain Logan's remaining veterans. In the estimation of Colonel Lawton, Logan's scouts were "a cocksure outfit with a hunger for the fight."

The temperature dropped into the midthirties and frost whitened the ground when I came to my feet the next morning, jaw clamped to keep my teeth from chattering. I envied Morgan's blanket and Jacks's sleeping spine to spine with him. Even a lean hound exuded a touch of warmth in freezing night air.

I witnessed about me a cavalry brigade on campaign preparing to move out. Cooking fires of squads were alight and a host of troopers visited temporary sinks to relieve themselves before trumpeters blew "Reveille." After roll call, details visited creeks and springs with pails in hand to water the horses. Other details visited supply wagons for future rations of cornmeal, bacon, coffee, and salt, or ordnance wagons for stocks of powder, caps, bullets, and paper cartridges. Troopers checked the loading of the extra cylinders for their revolvers they carried in oversized shirt pockets as they munched on smoking-hot bacon and corn bread, baked in the same fry pans, and sipped black coffee. They cared for their hand weapons and carbines with the same passion they evinced for blooded horses, sweethearts, and wives.

Captain Logan's polling of our two sergeants turned up a single horse with a loose shoe that needed the attention of my hammer. The horseshoeing at Waverly had paid off handsomely.

Morgan Holloway and I manned the cooking pans and the fire and served breakfast to Captain Logan, Lance and Lieutenant Donovan, and Sergeants Holloway and Whitman. First order of business was the day's marching orders delivered minutes earlier by General Shelby's courier. General Marmaduke's brigade would lead General Shelby's division with the Iron Brigade in the center, and General Fagan's brigade remaining in the rear with the Confederate wagon train. Shelby's orders pointedly warned he anticipated heavy action with General Blunt's Union forces in the vicinity of the Little Blue River, seven miles east of Independence, short of the noon hour.

The sergeants then reported the morning roll call, rounds of ammunition available per man, daily rations available per man, and physical status of their squads for Captain Logan's orderly book. "Except for Private Decker's minor arm wound, we're still at full strength," Captain Logan concluded with a final flourish of his pen.

"Doubt that will last if we engage in a close-quarter fight," Lieutenant Donovan asserted. "I can't fault the bluebelly Yankees. They got a beak sharper than a rooster since they laid that whipping on General Price at Pine Knob."

"A little pluck can keep a soldier upright now and again, no matter the enemy," Sergeant Whitman contended. "If the rumors are true, your young aide-de-camp here can swear to that, can't he, Captain? I mean, he challenged three armed men by moonlight in a dark alley and survived."

Captain Logan chuckled. "The rumors are true, and I advised Owen he best seek some reinforcement first, if there's a next time."

"Kinkaid brothers never possessed more than a smattering of brains," Lance said. "Robbing a bank at midnight in a town full of soldiers is a fool's errand. Owen hadn't been handy, Shelby's men would have had them hung by daylight."

"I was talking about your brother's show of guts," Sergeant Whitman said. "Most pups his age would have stayed clear, it not being any of their business."

I kept my head down, embarrassed at being publicly extolled, for courage I hadn't known I had, before superiors I hardly knew, and hurt by Lance's unwillingness to acknowledge a good deed on my part. I chanced a glance his direction and the hate in his eyes was molten as ever. Morgan's slight gasp told me he saw the hatred too.

Captain Logan ended my distracted thoughts by holding up his orderly book. "Study the contents and entries. I intend to make a clerk of you. I have after-action reports that need writing and I won't incur General Thompson's wrath."

I accepted the orderly book and the saddlebag in which Logan stored it. He stood and announced, "Gentlemen, time to saddle up."

Morgan and I hustled to pack cookware and douse the breakfast fire. "Captain Logan has a lot of faith in you. That shouldn't surprise me," Morgan ventured. "The captain trusts you to tell him if you decide to run off. After all, you owe him your life."

I nodded and kept packing.

"As for your brother, someday you'll have to kill him before he kills you. Don't give him the advantage by feeling sorry for him or thinking you should love him because he's of your blood. There's not an ounce of honest love in Lance Wainwright. He knows Jacks smells the coldness in him, and he'll shoot Jacks first chance he gets."

I might have contested Morgan's blunt assessment of Lance, had it not been for the haunting memory of the dead Shep sprawled across my chest. A man's willingness to unfairly kill a dog said a lot about his character, none of it good.

"We're going in! We're going in!"

The ascending yell swept through the ranks of the Iron Brigade. My watch read half past twelve. The fighting on October 21 had commenced at seven in the morning, with a clash of our skirmishers and Union forward defenses at the covered bridge spanning the Little Blue River on the Lexington to Independence Road. In the intervening hours, the Iron Brigade had languished in the roadway short of the bridge, while Marmaduke's division and the balance of Shelby's division had waded the Little Blue and engaged the enemy in a vicious slugfest after the Yankees fired the wooden bridge. The rolling thunder of cannon and crack of small arms floating to us from near and then afar in sporadic bursts told us ground was being gained and lost and won again by the combatants.

General Shelby's courier delivered orders that we were to turn back to the east and cross the Little Blue at the first available ford. There was a delay in our execution of this maneuver, for it necessitated the splitting of General Fagan's division, thousands of new unarmed recruits, and the wagons and personnel of General Price's headquarters to both sides of the road. Once again, those watching us pass through them at a trot to the sound of guns, bound for glory at their inconvenience, expressed their displeasure. Convinced they were superior to every other unit in the Army of Missouri, the Iron Brigade once again spent considerable breath assuring those berating them that without their intervention there would be no victory and no pleasure of visiting the taverns of Independence.

The banks of the Little Blue were heavily wooded, steep, and slippery; the water of its fords belly deep. Each Iron Brigade regiment dismounted at ford's edge, passed their reins to designated horse holders, and waded into the water. In ten minutes, the entire brigade, except for the horse holders, every fourth man, was across and into the fight.

Logan's scouts were first to reach the far bank, leaving Morgan and me with the horse holders on the near bank. We waited the hour specified by Captain Logan, mounted, and hupped our horses into the chilly Little Blue. Once across, we dismounted, dumped water from our boots, wrung out filthy socks, and pulled our empty but sodden boots back on. While the horses of the rest of Iron Brigade were held on the near bank of the river, on Captain Logan's orders the scout horse holders proceeded afoot, advancing slowly so as to avoid capture and the loss of their animals. Per the same orders, Morgan and I advanced with them.

Beyond the Little Blue, the terrain lifted gradually for two miles. Deep hollows, ravines, and stone-walled fence lines ran perpendicular to the road, a maze of obstacles favoring the defender. Early on, it was a frustrating afternoon for an observer with undying curiosity. With my Dollond telescope, I caught mere glimpses of distant troop movement and maneuvers between random tree trunks and atop high points of undulating ground.

I guessed at what was happening by sound and echo. The initial confrontation of blue and gray proved a stalemate till Captain Collins's battery was worked across the Little Blue with great difficulty and opened fire on the exposed Union line from a low ridge. The fading discharges of revolvers and repeating rifles told of a Union withdrawal to better cover, which switched then to ferocious volleys, indicating the retreating bluebellies were making another stand.

The back-and-forth, charge and countercharge, continued unabated for ninety solid minutes. Morgan and I hunkered down with the five scout horse holders out of rifle range, an iron grip on the reins of our hoofed charges, always ready to fall back on the run. A gap opened between our position and the fighting, and Morgan and I posted ourselves on a brow of high ground that gave us a forward view of a quarter mile. With the Dollond, I finally spied the lines of the charging Confederates and the withdrawing Federals.

Morgan's naked eyesight was phenomenal. "Why do Yankee uniforms and kepis always match and make them look like soldiers on parade, while our soldiers seem to be dressed in mismatched tatters from a rag pile? I swear our companies are wearing more blue than gray from robbing the Yankee dead."

The immediate objective of the withdrawing Federals was a

lengthy stone fencerow. A slam-bang small-arms fight developed that lasted a solid hour. Horses suddenly appeared on our left and a mounted Iron Brigade contingent, bearing the colors of Jackman's regiment, launched a direct assault on the fortified Federals. The pressure of galloping horses and blazing revolvers and the screeching Rebel yell was too great to withstand, and the bluebellies abandoned the protection of the wall and fell back rapidly.

"They're on the run," Morgan gushed.

We expected the balance of the Iron Brigade to wait for their horses to be brought up. But they clamored over the stone wall instead, and pursued the Yankee rear guard down a descending grade to farm acreage dominated by cornfield and pasture. I soon learned the land extended westward to Independence. The retreating Yankees were stubborn as bank mules on a hunger strike. Across the road, the commanding Union officer formed half his command at a time whenever he encountered a stone fencerow, swell of ground, ditch, or patch of woods that provided cover.

The dismounted regiments of the Iron Brigade fought thirst and hunger and dwindling ammunition and pushed the Yankee rear guard five miles to the outskirts of Independence. I would later read the story of how a company of mounted bluebelly militia armed with sixteen-shot Henry repeating rifles interceded at sunset on behalf of the withdrawing Yankees. Undaunted, fighting street corner to street corner, the relentless Iron Brigade drove the superbly armed Union company and their supporting comrades beyond Independence to a railroad bridge west of town.

Darkness fostered a cessation of hostilities. Morgan, Logan troopers leading the scouts' horses, and I were following the rearmost elements of the Iron Brigade, short of Independence, when a voice hailed us. It came from the gate of a wagon-wide lane leading to a torched frame house surrounded by barns and smaller structures that had suffered a similar fate. A fire was burning in the front yard of the destroyed home.

"Logan's scouts, this way to camp."

The hailer was Colonel Lawton; the wily, tireless Gray Fox, I swear, appeared everywhere and nowhere at his whim. We followed Lawton up the lane and were cheered in the barnyard by exhausted troopers, who hated fighting on foot. The battle-fresh horse holders were detailed to unsaddle the scouts' horses. Thankfully, per their training, they had watered their charges at a hillside spring before exiting the high ground bordering the Little Blue, for the farm's well had been bucketed dry by passing soldiers, both friendly and otherwise.

Our having exhausted the bulk of the foodstuff purchased by Captain Logan from Aunt Emma, and the cattle herd being miles behind us, what we had for a late supper was the standard ration we'd eaten at breakfast: bacon, corn bread, and coffee. Colonel Lawton followed Morgan and me to Captain Logan's fire on the brown-grass lawn of the blackened home. The limp posture of Logan and Lance and Lieutenant Donovan bespoke total exhaustion.

Captain Logan asked, "Frank, now that we've secured Independence, what's General Price's options looking forward?"

"Not many," Colonel Lawton declared. "He's got a large body of the enemy to the west of us anchored on the Big Blue River, and another coming up behind us from the east under General Pleasonton. The Missouri River cuts us off from the north. Price attacks the closest enemy or he withdraws to the south and preserves his army for another day. I believe he'll fight on the morrow."

Colonel Lawton, gray eyes bright and calculating, sipped coffee and swirled it in his mouth to cool it before swallowing. "I surveyed land for the Missouri state government before the war. Three roads run west from Independence. One to Kansas City, a second to Westport, just south of Kansas City, and a third runs southwest to Little Santa Fe on the state line with Kansas. They all cross the Big Blue River. The Big Blue's west bank is covered with brush and thick timber and too steep for cavalry and artillery, and very few fords are available to them. Major General Sam Curtis, an old chum of mine, commands the Union's Kansas Department. I suspect he has been fortifying the ford on the Kansas City Road the heaviest. It's the ford farther south on the Santa Fe Road that concerns me. I figure General Price will attempt to cross the Big Blue there and try to flank Sam, rather than fight him nose to nose. Such a strike would open a path for our supply wagons and cattle herd to slip away to the south, safe from capture if need be."

"What's your role if that scheme unfolds?" Captain Logan inquired, accepting a second cup of coffee from Morgan's pot.

"More like before it unfolds," Lawton said. "I want an advance peek at what fieldworks Curtis has constructed at Byram's Ford on the Santa Fe Road. Given how much faith Price has in General Shelby's division, he'll assign them to launch his flank attack, and since Shelby, in turn, trusts General Thompson and his Iron Brigade not to falter, he'll dispatch them to make the initial assault."

"How do you intend to have your peek beforehand?"

"In person before dawn. I'll need a courier on a fresh horse to report what I find."

Captain Logan's brows knitted together. "You have anybody particular in mind to ride with you?"

"Yes, I do."

To my amazement, Lawton's gray eyes settled on me. "Your aide-de-camp and his horse spent the day with the horse holders. Both are well rested."

"He doesn't have much field experience, Frank."

I had expected Captain Logan to flat refuse my services, what with me being a prisoner absent any sworn loyalty to the Confederacy.

The habitual persistence of Colonel Frank Lawton wasn't to be denied. "If what I heard via the rumor mill holds water, he acquitted himself quite nicely in a dark alley at Waverly the other night."

I was stunned. Had General Shelby's entire division heard of my lucky escape from death? Hell's bells, I had acquired a reputation and I wasn't sure I could ever conjure up that much courage again on the spur of the moment.

"I suspect young Owen here can backtrack on roads he's traveled without a problem," Lawton continued, "and, besides, every regular trooper in your command shot his bolt, fighting afoot under fire for seven miles today."

I sensed the heat of Lance's stare. I glanced his way and the scarlet of his cheeks matched the inherited red of Wainwright hair. God protect any Yankee enemy subjected to rage of that magnitude.

"You should have been a lawyer, Frank," Captain Logan conceded. "If you have that much confidence in Owen, I'll trust him to do your bidding and not wander off on us."

Colonel Lawton shot to his feet. "Then we'll be about our business."

I could have refused such service, I'm certain, but I wasn't being asked to assume a combat role, and, quite frankly, a nighttime spying mission with lean, mysterious Colonel Lawton excited my young bones something awful. I had yet to see enough blood spilled to instill in me the numbing horror of war known to the veterans of a long conflict.

Morgan Holloway joined me as I tightened the girth of Badboy's saddle. "Be careful, and pay careful attention to what the colonel orders. He appears a chancy officer, but he's not. He's very calculating and believes spontaneous derring-do has earned many soldiers a cold grave."

Morgan's concern for my welfare was touching. The advice he offered had obviously been garnered during his year at war with his father, listening and paying close attention to what happened and what was said around hundreds of campfires. Trust me, I took it to heart. Morgan and Jacks were there to watch Colonel Lawton and me start out on the Independence Road.

The chill of the night air promised a long, cold ride and another frost-laden dawn. Campfires of bivouacking Confederate forces formed a blazing ring around Independence. The streets of the town were free of fires and populated by roaming soldiers reveling in their victory with minor looting and pillaging. Bullet holes in walls and doors, broken windows and splintered awning posts, revealed the intensity of the earlier blue-and-gray struggle for control. Burial details collected both blue and gray bodies.

We saw no sign of the Iron Brigade while passing through the whole of Independence. As we exited, Colonel Lawton remarked, "General Thompson will be pleased. Whatever happens in Independence tonight, his men won't be blamed."

General Thompson's campfire was near the railroad bridge west of town. I waited in the saddle apart from the general and his entourage, while Colonel Lawton informed his superior officer of his intentions and secured his approval. Lawton was apologetic when he rejoined me. "Sorry for your wait. Thompson and I are on the same page now. We agree General Price might follow a different strategy than what I anticipate, but there's enough logic in an attack at Byram's Ford by the Iron Brigade to warrant a look-see beforehand. So off we go, Private Wainwright."

We returned to Independence, circled the courthouse, and exited the town square on Liberty Street. We departed town on the Santa Fe Road. Once we were beyond the lights of campfires and Confederate pickets, Lawton reined his horse into a grove of blackjack saplings beside the road, bisected by a small brook, and dismounted. "Step down. A little preparation is in order."

Dismounting, Lawton freed the rolled blanket tied behind his saddle, unrolled it on the ground, and held up a uniform coat. Even in the wan moonlight, I could identify the blue coat worn by Union cavalry. "We may need to impersonate those Union boys before the night's over."

I wasn't surprised Lawton had stored a second Union coat his size in his blanket, one bearing gold lieutenant bars at the shoulders. While we exchanged our gray jackets for blue coats—actually my new blue one fit over my gray one—Lawton explained, "We stopped a Yankee supply train on the Missouri Pacific line a year ago and I helped myself for occasions such as this."

Last from the unrolled blanket were two forage caps. A glimmer of what Colonel Lawton was planning prompted me to ask, "Have you done this before, sir?"

Lawton's chuckle was as carefree and bubbly as the water pearling over stones in the brook behind us. "Never fear, young chap. Spying is an art best practiced by the cautiously bold soul."

I decided I would be less nervous if I left the worrying to the colonel. Morgan Holloway had claimed Lawton was an officer who didn't take unnecessary chances. There was also some solace in knowing he had fooled the Yankees before . . . and any way you cut the bait, it was too late to back out on him.

"Best hand me your Dollond telescope," Lawton said. "That's an expensive piece of gear for a Yankee private to own."

Pocketing my telescope, Lawton retrieved the revolver, holster, and belt he'd looped over his horse's neck, while we changed clothes, and buckled it about his waist. He pointed at the stock of the breech-loading carbine protruding from the rifle boot tied to his saddle. "Switch the carbine and its boot to your horse, Private," Lawton ordered, removing the carbine's cartridge box from his uniform belt and passing it to me. "Your being unarmed might appear suspicious to a Yankee sentry."

While I was making the switch, he rolled his gray jacket and our old headgear in his blanket and tied it behind his saddle again. "Damn tired of stinking worse than an unwashed polecat. We don't smell sweet enough for a wedding day, but we won't wilt roses with the first sniff neither."

Our riding gear and weapons complemented our disguise as Union troopers. Both the colonel and I were seated on the McClellan saddle issued to the U.S. Cavalry. Both of our horses sported a USA brand. Lawton wore U.S. Cavalry spurs without rowels, instead of the Mexican spurs with large rowels worn by Missouri bushwhackers. He also shunned the bushwhackers' penchant for arming themselves with multiple handguns. My carbine was an arm common to Yankee cavalry. And, lastly, Lawton, born in Illinois, had no Southern burr in his voice.

Moonlight turned the dirt of the road ahead of us a ghostly white. An animal scream and a wild rustling and crackling of brush indicated two night creatures were disputing territory or a mating partner. A breeze stiff enough to blow aside the dust raised by our horses arose. The warmth of the heavier blue cavalry coat atop my thin Rebel jacket kept me shiver free.

To my surprise, the strangeness of accompanying a Confederate intelligence officer in disguise on a nighttime reconnaissance of enemy lines didn't alarm me. My existence had been overtaken by events beyond belief and my control. The comfort and security of life at the Wainwright Hotel and the lush dreams of Laura Kellerman seemed to have happened to someone else eons ago. My future was untethered and I felt I had enough faith in the Lord to trust I had the courage to face whatever confronted me next. Leastways, that's what I told myself, over and over again, as I followed a veteran soldier down the Santa Fe Road in the dead of night. Here was a man who eschewed a confidence that defied description and gave me hope he could lead us through Union lines and out again without our being imprisoned, hung, or killed outright.

I dozed off for brief periods riding behind Colonel Lawton till he halted and trained my Dollond telescope on what appeared a tall, solid black barricade eighty yards to our front. He handed me the Dollond and said, "Look close. See the flecks of red light reflecting off the trunks of the trees? Those are the dying embers of campfires. That whole long tree line is infested with sleeping Yankees. That's the west bank of the Big Blue you're looking at."

I came fully awake powerfully fast. We had covered five miles at an alternating trot and walk. A mile back, we had encountered the first sign of enemy activity. Trees had been felled where the road had narrowed, effectively blocking it to cannon and wagon traffic till it was cleared. The same type of defensive barrier blocked our path at what the colonel estimated to be a half a mile later. The final barrier straddled the road twenty yards to our rear.

"Byram's Ford is straight ahead. There will be a picket line on this side of the river. I would have stationed sentries at the last barricade. I don't want to surprise the Yankees and spook them into shooting one of us. We need to get close enough to the river to answer two questions. Have they fouled the ford? And what defensive measures have they taken on the far bank where the road leaves the river? With that information, General Thompson can lay out a strategy to crack the proverbial egg and win the day."

Lawton stood with one arm draped over the neck of his horse. "First off, let's try the easy way. The near bank is fairly free of trees and brush, but there are spots offering good cover. Might behoove us to angle upstream to our left and hole up along the bank. Using your telescope, we might be able to learn what we're after without drawing any closer to the ford. Then we'd only have to deal with Yankee pickets and scouts we might meet when we light a shuck for home."

I expelled a chest full of air as half the muscles in my body relaxed. I had visions of our bracing the Union sentries at the ford and bluffing our way into Union lines and scouring their fortifications without somehow raising suspicion as to who we were and what we were about. I believed Colonel Lawton was bold enough to invade the Union camp day or night. It was just comforting to know he really did pursue the course of action least dangerous to himself, as well as those serving under him.

Lawton picked a course to the near bank of the Big Blue, which arched away from it like the curve of a long bow, to avoid any pickets at the ford, taking advantage of the spots of low ground and trees and brush that offered cover. At the riverbank, he dismounted and searched afoot, never making a misstep in a night darker with the setting of the moon, and located a wall of debris plastered against two trees by past floods. The wall was in the middle of a slight bend of the waterway and allowed us a view downstream to the ford.

I tied the horses in a narrow ravine out of sight and fetched Colonel Lawton his saddlebags. We munched on chunks of corn bread, waiting for the first stain of dawn light to brighten the eastern sky. The breeze of the prior evening strengthened to a gusting wind out of the northeast, which brought with it penetrating cold that seeped through my blue cavalry coat.

As the outlines of the forty-yard-wide, breast-deep ford became visible in the growing light, the fieldworks the Yankees had built didn't bode well for future Confederate attempts to force a crossing. The water of the ford had been obstructed with piled timber. Across the way, howitzer cannon were posted above the twelve-foot-high bank behind a breastwork of abatises, with the points of the logs facing the attacker. The abatises blocked the muddied exit ramp from the river and extended for yards upstream and down. With a snort, Colonel Lawton snapped the Dollond closed and declared, "Like fighting the devil one-handed. Damned Yankees are so confident, they're lax with their picket line."

Yankees began stirring behind the trees of the far bank. Lawton pocketed the Dollond and slipped backward toward the ravine and our horses. "Easiest sneak of my career. Time to make our getaway. Pickets or no pickets, they'll be sending out scouts shortly."

We headed directly away from the Big Blue, leading the horses. The lone, foot-stomping Yankee picket we saw wasn't paying attention to anything beyond the Santa Fe Road. I found myself having to hustle to maintain the pace of the shorter-legged colonel. He was a coiled wire that never lost its tension. We marched afoot till half of a brilliant sun was shining in a cloudless sky over the eastern horizon. At a juncture of faint game paths, Lawton changed course and in fifteen minutes by my watch we were standing in the middle of the Santa Fe Road, him fresh as ever, with me wind-busted.

"We'll ride a mile or so to be certain we're beyond the reach of the Yankees," Lawton said. "Then we'll need to rid ourselves of our blue coats before we chance an encounter with our own sharpshooters."

It was the fateful decision of a fine soldier's career. Not two hundred yards farther along, Lawton's body seemed to collapse like a ruptured blister in time with the far-off slam of a rifle. He fell from his horse, slack as a bag of grain, telling me Colonel Frank Lawton, Confederate States of America, was dead before his body tumbled into the dusty domain of the Santa Fe Road.

Not being naive about what was coming next, a second bullet whisked by my ear as I left the saddle in a sideways dive, pulling the Sharps carbine from its boot as I abandoned Badboy for cover of any size and thickness, flat down on bare earth sufficing, if I'd no druthers.

I landed on my backside, the impact spinning the sun in a wild circle, my grip on the carbine iron tight. I squirmed, peered in every direction, saw nothing, not even a rise in the ground that offered protection. I fished my brain for a means of escaping certain death.

I slipped my arms into my pockets, pulled out a handkerchief, tied it around the barrel of the carbine, and waved it over my head—what Sam Benson said was "the universal surrender sign."

After what seemed an eternity, a bull-shouldered Confederate-uniformed soldier, with a chaw the size of a fist clamped in one jaw, spat a purge of brown tobacco juice that raised a dust cloud at the edge of the road, and said with the swipe of a hand across his mouth, "Twitch and you're dead, pup. Let go that carbine."

I followed his bidding and said, "I'm not who you think I am," praying if I could take his mind off killing me for a moment, I might be able to explain who I really was. The wrinkles that puckered the skin of his forehead gave me a sliver of hope.

His bent-backed gray-uniformed companion stared a hole in me and said, "Why should we care who you are, yuh damn Yankee!"

"Because I'm one of you," I said. I figured I had one chance to survive. "Have either of you ever laid eyes on Colonel Lawton, General Thompson's intelligence officer? The man you just killed is Colonel Lawton disguised as a Union officer."

"Aw, owl shit, Yankee," Tobacco Chewer said. "How would we know that?"

"Unroll his blanket and you'll find a Confederate uniform with three gold stars on each collar."

Tobacco Chewer spat again, dust rose in a column again. "That doesn't prove dog shit, Yankee. Maybe you kept that uniform as a trophy."

A thin, reedy voice from the other side of the Santa Fe Road spared my life. "Dugan, he ain't lying. By damned, it's Colonel Lawton in a Yankee uniform. Didn't think the bullet had been cast that could kill him."

Tobacco Chewer Dugan spun on his heels. "How can you be so dead certain, Monk? You been wrong afore."

"I saw him riding through our lines more than once, that's why. Ain't a man in camp hasn't heard of Colonel Lawton—except maybe you."

The three sharpshooters stood long-faced, transfixed by Lawton's lifeless body. "What now?" the shooter named Monk asked meekly.

Bracing a hand in the dirt of the road, I grabbed my carbine and swung to my feet. "We'll wrap him in his blanket and tie him across his horse. We scouted the ford on the Big Blue at daylight. I must report to General Thompson of the Iron Brigade straightaway. Will you help me?"

Relieved of any responsibility for the body of the renowned officer they had accidently slain, the sharpshooters were only too glad to wrap the colonel with his blanket and tie him as I'd suggested. They offered me Lawton's holstered revolver. Taking no chances with my own safety, I shed my Union cavalry coat for my familiar stained, bullet-holed, smelly gray jacket and strapped the revolver about my waist. Sensing Lawton's family, if he had any known relatives, might appreciate having his final Confederate gold-starred uniform coat as a keepsake, I bundled it in my lap with my blue cavalry coat, once I was atop Badboy and ready to move out.

Monk handed me the reins of Lawton's horse. "Do you know the password for the day? I don't want to be delayed passing through our lines."

"Pap Price, after our fearless leader," a smiling Monk answered. "We're with Shelby's division. Your Iron Brigade and General Thompson ain't but a mile behind us."

With a thump of Badboy's ribs, I set about finishing Colonel Lawton's mission with a heightened respect for the cold reality of war. When a man chose to don a uniform and weapons and fight for a cause, nothing about his person—not intelligence, military training, rank, or reputation—can shield him from physical harm.

Bullets and bombs make no friends.

# CHAPTER 13

I HUPPED BADBOY AHEAD, WONDERING HOW GENERAL THOMPSON would react to the good news, as well as the bad news I was bringing him. Besides their soldierly duties, he had shared a deep, respectful friendship with Colonel Lawton, as had Captain Logan. I suspected veteran, risk-taking, skilled intelligence officers were invaluable and doubly difficult to replace. And somewhere down the road, Lawton's absence might result in a loss of men that his counsel and experience could have spared.

Sharpshooter Monk hadn't lied. Shouts of "Halt right thar" soon had me tugging on Badboy's reins in a whipstitch. The voices on either side of the road belonged to Lance and his fellow scout Pat Shannon. They trained revolvers on me held at the end of outstretched arms, their expressions deadly serious and mouths drawn tight like they didn't know who I was.

They damn well recognized me. I was dressed the same and riding the same distinctive horse I was astride the last time they saw me. They were attempting to frighten and bully me. I realized then and there that I must always remember Pat Shannon was no less dangerous and ruthless than my half brother.

Without a gulp or a blink, I said in an even voice that did me proud, "Lest you two want to explain to Captain Logan how you shot one of your own in broad daylight, I'd suggest you cage the tiger right smartly."

Pat Shannon snarled, "'Cage the tiger right smartly'? What the *H* does that mean, Lance?"

"That's what our good-for-nothing, whip-happy father said if he even thought you were thinking of defying him."

I sensed I could gain control of the situation, particularly since I saw other curious scouts closing on the scene. I pointed and said, "That's Colonel Lawton wrapped in his own blanket."

Lance flashed his meanest smile and said gleefully, "I told Logan you were too green. That you'd get Lawton killed."

"I didn't get him killed. One of our sharpshooters shot him a quarter mile down the road. Now, if you two will step aside, I have important intelligence for General Thompson. He'll be expecting Colonel Lawton's report. I don't believe you'd want it known you delayed me."

I had my fingers crossed in my head. Pat Shannon caved first. "Better let him go about his business, Lance. We can't afford public trouble with Thompson or Logan. That would spoil our plans."

Lance shrugged and holstered his revolver. "Go be Logan's hero again. We'll have our chance at you later when nobody's around."

I waited to enjoy a relieved gulp and satisfied smile till I was well under way. I found Captain Logan in his usual spot in the center of the road behind his advancing scouts. The color drained from his face when he recognized Badboy and me. He had no trouble guessing the identity of the wrapped body beside me.

"What happened?"

"We were returning from scouting Byram's Ford disguised as Union cavalry soldiers. We were planning to shed our blue coats before we got too near Confederate lines. We encountered Confederate sharpshooters sooner than Colonel Lawton expected. One of them shot the colonel. They were remorseful and wrapped him in his blanket for me."

"What did you find at the ford?"

"The Yankees have fouled the ford with timber and built fortifications on the far bank supported by a section of howitzers. I believe that's how Colonel Lawton would describe it, sir. He said crossing the ford would be akin to 'fighting the devil one-handed.'"

Captain Logan glanced at the draped remains of his fellow officer and friend and chuckled. "Damn if that doesn't sound like Frank."

Face sobering, Logan said, "I'll send a courier to General Thompson with your report. In the meantime, there's the question of what to do with Frank's body. Damn if I'll have him buried alongside the road in the middle of nowhere. A career officer's family deserves better than that."

Logan dispatched his courier and we settled at the side of the road with Sergeant Holloway and young Morgan, while the foremost elements of the Iron Brigade filed past us. Finally Logan's head nodded vigorously.

He reached into a coat pocket and said, "Wainwright, here's enough money to bury Lawton in grand style. I want you and Morgan to escort his body to Independence and find an undertaker. I want Frank embalmed and buried in his Confederate uniform with a grave marker where his family can locate him later. I want you to witness the burial. Independence is supposedly a Southern-leaning town. You have any problem with my intentions, Micah?"

"No, sir, the boys were joking that they'd seen a big gold sign with black letters reading 'Eli Witten, Embalming, Undertaking, and Burial Services, 480 South Fourth Street.' They were wondering if his caskets are as fancy as his sign."

"That's our man, Owen. Listen carefully. Don't worry about time. I'm not expecting to see the two of you again before tomorrow. Don't travel at night or in the early morning when pickets are nervy and trigger prone. You're armed and can protect yourself and Morgan and guard my money. Hand me my orderly book."

Using his saddle horn for a desk, Captain Logan opened the book and wrote on a blank page in a fine, neat script: *October 22, 1864, Aide-de-camp Owen Wainwright is traveling on official business and is due all assistance and courtesy in the completion of his duties, Captain B. Logan, Shelby's Iron Brigade.*

Logan ripped the hastily prepared pass from the book and handed it to me, saying, "Keep this safe and handy in case an officer questions your status or what you're about."

I'll not deny that we weren't a curiosity point that attracted the attention of every trooper on the move. Besides the colonel's body and the long black hound trotting beside Morgan's horse, we were traveling the opposite direction of those bound for the day's battle. The muted boom of cannon and the random ripple of small-arms fire drifted from the southwest between gusts of wind. The assault on Byram's Ford was under way.

Once past the marching brigades, we encountered General Price's supply trains on the outskirts of Independence, making for little conversation between Morgan and me. Though I wouldn't have mentioned it for fear of hurting Morgan's feelings or belittling him, I didn't require any assistance arranging Colonel Lawton's burial. It appeared likely Sergeant Holloway had approved him accompanying me to protect his son against the stray bullets and cannonballs that threaten even those in the rear lines during a battle.

The general's trains traveling in one column stretched over three miles of roadway. I counted nearly 250 wagons, most of which carried food, forage, ordnance, quartermaster supplies, medical equipment, and iron forges. The rest of the wagons were loaded to their sideboards with the wounded and sick. Following the wagons were a group of guarded Yankee prisoners I estimated to total two hundred; a horde of three thousand new, unarmed recruits, whose value Captain Logan sincerely questioned; and, finally, one thousand head of plodding, lowing cattle. It was equivalent to passing an entire town on the move.

Independence's fifteen hundred inhabitants were trying to recover from the hours of street fighting between blue and gray forces that included the pillaging and looting of groceries, butcher shops, saloons, and clothing stores, scavenging their inventories to the final morsel of food and drink and last item of male apparel. The front lawn, steps, and pews of a church had been converted to a hospital. The groans and cries for water and mercy from wounded soldiers reached our ears in the street. All dead bodies and the wounded had been removed. At one street corner, a bewhiskered, balding gnome swept glass into a pile on the walkway of a brick building. At another, three men with a pull-along and a team of horses were winching the body of a dead horse onto a flat sled.

The second story of a structure at 480 South Fourth Street did indeed display a large gold sign with black letters announcing EMBALMING, UNDERTAKING & BURIAL SERVICES available within its walls under the guise of one Eli Witten. I left Morgan and Jacks at the hitching rail with Lawton's body and his bundled uniform. Inside the front door, I found two blanket-covered bodies on the floor and two wooden caskets resting on upright stands. Doors on the opposite sides of the room led to the interior of the building and what I assumed was embalming and storage space.

A rope hanging by the front door was attached to a bell with its armature bolted to the wall. I rang the bell twice. Nobody answered in person or by voice. I rang it three more times with solid yanks of the rope.

"Hold your horses," a hoarse voice shouted in the interior of the building. "Be there in a minute."

A minute of silence ensued, followed by "Herb, I'm finished. Put the body in the casket," and an individual with wild black hair standing straight up, wearing a white apron and tan gloves, and reeking of a strong chemical smell stepped into the front room. The undertaker's eyes were bleary with fatigue and his shoulders slumped as if bearing a great burden. His brown eyes were neither hostile nor friendly, hinting at a serious man mindful of wasting his professional time. I plunged ahead accordingly.

"Sir, I have a slain Confederate officer I wish to have embalmed and buried per specific instructions. I'm aware you're extremely busy, but my captain wants this officer interred properly and promptly. He will pay handsomely for your services with Federal greenbacks."

The words "handsomely" and "Federal greenbacks" snagged the undertaker's attention. "Just who is this Confederate officer?"

"Colonel Frank Lawton, General Thompson's intelligence officer."

"Good God Almighty, I thought I read Frank Lawton was killed two years ago at Pea Ridge. We served together in Arizona before I gave up army medicine for civilian embalming. I'm Eli Witten," the undertaker said, removing his right glove and extending his hand. "And you are?"

"Owen Wainwright, aide-de-camp reporting to Captain Brett Logan."

"My pleasure, Aide-de-Camp Wainwright. Now, let's discuss my fees. They don't need be 'handsome' for a true Confederate like Frank Lawton. How about sixty dollars for the embalming, fifteen dollars for the casket, and fifty dollars for a burial plot in the town cemetery."

"How much for a plain wooden marker bearing his name? His family may want to visit his grave or move him home later."

"Skaggs, the casket builder, does a fine cross for five dollars."

I had counted the money provided by Captain Logan earlier, a grand total of 180 greenback dollars. "Deal," I said, offering Witten my hand this time.

"Let me view our colonel. I don't anticipate any problems, but certainty demands evidence. Herb, if you will, please."

The undertaker's assistant was a hefty soul with the blank face of those diminished in their faculties, but able to perform menial tasks with training. Once we had untied the colonel's body from the horse, Herb had no trouble lifting Lawton by himself. Morgan handed me Lawton's uniform and I motioned for him to remain in the street.

Unwrapped in the embalming room, Colonel Frank Lawton, with his hawkish nose and narrow frame, resembled a downed bird. He showed no sign of having suffered physically. Blood ringed the bullet hole in his chest. "He died instantly," Eli Witten judged.

I was embarrassed I hadn't mentioned the necessity of changing out Lawton's blue uniform during our previous negotiation. I explained to Eli why a Confederate colonel was disguised as a Yankee lieutenant. "I'll make the switch at no additional cost to you," Eli Witten said graciously. "I expect to be paid for my services in advance. I will be finished with my preparation of our colonel by five tonight. I will have at that time a dated and paid deed for a burial plot in the town cemetery for you. The grave will be dug overnight, if not sooner, with interment early tomorrow morning. Does that suit you?"

"Yes, sir, Captain Logan is expecting us to return to camp before noon tomorrow."

I started counting out the agreed-upon amount for services to be rendered. The front door swept open and crashed against the wall. Two blond-bearded adult white males so similar in facial features and build they had to be brothers, if not twins, wearing heeled boots, twill trousers, broadcloth shirts, leather vests, Texas hats with snakeskin bands, and carrying twin holstered handguns, barged into the embalming room. "Where's our uncle Tom? He ready for our wagon yet?"

One of the intruders stared at the greenbacks I was holding. The other stared at Lawson's blue-uniformed body and demanded, "Did you charge the same for this Yankee you did for embalming Uncle Tom? You cleaned out our purse."

Eli Witten's expression never changed. "Yes, the same fee of sixty dollars."

The intruder staring my direction licked his lips and said, "Looks like a lot more money than that to me."

"You brought your own casket, Chauncey, and you're not paying for a town burial plot and a grave marker with Tom's name on it. You boys granted your uncle his last wish. You should be proud of yourselves."

"Proud don't taste for shit when you're hungry. What about Uncle's body?"

"He's in your crate in the back room. Herb will show you."

The disgruntled blond-bearded intruders departed with Herb without the customary "good day" and gentlemanly tip of the hat.

"Who were those two?'

Eli Witten said, "Chauncey and DeWitt Woodman. They and their father and their uncle Tom had a going place south of here till General Ewing's General Order Number Eleven pushed them off of it. Their father was killed in a skirmish with Union cavalry. The boys drove their mother and sisters to Memphis. When they returned, they took to the woods with their uncle Tom. They've ridden with bushwhackers and robbed by themselves. Their uncle caught a bullet in the back a week ago. He'd been dead a day or two when they finally brought him to me."

Eli Witten looked me square in the eye. "Those boys may have empty pockets at the moment, but their dress, horses, and saddle gear tell me they've succeeded at robbery more than once. I'm giving you fair warning. Your greenbacks might prove mighty tempting bait for bad characters, such as Chauncey and DeWitt."

"I'll remember that, sir, and thanks for the warning."

"No problem. Run along and let me get to my work. If you and your companion are hungry, Billy Bull's café around the corner to the right is open."

* * *

The mention of food plastered a smile on Morgan Holloway's face that threatened the brightness of the sun. "I've always told Jacks I'd never eat dog meat, but he was beginning to worry I was lying to him."

We left Jacks in the street in front of the café to watch our horses, for Morgan swore that at the word "guard" he was trained to attack anyone that came near his person or his property. I wasn't inclined to believe that, but when I checked from inside the Billy Bull Café, Jacks was stationed under the hitching rake beneath the horses' noses, alertly watching passing street traffic and sidewalk pedestrians.

Inside at the café's busy counter, I never witnessed another soul take the sincere pleasure Morgan Holloway did in a meal of fried beefsteak, whipped potatoes, oven bread, and apple pie with a cinnamon-dusted crust. Watching him in the wall mirror behind the café counter, I was again struck by the delicacy of his features and the near perfection of his skin, attributes normally observed in females. His insistence on privacy when relieving his bladder and bowels, behavior that had provoked wondering comments among Logan's scouts, I attributed to his youth. Thankfully, the comments had been ignored by scout officers for courtesy's sake in light of him being Micah Holloway's son.

Morgan cut short my study of him with a pointed question that had lingered in the back of my mind since our departure for Independence. "You know you could just ride on home from here. Your horse belongs to you, so you couldn't be accused of stealing him, and you've never taken an oath to fight for the Confederacy. Have you thought of that?"

"Yes, I've thought about it."

"And you'd be free of Lance and his toadies."

I sat pondering, sipping the coffee Billy Bull had laced with sugar, a treat worth hovering over. I would miss the excitement of riding with Captain Logan and watching the cat-and-mouse fighting unfold between the two opposing armies. But my sentiments inclined to the Union cause and my situation wasn't akin to two boys playing soldier behind a barn with stick rifles. I could catch a killing bullet as easily as sipping water from a canteen.

There was also Uncle Purse, Aunt Emma, and Laura Kellerman waiting and praying for my return. Had Uncle Purse recovered from his wound? How was Aunt Emma faring without my help? Was Laura Kellerman's affection for me holding firm in my absence?

The screech of a wooden brake applied to the iron rim of a wheel on a freight wagon drew my attention to the street. A mother holding a small boy was shouting at the frowning face of the wagon's driver. It was obvious the boy had darted into the path of the freighter's wagon and his mother was too frightened to realize only the driver's quick halt had spared him. The driver shrugged, snapped his whip over his teams, and shed the unfair abuse with a nod and a smile.

The tailgate of the freight wagon cleared the café window and a more riveting sight replaced it. Texas hats shading their eyes, the Woodman brothers were leaning against the porch posts of a storefront across the street. They weren't loitering there by chance. The brazen bastards were counting on the foot, hoofed, and wheeled traffic of the street to shield the stalking of their intended victims.

Their presence set my course for the immediate future. If the Woodman brothers believed I'd noticed their acute interest in my Federal greenbacks, they couldn't be certain I hadn't given whatever funds remained to Morgan to lure them off my tracks. If we split up, they would do the same, unwilling to chance missing out on even a few dollars of the only universally acceptable currency in circulation. I had no choice but to escort Morgan back to camp. They wouldn't hesitate to shoot Jacks and I couldn't let Morgan tackle a Woodman with his old, single-load shotgun. Running for home would have to wait.

Morgan Holloway tugged my sleeve. "Are the two men across the street wearing Texas hats the same two men that followed you into the undertaker's?"

Impressed as usual with Morgan's alertness, I nodded.

"Are they following us?"

"I believe so. They saw me counting out Federal notes to pay Mr. Witten. They're out to rob us of what remaining monies I might still be carrying. We're meeting with Mr. Witten in an hour. We'll know if they follow us again, we have a problem."

"What can we do?"

"Save ourselves. Shelby's division has passed through Independence. We're in a town full of strangers. We don't know who is in charge. We can't just run to a Confederate officer or a sheriff and claim two strangers are planning to rob us because they like Federal money. *Whoever* we complain to might ignore Captain Logan's pass and take his money. Fifty dollars Federal is four months' pay for a regular Yankee soldier, a small fortune for Rebels paid with worthless Confederate paper money."

I sipped more of Billy Bull's coffee. "Are you afraid of being close to dead bodies?"

Morgan Holloway's cobalt blue eyes widened with alarm and disgust. "You're not suggesting we sleep at the undertaker's? I saw those bodies on the floor when you opened the door."

"But you've walked right past dead bodies blown to bits," I countered, struggling to keep my voice lowered.

"But I didn't have to spend the night next to them and smell the blood and the stink."

I almost cursed aloud. It was the kind of objection I would expect from a female. Were my suspicions true? Was Sergeant Holloway hiding a daughter under that oversized shirt with a name fit for boy and girl by counting her on the official company roster?

"Why should Mr. Witten help us? We'd be bringing him our trouble."

"Independence is in a state of flux, just like parts of Missouri have been for most of four years, subject to the looting, pillaging, and burning of one army or the other. The Confederates had the streets at their whim early today. Tomorrow the Union will have the upper hand again. Master Schofield's history books talked at great length about the soldiers and armies of past wars. They didn't say much about the civilians caught up in the throes of the fighting who suffered the consequences when their towns became part of the battlefield and were subsequently occupied by soldiers and ruffians alike looking to enrich themselves whenever possible."

I drained my coffee cup and held it up to signal Billy Bull's male waiter for a refill. "Mr. Witten's in the same boat with us. Think about it. The Woodmans have some idea how much money I gave him and he has whatever they paid him, too. What's to stop them from robbing him in the middle of the night?"

I let Morgan digest that before continuing to say, "And you wouldn't have to sleep with any dead bodies."

"How's that?"

"Because I suspicion the stovepipe and windows on the alley side of the second story of Mr. Witten's building suggests he lives above his business."

Morgan's smile was that of a cat after he's licked cream from your fingers. "I will abide by your wishes, Master. A night in a bed would be nice."

I resisted mentioning I was suggesting a night under a roof with no dead bodies, not a night under a roof in a feather bed with pillows. "Let's skedaddle. Watch your shotgun. Folks get nervy around a youngster with a blunderbuss nearly as tall as he is."

I figured the Woodman brothers would split up and down the street to make themselves less obvious, and they did. Chauncey was peeking over the bat-wing doors of a saloon, forgetting the distinctive curve of his Texas hat brim. I didn't bother to locate his brother, since the bastards were inseparable, and I didn't want them to realize we had discerned their intentions.

Morgan agreed with Eli Witten that Colonel Lawton looked natural and composed in his new casket. When I broached the idea of our helping secure the Federal funds he had been paid for the night, our offer mirrored Eli's concerns.

A surprise awaited us at the top of the stairs accessing the undertaker's personal quarters on the second floor. I had somehow judged him a confirmed bachelor. We were met, instead, by a buxom, twinkle-eyed older woman, in a blue cotton dress, with the unlined face of a much younger woman at odds with her gray hair.

The warmth of Janine Witten's welcome matched that of Aunt Emma. She asked for no explanation for our staying the night. While she mostly recognized me with a smile and a little bow, she examined Morgan in detail. Ignoring the presence of Morgan's long-barreled shotgun, her solicitous tone making her sound to me like a mother talking to her daughter, she said, "Why, my dear child, you are in desperate need of a bath."

That sentiment unloosed a chain of late-afternoon events. The next thing for me was tying our horses in the high-fenced yard behind the mortuary. I drew water from the well for Badboy, Morgan's bay, and the colonel's horse, and fed them a mash of oats from Janine Witten's pantry, slim fare but enough to hold them overnight. Janine Witten fell in love with Jacks, who was invited inside and upstairs for what I heard called "table scraps."

Handyman Herb took a break from assisting in the mortuary and toted buckets of water upstairs to be heated for Morgan's bath. Though he appeared no worse for the effort, based on the number of buckets he toted, the bathing tub was large, Morgan was extremely dirty, or both those possibilities applied.

While work resumed in the mortuary and Morgan soaked in the tub, I stationed myself where I had a view of both front and rear doors in case the Woodman brothers had the nerve to attempt a robbery before we retired for the night. At eleven o'clock, per Laura Kellerman's gift watch, Janine brought me a mug of coffee and a wedge of lemon cake, which had me smacking my lips. Thirty minutes later, Eli and Herb finished embalming the two bodies I had witnessed on my arrival. As Herb wheeled the last casket to the rear storeroom, his boss finished what was, by then, cold coffee and said, "Isn't often I'm commissioned in the immediate aftermath of a battle to prepare bodies for shipment home. Those two Confederate families must revere their offspring."

Eli Witten stretched his tired back and said, "You have the back door and I the front, right?"

I nodded. "Just as we planned. Remember, no warning. We can't take chances. They won't give us one."

"You figure around two hours after midnight?"

I nodded again. "Thieves favor the darkest part of the night, according to Marshal Forge Bannister. Fewer unknowns to deal with."

They came right on schedule. I was prone on the floor in the doorway of the embalming room facing the rear door of the building. Eli Witten was in the same position on the opposite side of the embalming room facing the front door. I was armed with Colonel Lawton's 1855 Colt Navy revolver, Mr. Witten with an 1860 Colt Army revolver, both weapons cleaned and freshly loaded. I figured twelve shots between us would handle the Woodman boys. Morgan,

Janine Witten, and Jacks were upstairs with explicit orders to stay put, no matter what transpired beneath them. There was bound to be shooting and I wanted no accidental killings.

I waited for what was to unfold with calm nerves and no fear of remorse or regret for what I was about to do. Chauncey and DeWitt Woodman were no better than the bushwhackers riding with Quantrill and Bloody Bill Anderson. I had learned that while Shelby's Iron Brigade dressed and bore arms in a fashion similar to Quantrill's and Anderson's followers, they didn't shoot, scalp, and hang helpless Union prisoners and defenseless civilians. Nor did they collect the noses and fingers of their victims or count each man slain by tying knots in a bandana or notching a pistol or rifle butt. I was learning the hard lesson that killing to better only oneself, and not in pursuit of a national cause that justified such an act, if that were possible in the eyes of the Lord, was what separated the evil man from the good man.

The rasping squeal of a hinge on the backyard gate carried enough in the silent air to alert me. "They're here," I whispered to Eli Witten.

We had left both the back and front doors of the mortuary unlocked. I didn't want any doors kicked down and robbers busting in with pistols blazing away. I wanted their minds thinking how easy the pickings were going to be. The rear door opened slowly after the fright of the squealing gate hinge and a hard shadow stepped inside the storeroom, followed by a second shadow. The forward-thrusting right hands of both shadows gripped pointed black objects.

Were the Woodman brothers breaking in together?

I gave the shadows one more step, pointed my Lawton Colt Navy at the rearmost shadow, and figured that, if more robbers were entering from the front door, it was time to begin the dance. I squeezed the trigger and the blast of the shot reverberated off the walls with the boom of a cannon. A second reverberating shot behind me meant the Woodman boys *did* have help.

My initial target stumbled backward, fell, and his body slammed the rear door shut. The foremost robber fired at the flash of my shot and a bullet thudded into the doorjamb by my shoulder. I fired three times in succession, pointing the leveled barrel of my weapon at the mass of the target per Theo Corson's training. The object of my fire danced in the air like a puppet on strings held by a clown with the slam of each bullet before crashing to the floor with the meaty thud of a lifeless body.

The exchange of fire behind me was ongoing. I turned to help Eli in a moment of dead silence. The roar of a shotgun deafened me. I saw a shadow near the open front door explode off its feet and land with its top half resting on the front stoop.

The dead silence returned.

I crawled toward Eli through a cloud of stinking, eye-watering gun smoke, ready for more action if necessary. Nothing moved ahead of me. I chanced calling, "Eli, it's me, Owen," and was delighted a bullet didn't answer me.

Again . . . no sign of movement near the front door. I knelt beside Eli. "I'm hit in the forearm, lad, not bad, but enough of a blow I lost the grip on my pistol. It was the shotgun that saved me."

I looked around and, sure enough, there stood Morgan behind me with smoke curling from the barrel of his shotgun, precisely where my orders had explicitly forbade him to be under any circumstances. "Did you not understand my orders?"

Morgan huffed and shrugged his shoulders. "I was watching from the top of the stairs. Everything went quiet. A shadow stood up straight in the doorway and Mr. Witten didn't shoot. I thought he was dead or hurt and fired away and hit right where I was aiming, right in the chest. Not bad for a waist-high snap shot, huh?"

Lamplight bloomed and starved the darkness. I realized a barefoot Morgan Holloway was wearing a cotton nightgown and a robe of dark thick cloth. Holding her lamp high, Janine Witten halted at the bottom of the steps to the second floor. "Mr. Wainwright, this young lady was quite courageous saving my husband's life, wouldn't you agree?"

That question shattered the deception perpetrated for months by father and daughter. But as I stood staring openmouthed at *Miss* Morgan Holloway, I felt neither anger nor disgust. The courage to sustain her disguise, despite the crude roughness of soldiers operating without the mitigating influence of society and other females, was an admirable feat. Aunt Emma would adopt her in a second.

Thudding boots raised dust and lanterns bobbed in the hands of running men. It had taken a while for the violence of gunshots in the darkest hour of night to awaken the citizens of Independence, but they were awake and coming on the run to gape and ask questions.

"Upstairs, young lady. You need not be part of the aftermath in a state of undress. Leave that shotgun with us. I trust you to keep her name out of it, Mr. Wainwright," Janine said, kneeling beside her wounded husband.

Stepping over the dead body gracing the front stoop, the first person through the door of the mortuary sported a pointed star on his chest. The second wore a Confederate uniform. The officer of the law had muttonchop side-whiskers, an unlit cigar clamped in his teeth, and a rifle cradled in his left arm. The Confederate officer had the jutting jaw and ramrod posture of an officer accustomed to wielding authority. I warned myself to tread water carefully. Local law enforcement could be finicky when enduring a military occupation, even when the two bodies agreed politically and the occupying military forces might be gone the next morning.

"Marshal Deane, there's obviously been a shooting," Eli Witten announced as his wife helped him to his feet.

Attracted by the commotion behind the mortuary, the Confederate officer crossed the room and peered at the crowd gathering at the rear door and the fallen bodies blocking it. "Dead out back too. You know any of them, Marshal?"

"Yes, Major, the gent over here, resting half in and half out of the building, or what's left of him, is Chauncey Woodman. Don't know the second one. Odds are, one of them on your end is Chauncey's brother, DeWitt."

"You fit to tell us what happened here, Eli?" Marshal Deane inquired.

"Chauncey and DeWitt were aware I have a stash of Federal greenbacks from fees received and tried to rob me of it. Aide-de-camp Owen Wainwright," Eli said, pointing at me with his good arm, "is on official military business attending to the embalmment and burial of Confederate colonel Frank Lawton, who was killed in action this morning. Owen was our guest for the evening."

The Confederate major surveyed the scene. A haughty doubtfulness invaded his voice when he spoke. "And you and Wainwright awakened during the attempted robbery just in time to intercept the bandits at the back and front doors?"

I wasn't about to let Eli row the boat alone. "No," I said, "we were waiting on them."

The major spun on his heels and his gaze wasn't the least bit friendly. It was a guess, but most likely he was a provost officer accustomed to investigating military crimes versus civilians, and holding sway without question. "Say what, did they send you a note stating their intentions and time of arrival?"

I couldn't resist an opportunity to prick his arrogance. "They might as well have."

"Meaning exactly what?" the major demanded.

"Mr. Witten is acquainted with the Woodman brothers' reputation for riding with bushwhackers that won't hesitate to rob if their purse runs empty. They were here earlier today to fetch their uncle's body for burial and stared like hungry wolves while I was paying for Colonel Lawton's services in Federal greenbacks. Then they followed me to Billy Bull's café. It didn't take more than that to figure they were planning to rob the both of us."

"And you were waiting for them in the dark. Did you warn them before you started shooting? If you didn't, it looks like you fostered a massacre to me."

"No, there was no warning," Eli said. "They snuck into my business in the dark with guns drawn. They still got off a number of shots, but they're dead and we're not. You got any trouble with that, Marshal Deane?"

"No, I surely don't, Eli. The county is short four ruffians and not a soul will shed a tear."

The Confederate major had one last bone he had to chew. "Aide-de-camp Wainwright, do you have written orders justifying your presence in Independence?"

Inwardly thanking Captain Logan for his thoroughness, I dug his pass from my jacket pocket. The Confederate major read it twice, loosed a resigned sigh, returned my pass, said with all the authority he could muster, "The Army of Missouri has no further interest in this matter," and stomped from the room.

Marshal Deane chuckled. "We won't miss his pompous ass down at the courthouse once he's gone. Eli, I'll have lads here within the hour to remove the bodies. We'll mail the Woodmans' possessions to the family in St. Louis. The other two are bound for paupers' graves if we can't identify them. I'll tell Skaggs the county will pay for their caskets. My deputy and I will clear your yard of the gawkers. Wainwright, I thank you for standing by an old friend. Sorry your introduction to Independence cast us in such a poor light. Eli, Janine, it's been an interesting night."

And so ended a confrontation reeking of death and gun smoke that had ramifications for my future beyond my imagination.

# CHAPTER 14

*F*ROM THE BEGINNING, I WAS ENTRANCED BY THE NEW MORGAN HOLLOWAY. I mean, I couldn't stop staring at her during breakfast in the Witten kitchen on the second floor of the mortuary. Now that I knew, I found it hard to believe I hadn't known she was a girl immediately, despite her being dressed and armed like a man and traveling with a body of soldiers. She lacked the stunning beauty of Laura Kellerman, but Morgan Holloway's black hair, cobalt blue eyes, sculpted nose and mouth, and the dusky coloration of her skin, which I realized as I studied her across the breakfast table, was inherited, not brown from the sun. All combined, it still stirred a man's loins right proper. Even the slight natural quake in her voice helped hold a male's attention.

"Morgan, my offer stands," Janine Witten was saying. "You're welcome to stay with Eli and me till this nasty war staggers to its bloody end. No lady nineteen years old, or any age for that matter, should travel alone in the company of male soldiers."

Nineteen? It was good no one was looking at me just then, for there had to be red skin on me somewhere for misjudging her age so badly. But then so had everyone else in Captain Logan's camp.

Sipping tea from a small cup decorated with delicately painted flowers, Janine Witten said, "Your father would know you're safe and have a home if anything were to happen to him. You would want for nothing."

We certainly hadn't wanted for anything at Mrs. Witten's breakfast table. Without embarrassment and at her urging, I consumed three helpings of cornmeal pancakes with syrup, poached eggs, fried bacon, bowls of boiled grits, and half a pot of tea. If poked in the belly, I would have exploded.

Morgan placed her teacup in its saucer. Her face had a somber cast, a mixture, I determined, of thanks and sadness. "I appreciate your offer, but I must return to my father. I never wanted for anything till the war came, not for food, not for a warm bed, certainly not for love. Then overnight, we lost everything—our land, our home, our way not only of surviving, but prospering—wiped away by bullets and fire in mere minutes. Not for a second did he consider abandoning me, of leaving me in the care of another family and depending on their charity. He dressed me in a man's clothing, had me tie my breasts down to make me appear more boyish in my big shirt, and convinced Captain Logan he would eat much better and make his wife happy when she learned he had a camp cook."

Resigned to disappointment, Janine asked, "Does your father have plans for after the war?"

"He's mentioned California. He says the passion for the war appears less on both sides there. His men talk of accompanying General Shelby to Mexico if the Confederacy doesn't prevail. Whatever he decides, I must stand beside him. I can't do to him what he refused to do with me."

Childless Janine Witten nodded, her eyes warm, her smile approving. "I understand, and I thank you, dear girl, for letting me glimpse the joy a daughter would have brought to our home."

I should have guessed I would be the next topic of discussion. "And what about you, young man?" Janine asked with another radiant smile. "Morgan tells me you have no sworn allegiance to the Confederacy and actually are a Yankee at heart."

"She told the truth, Mrs. Witten. My problem is, I promised I would look after Morgan and accepted responsibility for her safe return to camp, even though the camp is in the middle of a war. Enemy or not, I respect her father and Captain Logan, both as men and soldiers. Maybe I can't explain it better, but I don't want to fail them."

"I can understand your situation. I live with a man of principle. He keeps his promises and his loyalties never waver."

"Captain Logan said Independence is a Southern-leaning town. Will the Yankees' eastern army chasing General Price give you trouble when they arrive later today?"

Janine laughed. "No, everyone needs the undertaker. Eli is adept at staying out of politics."

Boots thudded on the stairs outside the second-floor kitchen. Herb's head appeared in the doorway, announced, "Horses are ready," and disappeared just as quickly.

Janine rose from her chair, lifted a cloth knapsack from a sideboard, and handed it to Morgan Holloway. "I prepared a few nibbles for the road—corn dodgers, hard candy, sweet sugar cakes, and a bag of tea leaves."

I fled, leaving the teary good-byes to the females. Downstairs in the fenced rear yard, Herb had Badboy, Morgan's bay, and Colonel Lawton's mount watered and fed, per Eli's instructions. Rolled blankets were tied behind the saddles of Badboy and the bay. "October nights are right chilly," Eli said by way of explanation. "I rolled your blue coat in your blanket," he added with a conspiratorial smile. "Never know. You might need to play Yankee again."

Eli and I had decided earlier that I would retain possession of Colonel Lawton's Colt Navy, breech-loading carbine, McClellan saddle, saddlebags, and USA-branded gelding, assuming they were the property of the Confederate government. Final disposition of the colonel's property at the time of his death rested with General Shelby, Lawton's superior officer, and the division quartermaster.

Eli turned to Herb. "Fetch the ladies, please. Situation in town has changed. Rebels are gone and the Yankees are starting to file in. I know this country from my autumn bird hunting and fishing. Was I you, I would hustle down South Fourth Street and keep that direction a good piece, once you're clear of town before turning southwest to Byram's Ford, where you expect to find Morgan's father. You need to move quick to avoid the bluebellies."

Earnest Herb shooed the ladies from the mortuary. I motioned for Morgan to mount up. Once we were in the saddle, I apologized to Janine Witten for our abrupt departure, thanked her for her hospitality, and nodded at Herb to open the yard gate. South Fourth Street was lean on street traffic at that early hour, and with not a blue soldier aboard on foot or horseback, I booted Badboy into a gallop.

Morgan Holloway met my challenge without a tick of indecision. When I glanced over my shoulder, she was leaning forward in the saddle with the bay's reins clenched in her teeth, the reins of Colonel Lawton's horse in one hand, and her tall shotgun in the firm clasp of the other.

Bounding on the bay's heels came her inseparable bodyguard, Jacks.

Never before had I met a female that totally defied how she was expected to comport herself.

*Tomboy* came into my mind.

We were side by side, belly down atop the brow of a hill, and I was studying Byram's Ford with the Dollond telescope. "Not what I expected," I muttered, scanning the banks of the Big Blue.

Morgan Holloway had no objection to leading the colonel's horse, but she had no intention of playing horse holder in the patch of trees where we'd hidden our animals. Neither did the hound on her other hip. "What did you expect to find?"

"Yesterday morning before sunrise, the Yankees had the far bank of the river bristling with abatises backed by howitzers. The ford was filled with felled trees. The ford has been cleared, Yankees are now on this side of the river, and lest my eyes are failing me, gray uniforms are defending the ford's west bank. I'm trying to figure what that means."

"May I have a look?"

I handed her the Dollond, the flowery smell from her Independence bath tainting the air between us. I wondered what the reaction would be among the regulars surrounding Captain Logan's fire when they got a whiff of her.

She studied both blue and gray soldiers a goodly while and said, "We know the Yankees didn't clear the ford and there are fresh hoofprints by the score and wheel ruts in the mud on the far slope of the ford. I'd say General Thompson's men overran the Yankees, and then cleared the ford for their horses and cannon. They got across and left a force to hold the ford. Didn't Captain Logan mention a division of Union cavalry was chasing General Price from his rear? That would account for the Yankees on the near bank."

The series of booms off to the north we'd been hearing for at least an hour had to be cannon fire, given the clear sky, and supported her theory. General Thompson's Iron Brigade was the lead force attacking the Yankees dug in at the ford yesterday. They had fought their way across the ford and pushed the enemy to the north toward Westport, as she'd said, and were engaging them again this morning. Confederate rear elements had remained behind as a rear guard to defend the vital river crossing against any Yankees approaching from the east.

An ornery urge to test her beset me. "Wonder what happened to the general's supply trains?"

"Well, since the southwest road we're traveling runs clean past the ford and is free of fresh wheel ruts and cow manure, I'd say they followed the Iron Brigade across the ford yesterday."

My mind was racing, trying to map out a course of action that would put her in the least danger. That aspect played a much bigger role in returning her to her father than it had before our trek to Independence. She would deny that and claim she could watch out for herself as before, undoubtedly pointing out how'd she saved my life in a certain dark alley not long ago. But that didn't allay the additional responsibility I'd felt since her unmasking.

The Yankee assault on Byram's Ford below us met with stiff resistance. Confederate skirmishers were peppering the Union boys from a limestone escarpment, twelve to fifteen feet high, beyond the Ford. Sharpshooters stationed in two log houses and in treetops on the grayback left flank picked their targets with care, while Confederate cannon concentrated on the ford itself.

The Union batteries continued their barrage and their dismounted cavalry ignored the accurate fire of enemy cannon and waded the river, one at a time, with rifles and cartridge boxes held over their heads, till they established a stronghold on the opposite bank. A burst of small-arms fire on the Yankee right presaged a breakthrough of the grayback lines by a Yankee regiment that had scooted upstream, swam the river, and attacked from a ravine, out of sight to the Confederates.

The fierceness of the fighting made the decision for me. It was too deadly for us to cross the river within range of the battle, and if we did make the opposite bank and circled the two opposing armies, we had no idea where any of the brigades fighting farther north were located. We could be slain by either side, for in the heat of battle, pulling the trigger was safer than chancing a conversation with an unknown opponent.

"Follow me," I ordered, sliding backward belly first on the ground to avoid sky-lining myself above the brow of the hill, knowing Morgan would follow me in the same manner.

At the horses, I offered an explanation without waiting for her to ask. "It's too dangerous to cross the river upstream or down and hunt for your father and Captain Logan. Remember Captain Logan saying if General Price failed to take Westport and Kansas City, his only recourse was to escape to the southwest. Sam Benson traveled the old Santa Fe Trail that ran past this ford through a town called Hickman Mills to Little Santa Fe on the Missouri-Kansas state line. The general's trains may be across the river, but they're bound for Little Santa Fe. We circle around behind these hills, and stay on the road down there, we can intercept General Price's supply train at Little Santa Fe. No matter what else happens, sooner or later, Thompson's brigade has to requisition ammunition, rations, and beef from Price's wagons and steer herd. We can follow those supplies to your father's camp from behind Confederate lines, with the least exposure of ourselves, or send word that you're well and where he can find you. Does that make sense to you?"

"Yes," she agreed, returning the Dollond. "Comes to mind Private Smithson was from a town called Hickman Mills and he said it was on the old Santa Fe Road, same as your Sam Benson. He bragged about his favorite fishing hole on the Big Blue River." Her voice trembled. "Smithy was killed at Prairie Grove."

We set off downhill, and after covering two miles of rough, broken country, circled back to the old Santa Fe Road when the terrain leveled mostly into agriculture acreage, alternating between a walk and a trot. We kept watch in all directions, stopping to study the road ahead atop every significant swell of ground, again without sky-lining ourselves. The always-hungry Jacks ranged to the left and right of the road in search of game. He trailed without barking, precluding the chance he would alert the enemy to our presence.

A side road from the southeast joined the old Santa Fe Road and the churned surface of the combined roadways suddenly showed much use by wheel, hoof, and foot. It was free of traffic. "They must be Yankees," Morgan judged. "I'm surprised we're not meeting any stragglers. Whoever's in command must rule with an iron fist."

Burned-out dwellings, barns, and crops told me the war had been as cruel here as it had been farther north in Jackson County. I didn't consider my wondering who the families were that had been forcefully denied the legal use of their property a weakness. When the smoke of battle cleared, a measure of legal redress was due the displaced. But who would guide such an effort? Who would care that much, particularly if a family had supported the losing cause?

My gosh, how I missed listening to the discussion and debates of Uncle Purse, Mr. Kellerman, and other Sedalia town leaders over and after dinner in the Wainwright Hotel dining room, before war muddied beliefs and strained convictions. I was beginning to understand the value to a community of learned, reasoned citizens. To quote Master Schofield, they were the lifeblood that sustained the equal rights of all men.

Badboy missed a step and I cursed myself. Yankee troops separated us from our proposed destination. *Clear your head, damn it, before someone shoots it full of holes.*

Aware a Yankee column might loom ahead of us, we kept our pace at a walk. A church steeple and the ridgelines of two second-story buildings peaked over the horizon. "That must be Hickman Mills," Morgan announced.

I slanted off the road to the south and wove a path across empty pastures and uncultivated fields, slowed by stone-walled fences and diverted by dense woods. An upward slope topped by a smattering of trees caught my eye. I went for it arrow straight, tugged on Badboy's reins short of slope's crest, and dismounted. Our caution was rewarded when I trained the lens of the Dollond on Hickman Mills.

What jumped out were the supply wagons and ambulances

marked USA parked astride the old Santa Fe Road at the west end of the village. On closer inspection, blue uniforms moved about on the main street. Whatever the Union command, an occupying force was in place and making use of the water and shelter available. Three long-ago burned-out buildings on the southern flank of Hickman Mills indicated that its citizens hadn't been spared the presence of armed combatants in the past.

I handed the Dollond to Morgan Holloway and eased along the crest of the slope till I had an unobstructed view to the southwest. What I sought was barely visible to the naked eye, but I spied a long smudge of dust that lingered just short of the horizon. Morgan joined me. I pointed that direction. She leveled the Dollond, feet staggered to hold the telescope steady.

Without knowing what she was looking for, she said, "A huge dust cloud way off, far as I can see. Do you suppose it's General Price's trains?"

"Yes, only a procession of hundreds of wagons trailed by a thousand head of cattle can raise that much dust."

In the silence of deciding what to do next, a rumble mimicking faint thunder could be heard to the north of Hickman Mills. "Sounds like the big battle might be moving our way instead of toward Westport," Morgan suggested.

I nodded, linked together the Yankee presence in and near Hickman Mills, the dust cloud to the southwest, and the possibility the Yankees might be forcing General Shelby's division and the Iron Brigade southward. I determined a new strategy was necessary to ensure our survival. "We need to hole up till dark. We can't pinpoint the location of either friend or enemy in broad daylight. But come dark, every military unit will make camp and light fires. After the sun sets, we can determine how to best avoid the enemy and make our way to the southernmost fire."

A skeptical Morgan Holloway wasn't as certain. "Just where will we do your holing up?"

I pointed at what I estimated to be a degree smack between south and southwest on a compass. "That direction, as far as we can ride by sunset."

Morgan Holloway pursed her lips, put her hands on her hips, and fixed a cobalt blue–eyed stare on me that could have melted glass, showing heated feelings heretofore unknown to me. There was definitely a grown female lurking inside that oversized shirt and baggy trousers. "I don't really know you from Adam, but somehow you seem to know what you're talking about, and I'm trusting you with my life. I'll stick with you till I learn otherwise. Then Jacks and I are on our own. Agreed?"

Hell's bells, the shotgun she never relinquished was leaning against her hip. I had witnessed what damage to the human body the lethal charge of that weapon could render on two separate occasions, and had no interest in inviting a blast aimed at me. Had she wanted to push the issue, she could have ridden away, then and there, with my blessing. My mother may have raised a foolhardy lad, but not an out-and-out fool.

I raised both hands. "Agreed, I'll abide by your wishes."

Morgan Holloway had taught me an invaluable lesson when dealing with a strong female. Never change your mind lest it's absolutely necessary.

Our holing-up camp was taking shelter atop a wooded hill affording a panoramic view of the western horizon. A spring and small meadow at the bottom of the hill's back side provided water and graze for the horses. We loosened their girths, but kept them saddled.

We dined on the corn dodgers, hard candy, and sugar cakes in Janine Witten's knapsack. Morgan brewed tea over a fire the size of cupped hands and served it in the tin pail Mrs. Witten included in her knapsack. With the skill of an Apache, my female companion started her fire with a piece of flint and a rock.

The previous morning, a skim of ice had coated the rainwater barrel behind the Witten residence, and the early-night air, twelve hours later, was raw and chill as our vigil began. I unrolled my blanket and offered Morgan the Union cavalry coat. She accepted the coat with a grateful nod and we settled on opposite sides of the fire wrapped in our blankets. Jacks had apparently partaken of wild game, for he showed no signs of hunger and curled up at his master's hip. The hound's near independence was rare in a domesticated dog.

In short order, fires bloomed due north of our chosen hill and on the low ground facing us from the west, probably a distance of five miles. I searched and searched to the south and southwest with the Dollond and discovered nothing but utter blackness. Were the general's trains fleeing under the cover of darkness after a full day's march?

"What now?" Morgan asked.

"We sleep till midnight. The sky is clear, and by then, the moon will be up and the stars showing. Our line of travel will be to the south of the western fires."

Her tone ripe with worry and doubt, perhaps a little outright fear, Morgan said, "How can you be sure of the direction we're traveling, once those fires die out? We won't even be able to see their embers, once we're down on low ground."

"The stars will guide us. When Sam Benson and I hunted at night, he taught me to read the autumn stars. He would make me lead the way back to our camp."

"Is Mr. Benson a relative of yours?"

I realized with her question that we had engaged in no private conversation since our meeting in Sedalia. What she knew about me was what she'd heard said by others in her presence if she'd been listening. I really could be as strange to her as Adam.

"No, Sam Benson served in the Mexican War with my grandfather. He's the hostler and horse handler for the livery stable attached to the Wainwright Hotel. He's a learned man when it comes to horses, guns, men, and Shakespeare. He offends no one and will not be slighted."

"He sounds like a fine friend and mentor for a young man," Morgan surmised.

In the next half hour, she plied me with questions and absorbed brief histories of Uncle Purse, Aunt Emma, and Titus Culver, the operation and living arrangements of the Wainwright Hotel, and my studies under the tutelage of Master Schofield. I answered her questions earnestly, but evaded inquiries into my personal romantic involvement with Sedalia's eligible young ladies.

Her fire was out and the cold increasing. I suggested a few hours' sleep would put us both in good stead for our upcoming night march. She agreed and edged closer to the snoring Jacks.

I remember glimpsing shining stars and a bright moon when the first tug on my blanket brought me half awake. The second tug was stronger and plowed through the sleepy haze gripping me. "I'm cold," a voice whispered.

Jacks couldn't talk and recognition of my intruder snapped me awake. Hands pulled my blanket open, a body slid in place beside me, and the flowery smell of my after-the-bath visitor washed over me. A hand gripped mine and thrust it between us. My fingers touched warm, bare flesh instead of cloth. The guiding hand made a circle and my palm grazed the nipple of a breast no longer bound by cloth to diminish its size.

Lips touched the side of my neck, and a voice huskier than usual said, "You wouldn't disappoint the girl who saved your life, would you, Owen?"

Before I could answer, her lips covered mine. She left my hand holding that loin-stirring breast and began tugging at my belt buckle. While I had enough sense remaining to fear I might freeze to death, there was no earthly means of stifling her desires—not and face her with my manhood intact come daylight.

Morgan Holloway taught me another invaluable lesson about females during our dark-of-the-night tryst. They know how to awaken a man to their desires and draw him into an all-encompassing whirlwind of pleasure that at its peak blots out the universe.

Afterward, she held me close and said, "Nothing lasts forever. Remember this night when you think of me."

Before I could decide how to respond, she was sound asleep.

"Halt! Who goes there?"

The shout jerked me awake in the saddle. Against all my will, I had fallen asleep at the most inopportune time. We had made a star-guided sashay around to the southwest and, in the fish belly color of early dawn, turned north after sighting wheel ruts in a double line, tossed-aside luggage, lost cattle, and a dead horse. I was as certain as I could be that we were located between General Price's fleeing trains and what remained of his fighting army.

I motioned Morgan forward and raised both hands. "Owen Wainwright, aide-de-camp to Captain Logan of the Iron Brigade, and Private Morgan of the same unit."

Two gray-uniformed troopers, Enfield rifles sighted on us,

emerged from the ground-hugging mist. A rustling in the brush behind me told me the two sentries weren't alone. They had seen us coming and arranged a quick trap. And I had blundered smack into it. At least they wore gray and not prisoner-taking blue. When I chanced a glance at Morgan, I thought I saw a sheepish look on her face. Had she fallen asleep too?

The taller sentry jabbed at me with his Enfield. "Elmer, disarm them."

We sat stock-still in the saddle while Elmer lifted my revolver from its holster and took charge of Morgan's shotgun. "Leave the carbine, Elmer. He'll be dead before he lifts it free."

The sights of the taller sentry's Enfield never wavered. "You're wearing the right uniforms and coming from the right direction, but Corporal Varner has a mean-bull temper. It would save us a heap of trouble if you had identifying papers on you?"

I remembered Captain Logan's pass. The sentry's grammar pegged him a reader. "I have your paper. Can I reach in my pocket?"

With his crisp nod, I slowly lowered my right arm, pulled the pass from the pocket of my jacket, and leaned forward. "Elmer, bring me his paper. Evans, light your lantern and fetch it over here."

I sighed thankfully. I'd been afraid we'd have to wait on brighter daylight so the sentry could make out the wording of Captain Logan's pass. "Chaffee, you always bragging about your education," Elmer said with a snort. "Now you can prove you ain't a liar."

Chaffee did himself and his teacher proud. He clasped the pass, told Evans to come closer with the lantern, and read aloud, "'October 22, 1864, Aide-de-camp Owen Wainwright is traveling on official business and is due all assistance and courtesy in the completion of his duties, Captain B. Logan, Shelby's Iron Brigade.'"

A doubtful Evans scoffed, "What the hell does 'all assistance and courtesy' mean?"

"Means whatever this young feller asks for, he gets, or you deal with a captain of General Jo Shelby's Iron Brigade, and we ain't raisin' any dust on that road, you dunderhead. Elmer, hand back their weapons," Chaffee ordered, returning Logan's pass.

Once we were in possession of our weapons, Chaffee asked, "Anything else we can do for you, Wainwright?"

"I was occupied in Independence tending to Colonel Lawton's burial. Can you tell me what happened yesterday? Are General Price's forces retreating before the Yankees?"

"Damned if we ain't," Evans asserted. "Them Union boys laid a royal ass whipping on us. Even the Iron Brigade was routed and ran to save their scalps. I tell you—"

"Wainwright, you looking to rejoin your company?" Elmer said, his disdainful expression hinting Evans was a blowhard who liked to talk and talk.

"Yes, I'm to report to Captain Logan by noon today."

"Whatever's left of the Iron Brigade is back up the road a ways. They may have been routed like the rest of us, but I heard Major Franklin tell Lieutenant Hoffman the whole of our army would have been lost if it hadn't been for their last stand. They held the Yankees at bay long enough for the rest of us to get clear."

The ride to the rear of the Confederate column wasn't a pleasant excursion. It was quickly apparent the flight from the attacking Federals had mixed brigades and companies, wagons, artillery, and refugees in a scrambled mess requiring considerable sorting out before the column could march and fight again. The hangdog appearance of troopers surrounding meager breakfast fires, with little concern for the state of themselves or their weapons, was proof of how devastating the defeat at Yankee hands had been. It was impossible for me to shun the notion that General Price's planned retaking of Missouri was a bust, and though there would be more fighting as the blue pursued the gray to the bloody end, he was left with nothing but a painful retreat into Kansas and the Indian Territory and beyond.

At seven twenty-seven by my pocket watch, General Ackerman's staff courier was able to give us directions to the middle fork of the South Grand River and the camp of the Iron Brigade. It was then a matter of a short ride and a scouring of the breakfast fires on South Grand's bank to locate Captain Logan and his scouts.

As we neared the scouts' breakfast fires, I realized the odds of General Price's army being scattered to the four winds by the more powerful Union Army at any moment could squash forever any chance of my being alone with Morgan Holloway again, even just to talk with her. In the meantime, I had a suspicion her father would be more inclined due to the heightened danger of our situation to keep her within his sight or in the company as much as possible to protect her.

We hadn't exchanged a dozen words since awakening that morning. It was as if the previous night had never happened. But it had and, Laura Kellerman or no Laura Kellerman, I didn't want it to end there.

# CHAPTER 15

Captain Logan's detail was arranged as usual for the morning meal in a grove of widely spaced trees: squads with their sergeants, and lieutenants with their captain. Lieutenant Graham Donovan spied us first. He bounced to his feet and saluted us with his coffee cup. "I be damned, the young pups found their way back to the trough with no blood lost."

Red bandana binding her hair, a slash of scarlet against falling autumn leaves, Morgan Holloway dismounted and made a beeline for her father. I unsaddled our horses and walked to the officers' fire, wearing Colonel Lawton's pistol and carrying his breech-loading carbine and the saddlebags containing Captain Logan's orderly book, pen, and ink bottle. For safety's sake, the Union cavalry coat was rolled in my blanket once more.

The swollen bruise radiating a bright purple color on my half brother's forehead testified that the previous day's fighting had involved close-quarter, hand-to-hand combat at some point. Lance's tone was ice cold when he quipped, "Playing soldier for real now, huh?"

Captain Brett Logan ignored Lance's hostility. "Welcome back, lad. Is Colonel Lawton resting peacefully, per my instructions?"

"Yes, sir. Mr. Witten, the undertaker, was most accommodating. He was acquainted with Colonel Lawton from prior military service and he much appreciated your Federal greenbacks."

Captain Logan said, "Have a seat," and held forth a hand. "If you'll pass me my orderly book, I'll do the honors. You haven't had time for much training or practice yet."

I gladly relinquished those items. Captain Logan called for his sergeants and his morning "skull jabber," as he jokingly called it, commenced. Sergeants Holloway and Whitman showed no sign of injury. As a unit, the scouts had not fared equally well. "Sergeant Holloway, you lost Private Boyd," Logan began. "Sergeant Whitman, Privates Lake, Stewart, and Decker. Four good men, gentlemen, they'll be missed."

I saw a brief flicker of interest in Lance's eyes at the mention of Tom Boyd's name. It was the first death among the trio that had robbed the Kellerman Mercantile many weeks ago. Whatever monies remaining from the crime would now be split two ways between Private Pat Shannon and Lance. The thought crossed my mind that Lance wouldn't hesitate to kill Shannon and take all the money if the notion struck him. It surprised me that I felt no guilt over believing a person carrying my blood could be so sinfully ruthless, but I shuddered at the depth of Lance's wickedness.

The scouts were breakfasting on hardtack biscuit and weak coffee. Morgan assumed her usual duties and refilled everyone's cup, including one for me. "Not to hurt your feelings, Captain," Graham Donovan said, "but this coffee of yours would cause a riot in a Fort Worth cow camp."

During the chuckles around the fire, I saw Lance's nose sniffing the air while Morgan poured his cup. He apparently assumed the flowery smell of her was his nose playing tricks on him and held his tongue. The other scouts were either too tired to notice or their days-old stench overwhelmed their senses.

"Lance, Private Boyd fell to a Union bayoneting after we broke their line, correct?"

"Yes, sir, a bullet broke his shoulder. He lost his revolver and was helpless in the saddle."

"Damnably clever of those Yankees to hide those dismounted troopers with bayonets at the ready behind their mounted lines," Graham Donovan said. "My guts like to froze at the sight of 'em."

"That didn't keep you from saving Lance's bacon, though," Sergeant Whitman said, head shaking in awe. "I ain't never seen a trooper pick a fellow off the ground with one hand from the saddle of a running horse afore."

Though I hadn't witnessed that miraculous feat, only a man with the massive shoulders and hands of Graham Donovan could have accomplished it. A slight twinge of red stained Lance's cheeks. I suspected it wasn't embarrassment. Most likely, it was anger he'd made a hero of latecomer Graham Donovan.

Captain Logan's pen scratched hurriedly on the open page of his orderly book. "Graham, what about your lost men?"

"Rifle fire cost us Stewart and Lake. Decker's horse tripped and fell on him during the charge, breaking his neck."

Captain Logan allowed a few moments of silence and then said a short prayer for our fallen comrades before continuing. "Ammunition, Sergeant Holloway."

"Twelve rounds per man, sir."

"Sergeant Whitman?"

"Ten rounds per man, sir."

"Shame General Shelby burned our ammunition wagons to keep them from Yankee hands," Graham Donovan observed. "Now it is beg from General Price's precious supplies. His bloated supply train is an albatross dragging us to our knees. Instead of fighting, we retreat to spare flour and cows."

Whatever his faults, Lance never quibbled over details when the full story loomed in front of him. "The truth is, supplies are less important than sweat on an ant's balls. This war is lost. There'll be a few final tussles and skirmishes, but the Yankees have more men, horses, cannon, small arms, and ammunition, and there's not an ounce of quit in them."

Lance's frank, brutal assessment of the Confederate Army's future prospects in Missouri, beginning that morning, stymied conversation for five long minutes that seemed an hour. Aware he was commanding mature soldiers and not early-war recruits enthused by the promise of certain victory, Captain Brett Logan made no attempt to diminish the validity of Lance's words.

"Gentlemen, our situation is indeed bleak. Nevertheless, we must do our sworn duty. We can't quit our brothers so long as we have the means to fight. When the time comes that nothing remains for us but hopeless defeat, it is your decision to surrender to the enemy or take your leave and avoid a stretch in a Yankee prison camp."

Those were big judgmental words requiring time to swallow and chew over. The coffee sipping grew noticeably louder. "One last consideration, gentlemen," Captain Logan said. "Most of you are aware General Shelby has vowed he will never surrender. He plans to lead the last holdouts to Mexico and forge a new settlement there. Bear that in mind. It might be more appealing than returning home a defeated soldier if you survive Yankee imprisonment."

A courier riding a paint horse jumped from the saddle and hustled before Captain Logan. "Orders from General Thompson, sir."

Logan read from the proffered document. "We depart at high noon. Sergeants, see that the horses are watered properly and allow the men a quick swim sans boots, jackets, and shirts. They need something different. Graham, take Private Townsend and the pack mule, find the nearest ordnance wagon in General Price's trains, and replenish our supply of ball and powder. You can catch up to us on the trail. Lance, you and Private Shannon fetch three days' rations from the quartermaster wagon, which just parked down the bank yonder. Hunger isn't on our schedule today."

I saw a brief twist of disgust on Lance's features, which I attributed to the assignment of duties. His kept him in sight of his commanding officer, while Graham Donovan was being trusted to use his discretion in locating a supply of ammunition that might be miles away, and then finding us after the march resumed. I wondered if Captain Logan had any concern over Lance's sticking with the scouts till the bitter end.

Men scattered as assigned. Captain Logan held Morgan and me at the fire with a raised hand. Her sigh of relief was a near hurricane. She had no interest in suffering the mortal embarrassment of swimming shirtless with her male companions.

Captain Logan settled on his deadfall seat. "Tell me about your trek to Independence. It surely didn't come off as easily as you intimated. You said the undertaker Witten was very accommodating."

Between us, Morgan and I painted an accurate picture of the hospitality of the Wittens, the fees I agreed to, how fine Colonel Lawton looked in his burial uniform, the grave plot and marker, the sumptuous meals at supper and breakfast provided by Mrs. Witten, and their providing us quarters overnight.

My not wanting her father to hear of the degree of danger she'd encountered, I omitted any mention of the shooting inside the mortuary. Imagine my shock when she spun a complete circle on me. "We did have some trouble with the Woodman brothers."

A half-drowsing Captain Logan's ears perked up immediately. "Who are they?"

"They came to secure their uncle's body for private burial and saw Owen counting out your money to pay Mr. Witten. Mr. Witten told Owen they were bushwhackers and robbers who belong to no army. They followed us while we ate at a café. Mr. Witten agreed with Owen they'd be back to rob him and Owen that night. So we laid a trap for them."

That assertion perked *my* ears. She was including herself in the planning of the trap, and that was an outright lie. She was not to be involved under any circumstances.

When I studied her and caught the solid set of her jaw, it was clear to me she was trying to confirm her value as a bearer of arms, not a mere camp cook who had luckily shot a bank robber in a dark alley. She was out to prove herself as much a soldier as any man riding with Logan's scouts. And I naturally went along with it and let her finish the tale-telling.

She didn't waste a word. "The Woodman brothers and their fellow robbers, all armed, came at us from both the front and the back doors in the middle of the night. Owen shot the two at the back door. Mr. Witten and I did for the two at the front."

Genuine surprise raised Captain Logan's brow and he whistled softly. "Did they return fire?"

"Yes, sir," Morgan said.

Unlike the Confederate provost officer at Independence, the idea we had ambushed the unsuspecting Woodman brothers never occurred to Captain Brett Logan. Defense of self and property took precedent over the question of who fired first. The welfare of those perpetrating the crime wasn't a priority worth the bother, and I didn't doubt the harsh cruelty of the war had hardened his outlook on the subject.

"Must have been a right touchy go for a bit," Logan concluded. "And the Wittens survived without injury?"

"A bullet grazed Mr. Witten's forearm, sir," Morgan reported. "It wasn't a serious injury."

I decided to drive the last nail home for her. "Except the wound caused him to drop his revolver and he'd be dead if Morgan hadn't killed the last standing robber."

Captain Logan chuckled. "It seems you have a knack for shooting at the most opportune times, young man. Maybe I should make you my bodyguard."

Morgan Holloway's smile gave a new meaning to the concept of happiness. It was the pupil receiving the highest grade from her mentor; it was a feeling I experienced on the rare occasions Master Schofield praised one of my essays expounding on Blackstone's legal commentaries.

"I'd be honored, sir, except you'd need a new cook and I don't believe your stomach would find that a fair trade."

Their shared laugh and the captain draining the last of his coffee signified the morning was advancing and other matters needed our attention. Captain Logan updated his book, Morgan cleaned and repacked the coffeepot and tinware and doused the fire, and I saw to the watering of Badboy, her small bay, and Colonel Lawton's seal-brown gelding.

The hooting and hollering of the half-naked scouts enjoying the cooling waters of the South Grand River lent a picnic atmosphere to a few hours of leisure snatched from the grind and sweat of a murderous conflict. Leave it to Lance to spoil those relaxing moments for me with the keenness of a knife stab to the heart.

He crossed my path returning to camp from the quartermaster wagon. He halted and his devilish grin whitened the scar running from the corner of his mouth across a cheek dense with flame-red beard. "Tell that whelp of Holloway's, she keeps staring at you with cow eyes when she thinks no one is watching, the whole camp will soon know her for what she is."

Our march led us across the state line into Kansas. Smoke rising in swirling smudges in the rear of General Price's army told of burning homes, barns, and haystacks. Morgan kept turning in the saddle to scan the horizon behind us. "Confederate stragglers burning and looting homesteads," Graham Donovan explained. "Revenge for what Kansas Jayhawkers did in Jackson County and elsewhere in Missouri."

It was a sight that tightened the chests of men not prone to tears who sought the peace of a home hearth and land on which a family could grow and prosper. The finality of war and its ability to abruptly end lives and destroy whole families weighed more heavily upon those away fighting in uniform, and helpless to intervene, than the loss of their own lives and promising futures. It was a fate endured by countless Southern families, unknown to Northerners far from the battlefield.

We were two days into flight from the Union foe and the Iron Brigade was stationed on the right flank, four hundred yards from General Price's column, precisely where an enemy attack was considered most likely. It was October 25, 1864, ten days after my departure from Sedalia as a purported prisoner of war. I was now riding with Logan's Confederate scouts, wearing gray and armed with revolver and carbine, having yet to fire a shot at my *non*enemy, the men in Yankee blue. I swear, even my Maker didn't know how long such a concocted, odds-defying stalemate would continue.

General Price apparently considered his cumbersome trains the sole gain of his collapsing Missouri raid and refused to abandon a single wagon or head of beef. Our pace was further slowed by the myriad of rivers and streams, large and small, bisecting our path. While riders on horseback could swim all but the deepest waterways, large numbers of them churned the beds of those streams into slippery, sticky substance, rendering them impassable for the balance of the Rebel army. Supply wagons and artillery had no choice but to ford where streams were wider, shallower, and offered a gravelly, solid base. Anxious with his men to push forward and attack the huge Union supply depot at Fort Scott, a cursing Captain Logan proclaimed in long rants to everyone within earshot that we'd pay the piper dearly for General Price's greed. The captain had no idea the fruition of his prediction was boiling in frustrated Union bellies tired of trailing after us.

About noon, General Thompson moved farther to the right and dismounted the Iron Brigade in a cornfield near the Little Osage

River ford, intending to make camp and wait for fresh orders. Horses were being unsaddled and wood collected for fires when a galloping courier arrived with orders requiring Thompson to form his troops and return immediately to the right rear and drive off the fast-approaching enemy. Buglers blew "To Horse" and the disorder caused by camp preparations was reversed and the dismounted regiments were quickly back in the saddle and moving to the northwest.

Within a mile, a long blue line of soldiers materialized in the tall grasses ahead of us, advancing across the rolling prairie at a measured pace. General Thompson brought his brigade into line and started us forward, but the Yankees fell back. We descended a ridge, which moved us out of sight of the road. It was a joy to watch General Thompson exploit the terrain by deploying Slayback's regiment to the far left and Erwin's regiment to a nearer field on the left, intending to flank the Federal line, while the main line, consisting of Smith's, Elliott's, Gordon's, and Williams's commands, continued their advance.

"Neat strategy," Captain Logan said. "It would be a real surprise for our bluebelly friends."

But the inevitable General Shelby courier came galloping from behind us with orders to withdraw, without being seen doing so, if possible, and beat a hasty retreat to the Little Osage River. A dismayed but pliable General Thompson sent our main line back to the ford and sent orders to Slayback and Ervin to take advantage of the first low ground and withdraw. Both Slayback and Ervin withdrew, without drawing the attention of the Federals under the watchful gaze of their general, his staff, and Logan's scouts. After that, we followed that same general back to the ford at a leisurely walk, the only sign of agitation exhibited by our commanding officer.

General Thompson remarked during our return, "Odd we haven't heard a gun fired in an hour," an observation that sparked speculation that the enemy wasn't about in any force or the Rebel army was changing position.

Shocking news awaited us at the Little Osage. General Pap Price's army had suffered a brutal routing. Union cavalry had defeated the divisions of Marmaduke and Fagan at the Mine Creek crossing and seized Generals Marmaduke and Cabell personally.

Hundreds of gray-clad men and many officers had been killed, wounded, or captured, along with eight pieces of Union artillery. An estimated two-thirds of the Confederates in the battle had thrown down their weapons and fled down the Fort Scott Road.

"Good God Almighty!" Graham Donovan exclaimed. "Shelby's brigade is the only thing between Price's army and total disaster. We're being asked to protect his rear till he escapes again, something two whole divisions failed to do. This is insanity."

The truth of Donovan's rant was plain to the eye, once General Thompson and the small party of us riding with him forded the Little Osage and deployed on both sides of the crossing in a skirmish line. Large numbers of Federal cavalry soon appeared. Their wide lines exceeded both of our flanks and we withdrew without firing a shot.

General Shelby had formed his brigade in three lines, one after another, astraddle the road where it left a timbered hillside and passed between two cornfields. Elliott's regiment and Johnson's battalion formed our first line on the side of the cornfields nearest the enemy. The regiments of Williams, Gordon, and Smith formed our second line on the opposite side of the cornfields. The third line consisting of Ervin's and Slayback's regiments was farther back, positioned where the road crossed a prairie ditch.

Comparing the two cavalries via the Dollond telescope gave me the shivers. The mounted Federals were fully equipped with revolver, carbine, and saber. The arms of the bulk of Shelby's brigade amounted to long-barreled, muzzle-loading Enfield rifles extremely difficult to reload on horseback, making hand-to-hand combat a one-sided contest. General Thompson would have to rely on a delaying strategy that never fully confronted the enemy for any period of time.

Before a shot was fired, Sergeant Micah Holloway corralled Morgan and me. "To the rear, the both of you. Stay clear of the action. Your guns won't make a whit's difference in this battle. If anyone challenges either of you, you're serving as ammunition runners for Captain Logan's scouts and keep riding. Get a move on. The dance is about to begin."

"You heard him," Brett Logan seconded in a near shout.

I didn't miss Lance's disgusted snarl as we turned our horses and departed the first line. I ignored him. I'd risk Lance's wrath rather than be found at fault by Captain Logan or Micah Holloway.

In the ensuing five hours, I developed a towering respect for the tactical knowledge and skills of General Jeff Thompson. Key to Thompson's rear-guard strategy was the constant awareness that once a mounted infantryman fired his single-shot weapon, he cannot load again on horseback. Therefore, Thompson's only chance at holding the Federals at bay was single-shot volleys and then falling behind the next line to reload. To dismount in the open prairie with charging dragoons to the front meant certain capture.

Morgan and I found cover on uptilting ground, well behind the third line, just as the Union dragoons drew within two hundred yards, booted their carbines, drew revolver or saber, and sounded the charge. General Thompson was conspicuous at the center of the first line and gave the order to fire with the Federals within a hundred yards, wheeling to lead the retreat before the blast and smoke of the blazing guns died away. Retreating was dangerous, for as Thompson's men approached their second line, some anxious Confederates banged away, endangering their comrades. The charging enemy came on like a rolling wave, and despite the exhortations of Thompson and his fellow officers, the second line broke and both lines rushed in a confused mass for the third.

I kept my Dollond trained on General Thompson, his white horse a convenient focal point. He never evinced a second of panic. He corralled officers individually, instructing them to get in front of their fleeing charges and rally them, once they weren't under fire. Once the leaders of those in flight were under control, they helped form new Confederate lines, an action aided and abetted by our well-posted third line holding fast when the Union dragoons had to halt and dress their own lines before renewing their charge.

In the distance, I spied mounted Yankee regiment after mounted Yankee regiment crossing the Little Osage, and the weight of their superior manpower pushing against our third line soon compelled it to fall back. At that juncture, Morgan and I hustled and found a new observation point farther to the rear. Ahead of us, we could see Confederate forces from the very rear of Price's main army manning defensible positions behind ditches and fences and natural obstructions. They were preparing to assist Shelby's Iron Brigade with its slowing of the inexorable Yankee advance.

The additional support wasn't sufficient to arrest our withdrawal. What saved us from being overrun was the Union high command's failure to appreciate the weakness of their enemy, that every third man from Price's army was unarmed. Their overestimation of our strength kept the Federals from charging two of our lines in succession without halting to dress their lines. Those brief lulls allowed us time to reform our lines, absorb the shock of the next attack, and then withdraw again. Our supply trains used the slow pace of both armies to gain a lead of six miles in the race to preserve themselves.

A portion of the Shelby Brigade was in every front line, and General Thompson, Captain Logan, Lance, and Graham Donovan remained with each successive line as the others passed back. Thus, they received more than a dozen charges with bullets flying by them like enraged hornets, without person, clothing, or horse being touched. Morgan Holloway deemed it a miracle the moment she learned her father was also unharmed. Three more of Logan's scouts perished that long afternoon.

Darkness closed in and ended the day's hostilities for men and horses whose stamina and fighting zeal were worn razor thin, but the flight of Price's army continued. In a few miles, we came into contact with the very rear of the column and were forced to halt. Word was passed back that the train was crossing Marmiton Creek and establishing camp on the other side. At this juncture, the horse-killing practice began: Thousands of mounted troopers moved forward twenty feet, every five minutes, when another wagon made it across the creek. Men, virtually asleep in the saddle, appointed a fellow to watch over them while they slept along the roadway; then they were jostled awake to walk twenty feet, then slept again.

This bug-crawling pace continued for a couple of hours till General Thompson's patience was exhausted. He went forward with Captain Logan and thirty minutes later the column began moving steadily forward. Our frowns went without explanation till Captain Logan rejoined his scouts just short of the Marmiton Ford.

"The creek runs between steep banks and is only thirty feet wide and two feet deep. Every team entering the water would refuse to move without drinking first, and then stalled going up the opposite bank. Once a team was clear of the far bank, the volunteers helping it moved on with it. General Thompson cajoled and threatened and secured twenty men to stay put and help each wagon up the bank," he reported.

It was midnight when we located our brigade wagons. Bad news accompanied their discovery. General Thompson ordered us to select indispensable baggage, burn everything else, and be prepared to move at 2 a.m. Having nothing in the wagons of value or importance, I grabbed two hours of sleep with Morgan and Jacks on the far rim of our supper fire. We didn't share blankets, and not a soul commented on our sleeping arrangements.

We were mounted and just clear of camp when flaring plumes of light propelled by the explosion of extra ammunition shot into the sky. Totally startled stragglers and those half asleep soon stampeded by us afoot, gaping mouths uttering wild stories of narrow escapes from the battle raging behind them. The enemy had been within bayonet length of slitting their throats in their beds and burning their bodies. We laughed and joked with the tale-tellers, enjoying the humor of their false terror.

Lance seized the opportunity to gnaw on me and reined his rangy black gelding, stirrup to stirrup, alongside Badboy. "Maybe you'll have to shoot at a Yankee one of these days to save your own butt. Be interesting to learn if you've got the guts for it."

# PART IV

# IN YANKEE HANDS

# CHAPTER 16

IT WAS 11 A.M. ON OCTOBER 28, 1864. I WILL FOREVER REMEMBER THE events of the next hour in a second-by-second sequence. We sat our horses on a slight knoll overlooking a ten-acre tract of flat ground surrounded on three sides by a brush-covered swale twenty feet high. A thin tendril of smoke drifted from the chimney of the cabin tucked into the midpoint of the natural swale. A vegetable garden filled a side yard and a lone horse occupied the stock pen on the other side. The sight of the windlass, rope, and bucket of the water well centering the cabin's front yard was mighty appealing to a thirsty party searching for enemy troops attempting to flank their fleeing army.

We were five in number—Lance, Sergeant Holloway, Pat Shannon, Morgan Holloway, and me—a small detail meant to travel fast and light on rations, capable of reporting a sighting of the bluebelly enemy accurately and with utmost speed. Our first priority was to spy on Union troop movement and engage the Yankees, only if our safety was imperiled.

"Seems this piece of paradise is far enough from the road it missed out on the war," Pat Shannon surmised. "Bet the water is mighty cool on the tongue. We haven't seen mud-free drinking water for nearly a week."

"Be best if one of us scouts the place first," Sergeant Micah Holloway cautioned. "Yankees can be damned wily, if you let them."

"No need to waste time," Lance snapped. "One horse in sight

and the cabin can't hold more than three or four stragglers at the most. But we will form a line at the bottom of the knoll."

Sergeant Holloway nodded at that concession and we moved, single file, to flat ground, and then lined out as ordered, Jacks following after us. Thick clouds filled the western sky and, given our lack of rain gear, I wondered if Lance intended to take shelter in the cabin during the coming storm.

Twenty feet short of the well, the shutters on the cabin's front windows were pushed open by rifle barrels, and a dozen armed men in piecemeal blue uniforms, with aimed weapons, rose simultaneously from the brush atop the swale behind the cabin. The singular scream of "Fire" rent the air, igniting a sweeping volley that blasted away without any warning or chance to surrender.

I felt that familiar jolt to the side of the head that I'd suffered from the flying bullet on the porch steps of the Wainwright Hotel. I fought the blackness that threatened my senses and tumbled from the saddle. I landed on my shoulder. Though my vision was fuzzy around the edges, I made out the prone body of Morgan Holloway on the far side of Badboy's legs.

She lay in a heap, unmoving, a stain of red blood widening on the rear of her shirt. I had the wherewithal from observing numerous battle wounds to understand she was dead or dying. I tried to move, wanting to comfort her, if possible, but my muscles refused.

More shots rang out and a voice yelled, "Shoot the bastard. Don't let him get away."

Hoofbeats pounded packed earth between shots and receded into the distance. "I don't believe it, Olney, the biggest target shoots two of us and rides free. Next time, it might be wise, Sergeant, for you to wait on my command to fire, instead of buggering things up in your usual doltish style."

I knew it was Lance escaping. He was the biggest member of our detail physically and rode a large, rangy black horse.

"True, Captain," Sergeant Olney said, "but these other four aren't going free."

I watched fingers reach to touch Morgan Holloway. A streak of black shot past me, spooking Badboy. With a vicious growl, Jacks clamped his jaws on the arm of the hand's owner. The hound's weight bowled over his target and they crashed to the ground together. A quick-thinking ambusher drew his revolver, stepped alongside the two wrestling figures, and shot Jacks through the body to avoid accidentally wounding or killing his comrade. Jacks's death was as terrible and as unexpected as his mistress's, but he died attempting to protect her from harm, a noble achievement for a once-homeless canine.

Another ambusher rolled Morgan Holloway onto her back to check her pulse and wound. "Something's wrong here, Captain Foster."

"What's the problem, Haney?"

I heard cloth ripping. I forced my eyes open. The front of Morgan's shirt had been torn open, exposing her bound breasts. Haney pulled at the wrappings. "This dead Confederate ain't a man. He's a woman."

Captain Foster snorted as he stepped beside Haney. "You better not be rattling my chain for the fun of it, Pete Haney."

I saw Captain Foster's eyes bug. "Holy mother of God, it *is* a girl!"

He stood staring at Morgan Holloway, pulling at his earlobe. "Haney, close her shirt. Sergeant Olney, our horses are worn out and tucked up. Tell the men to break out the tents and set up camp. Us Kansans may not show much mercy to our enemies, but we can't leave a woman unburied, even if she fought for the slaving Confederates. We just can't. I'd love to hear her story. Are all her fellow Rebels dead?"

Pointing a finger in my direction, Haney answered, "No, sir, that one is staring at us."

Captain Foster walked around Badboy and yelled, "Zeller, check this man's wounds."

A grizzled, blister-skinned, goateed individual knelt on a knee and turned me onto my backside none too gently. Grabbing a handful of my hair, he lifted my head and felt above my right ear with his free hand. "Bullet grazed his skull," Zeller determined, fingers probing hard. "Lot of blood lost, but it doesn't feel like it broke bone. He's dazed from the blow. He should regain his senses here shortly."

Zeller was lowering my head when he noticed the scar above my left ear. "He suffered the same wound before, above his other ear. Hardheaded youngster, if you was to ask me."

Haney quipped, "Glad you're sober enough to tell what's wrong with him, Doc. Ain't that blood on his forearm too?"

Doc Zeller's blistered skin darkened, revealing the depth of his anger. "That's blood from his wound, you dang fool. Fetch me a rum jug from the supply wagon."

Haney hesitated. "Sergeant Olney?"

"It's for his wound, not me," Zeller contended. "And grab my satchel too."

"Sergeant Olney?" Haney repeated.

Captain Foster squelched the quibbling as a drop of cold rain wet my cheek. "Fetch the rum and bag, Haney," Foster ordered. Pointing at me, he continued, "Griggs and Anders, grab hold of this wounded Rebel's shoulders and feet and tote him inside the cabin."

I overheard further orders from Foster while his underlings rough-handled me from the ambush site. "Sergeant, I want the woman wrapped in her blanket for now and a grave dug for her, along with a common grave for the other Rebels, and a second one for our men soon as the rain passes. We'll bury the dog beside the woman. We'll leave nothing for the wild hogs."

Flickering candles lit the cabin. The heat of the hearth fire was warm on my cheek. The two Yankees laid me out in front of the hearth, per Doc Zeller's instructions. I was awake enough to feel every stitch he inserted, closing the tear in my scalp after flushing the wound with rum, the sting of which made me gasp. Surprisingly, for a medical physician long committed to the numbing comfort of the bottle, he was as gentle as Sedalia's Dr. Gribble. He tugged the last stitch tight and joked, "Not many patients realize sewing loose skin is no harder than hemming a dress."

Captain Foster dragged a ladder-back chair from the cabin's small dining table to a position near my feet, lit a cigar with a sulfur match struck against his thigh, and seated himself. "Give me a jolt on that jug, Doc. It's been a long day to this point."

Doc Zeller placed his needle in a tin box, closed his medicine satchel, handed Foster the rum jug, stood, and said, "I'll check on him later. Wilson finally wants that rotten tooth yanked."

Senses clearing, eyes seeing in detail again, I studied my captor. Firelight shone on his boney forehead, cheekbones, long jaws, and square chin. The two or three days of whiskers suggested a man who shaved regularly. His large brown eyes and warm smile dampened the impact of his stern countenance and lessened the impression you were dealing with a man devoid of emotions and capable of great cruelty. Had he not just ordered the burial of an enemy combatant because of her sex?

Puffing on his cigar, Foster said, "Can you hear me, young man?" At my nod, he said, "What's your name?"

"Owen Wainwright."

"I'm Captain Dayton Foster, Company D, Fifth Regiment, Kansas Mounted Militia. We're bound for Little Santa Fe, and then Kansas City to be mustered out. We've been fighting for three years. Company D was sworn in with seventy-five on the roster; there are thirteen of us left after losing the two your man killed. Never seen a man shoot faster with a revolver. He related to you by any chance?"

Before I caught myself, I blurted, "My brother, Lance."

Foster's frown resembled boulders sliding together. "Maybe you better tell me the name of your company and regiment, or are you freelance bushwhackers?"

"We're not bushwhackers, sir. I'm aide-de-camp to Captain Brett Logan. Captain Logan was the lead officer of a scout company reporting to General Thompson . . . commanding General Jo Shelby's Iron Brigade."

"Shelby again, that fighting bastard. I thought we would never break through his line, and when we did, he managed to wriggle loose and reform, no matter how hard we pushed at him. We hold the upper hand now, though. Even a genius cavalry officer like Shelby can't last forever against superior manpower and guns." Foster touched my leg with a boot toe. "You awake, lad?"

I popped my eyes open. "Yes, sir, I'm just resting."

"Good, because pain or no pain, wounded or not, you present a problem that we must deal with. That is, if you want to live."

I bit my lip as another wave of pain beset me. "I want to live."

"Here's my problem. Every trooper making camp outside has a scarlet patch on his chest. It means he's engaged the enemy at least a dozen times, no matter the color of their uniforms. They're veterans trained to kill and don't hesitate to do so. You ride in here with comrades dressed in gray and bearing arms. Had the situation been reversed, you would likely have ambushed us. I know without asking what my men are thinking. Why should we fuss with a prisoner on our way home after our unarmed boys have been murdered and scalped by Confederates and bushwhackers again and again? Why not just shoot you and be done with it?"

The pain in the top of my head was suddenly bearable. I had to stay awake. My life was dependent on my giving Captain Foster reason to convince his men I deserved fair treatment as a prisoner of war, not a firing squad. Hard as it would be to tell in my lame condition, and unbelievable as it would sound if I had the strength to tell it, the truth was my sole option.

But how would I even begin?

"Well, young man, do you have any reason why you shouldn't be shot in the morning?"

It was leap from the cliff or perish. "I was taken captive by Captain Brett Logan's scouts at Sedalia on October 15, 1864. Unlike my brother, I have no Southern leanings. Captain Logan made me his aide-de-camp to help him with his company books and make use of my horseshoeing skills."

My strength was ebbing quickly. Captain Dayton Foster puffed on his cigar. "Is that why you're not armed like the rest of your detail?"

*Oh, thank you, dear Lord! Thank you for Lance's hatred and bullheadedness.* I'd forgotten in the crushing terror and excitement of being ambushed and wounded that Lance had insisted I hand Colonel Lawton's revolver, holster, and carbine to Morgan before we left camp that morning. I was so relieved I nearly burst into tears. "Yes, sir. I was left with the horse holders whenever the scouts were engaged."

Captain Foster stared at me. His crumbled-boulder frown returned. Maybe he would accept me at my word. Maybe. I was too exhausted and hurting too much to say another word.

Leaning back in his chair, a deliberating Foster blew a series of smoke rings and watched them float upward in the candlelight. His body jerked forward and a slight smile gave me hope. "All right, you tell a tale I've never heard before. You'll travel to Little Santa Fe with us. I'll turn you over to a Union provost officer. You can tell your story to him. He'll decide your fate. Understood?"

Waving a hand in agreement was easier than a pain-racking nod or speaking aloud.

My eyelids were suddenly too heavy to hold open.

As with my first scalp wound, a throbbing pain lingered above my ear and I had trouble staying awake. But the pain was less harsh, the periods of drowsiness shorter in duration, and I had no fever, leading me to conclude the second wound wasn't as deep or as severe.

I remember hands moving me to a blanket at the side of the hearth and covering me with a blue overcoat to clear a path to the fire. Pots and pans clanged and the heat of the fire plastered a sweaty sheen on the forehead and cheeks of a handsome black male wearing a white apron, of all things. I swore I was dreaming when I smelled the hearty aroma of beef hash, lima beans, sardines, stewed tomatoes, peaches, and spiced apples, till I identified the snip of a knife opening cans of tinned rations common to Union campsites, but known to Southern soldiers only by theft. I regretted having neither an appetite nor the strength to chew anything stronger than air.

I heard words that were music to my ears when darkness, instead of daylight, filled the doorway with the comings and goings of Captain Foster's subordinates. "We'll camp here for another full day to rest men and horses."

Doc Zeller's blistered features hovered over me while his fingers felt my forehead and the side of my throat. "No fever," he informed Captain Foster, "a good sign a quick recovery is achievable. He can ride with Boomer in the supply wagon without harm, day after tomorrow."

Dabbing a cloth in a pan of water, Zeller gently washed dried blood from the area around my wound and ear. "What are the men saying about our gray-clad guest?" Foster inquired.

"They found a Union cavalry coat wrapped in his blanket," Zeller answered. "They figure it's a keepsake or he spies on us for the Rebs."

Dayton Foster's amused laugh turned Doc Zeller's head. "What's so funny?"

"Our guest claims he was taken captive at Sedalia earlier this month."

"And you believed him?" Doc Zeller responded, his incredulous look spawning another amused laugh on Foster's part.

"Not sure, but I'm certain he wasn't armed like his companions, and that raises the possibility he's telling the truth."

"What are your intentions with him?"

"I told him I will turn him over to the nearest Union provost officer. I have reasons for why I don't want to determine his fate. Think the boys will accept my decision?"

I fought off a drowsy spell to hear Doc Zeller's answer. "Being skeptical of everything, like veteran soldiers, they may not agree with your decision, but I doubt they'll challenge you on it. Probably Haney will be the only one that bitches."

Foster sighed and said, "If we live to fight another war, Doc, don't let me try to make a sergeant out of a brother-in-law who can't hold his liquor or his tongue, no matter how much my wife pleads his case. I've broken him to private so many times, he's got scars from his neck to his ankles."

I found smothering my laughter didn't increase my pain. I slept then, a deep and abiding slumber that vanquishes hunger and pain and lets a body heal. When I awakened, Sergeant Olney, Doc Zeller, and Captain Foster occupied the dining table, and the handsome black cook was working at the hearth.

"Marvelous breakfast, Jules," Foster said. "What about the grave digging, Olney?"

"Rain has stopped. Men are eating breakfast. We'll start at daybreak."

The mention of grave digging attracted my attention and the suddenness of Morgan Holloway's death dealt me a savage, belated blow to the heart. I'd known her but thirteen days, but it seemed like years. She had wormed her way into my life and given herself to me boldly, without demanding anything in return. She'd shown herself incapable of deception and guile. Her forthrightness and passion matched Laura Kellerman's. She would have been the soul mate every man longs for, but seldom finds. I felt privileged to have known her and shared her bed. No man deserved to meet and love two beautiful women in a single lifetime, and it was a tribute to the one I'd lost that she made me want and appreciate the other all the more.

Heavy on my heart, too, was the loss of her father. No matter the color of his uniform, Sergeant Micah Holloway had been a true line soldier in the vein of Sam Benson and Theo Corson. Stubbornly loyal to their cause, skilled in arms, disciplined to the core, they put the training, success, and survival of their charges before their own well-being. Beyond his professional duties, Micah Holloway had been a loving father who cherished his wife and daughter. He had done his best to keep Morgan safe in the midst of a conflict in which there was no stable front and every soul was in danger day and night.

I tried moving my head to test for pain and found nothing unbearable occurred. Emboldened, I searched my jacket pockets beneath the blue overcoat serving me as a blanket and was delighted to learn my Dollond telescope and pocket watch had not been taken. I mouthed a silent prayer thanking the Lord I was still alive, still in one piece, and still in possession of the two practical worldly goods that meant something to me.

Captain Foster saw me stirring in my makeshift bed. "Ah, the young pup awakens. Perhaps before the day is out, he will find the strength to tell the story of our mysterious female soldier. Jules, would you ask our guest if he is hungry? Olney and I need to check on how the boys are coming with the digging."

Cold air rushed in with the departure of the captain and his sergeant. Jules didn't question my hunger, nor did he leave it to Doc Zeller. He brought me a small pail of a beef-based broth, held my head up, and fed it to me in small sips. His behavior and judgment were those of a freeman with experience treating the sick and wounded.

I ate greedily and slept till a new blast of cold air awakened me. "Never heard such bitching and griping over a little shoveling," Captain Foster said, tossing his overcoat across the spine of a ladder-back chair. "They didn't carp about the graves for the woman and our boys. It was having to throw a single shovel of dirt for a dead Rebel that lit their fuse."

Doc Zeller chuckled. "And I bet Haney struck the match."

Accepting a cup of coffee from Jules, Foster seated himself and said, "He did, and ignited an argument over who had the right to the long-bladed knife one of the Rebels wore inside his shirt."

I heard a thump and knew Sergeant Micah Holloway's "toothpick" knife now rested on the dining table. I fought back the sadness that welled in my chest, but my half-choked voice was understandable. "The knife belonged to Sergeant Holloway."

Captain Foster stood and one-handedly set his chair alongside my bed without spilling his coffee. "Did he eat, Jules?"

A smiling Jules said, "Yes, sir. He did himself proud."

"If I'm to help you, lad," Foster said, "I'd like some information from you. You up to talking a mite?"

With my nod, Foster placed his coffee cup on the corner of the hearth, yanked a long-stubbed cigar from a shirt pocket, and used a thigh-struck sulfur match to light it. "I'm most fascinated by the gal riding with you. That's a rare situation in any war. Who was she?"

I steeled my nerve and avoided biting my lip. "Morgan Holloway, Sergeant Holloway's daughter. Her mother died of pox, the war took her brother, and your soldiers burned her home." I paused to catch breath that seemed in terribly short supply, and then said, "Sergeant Holloway had no relatives to send her to, so he disguised her as a man and talked Captain Logan into making her his personal cook."

"She was armed with a pistol and carbine. Could she shoot?"

"Yes, sir, quite well, but, like me, she stayed back with the horse holders when the mean fighting took place."

Foster puffed on his cigar and spoke with smoke curling from his mouth. "Chapman is a cabinet maker. He's fashioning a cross for her grave. We'll tie her red scarf on the cross as a marker."

I swiped at sudden tears and Foster politely looked away from some long moments. When his gaze sought me next, he changed the subject. "You mentioned Logan's scouts. Just who the hell were they?"

"A special scout company attached to General Thompson's Iron Brigade."

"How many of you were there?"

"At full strength, Captain Logan, two lieutenants, two sergeants, and twenty troopers."

"I take it Logan and his men engaged in field recognizance, scouting of towns, sharpshooting and skirmishing, duties that kept them in front of the Yankee army?"

"Yes, sir, whatever General Thompson and his staff wanted done and, if necessary, on the sly."

"Lad, I'm a duly elected county sheriff with a college education and, for your age, you talk like you've had considerable schooling."

"Yes, sir, my uncle Purse Wainwright pays for a private tutor."

"The same Purse Wainwright that owns the hotel in Sedalia, where you claim Logan and his men captured you?"

My head barely nodded. What strength I'd gained overnight was about gone.

"Better let him rest awhile, Dayton," Doc Zeller suggested. "The wagon ride will be a tough nut to chew for him, as it is."

Captain Foster shot to his feet, coffee cup in one hand, and cigar in the other. "I was only going to tell him I stayed a night in his uncle's establishment. This lad's no Rebel, Doc. Purse Wainwright isn't an outspoken abolitionist, but there's never been a better Unionist."

I drifted off to sleep, feeling much better about my situation. Dayton Foster believed my story that I had been a prisoner and had served in a passive role while with Logan's scouts and wouldn't hesitate to support my release when we reached the office of the Union Army's provost marshal. And the fact he was an officer of the law was another plus on my side of the ledger. The odds appeared to be stacked somewhat in my favor.

A rough three days followed our brief stay at the cabin. Company D, Fifth Regiment, Kansas Mounted Militia, had one goal on its collective mind: mustering out at Haneytown, Kansas, in time to vote in the presidential election on November 8.

Nourished and bolstered by Union Army hardtack soaked soft in black coffee and canned peaches, I listened closely while Captain Foster explained to me the constraints I must endure to travel with his company as a prisoner of war without disrupting the harmony of his men. "No boots. Manacle on wrists and ankles. You'll ride in the supply wagon. Boomer Harmon will do the driving. A bullet hit him in the throat next to the vocal cords and Boomer sounds like a cannon firing when he talks. You want peace and quiet, pretend you're mute and don't answer his questions."

Wise advice and, thankfully, I followed it, nothing against the naturally gregarious Boomer Harmon. We traveled twenty-eight miles that first day and I learned there was no comfortable position for a passenger confined to a strap-spring supply wagon. Every rut, every bump, and every dip in the road jolted the hard wooden bed beneath me, and with it, my throbbing head. We made brief halts to blow and water the horses and reached Little Santa Fe at dusk.

Riding next to Boomer Harmon, Jules surprised me with a brief history of Little Santa Fe as we drove to our campsite. "I came through here in '49 with my aunt and uncle. Wasn't anything beyond the supply depots here but wild Injuns till you reached New Mexico's Santa Fe. Don't recall a dentist office, barbershop, and a school. Right civilized place now."

A frustrated Captain Foster arrived as Jules finished preparing his supper. "Damn shavetail lieutenant they left behind to garrison this burg doesn't know his brow from his butt. Looks like you're traveling to Kansas City and Fort Leavenworth with us, Wainwright. The regular army provost marshal there will have the final say where you're concerned."

Chewing tenderly, I ate solid food that night. Salt beef never tasted better. Doc Zeller insisted on flushing my wound with carbolic acid and afterward decided the Lord had gifted me with a bullet-defying skull. "And some people claim granite is hard."

Captain Foster spent the evening writing a description of the particulars of the ambush that he intended to present to whatever Federal officer decided my fate. He wrote in a clean legible hand with a solid command of our English language. He had me sign under his name on the second page as proof I stood in agreement with his recounting.

I thought of home and Laura Kellerman that night, but the blunt awareness of how quickly the course of our days on the Lord's earth could change direction, or end forever with the speed of snuffing a candle, curbed my excitement. I'd hoped for a quick release from Captain Foster's custody after a hearing before a field provost officer who would accept Foster's explanation of my circumstances. Now we would deal with a professional, experienced provost officer who'd perhaps dealt with hundreds of pleading prisoners whose stories of their purported innocence might have already drained his last vestige of mercy and sympathy. I was where Aunt Emma would say with great timeliness, "Keep your spunk up, stay alert, and pray like you mean it."

The second day we clung to what was called the State Line Road running to Westport and on to Kansas City, encountering little traffic in either direction. The rising spirits of battle-winning soldiers, homeward bound for a mustering out, with a fever to vote for the man in Washington who'd saved their beloved Union, didn't flag for an instant. The weather was cool and dry, the rainbow colors of the fall foliage spectacular, the road dust moderate, rations plentiful, water handy, and no armed enemy lurked in ambush in any direction. It was the beginning of a peaceful lull that pushed the blood, pain, terror, and death I'd observed and experienced to the back of the mind and let my innards relax and the nightmares give way to dreams of feminine love, hearth, and home.

We were twenty miles beyond Kansas City late in the afternoon of the third day. We located a clearing on the bank of the Missouri River, below Fort Leavenworth and Leavenworth City, capable of accommodating a wagon and fifteen men and their horses, and went into camp. Captain Foster had decided earlier that we would seek out the fort's provost office in the morning while his command undertook the final journey of ten miles to Haneytown.

Before the sun went down, Captain Foster insisted Jules cut my hair. He provided scissors, razor, shaving soap, and mirror for the removal of my beard; then Jules washed my gray jacket and trousers in the creek at the edge of camp and dried them over a fire while I bathed in the same waters. His explanation for these "necessary" personal chores stilled any protest on my part.

"I was sheriff of Leavenworth County before I enlisted and had my share of dealings with the provost office at the fort. The Federal regular officers assigned to that court hate the bushwhackers and Jayhawkers who refuse a uniform and kill and loot at their whim. They want to hang them without a trial, same as their brethren in the field, no questions asked. I want you looking like a young, not yet dry-behind-the-ears Confederate regular, not a young, unwashed, unshaven border ruffian with blood on his hands," he revealed.

Later, while we enjoyed Jules's supper, with me dressed in a Federal overcoat while my clothes finished drying, he said, "You've had to wonder why I don't assert my authority over my men and tell them who you are and how you came to be riding with men dressed like bushwhackers against your will and set you free, haven't you?"

I admitted to having such thoughts.

"Here's my problem with arbitrarily setting you free on my authority, Owen. One of the men your brother killed was Hayden Chandler, the youngest son of the wealthiest banker in Leavenworth City. Standing next to Hayden in the firing line was Lonnie Hoffer, his best friend. Understand me, in my opinion Hayden Chandler was no more a soldier after two years of service than a four-legged jackass. His father foisted him on me, praying I'd put some iron in his spine. Old Maynard will want to know every detail of his son's demise, and Lonnie will be only too happy to accommodate him."

Captain Foster licked his lips and enjoyed a swallow of his coffee. Doc Zeller inched closer on his deadfall log to better his hearing. Otherwise, we were alone at the fire. "Lonnie will tell Maynard that we captured one of his son's killers. It won't make any difference to Maynard you weren't carrying a gun. You were with the bushwhackers that killed his son. I'll have to account to Maynard for how I extracted justice for Hayden if I want to hold an elective office in Leavenworth County again. He'll accept the opinion of a Union provost officer."

My jaw dropped; luckily, not enough Captain Foster noticed it. Was he truly interested in my freedom or protecting his own reputation and future?

What if the Federal military threw me in prison or condemned me to death? What could he do for me then?

And damn my half brother! How could his escaping a deadly ambush leave me in the lurch?

Captain Foster sensed my growing uncertainty and raised a calming hand. "Don't fret. I know the colonel commanding Fort Leavenworth and the lead provost officer. If the provost office gives us undue grief, which I'm not expecting, I'll talk to Colonel Whittaker and demand a trial. We'll obtain statements from those in Sedalia that can swear you were taken captive. And there are those in my company who sleep with the truth and will testify only one man in your party returned fire, and it wasn't you."

Tossing the final drops of his now-cold coffee into the fire with a flip of the wrist, Foster chuckled at the relief I was feeling, which had to show on my face, and said, "Never fear, Aide-de-Camp Wainwright, Dayton Foster is too much of a lawman to allow a young chap to suffer punishment for an act of war he didn't commit. Nor would Dayton Foster feather his own nest at that young chap's expense."

I didn't doubt the sincerity of Captain Foster's vows. But a smidgen of doubt lingered in a corner of my mind. He was counting on the principals who would determine my fate to be as honest in the performing of their sworn duties as he was, and I'd watched the passions of war turn honest men into brutes who trampled the rights of honest citizens for their personal gain without hesitation. I reckoned another nighttime round of Aunt Emma's "pray like you mean it" wouldn't hurt my cause any.

The sun was clearing the eastern horizon on a frosty morning when Captain Foster and I departed Company D's camp, with me riding Badboy. Leavenworth City was situated on the west bank of the Missouri River below the high bluffs on which Fort Leavenworth was erected in the 1820s. According to Captain Foster, Leavenworth City, the first city incorporated in the state of Kansas, was a thriving community of eight thousand residents; it served the needs of the locals and the soldiers stationed atop the bluffs quite handsomely. Freshly paid soldiers were more than happy with the city's numerous stores, saloons, and brothels. Foster took pride in pointing out the four-story stone-built Planters Hotel he deemed the finest resort establishment between the Missouri River and San Francisco for its sleeping quarters, cuisine, and fine wines. We passed large wagon yards and corrals for draft animals; these bore signs reading RUSSELL, MAJORS, AND WADDELL, entrepreneurs to whom Foster credited a major expansion of the trade over the Santa Fe Trail and points west.

We ascended the winding road leading to Fort Leavenworth. There was no wooden stockade surrounding the commandant's headquarters, soldiers' quarters, officers' quarters, hospital, quartermaster warehouses, military prison, horse stables, blacksmith shop, western arsenal of the U.S. Army, and parade ground. At midmorning, uniformed soldiers on foot and horseback moved like honeybees working the hive, companies of mounted soldiers drilled on the parade ground, and wagons were being loaded and off-loaded at warehouse docks.

"You're looking at the major supply and replacement depot," Foster observed, "and the source of every gun installation west of the Missouri for the entire Union Army."

From his prior experience as the sheriff of Leavenworth County, Captain Foster knew the location of the provost marshal's office at the rear of the commanding colonel's headquarters. We hitched our horses to iron rings embedded in the front wall of the building and entered without knocking. Two corporals manned desks in an anteroom with filing cabinets lining its walls. Behind the two corporals, a lieutenant with a desk that flanked a door at the rear of the anteroom recognized Captain Foster's rank and came to his feet. He studied my gray uniform before saluting the captain and asking, "May we be of assistance, sir?"

"I'm seeking an appointment with Major Cass Fielding."

"Sorry, sir, but Major Fielding's malaria beset him and he's confined to the hospital. Captain Brian Howard is temporarily in charge of our office."

"Is Captain Howard present?"

"Yes, sir. If I may have your name, I will inquire as to his availability."

"Captain Foster, Company D, Fifth Regiment, Kansas Mounted Militia."

The lieutenant disappeared via the anteroom's rear door. He returned and waved us forward. Captain Brian Howard was my height, broad in the shoulder and the hip, and sported a dense black mustache. His deep-set blue eyes had the keen sharpness of a predatory bird on the hunt. Before speaking, with jabbing fingers, he pointed to two wooden unpadded chairs before his desk, extending a courtesy I didn't expect, given my gray uniform. From those first few moments in his presence, I could only conclude that Captain Brian Howard's business was the business of command and duty, period, and he didn't disappoint me.

"Captain Foster, what is your business?"

"Captain, I require an opinion as to the status of my Confederate prisoner, Owen Wainwright. He was part of a Confederate scouting party ambushed by my men. The Confederate's return fire killed two of my company. Young Owen here suffered a head wound.

When he regained his senses, he claimed the Rebels he was riding with had taken him captive at Sedalia, Missouri, on October 15, 1864. Other than his word for that, the only other possible proof of his captivity was the fact he was the only Rebel not bearing arms. He, in fact, might be a Yankee."

"Did any of the other Confederates survive?"

"Yes, sir, one, but he managed to kill two of my men and make his escape on horseback."

Captain Howard drummed fingers on the top of his desk, thinking. "I must ask, Captain, given the thousands of Confederate soldiers we've killed and wounded to date, why is the fate of this particular 'might be a Yankee' so important to you?"

"His scouting party was dressed in the garb of Rebel bushwhackers, not the gray uniforms we're accustomed to seeing," Foster answered. "My men despise the bushwhackers and would've cheered me on if I'd shot him in the head." Captain Foster paused, swallowed hard, and said, "Captain, after three years of killing, and on my way home to be mustered out, to have cold-bloodedly shot this lad would have been one shot too many. I figured he, at least, deserved a chance to prove his story. I assuaged my company by telling them I would leave his fate to the provost department."

I knew nothing of Dayton Foster's personal life, but whether he had children or not, I wondered if the ambush death of Morgan Holloway, a female fighting in a man's war, hadn't softened his resolve in my favor. I wanted to believe consideration of banker Hayden Chandler's political clout came later. But then, I did tend to give those I liked the benefit of the doubt.

Captain Howard's fingers drummed a second time. His bristling mustache nearly hid his slight smile. "I can understand such sentiment, Captain. I've lost two sons in two years."

Sliding a writing pad in front of him, Howard dipped a steel-tipped pen in an inkwell, and fixed his eagle eyes on yours truly. With terse, short questions, he obtained my full name, age, mail drop, the names and locations of witnesses that could swear I had been taken captive, and to complete the record, the names, company, and regiment of my principal captors. When Howard turned to the details of the ambush itself, Captain Foster presented the report he had prepared and had me cosign in advance. Howard read through the report and thanked its author for its thoroughness and keen insight.

Captain Howard laid his pen aside and leaned forward, elbows resting on his desk. "Major Fielding will return next week. We shall start without him. We will request that a representative of the United States Marshal's Office—in this case the jurisdiction is Kansas City—proceed to Sedalia and seek statements from the captivity witnesses identified by Mr. Wainwright. Once that investigation is complete, we can reconvene on a date suitable to you, Captain, and conduct a hearing. I'm certain Major Fielding's ruling will suffice in this instance."

The force of my relieved sigh wasn't so great it rustled the top sheet of Captain Howard's writing pad, but its whistling sound did lift his brow and provoke another half-hidden smile. "There is one catch, gentlemen. Since Mr. Wainwright has become the subject of an official provost office investigation, it will be necessary to hold him in our guardhouse till his case is resolved."

Howard's eagle eyes switched to Captain Foster. "You need not fear for his safety. We have separate cells for those facing serious charges and those involved in minor scrapes as defined by post rules and regulations. His fellow prisoners in the main are trying to sober up and get a grip on how to pay their fines."

The idea of being held in the guardhouse for a week or more didn't bother me, for Forge Bannister was the U.S. marshal for western Missouri. Him I could trust to honor the requests of the Fort Leavenworth provost office as expeditiously as possible. Bannister had the same devotion to duty Captain Brian Howard exhibited. Maybe I was closer to holding the waiting Laura Kellerman in my arms than I'd thought possible just an hour ago.

It was the first good news regarding a possible return to what for me was a normal existence. I should have known, however, that in a world suffering through the turbulent disruption of a civil war, nothing is certain or guaranteed, and the conflict and events related to it may demand a man find a well of courage he thought beyond his reach in order to survive.

My quest for that special well of courage began before dawn the next morning.

# CHAPTER 17

THE RATTLE OF A KEY IN THE LOCK OF THE CELL DOOR PENETRATED the fog of deep sleep. Next, a hand clasped my arm and yanked me from the straw-stuffed mattress of the wall-hung bed. A gruff voice spoke so close to me I felt flying spittle on my ear. "One sound and I'll split your skull wide open."

My hands were manacled behind me and the same rough hand jerked me into the hallway fronting the cell. It was pitch black beyond the cell window and the oil cold in the guardhouse's wall lamps. My escort shoved me ahead of him with pointed blows of what had to be a club. He knew our course and had no problem guiding me through the darkness to the front door of the guardhouse. Our passage was quiet enough; not a prisoner stirred in the cells we passed.

Outside, a wagon pulled by a team of horses awaited us. A lit lantern hung from the rear corner of the vehicle's enclosed bed. Iron bars lined side windows and the rear door, and the vehicle's roof overhung the driver's box. Two soldiers in blue uniforms, one displaying lieutenant's bars, the other a corporal's insignia, stood at the rear of the prison wagon. The lieutenant was holding a handful of documents and a pen. The corporal held a shotgun and a large key ring. The document-bearing officer said, "This is Wade Purcell, the last of the four, right, Hinkle?"

"Yep," Hinkle responded.

The lieutenant peered at me and read from his sheath. "Wade Purcell, five feet nine inches tall, weight one hundred sixty pounds, red hair. I've never seen anything redder except fire. Load him up, Hank."

I opened my mouth and Hinkle rapped my elbow with his baton, igniting my crazy bone. I barely kept from screaming aloud. The shotgun-wielding corporal had size, weight, and reach on me, and I decided not to raise a fuss.

Hank gave me a hard shove from behind and I landed on the floor of the wagon between rows of wall-mounted benches occupied by the other three prisoners. All three welcomed me with a baleful stare. I hauled myself off the floor and plopped on the least-occupied bench, rubbing my elbow and asking myself, *Who the hell is Wade Purcell?*

Hank slammed the wagon's rear door and padlocked it. The lieutenant signed his signature with a flourish and handed the top copy of his paperwork to jailer Hinkle. Both blue soldiers mounted the box. There came the snap of a whip and the wagon lurched forward. We were off to a destination unknown to me.

My fellow passengers were manacled at hand and foot, hands in front of them. Two wore drab shirts and trousers that I assumed were prison-issued; the third prisoner was dressed in Confederate Army gray with the single star of the rank of major on his collar. His long beard was a combination of black and gray and his nose oft broken. There was a sorrowful cast to his features in the growing morning light. Seated next to me, he appeared the friendliest soul in the prison wagon.

"Do you know where we're bound, sir?"

The skinny prisoner with a beard tangled enough to hide a rat's nest, and missing his upper front teeth, blurted, "Told you, Ivey, he's a dumb young shit. Going where we are, he probably got caught after he killed himself a Yankee general with a lucky shot."

"Hell no, Elmer," his companion chimed in, "he's too clean to be anything other than an office clerk caught with his hand in the company cookie jar."

The Confederate major stiffened beside me. "And you two were lucky you survived the first volley. I'm betting you're deserters."

Much squirming by the two in drab dress followed the major's retort, but the resulting silence indicated the truth of his supposition. Gray eyes shadowed by sadness sought mine. "We're bound for a most unhealthy destination, lad. No Yankee jail west of the Mississippi has a worse reputation than St. Louis's Gratiot Street Prison. The brick walls are said to bleed real blood."

Unfortunately, try as I might, the image of Gratiot Street's bleeding walls was never absent from my thinking the whole journey to St. Louis. We traveled virtually nonstop. Our military guards shared the reins in alternating shifts while we passed through Leavenworth City and Kansas City the first full day. We sped along country roads to Warrensburg the second day, where we found the construction crews of the Missouri Pacific hard at work, the village having superseded Sedalia as the MP's westernmost terminus.

The passes of our escort bore the signature of a high-ranking Union officer. After a short haul to Sedalia aboard an open rail carrier, we had prime seating in a passenger car of the next train headed east. It was while the engine of our train set under the spout of the watering tower at Sedalia in the dead of night, with the Wainwright Hotel and the home of Laura Kellerman mere blocks away, that I found a longing pain in a man's heart could hurt damn near as bad as a toothache.

I finally engaged Major Mack Somers of the Confederate Army in conversation on the stretch of track after Otterville. He possessed a sharp, nimble mind, and once he knew who I really was, and heard the story of how I came to be in the Fort Leavenworth guardhouse and the details behind my short stay there, he concluded that I had been substituted for another prisoner matching my description to facilitate his escape. In Somers's opinion, the whole scheme centered on night jailer Hinkle. Hinkle had orders to produce four prisoners per the names and descriptions provided him and he had deliberately violated those orders and delivered me to our escorts.

"But how much time would handing me over gain Hinkle and the prisoner he wanted to help?"

"Maybe two or three days if he put a prisoner in your place and no one inquired about you. They don't call roll or take a head count every day at Leavenworth. If we ever had a chance to ask, I'd bet Hinkle disappeared the other morning with his buddy before daylight. He had this planned down to the nubs."

From that juncture to St. Louis, I tried to keep from lingering on such questions as to how Captain Howard would react when informed of my sudden disappearance. More important, would anybody seriously seek the truth behind my disappearance and spare me a stint in a distant Yankee prison on charges as yet unknown to me? Or would my disappearance prove so mysterious and clueless to everyone not involved, no one would solve it?

Good, it was, that I had finally crossed the threshold that tells a grown man he is too old to cry wet tears.

I paused my early-morning chewing and concentrated on watching a many-legged bug trying to swim to the side of my tin cup through the thin liquid the cooks dared call coffee, the sign of a man on the verge of death from sheer boredom. Nothing changed from day to day inside the walls of the Gratiot Street Prison. A tin cup of the less-than-poor-man brew, one-fifth of a loaf of baker's bread, and a small portion of bacon constituted breakfast. The evening meal consisted of the same amount of bread, a hunk of beef, and a pint of water the beef was boiled in, which was called soup, and, once in a while, a couple of boiled potatoes. Our tin cups and plates were never washed. Knives, forks, and spoons were prohibited. Food was dished out by hand and we ate with our fingers and wiped them clean on our clothes for lack of napkins. It was not unusual for prisoners to carp, to no avail, that they left the table as hungry as when they arrived.

After the morning and evening meal was served to eight hundred prisoners in three shifts in the mess hall, we were herded back to filthy interior pens holding thirty men each and barren of furniture and beds. Your pallet was the bare floor and a thin blanket. Dirt-covered windows meant little natural light, producing a constant gloom, and wall lamps for night illumination, except in hallways, were taboo. A dearth of newspapers, books, mail, writing paper, and playing cards equaled intellectual starvation. The prison privy in an open yard, surrounded by a fifteen-foot-high fence, was so foul, prisoners swore it could grow hair on a dog with the mange. Even the guards feared the midnight-black pit of the dungeon in the basement, which was reserved for severe prisoner punishment short of hanging.

The exceptions to placement in the pens was the second-floor hospital, filled with sick and dying inmates; constantly guarded rooms on the third floor, for those condemned to death for their crimes; and attic space for dead prisoners awaiting shipment elsewhere for burial. Prisoners supplied the labor for the kitchen and laundry. Given its filthy conditions and disease-ridden quarters, it was hard to believe Gratiot's gracious two-winged building, with its four-story conical tower, located in a wealthy St. Louis neighborhood, had once been the McDowell Medical College.

From snatches of overheard conversation, I learned the pens of Gratiot held Confederate prisoners of war, Southern sympathizers, political prisoners, mail runners, bridge burners, and Union deserters, often thrown together indiscriminately. Upon arrival, I learned that the crime of Wade Purcell was assault on a commanding officer. His sentence was imprisonment for the duration of the war. My protest that I was not Wade Purcell was brushed aside with the explanation that particular contention to evade jail time had worn thin and been discredited months ago. I sensed an intense dislike on the part of the prison staff for Wade Purcell's type of crime from the outset and deemed it advisable to attract as little attention as possible to myself.

My sole hope for rescue rested on my trust that Captains Brian Howard and Dayton Foster were both stalwart, upright, honest men, as well as officers devoted to their sworn duties. I hoped they wouldn't dismiss my mysterious disappearance as happenstance, something beyond explanation, for I'd had nothing to fear from spending a few days in the Fort Leavenworth guardhouse. That hope, the centerpiece of my nightly prayers, began to fade as the days and nights ground by without relief. Was I blowing smoke into an empty bee tree? Was I expecting too much of busy officers, one now mustered out, that I'd met by chance and to whom I'd contributed nothing?

My sole companion of note during those lean, mean days was a tall gent with hair the color of dried corn husks, an ax-handle-wide chest, a waist befitting a corseted female, long legs, and a fist that, when balled, matched the size of a small pumpkin. The only open space on the floor of my assigned pen the first morning, or what I judged an open space, was beside the tall stranger with a touch of menace about him.

I drew the same baleful stare from him I'd received from the prisoners in the Fort Leavenworth prison wagon. "What makes you think that space hasn't been claimed?"

Despite his size, his soft Southern tone wasn't threatening and I didn't shy away from him. "I didn't see anybody sitting beside you, sir, and being new here, I figured the safest place in the room appeared to be next to the biggest and strongest man in the room. My aunt Emma taught me to never be bashful about looking after your own self."

To my surprise, a wide smile bunched the corners of the big stranger's mouth. "You can be a charming bastard for a young fellow, can't you, a breath of fresh air in a stale hole? What's your name?"

I answered, "Owen Wainwright," and extended my hand.

His huge palm engulfed mine. "Amos Blackman, but you can call me Blackie."

I judged Blackie to be in his late thirties. I would learn it was a privilege to address him by his nickname. He was wearing a Confederate uniform with no insignia or designation of rank. "What's your crime, Owen? You look too innocent to be in jail."

I threw caution aside and risked sounding foolish and naive to the war-hardened prisoners surrounding Amos Blackman. "I've been jailed under another man's name for a crime I didn't commit."

The blinking of Blackie's eyes was nearly a comic exaggeration. He lowered his head and said, "Say that again, Owen."

I felt the heat of embarrassment redden my cheeks. "I've been jailed under another man's name for a crime I didn't commit."

The guffaws I expected didn't explode around me. Curious gazes settled on me instead. I realized then that the exaggerated charges that had jailed Union and Confederate civilians and soldiers without trial under the guise of military law throughout the war had made what might have once seemed laughably impossible a serious matter.

Blackie settled against the wall of the pen. "Explain to us exactly how that happened, Owen."

I didn't know what, if anything, it would gain me, but if I were to be the unexpected, entertaining diversion for the morning, I decided nothing but a memorable telling was worthy of my audience's time. I stuck to the main details of how I came to be available for abduction and transport to Gratiot Prison under another name. Most fascinating for my listeners was the odds against my height, weight, and hair color matching those of Wade Purcell, the key factor in the prison wagon officers accepting me as the genuine article. There was anger at the injustice done me showing on more than a few faces when I finished.

Amos Blackman's questions confirmed he agreed with my conviction that the initiative to free me had to come from Fort Leavenworth. I had not a single document in my possession establishing my true identity. The officers delivering me in person had confirmed my identity on both ends of the trip and their paperwork was cosigned by the Fort Leavenworth jailer, additional proof I was the *real* Wade Purcell. For the Gratiot guards and their superiors to accept my story solely on my word was akin to their suddenly believing a child's fairy tale.

I spent twenty days with Amos Blackman. He learned everything he wanted to know about me and I learned a lot about him, but nothing as to his rank and military service with the Confederacy. We talked history, philosophy, and literature, and I found him the equal of my learned tutor, Master Schofield. His knowledge of the law led me to believe that, while he hadn't practiced law personally, he was from a family of lawyers, and perhaps judges. He was that rare man who had the ability to succeed either physically or with his mind as he wished. He was the most confident man I ever met and he constantly encouraged me to never give up hope that help for me would be forthcoming.

My last contact with Blackie occurred in the middle of the night. He shook me awake and whispered, "I'm leaving you, Owen. Been a pleasure palavering with you, but I have a new life waiting for me in another country."

Leaving me? How could he escape from a guarded prison in the middle of the night at an hour of his choosing?

But he did.

The news of the prison break spread through the pens like a prairie fire the next morning. Eight inmates had cut a hole through the north wall of the prison on the second floor, where it abutted the Christian Brothers Academy. Six of the eight were in manacles by noon. The other two apparently found homeowners in the immediate neighborhood willing to hide and assist them and escaped capture. One of them was surely the capable Amos Blackman. Other than a few whispered conversations with our fellow prisoners in the mess hall line, I had witnessed no other evidence that Blackie was planning to flee in the night. He was that secretive.

It didn't hurt my feelings that he'd left me behind. If I was forced to serve the duration of the war in a Yankee prison and survived, I would emerge a freeman absent any further charges. Escaping with Blackie would have resulted in a Federal warrant for my arrest and additional time behind bars. He had acted in my best interest, the mark of a true friend.

A long, lonely week later to the day, two guards sought me out as I stood in line for breakfast by calling for one Wade Purcell to step forward. I did so and was led down the south stairs.

We turned the corner at the end of the corridor and my glance ahead, past the lead guard, into the office of the commanding warden, had me fighting those tears I'd sworn were a thing of the past, for my days confined in the Gratiot Street Prison had run their course.

# PART V

# PURSUING JUSTICE

# CHAPTER 18

His shoulders were still broad, his body well muscled, his shirt white and starched, features ruddy, Vandyke beard and mustache neatly trimmed, and eyes a disconcerting steel gray. The only difference in the appearance of Marshal Forge Bannister from the time he'd visited with me in my room at the Wainwright Hotel was a fur-collared overcoat, which hid his standard black suit, and brand-new shiny black boots in lieu of a pair that was scuffed and worn down at the heel. And his authoritative voice had not lost its deep tenor.

"The injustice didn't happen on your end of the stick, Warden," Marshal Bannister was saying. "A clever Fort Leavenworth jailer outsmarted his superiors."

Both men, one broad and one tall and spare, turned as the guards led me into the warden's office. The warmth of Marshal Bannister's greeting smile contrasted sharply with his usual business-first demeanor. "Mister Wainwright, it's good to find you hale and hearty after your unfortunate incarceration. I'm here to correct that error with the assistance of Colonel Thomas."

In a few short minutes, I was standing on Eighth Street in front of the Gratiot Street Prison with Marshal Bannister, shivering from the cold. "Come along, lad. We have a busy morning ahead of us."

Glad to be free as a gliding bird, I followed Marshal Bannister's lead. Questions on my part about his securing my freedom would have to wait till his plans for the morning were completed. He had a carriage and hired driver waiting at the curb. Our first stop after a four-block journey was a men's haberdashery. Here we purchased long underwear made of cotton, quill trousers, a long-sleeved woolen shirt, a canvas jacket, a fur-collared overcoat that matched Marshal Bannister's, and a flat-brimmed, flat-crowned hat, all fitted to my size. On Bannister's orders, I toted our purchases to the hired carriage, except for the overcoat I donned against the November cold, and we were off to our next stop, a public bathhouse and barbershop. There I scrubbed with scalding-hot water and a skin-scouring soap, which left me jumping, foot to foot. The barber shaved me after my bath and applied a Florida Water scent, which might have appealed to a damsel of the night, but would have repelled a scenting hound. Outfitted anew from head to knees, we proceeded to our third stop, the Brass Steer Saloon, overlooking the Missouri River at Seller's Point.

By the time we were seated by a waiter, definitely acquainted with the marshal, my curiosity was threatening to bust its leash. Just why was Bannister paying a near fortune to outfit me and feed me like a king? He had no obligation to me as a law officer beyond righting the wrong done me. What, if anything, did he expect in return?

Bannister ordered for the both of us, the waiter nodding and smiling. Before I could initiate a conversation, the waiter returned with platters of ham steak, fried eggs, potatoes, grits, a bowl of cream gravy, a wicker basket of oven-hot biscuits, and steaming mugs of black coffee sweetened with sugar.

"We eat, then we talk," Forge Bannister said. "I reason better with a full belly."

I was near to choking on curiosity. What was there to "reason" about? Wasn't I a freeman homeward bound? I had no binding commitment, other than perhaps a few more months of duty with the Enrolled Missouri Militia, which might have disbanded with the defeat of General Price's Confederate forces.

One thing I never doubted about Marshal Forge Bannister after that Brass Steer breakfast—the man's appetite matched his size. And I admit that after nearly four weeks of prison fare, I didn't deny myself a single bite. We kept our waiter busy, plowing through second platters of the main courses and finishing the gravy. A lone biscuit resided in the wicker basket with my last swallow of a third cup of coffee.

Bannister leaned back in his chair, patted his belly, lifted a cigar from the waiter's proffered silver tray, and sniffed it, smiling broadly. I waved off the waiter's offer. Smoking and my stomach would never know peace. The waiter struck a match and lit the marshal's cigar.

A few smoke rings later, he straightened his chair and said, "Now, let's talk."

"How did you find me?" I blurted, hating my display of childish impatience.

"I delivered a pair of Union deserters to Captain Howard's office three days after you disappeared in the middle of the night. He was waiting for me to answer a letter regarding you that was mailed to my Kansas City office. He told me about his meeting with you, the agreement you'd reached, and the part I was to play in it. Since no cell keys had been missing, they suspected someone on their staff had unlocked your cell. A staff roll call of three shifts found the civilian jailer for your wing, one Purvis Hinkle, had not reported for work since the morning you'd disappeared."

Bannister enjoyed a long draw on his cigar. "The standard inmate roll call the next morning found they were missing a prisoner named Wade Purcell. A sharp clerk in Howard's office said that was impossible. He had signed documents on file stating Wade Purcell and three other prisoners had been transferred to St. Louis three days prior. Both regular army guards and jailer Hinkle had signed the transfer papers. It was Captain Howard who tied the knot in the rat's tail. He compared your admission slip to Purcell's and discovered you were both redheaded and the same weight and height."

A smile accompanied Bannister's next smoke ring. "That made Howard suspect the two guards assigned to transfer duties had never seen either you or Wade Purcell, and a switch by an authorized jailer possessing the appropriate keys accounted for both missing persons. Howard's dilemma was how to make sure a switch had taken place before he telegraphed Gratiot Prison and informed them. He'd look foolish if no switch had occurred. So, though three days had passed, he asked me if I would see what I could learn on his end. Since his staff knew where Hinkle boarded in Leavenworth City, I said I would."

The waiter refilled Bannister's coffee cup and placed a glass ashtray before him. I declined a refill. "Owen, if you ever decide to break the law, for the love of Jesus, never leave a trail running from the law that a hound can follow without using his nose. I located Hinkle's boardinghouse based on the directions provided by Howard's clerk. A little asking around and I learned Hinkle spent his free hours sipping beer and playing cards at a saloon up the street from his boardinghouse. To be honest, I got lucky. Turns out back in '59 I cleared the owner of the Square Peg's brother of a murder charge. Fritz Arnold shared with me that a gent claiming to be Hinkle's first cousin showed up there three weeks earlier. Hinkle eventually stopped playing cards and spent his time at the Square Peg at a corner table, jabbering with his newly arrived relative, and sometimes that led to red-faced arguments. Fritz felt Hinkle was maybe being pressured to do something he didn't want any part of. Then suddenly no Hinkle by himself or with his supposed cousin. When Fritz and I pinned down the date, it was the same morning you disappeared from Fort Leavenworth."

Bannister cleared his throat, snubbed out his cigar, and sipped coffee. "I figured that much information might satisfy Howard enough he'd telegram the warden at Gratiot Prison regarding his suspicions, but that wasn't all Fritz had to tell me about Hinkle. Seems Hinkle had bragged, off and on, about how his uncle operates a hog ranch at Turner's Crossing, thirty miles north of Leavenworth City. Hinkle, uncle, and first cousin rang a bell with me. The hog ranch not being a long ride for John L. Whitefeather and me, we lit out the next morning. We located the ranch late in the next day. We found cover on a hillock, where we had a view of its outlay. The corral by the barn, the structure nearest us, held half-a-dozen horses. Skinny hogs roamed the farm lot and nearby woods. Beyond the barn and farm lot, smoke rose from the chimney of a two-story structure situated on the south bank of a large creek. We waited till dark. The smoke coming from the chimney dwindled and we went in on the sneak. I left Whitefeather at the corral to cut off access to the horses. I entered the house without knocking. Not knowing what awaited me, I had a loaded pistol in each hand."

Bannister's chest pumped air, though his ruddy features were calm. "The smell of the place watered my eyes. A snoring, naked creature I determined was a woman was sprawled on a couch to the left of the fireplace. An older male dressed in loose farm clothes, bleary of eye, and unsure of his footing, saw me and leaped from a chair at a table heaped with dirty dishes and garbage. He was, unfortunately for him, unarmed and I laid a pistol barrel across his skull with all the force I could muster."

I found it fascinating to listen how a U.S. marshal thought and decided to act in an unsettled situation. "That left me with whoever was on the second floor to deal with, which could be three men—Hinkle, his first cousin, and fugitive Wade Purcell—and any other females inhabiting the house. I went up the stairs, one at a time, unsure if anyone above me knew of my presence. I cocked both pistols. There were three doors that opened off the hallway. I opened the first door, hoping the door hinges didn't sound off, and found a lone male, in what I deemed city clothes, sound asleep on a rope bed. I put manacles on his wrists and moved to the next door. The door hinges creaked like a croaking frog, warning anyone awake in the room, and I saw a male in farm clothes spot me with drawn pistols and shove aside a half-dressed female while lunging for a revolver on a night table next to the bed. There isn't much mercy in my business, Owen. I didn't shoot to disarm him. I shot him dead center in the chest."

Caught up in the excitement of Bannister's recounting, I swallowed twice to steady *my* nerves. "My shots alerted the man we later identified as Wade Purcell. Purcell had no scruples whatsoever—what you'd expect from a soldier who tried to beat his superior officer to death. He shoved the female in his room into the hallway ahead of him. I honestly don't think she was sober enough to appreciate the danger she was in. He came out with pistol raised, searching for a target. I slid down the hallway wall to confuse him and fired both of my pistols. The poor girl stepped into the line of my first bullet. My second went high. His only shot sprayed my neck with wall plaster. My next two shots didn't miss. One turned him sideways. The other knocked his feet from under him."

Bannister eased back in his chair, steel-gray eyes watching me closely, assessing my reaction to his unannounced invasion of the hog ranch. Had I myself not killed in self-defense, I would have been stunned by the violence involved and the killing of an innocent female. His justification for what he had done was straightforward without a hint of apology.

"I'm in a sudden business, Owen, with one cardinal rule. I have the law on my side and, in any circumstance, I intend to be the last man standing. If you don't want to deal with me, don't give me cause to come hunting you. I'm a dedicated lawman. I don't have any quit in me whatsoever."

Bannister signaled to the waiter with his empty coffee cup. He waved off the coffeepot and said, "Jacob, bring us a bottle of that Kentucky bourbon you're always overselling and a couple of glasses. We still have business to transact."

When Jacob returned, Bannister poured three fingers of straight bourbon in each glass, smiled at how carefully I sipped from mine, and continued to speak. "When it was said and done at the hog ranch, we were left with a first cousin, whose name I never bothered to learn, and a wayward female named Leona Phillips to bury. We carted the body of Wade Purcell back to Fort Leavenworth tied over a saddle. Purvis Hinkle traveled on horseback, tied hand and foot. Captain Howard was one happy jail overseer when I rode across the parade ground and presented him Purcell for burial and Hinkle for punishment. He was a tad astounded, though, when I announced my intention to personally fetch you from St. Louis."

He had me on the edge of my seat again. "Why was he astounded?"

"I told him I needed you for bait."

"Bait for what?" I asked, totally confused.

Face blank as that of a veteran poker player holding the winning hand in a $10,000 game, Bannister said, "Bait for your murdering half brother."

I had been entertained on countless occasions waiting tables in the Wainwright Hotel dining room by people so flummoxed by something said to them their chins dropped like a falling rock. It was a wonder mine didn't bounce off the table. I actually expected to find a bruise the next time I shaved.

"Marshal, do you have a clue as to where Lance can be found?"

"Not precisely, but we'll have a starting point if you can show me where you blundered into the Union ambush that started all your legal troubles. If you can't, we'll follow the course of General

Price's retreat and spread the word through the towns along that path that you're looking for him. Given the way gossip travels among wanted men, we spread the word and Lance will hear it."

"We'll have a lot of ground to cover to even get within reach of Lance. I can tell you General Shelby's remaining troopers will never surrender. They're Mexico bound."

Bannister drank more of his bourbon. "Somehow I don't believe Mexico fits your brother's tastes. He probably has a hunk of money left from the Sedalia robbery and there are places in North Texas where he could settle with no questions asked, as long as he has money to buy property. Everybody wants to forget a war, once the last shot is fired and you take that uniform off."

I couldn't help asking, "Marshal, just why are you so determined to bring Lance to trial, when there has to be other wanted men closer by and easier to track down?"

His gray eyes fixed on mine. "Lance is that rare bad apple, the curly wolf for real. He can kill without a qualm. He's smart and knows how to recruit men to ride with him. Bloody Bill Anderson is dead, but a large host of those who killed, plundered, and looted with the likes of him and Bill Quantrill are still on the loose. There will be a period of lawlessness across Missouri, Arkansas, Kansas, and Texas in which enforcing the law without the help of the army will require a supreme effort by all of us willing to pin on a badge. Not a train or bank or store with money in the till will be safe. The same goes for the common folk handling that money."

Marshal Bannister let me think on his rationale for pursuing Lance. I couldn't refute what he'd said, for I agreed Lance was extremely dangerous and quite capable of leading a large band of robbers and outlaws. Bringing him to justice as soon as possible might well spare lives. All else considered—his meanness, his insults, his attempt to drown me in the watering trough—the blunt truth was I would never forgive the bastard for shooting Shep.

I answered Bannister's implied question with Sam Benson's favorite poker game response: "I'm in."

Marshal Bannister's acceptance for my joining his venture was a simple nod of the head. Reaching down beside his chair, he lifted a leather satchel he carried with him, placed it on the table, and said, "All right, let's get to work."

Curiosity swelling like that of a child expecting a gift, I almost squealed with delight when he opened the satchel and retrieved my Dollond telescope, then Laura Kellerman's silver watch, and finally what had to be the Russell Colt Navy and holster I'd hidden under Sam Benson's bed before my departure from Sedalia with General Thompson's army.

I'd surrendered the telescope and watch at Captain Howard's prison office in lieu of being searched. The Russell Colt Navy was a different wag of the dog's tail. "You've been to see my Uncle Purse and Sam Benson recently, haven't you? How is my uncle? Is he well?"

Marshal Bannister did smile then. "Yes, he is. His shoulder wound healed with Dr. Gribble hanging over him day and night. I got off the train to St. Louis at Sedalia to have your aunt and uncle sign statements to the effect you were truly taken prisoner, in case that question ever raises its head again. I told them and Sam Benson where you were, that I believed your health was fine, and that I was hoping you would join the posse I was forming to hunt down Lance. They were delighted to hear news of you. I promised them a telegram if you decided to ride with us."

The real significance of what he'd done, beyond securing my personal property and the news about me he'd imparted to Aunt Emma and Uncle Purse, was, of course, unknown to Marshal Bannister. What Aunt Emma had learned about me would soon fill the ear of Laura Kellerman. I no longer had to worry she feared I was dead and lost to her forever.

"Our train leaves in an hour," Bannister said, knocking back another three fingers of bourbon. "We rendezvous with the rest of the posse Saturday morning in Otterville. Whitefeather will meet us there with the horses and gear we require. One last point, Owen—while I told Judge Appleby when he authorized this assignment that arrest and trial was our number one priority, we will not endanger our own lives if circumstances warrant taking a different course of action. In your case, the prize fish doesn't get to swallow the bait."

Marshal Bannister's posse sat round a campfire on the outskirts of Otterville, Missouri. Sedalia was just twenty-one miles to the west.

But we were headed south, negating any possibility for me of even a short visit home.

A chill breeze was rippling the surface of the Lamine River. The wooden bridge spanning the Lamine was a solid black line. Smoke from the tin pipe chimney of the railroad guardhouse on the opposite riverbank rose skyward in a straight line. The few light gray clouds lingering overhead promised a clear day for a long horseback ride. It was a late-November early morning most comfortable in an overcoat.

The Confederates had burned the railroad station and hotel in Otterville prior to their October siege of Sedalia, and only the station had been rebuilt; hence, our meeting over a riverbank breakfast fire. Two members of Bannister's posse, Will Strong and Cuff Parker, had arrived by train from Kansas City near midnight. Will Strong was dressed in a canvas shirt and trousers, a buffalo-hide coat, a woven naval cap, and the tall laced boots worn by North Woods loggers. The cinnamon color of his short-cut hair and chin beard matched that of his eyes. He flashed a ready smile and his bubbly chuckle belied the primary task assigned him by Marshal Bannister. He was the posse's sharpshooter. When necessary, he killed at long range to facilitate an arrest or to protect his fellow members operating in a country torn asunder by bushwhackers and guerillas. Day by day, Strong served as the posse's mule skinner and cook, responsible for the packing and transport of rations, cooking gear, and his personal long-range weapons.

Cuff Parker was short and thin of stature, and his clothes—at both first glance and closer examination—resembled the holed and patched cotton shirt, pants, vest, and thin overcoat worn by the dirt poor and town drunk. His white beard, pouty mouth, and squinty eyes completed the appearance of a harmless old duffer bouncing from pillar to post to find his next meal and survive. Even his horse, a seal-brown, slightly sway-backed animal, without a distinguishing feature, went unnoticed, just what Marshal Bannister wanted, for Cuff Parker was his "town spy" sent on the sly to ferret out who of the local populace might be of interest to a Federal officer on the prowl with warrants in hand.

John L. Whitefeather, the final posse member, had arrived by horseback and established the riverbank camp a day ahead of the marshal and me arriving by train from St. Louis. The half-breed brought with him the saddle stock and pack mule needed for our upcoming southern trek.

Over a second cup of coffee, Marshal Bannister outlined the tactics of our manhunt. "Will, Cuff, and John L., I have deputy U.S. marshal badges for you, along with a letter from Judge Appleby authorizing the arrests of Lance Wainwright, Frank McCabe, Samuel Clifford, and Henry Taylor for treason, murder, and robbery. Wainwright is the only soldier. The others rode with Bloody Bill. They hail from Carthage and Newtonia if our information is correct. The Federal army chased General Price's Rebel brigades through those towns to the Missouri-Arkansas border just a few weeks ago. What's happening in their wake is what concerns the judge and me. I intend to meet with county sheriffs and local marshals, give them copies of our wanted posters, and determine if I can count on their assistance once martial law is rescinded. If we can jail any of the known troublemakers straightaway, it might make for an easier transition to peacetime."

Marshal Bannister paused to drain his cup. The morning breeze put the flames of our breakfast fire to dancing. "I don't want to ruffle feathers unnecessarily, so Owen and I will call on Federal military commanders stationed in the area first. We'll make the courthouse and jail calls next. We'll give military and local officials copies of our wanted posters. Be good to know if the locals have experienced problems with deserters and ex-bushwhackers hanging about. Then we'll make a tour of the town drinking establishments and inquire after our four outlaws. I'm hoping our two-hundred-dollar reward for each man, five hundred dollars for Wainwright, will warm a few larcenous hearts. Bear in mind, all four are bold enough to seek hard spirits and fleshly pleasure in public right under the nose of the law. We're bucking big odds, but I'm betting my instincts are right, that the local boys will show close to home, and that Owen's brother has a stash of stolen money and won't stick with a defeated Confederate Army on the run forever."

Bannister's gaze settled on Cuff Parker. "Cuff, you do your usual thing. Hang out on the sly where the locals congregate and listen to the latest gossip, particularly what's said after Owen and I finish our public tour."

Will Strong chuckled and shook his head. "It never ceases to amaze me, Cuff, how many men are behind bars because of you that have never laid eyes on you."

Marshal Bannister said, "Will, you work the livery stables and the public corrals. Nobody but me shows a badge till I give the word, lest you need to identify yourself for your own safety."

"Understood, sir," Will said. "You're the boss."

"Now get the mule packed and water the horses. I don't know the status of the telegraph south of Otterville and Sedalia, and Owen and I have a message to send."

The Confederates had burned the Otterville station, forcing the relocation of the telegraph office to a small structure nearby till the replacement station was completed. Chimney smoke signaled the temporary office was occupied despite the early hour, as we expected. The operator opened a side window and placed a pad of forms and a pen and inkwell on the counter below the window. "Five cents a word, gentlemen."

Marshal Bannister leaned over the counter and scribbled with pen and ink, his tongue protruding from the corner of his mouth. When he finished, he straightened, reread what he had written, and said, "There, that will confirm to your aunt and uncle you're traveling with me and that I will return you to them intact."

Passing the completed form to the operator, Bannister offered me the pen and said, "Anyone you want to send a message, maybe a lady friend? I'll pay."

I accepted the pen and slid the pad of forms in front of me. I was at a loss for words momentarily, then decided on a short message that said exactly what I was thinking:

> *Miss Laura Kellerman, c/o Kellerman Mercantile, Sedalia, Missouri.*
> *Don't quit on me. I'll come for you soon as I can. Owen*

The seemingly endless wind stirred waves in the tall grass atop the slight knoll overlooking the tract of flat ground surrounded by the same brushy swale, just as it had on my previous visit. The cabin tucked into the midpoint of the swale was still intact and no smoke came from the chimney.

My stomach was unsettled despite a hearty breakfast. The thought of visiting the site of the deadly ambush that had altered the course of my life in a finger snap had sparked a queasy feeling, which was hard to handle. I found being there renewed the overwhelming sadness that had gripped me the morning I rode off with Captain Dayton Foster and his Kansas Mounted Militia.

The sadness grew a lump in my throat as we descended the knoll. No one emerged from the cabin to greet us. No guns suddenly appeared at flung-open windows. Riding point, Marshal Bannister raised an arm, halted his horse, and stepped down next to the well centering the dooryard. "Gentlemen, dismount and water your horses. Will, make sure the cabin is unoccupied. John L., Owen, and I have business to conduct."

Bannister gathered the three of us at the corner of the cabin where we could see the graves stretching along the brush line behind it. The sight of the red bandana atop its tree branch marker struck me a blow to the heart and it took me a few long moments to recover from it.

Bannister didn't speak till I looked at him. "All right, tell us what happened, including where everyone was located when the shooting started."

The details I remembered from the ambush surprised me. I was able to recall Captain Foster's rant as to how could his company's "biggest target" escape alive, the words that told me Lance had survived and shot his way clear of a certain death.

"So, given your brother's location, the location of those doing the shooting, and the surrounding ground," Bannister concluded, "his escape route had to be back uphill over the knoll, right?"

At my nod, he turned to John L. Whitefeather. "The ambushers came from the south. We came from the north. This is empty country. Ride south following any tracks from that direction and search for a sign someone riding away from here veered left or right within three miles of the cabin. If you don't find such tracks or a dead body, then we'll assume Owen's brother survived any wounds he might have suffered. I want to be as sure as we possibly can we're not chasing after a dead man."

In Whitewater's absence, the posse lingered about the yard and the stoop of the cabin. I finally caved to my roiling emotions and walked to Morgan's grave. Her red bandana fluttered in the breeze, reminding me somehow of her quick wit and lively tongue. She'd proven such a warm lass, too warm and too loving to perish so young. She'd freely given herself to me and showed me a depth of passion I would forever remember. I hated that she was laid to rest with no one to visit her grave and decorate it with flowers. She deserved better and I knelt and asked the Lord to keep His promise to never forsake His chosen ones.

Whitefeather's quest for veering hoofprints or a body to the south was unsuccessful and we rode that direction late that same morning. The now-familiar inquiry "Where to" of Will Strong was answered by Marshal Bannister with a crisp "Carthage."

Over two days, we traveled fifty miles of prairie roads bisected by creeks and ravines easily negotiated on horseback. Discarded luggage, mess utensils, small arms, and wagons, along with the rotted bodies of horses and mules that perished from exhaustion and lack of forage, continued to litter the countryside along General Price's path. What we found disconcerting were the emaciated bodies wearing blue uniforms scattered among the Confederate leavings that exhibited bare feet resembling raw meat, hollow jaws, and skin tight and yellow as parchment. Cuff deemed them "walking scarecrows." Forge Bannister solved the mystery surrounding their origin. "General Price released a horde of Union prisoners. Probably couldn't feed them or guard them any longer with a shrinking army. Those boys had a hard time of it."

We arrived in Carthage as the setting sun was nearing the western horizon to find the streets shy of traffic during the dinner hour. Marshal Bannister had informed us short of Carthage that Confederate-leaning guerillas had attempted to burn the city this past September and nearly succeeded, doing extensive damage to the town square. Piles of burned planks and beams filled empty lots, once home to frame-and-log residences and businesses. The empty shells of brick structures and a large stone courthouse thrust skyward like blackened fingers. A quick glance about confirmed the two-story Shirley House Hotel and a large blacksmith shop and livery stable had survived on the square's north side. The Franklin House Hotel, a grocery and dry goods store, the Masonic Hall, two saloons, a saddler shop, a law office, a diner, and a one-story brick building bearing a sign reading JAIL had survived the torchbearers on the balance of the square.

Never at a loss for a course of action, Bannister led our party to the livery stable adjoining the Shirley House Hotel. He dismounted and bent at the knees a few times to relax tightened leg muscles.

"Getting old, are we, boss?" Cuff chirped.

"Not as old as clotted dirt like yourself. Leastways I don't creak louder than a rusty door hinge the first hour of the morning."

Will Strong's chuckle matched the chime of a church bell. "He laid the wood to you with that one right fine, yuh old codger."

Cuff saw his opening. Pointing at the Shirley House, he said, "Though I'm young for my age, I do tire now and again when I'm rode hard and put away wet. Boss, is it possible we could sleep in a real bed tonight? Such a luxury is becoming a distant memory for me."

Bannister's gray eyes rolled back in his head; then he loosed an exasperated whistle. "Next thing you'll want meat cooked over a fire with every meal."

Cuff's feigned downcast expression earned him a rare Bannister smile. "I suppose Judge Appleby could spring for one hotel night. In the meantime, leave your horse and scoot across to that diner yonder before the whole town sees you're with us. We'll sneak you in the rear door tonight."

Gray beard crusted with tobacco juice, a balding oldster dressed in bib overalls and blue shirt shuffled from the livery. "Just stalls or a bait of hay too, gents? You do the unsaddling. Fifty cents a night per animal, including the mule."

Once our horses were stripped, stabled, and hayed, and the pack mule unloaded, Will and John L. waited at the livery while Marshal Bannister and I booked rooms at the Shirley House. The night clerk's wire-rimmed spectacles reflected the light of the lobby's wall lamps. Marshal Bannister paid for two rooms for four men at the rear of the first floor and then signed the ledger for the four of us.

The night clerk frowned at the mass signing, but Bannister's badge stayed his tongue.

Bannister made no attempt to reserve a room for John L. Whitefeather, which wasn't a surprise. I'd never heard of a hotel in Missouri that allowed Indians on its premises. Free and slave black men and women were as workers, those red of skin never in any capacity.

Bannister inquired as to the best place to enjoy an evening meal and the clerk quickly answered, "The Saddleback Saloon directly across the square offers free food with their beer and whiskey. Word is, the building didn't suffer much smoke damage."

Back in the livery stable, Bannister retrieved his leather satchel and said, "Will, cross over to the Saddleback Saloon and enjoy an evening on Judge Appleby's tab. Owen and I will visit the jail and then join you. John L., you guard the horses and gear. We'll bring you vittles on our return."

Light shone in the barred front window of the brick jail. Marshal Bannister entered without knocking, with me hard on his heels. A string bean of a young fellow, with a waxed, overly groomed mustache too mature for his soft, smooth baby face, jumped to his feet behind the office desk, slamming his wheeled chair into the wall behind him. On his chest, the four-pointed star etched with DEPUTY heaved with his heavy breathing. I suspected Bannister's surprise appearance and physical bulk had thoroughly spooked him.

"What can I do . . . do for you?" the deputy stammered.

I saw Bannister's shoulders square and back straighten, bringing him to the full attention of a military officer. "U.S. Marshal Forge Bannister, where might I find Sheriff Smart?"

"He's . . . he's home sick with the ague. Hasn't been out of bed in six weeks. He missed the big battle fought near here a month ago."

"Sorry to hear that. John's an old friend of mine. I needn't bother him on his sick bed. I'll leave my paperwork for him with you," Bannister said, opening his satchel atop the office desk. "Pay attention to what I'm about to tell and show you."

Bannister carefully laid copies of his four wanted posters in a precise line on the desk as he rattled off the name, charges against each lawbreaker, and the reward being offered, his own eyes never leaving the deputy. "Ever seen any of these boys or heard of any of them?"

"No, sir. No, sir, I haven't," the deputy answered, his voice trembling.

"What's your name, Deputy?"

"Lou Collins, sir."

"All right, Deputy Lou Collins, here's what you're going to do for me. Your next stop is Sheriff Smart's house. You will show John these posters and ask if he knows any of these men. I'm staying the night at the Shirley House. You bring any message for me from Sheriff Smart there first thing in the morning, no later than seven . . . not a minute later. Any message, understand?"

"Yes, sir, any message."

Closing his satchel, Bannister said, "Owen, our business is finished here. Let's proceed to the Saddleback and fill our bellies."

Out in the street, Bannister clasped my arm. "Collins couldn't hide his surprise. He knows two of the bushwhackers, McCabe and Taylor. He didn't expect to ever see their faces on a Federal wanted poster. If McCabe and Taylor are nearby, Collins may attempt to warn them I'm in town. Fetch John L. from the livery. Collins will bear watching."

I was only too glad to do Bannister's fetching. I'd started to feel like a fifth wheel on a four-wheel wagon. John L. showed no surprise at the sudden change of duty. He matched my long strides on the return trip across the square. Bannister's orders for his tracker after providing a description of Deputy Collins were terse and pointed. "Never out of your sight. I will send food to you by midnight."

There was no danger of John L. Whitefeather starving. He had jerked meat stashed everywhere on his person. In fact, he had meat smoking over our postsupper campfire every dry night.

The Saddleback Saloon had a generous main room that held ten tables for dining and gambling. A solid bar covered the left side of the room. Shelved bottles of various liquors appeared double rowed in the tall wall mirrors matching the length of the bar. Platters of what we soon learned contained piles of ham and cheese sandwiches, with vessels of mustard and horseradish for garnishment, and large jars of pickles rested on the ends and the middle of the bar. Two kegs of beer with pouring spouts facing the bartender sat between the platters of food. The light from oil-fired wall and table lamps made faces visible throughout the room and highlighted the bar's brass footrest and spittoons. A wood fire blazed in a wide stone fireplace in the far end of the room. The sawdust-covered floor dampened the sound of voices and clinking glassware. A dozen customers occupied the bar and half the tables were in use, for it was a Saturday evening.

Will Strong had chosen a table in the farthest corner of the room from the heat of the fireplace. The empty beer mugs and food plate on his table, coupled with the beer foam on his upper lip, indicated the sharpshooter was well into running a tab on Judge Appleby. "Solid eats, boss, and the beer's cold from the cellar."

"I'll bet you never missed the clang of the dinner bell as a child, Will," Bannister said. "You'd be the last man I'd cross a desert with. We'd be out of water and vittles the first half day."

I suddenly felt strange and out of place, downright uncomfortable. I had a view of half of the room from my chair and that's all I needed to see. The magnet for nearly every eye in the saloon wasn't me. The silver badge pinned to Bannister's broad chest as he sat facing the crowd, sans his overcoat, was no less attention grabbing than the sight of a solitary white star on a black velvet night. The watchers slowly resumed their individual pursuits, though I caught a few curious glances our way as the evening progressed.

Without being asked and knowing the boss wasn't picky when it came to eating, I secured three ham sandwiches slavered with mustard and horseradish and a pair of pickles for each of us and made a second trip for mugs of beer. The bartender accepted my word he'd be paid in full upon our departure.

"What did you learn at the jail?" Will asked, sipping beer from a fresh mug.

It was a while before the hungry marshal interrupted his meal. "The county deputy on duty, Lou Collins, knows McCabe and Taylor personally and might know where they're holed up. We'll need to keep track of his comings and goings. There's a lot of secessionist sentiment around Carthage and information about former bushwhackers may be hard to come by. Don't be fooled into thinking the locals turned to the Union just because pro-Confederacy guerillas were toting the torches last September."

Will Strong's crooked grin made question marks of the corners of his mouth as it always did when he had something important to share with the boss. "Best we talk with Pierre Fountain then. He owns this handsome establishment, and the bartender says Pierre can even tell you how to corn hole a bear without holding him by the ears."

Marshal Bannister's explosive guffaw turned heads at the bar. "And just where would I find your Pierre Fountain at this very moment if it were possible?"

"In his office, past the near end of the bar, according to Rex, the bartender. He said Pierre usually appears for a card game toward midnight. Shall I fetch him for you?"

Bannister pondered, stroked his Vandyke beard, and said, "Why not. We need to throw a wide loop to be sure we have a chance at our prey."

Pierre Fountain was portly and bald, except for a few strands of hair plastered to his bare scalp. His red-tipped nose was overly generous and his pencil-thin brows matched the width of the mustache that traced the curve of his upper lip. His suit was tailored blue velvet and his shirt snow white, the collar closed with a diamond stickpin. His black eyes were bold and bored into the person he was addressing.

The saloon owner seated himself next to Marshal Bannister. The bartender set a stemmed glass of what I assumed was red wine in front of his employer. "Marshal Bannister, much has been said about you at my bar. It is a pleasure to finally meet you."

Pierre made no move to shake hands, a decision I reckoned resulted from his having to deal with customers whose political beliefs ranged from ardent Unionists to those willing to die for the Confederacy. He could be forgiven for talking with a U.S. marshal. Shaking hands and playing the most gracious host might well invite scorn and the torch.

Bannister said, "Monsieur Fountain, I hope what you heard wasn't overly damning. We marshals are often misunderstood."

"No, I would say the core of what was said was truthful. You are by reputation a violent but fair officer of the law. One does not invite your official attention if he wants to retain a peaceful life free of nasty things like jails, judges, and nooses."

Pierre drank wine from his glass with delicate sips. "Marshal Bannister, I'm certain you are not here to exchange pleasantries with an old, fat, bald saloonkeeper, so what is it you wish to share with me?"

I smothered a grin. The two gentlemen before me were from different worlds pursuing totally different professions and would never reach a point where they called each other Forge and Pierre. Reaching down beside his chair, Bannister withdrew copies of his wanted posters from his satchel and laid them on the table, a move he had to know might terminate his conversation with Pierre Fountain. Did he dare ask Fountain to provide information on local citizens sought by the law and thereby risk isolating himself from a large portion of his community? Goodwill was a saloonkeeper's greatest asset.

Features blank, Pierre listened patiently to Bannister's spiel on the wanted bushwhackers. This go-round Bannister emphasized how each had gone beyond the accepted bounds of civilized warfare to rob and murder defenseless civilians far from the battlefield on more than one occasion. I must admit he painted a mighty black picture of the crimes involved.

Pierre Fountain sat so long without speaking, I deigned he was searching for how he could walk away from the table without insulting Bannister, or, worse yet, rousing his ire. Finally he finished his wine and said, "Marshal Bannister, I will not provide you information that might facilitate the arrest of those you are pursuing, or seek such information on your behalf. I cannot chance my customers thinking I'm interested in collecting the rewards you offer. It would be my ruin. But I cannot refuse a lawful request by your office. When asked, I will repeat what you've told me and share your posters, and, trust me, the word will spread quickly. Perhaps then someone will come forth and assist you on the sly. This war has been a pox on bravery and fostered much fear."

I was learning to read Marshal Bannister. His body spoke for him, not his facial expressions. A slight relaxation of his shoulders told me he was satisfied with Pierre's proposal. He had wanted help spreading the news of why a U.S. marshal had come to Jasper County, and had secured it from the owner of the most-frequented house of entertainment in Carthage, the county's seat.

Pierre Fountain rolled Bannister's wanted posters into a tube. "Marshal, be careful where you tread. With Sheriff Smart's illness, lawlessness in this county is enjoying free rein for the moment."

"I will heed your warning, Monsieur."

Fountain stood. "We've chatted long as I dare, Marshal. Perhaps we will meet again when allegiances are less important and proper manners are once again in vogue."

With Bannister's silent good-evening nod, Fountain had his wineglass refilled at the bar and returned to his office. "He's a fine gentleman," Bannister conceded, "trying to ride a neutral wave in a rough sea."

"What next, boss?" Will inquired.

"We finish our meal and retire. My old backside needs a bed for the night more than Cuff's. Owen, wrap a couple of those sandwiches for John L. He can drink from that flask he never shares."

We were at the door when, as if on cue, Cuff Parker sidled past us, paying us no attention. "They must have made him open his own purse across the street," Will quipped, though he knew Cuff was following his standing orders: if the gossip dried up, seek loose lips elsewhere.

The night sky was awash with winking stars, the air cold and still, the town quiet except for two barking dogs. The light in the window of the brick jail had been extinguished. The glow of the lobby lamps of the Shirley House across the square beckoned like a lighthouse beacon on a rocky shore. The prospect of sleeping on any kind of mattress versus a bare prison floor or cold ground quickened our pace.

"Wonder where John L. got to?" I wondered aloud.

I liked to jump out of my skin when a hand brushed my elbow and John L.'s lowered voice said, "Right here."

I swore under my breath. Damn, he floated across any surface with less noise than drifting smoke. John L.'s half smile revealed how much he enjoyed startling a man half to death. But it was impossible to stay mad at him. He was a tireless drone bee that asked little in return beyond sustenance and loyalty.

"What about the deputy?" Bannister said.

"Went two blocks south, in house there one hour your time. Then back to jail. No see again."

Conversing with John L. was akin to receiving a telegram with *stop* written between each short statement. Cuff Parker joked that the Lord had given John L. a set number of words that had to last him a lifetime and he had yet to squander a single one.

One thing his companions didn't joke about was John L.'s acute sense of what was happening about him, near and far, no matter the hour of the day or night. Still, the brutal shove that knocked Marshal Bannister into me and toppled both of us into the dusty street was a complete surprise. So was the gunshot that was suddenly echoing through the square.

I was pinned beneath Marshal Bannister. The crash of more shots pounded at my ears and the closeness of three of them, the squirming body atop me, and the acrid smell of gun smoke told me Bannister was returning fire. A pause . . . then a final shot . . . then silence except for Bannister's heavy breathing and the thud of my heart, which was threatening to dislodge itself from my chest.

Marshal Bannister rolled off me, braced an arm against the ground, and swung to his feet. A big paw grabbed a handful of overcoat and yanked me upright. "You hurt, lad?"

I resisted the urge to feel all over myself, for I felt no pain. "No, sir."

Marshal Bannister turned to John L. and Will. John L. was standing. Will was sitting. "Either one of you hurt? I thought I heard a grunt that didn't bode well for one of you."

"Took one in the left shoulder," Will said. "Flesh wound, I believe. Don't hurt god-awful, like a shattered bone would."

"Let's get you inside, where we can have a look at it," Bannister said.

John L. helped Will to his feet. Bannister's sweeping gaze surveyed the front of the Shirley House and the alley on each side of it. "Bastards waited till they had a good look at us in the light from the lobby. What warned you, John L.?"

"Shadow don't lift long gun to shoot. On his belly, you would be dead man."

"Wily Moore claims you have the eyes of a catamount," Bannister said, "and you've never given me cause to doubt his word."

John L. completed what for him was a long conversation. "Town no good. Woods is true friend."

A few curious townsmen were drifting to the scene, including Deputy Lou Collins. In the quiet following the shooting, Collins appeared more confident than he had at the jail. "Marshal, glad to learn you weren't hurt. So I don't forget, the sheriff is much better and wants you to call on him in the morning. He has information to share with you."

"Well and good," Bannister said. "Why don't you and Owen check the alleys yonder and see if we downed either shooter. If we did, maybe you can identify him."

Told what to do, Deputy Lou Collins could act decisively. "Yes, sir."

He sprinted off fast as a rabbit, leaving me to chase after him. One narrow hotel alley was empty. A prone body, slanted backside against the wall of the hotel, filled the other. Collins knelt, pushed fingers against the side of the ambusher's neck, and said, "Dead for certain."

Striking a match on the wall of the hotel, Collins lifted the dead shooter's chin and whistled softly. "By damned, it's Charlie Stafford."

The name, of course, meant nothing to me, but it might to Marshal Bannister, and surely would to county sheriff John Smart in the morning. "You go tell your marshal, sir," Lou Collins suggested, "while I help the undertaker whenever he shags his fat frame out of his house. Uncle John can answer whatever questions you have regarding Charlie here."

Inside the lobby, Marshal Bannister was wrapping a white bandage around the shoulder and upper left arm of a shirtless Will. Will's right hand was holding a long-necked brown bottle, the type that held brandy at the Wainwright Hotel. I chuckled, wondering if the brandy would appear on Judge Appleby's tab.

"What'd you find?" Bannister asked as he tied off Will's bandage.

"One dead body. Lou Collins identified him. Name is Charlie Stafford. Collins, who, by the way, is the sheriff's nephew, said his uncle can tell you about Charlie in the morning."

"That would be most helpful. We've done a grand job of attracting a couple of hornets. We best find their nest before the rest of them come hunting us."

# CHAPTER 19

WE IDENTIFIED SHERIFF JOHN SMART'S WHITE FRAME HOUSE TWO blocks south of the town square by John L.'s description of its green window shutters and red door and the burned-to-the-ground residences on either side of it. "Wonder if those guerillas lacked the balls to torch a lawman's home?" Marshal Bannister speculated as he knocked at the front door.

A pretty, smiling brunette woman, with apple-red cheeks, matching my height, answered the door. "Come in, gentlemen, John is expecting you."

We stepped inside the front door. Mrs. Smart said, "You may put your coats on the couch. I'm fixing John's breakfast. Thank goodness he's eating again. Have you two eaten?"

"Yes, ma'am," Bannister assured Mrs. Smart, sniffing like a hound on the scent. "But I wouldn't refuse a cup of that coffee you have brewing on the stove."

Mrs. Smart's smile widened with the marshal's compliment. She led us down a short hallway to a bedroom where a long-legged man, with sallow skin and hollow eyes, wrapped in a yellow robe, reclined on a brass bed. Given the leathery lines marking his cheekbones, I judged John Smart's earlier years were spent in the saddle, not behind a desk.

Marshal Bannister snorted and pointed to the quilt-lined golden Prince Albert slippers adorning Sheriff Smart's feet and said, "Bet you've never worn those to the jail, John."

The two lawmen enjoyed a hearty laugh while shaking hands.

"Forge, you big warhorse, has it really been ten years since we saw each other?"

"Yep, not since the day you rode out of Fort Dodd with the Kincaid gang in handcuffs with their horses tied, tail to bridle."

John Smart said, "Those were the days when the bad men among us were easier to sort out. Now a man you thought your friend yesterday might shoot you in the back today."

Shifting into a sitting position, Smart pointed at two wooden chairs at the foot of the brass bed. "Have a seat, gents, we need to palaver."

"How are you feeling John?" Bannister inquired.

"Better than I look. I'll be up and about by tomorrow or the next day."

Mrs. Smart appeared with a tray containing a breakfast of fried eggs, bacon, quartered potatoes fried in bacon grease, slabs of buttered bread, and a pot of coffee for her husband. She placed the tray on her husband's lap, the coffeepot on the dresser, and hustled back to the kitchen for coffee mugs for her guests.

Once we three men had our coffee, the conversation settled on serious business. "John, I believe your deputy showed you the wanted posters I brought with me. Do you know any of those men?"

"Yes, Frank McCabe and Henry Taylor have been roaming the whole of Missouri with various cutthroats for two years. Rumor has it, they were with Bloody Bill Anderson at the Centralia massacre, but that may be bogus. While vicious and deadly on their own, Frank and Henry like to brag a heap. The crimes your posters cite were committed well north of Carthage. Around home, they wear masks when robbing and murdering, and the local secessionists will feed and hide them whenever the law or the Union military tries to hunt them down. A number of the guerillas who tried to burn the whole town in September wore masks. I'm certain Frank and Henry were part of that bunch. You're the first Federal marshal to try and bring them to justice."

Marshal Bannister drank coffee and said, "Eat your breakfast before it gets cold, John. I don't want your wife upset with me."

Blessed with the appetite of a man recovering from a sickness, hollow-eyed John Smart made quick work of his breakfast. Mrs.

Smart appeared a second time with a fresh pot of coffee and retrieved her serving tray.

At that point, Marshal Bannister surprised me. Instead of asking Sheriff Smart where we might find McCabe and Taylor, he broached the subject of Charlie Stafford. "Who the hell is Charlie Stafford, and why would he ambush me and my deputies?"

"Before retiring last night, Lou came by and told me your deputy had been wounded. I have confirmed reports that Charlie Stafford and his younger brother, Mike, have been seen with McCabe and Taylor in recent days. The McCabe and Stafford places abut each other north of town. Buck Stafford, Charlie's father, pulled up stakes in early September. Lincoln's Proclamation cost Buck his slaves. He finally listened to the entreaties of his brother, Leland, to join him in Texas. Leland owns a sizable ranch outside Sherman, Texas. Charlie bragged in McKenzie's Grocery that he and his brother planned to join their father soon. That was before he and his brother started running with McCabe. Seems to me, the Stafford boys are enjoying a final toot before abandoning the chicken coop."

Sheriff Smart cleared his throat, sipped coffee, and said, "Forge, I've got a wild-ass notion as to why Charlie, and almost certainly his brother, ambushed you last night."

"And what would that be? I'll gladly listen. You've always had a feel for what makes men break the law after greed, pride, and anger."

"Frank McCabe's father was the most blatant secessionist in this county. He had no hesitation when it came to feeding bushwhackers in the dark of night and letting them sleep in his barn. A company of Union cavalry raided his farm one night, two years ago, and found half-a-dozen bushwhackers asleep in his barn. They hung the bushwhackers, one by one, in his yard, then hung McCabe himself, and set fire to his house and barn. McCabe's wife went to live with her sister in Kansas City and Frank became a one-hundred-proof Union hater."

Sheriff Smart's parched throat required more soothing coffee. "Bear with me, Forge, I'm about finished. Have you been showing those wanted posters along the way?"

Bannister nodded and said, "In every town and hamlet we passed through."

"Including Willow Crossing?"

"If you mean the cluster of three houses, a grocery store, and a blacksmith shop seven or eight miles north of here, yes. The storekeeper stared at the posters a long while, but claimed he didn't recognize any of the four."

"Did the storekeeper have a gap in his front teeth and a humped back?"

Bannister nodded again.

"He's a Stafford cousin. The Stafford and McCabe places are located a mile west of the store. Were you there long?"

Bannister's gray eyes narrowed. "Just short of three hours. Will's horse threw a shoe and Owen here made good use of the blacksmith shop. We'd ridden twenty miles by the time we reached the store and I wanted to rest the horses. So you think Charlie was warned we were headed for Carthage and what our business is?"

"Did anyone leave Willow Crossing while you were there?"

A prolonged sigh preceded Bannister's reply. "What I thought was just a tow-haired lad on a scrawny horse."

"Buck Stafford sold his place to a man named Federspiel. The German won't hide Charlie and his brother, but he will feed them and relay messages to them."

Bannister threw back his head and stared at the ceiling, lifting the front legs of his chair off the floor. The chair legs thumped back in place and he said, "All right, suppose what you're suggesting is true. Charlie Stafford or McCabe . . . or the both of them were informed my posse was bound for Carthage, but why would Charlie and his brother do the dirty work? Why not McCabe and Taylor?"

"The best answer I have for that is, young Charlie idolized Frank McCabe, the daring, law-defying bushwhacker, and would do anything to score favor with him. My deputy believes McCabe and Taylor will light out for Texas with Charlie's brother, Mike. Your arrival may have put the spurs to that possibility. Bushwhacking will become a thing of the past damn quick with General Price's defeat and the end of the war in Missouri. Hell, Forge, are you willing to ride to Texas to serve your warrants?"

Sheriff Smart's query lifted my chair legs off the floor.

"Yes, I am, John," Marshal Bannister said. "I've never abandoned a manhunt once I'm in the saddle, and Sam Clifford hails from Newtonia, smack in line with Sherman and North Texas."

"What's the story on the fourth man you're seeking?" Sheriff Smart inquired.

"Lance Wainwright is the half brother of young Owen here. He's a lieutenant in the Confederate Army, attached to General Shelby's Iron Brigade. He probably crossed into Texas with Shelby's men early last month. I'm expecting he'll set off on his own rather than follow Shelby to Mexico. Lance isn't one for hiding where there's no excitement and no women. Owen is my bait for him," Bannister said. "I know it's a long shot, but with the right lure, any fish can be caught."

Sheriff Smart's features slackened, indicating a growing tiredness, and he let out a long breath. "Take care, Forge. I'm disappointed I can't join you. Just don't get careless with your bait. Owen seems a fine young man. We've lost too many of them in the war."

Bannister stood. "John, I'm not wasting time riding to the Stafford place. I'm assuming our local birds have taken flight. One of my men, Cuff Parker, heard at the Saddleback Saloon that Price's retreating army robbed Carthage businesses of food and forage at will. Owen tells me his half brother's scout company often rode point for Shelby's brigade. On the hair-up-your-ass chance Lance's squad was in the lead that day, I asked your deputy to show the description of Lance on his wanted poster to your local merchants. His height, red hair, and scarred cheek are hard to forget. Probably won't amount to a pile of ant shit, but how many times did pure luck play a huge part in our making an arrest?"

Sheriff Smart's parting smile sent us on our way.

Deputy Lou Collins was waiting outside in the street. He was fairly jumping from foot to foot. "Marshal, please come with me. I have grand news for you."

Sheriff Smart's deputy led us back to the town square and across it to the Ferguson Grocery and Dry Goods establishment on the southwest corner. The smell of spices and the sight of sausages pickled in a barrel, loaf bread, and jars of sugar candies reminded me of Sedalia's Litzinger Market. An apron-outfitted male wearing a tight-fitting skullcap stood behind the counter. His bushy mustache was a thatch of wild growth. The dark eyes beneath brows equally wild had a sparkle like those of a mischievous child. His smile oozed friendliness. "And what can Rufus Ferguson offer you fine gentlemen this morning?"

"Information, Mr. Ferguson. This is Marshal Bannister and his deputy. He's interested in what you know about the Lance Wainwright on the wanted poster I showed you this morning."

Rufus Ferguson studied Marshal Bannister closely. "I'm tired of the killing and robbing destroying the peace of my adopted country, and that is why I will share what little I know. I have no interest in a financial reward for doing my civic duty."

Without waiting for a response, Ferguson continued his remarks. "Widow Juliet Harris lives at the south edge of town. Approximately a month ago, two soldiers knocked at her door. Between them, they held a soldier who had suffered a wound in his right leg. One of the soldiers introduced himself as Captain Brett Logan of General Shelby's Iron Brigade."

Brett Logan's name shot through me hotter than a bullet. I was nothing but ears in a heartbeat.

"Seems Captain Logan spotted the sign in front of Juliet's house reading 'G. Harris, M.D. and Dentist' and asked if her husband, the doctor, was there. Juliet told Logan the doctor had passed away. But, being a good soul and aware of the soldier's pain, Juliet said she had assisted her husband on many occasions, and if they brought the lieutenant to Dr. Harris's medical room, she would do whatever she could. They had just placed the lieutenant where Juliet wanted him when a voice in her yard yelled 'Yankees in sight.' Captain Logan told Juliet they couldn't linger. He said he and Lieutenant Wainwright thanked her for her help and they departed at a gallop."

I was certain the lieutenant left at Mrs. Harris's home was Graham Donovan.

Bannister said what I was thinking. "You have an excellent memory, Mr. Ferguson."

Rufus Ferguson grinned sheepishly. "No, sir, I must confess I became involved and heard all the details from Juliet when she came to my store for carbonic acid and turpentine to treat Lieutenant Donovan's wound. She has made more trips for fresh bandages and supplies since and has shared many war tales told by her patient. I've heard the name Lance Wainwright at least three times."

"Mrs. Harris is still doctoring Lieutenant Donovan then?"

"Oh, yes, sir," Ferguson confirmed. "He walks with a cane, but still needs care. His wound is finally healing."

"Would Mrs. Harris mind Owen and me calling on her?"

"No, sir, Juliet's door is never shut and locked."

Ferguson's blush colored his cheeks. "Frankly, I suspect she's become quite fond of Lieutenant Graham Donovan."

The G. HARRIS, M.D. & DENTIST sign hung from a post before a two-story brick dwelling, the last house on Fifth Street. A few dying blooms decorated flowerbeds that created a wide band of color on each side of the front walk in warmer months. The picket fence enclosing the yard and the shutters at the windows were stark white from an annual painting. Marshal Bannister and I dismounted and tied our horses to the nose ring of a child's stone pony.

Bannister knocked and we waited, hats in hand. The lady who answered was still a stunning beauty despite her fifty-plus years. Her light blond hair was tied in a bun, and without powder, her skin had a natural pinkish hue and was nearly flawless. Her eyes were cornflower blue. Despite her slim body and delicate appearance, I didn't doubt she was a woman strong enough to be a country doctor's wife and patient nurse.

She spoke in a soft voice with a touch of Southern drawl. "Yes, gentlemen?"

"Marshal Forge Bannister and Owen Wainwright, ma'am. If we might, we'd like to speak with Lieutenant Graham Donovan."

"Should I expect any trouble in my house, Marshal?"

Bannister's head wagged. "No, ma'am, we've come on peaceful business."

A delighted smile added to the warmth of Juliet's eyes. "Then follow me, please."

The front portion of the Harris home was a waiting room serving patients and family members, and six wooden chairs and two lamp tables sufficed for furniture. The balance of the ground floor was divided into an examination/operating room, a bedroom, and a storage room.

Without hesitation, Widow Harris led us to an upstairs parlor, where barefoot Lieutenant Graham Donovan, dressed in a loose-fitting cotton shirt and trousers, was seated in a padded chair, bandaged right leg propped on a short stool. He held a breakfast cigar in one hand and a mug of coffee, which he jokingly said was laced with brandy, in the other; his nurse said it was laced with sugar.

I marveled how out of place raw-boned, gray-haired, gray-bearded Graham Donovan, with his long arms, walnut-sized knuckles, and feet long as rowboats, seemed in Widow Harris's delicate armchair. He wasn't a handsome man, not with his violently hooked nose and ears the size of dinner plates. Still, he had struck a chord with beautiful Juliet Harris that produced accommodations far exceeding those normally shared by nurse and patient.

It would be fair to say that upon sighting me, an awed Graham Donovan nearly fell from his undersized perch. As it was, he dropped his cigar and spilled either his brandy or sugar-laced coffee. "Well, I'll be double damned and triple kicked in the ass. How can you be alive? Lance swore to Captain Logan that you and Sergeant Holloway and his son, Morgan, and Pat Shannon were shot dead by the ambusher's first volley . . . that you couldn't have survived . . . there was nothing one man could do against those odds."

Juliet Harris retrieved Donovan's dropped cigar from the carpet and dabbed at his stained trousers with a cloth. "Relax, my darling, we need not embarrass our guests."

"But Owen is alive, dear woman, a fine chap is alive."

Thankfully, before I started dancing from foot to foot, red-faced and stammering with embarrassment, Marshal Bannister had the wherewithal to resurrect the original purpose of our visit. "It's Owen's brother that brings us to your door, Lieutenant. I'm carrying a warrant for his arrest on charges of robbery and murder."

Graham Donovan's expression sobered and he said, "I'm sorry to hear that, but it doesn't surprise me. Lance had a lot of rough edges that angered even his few friends without his trying. His fellow officers and soldiers overlooked his brash conduct, so long as it didn't interfere with his duties. I never met another soldier that could take to killing the enemy quicker."

Juliet now in charge of his cigar, Donovan drank the remains of his breakfast coffee and said, "It was the ambushing of Owen and his party that brought all that smoldering resentment to a head for Captain Logan's men. Lance let it slip reporting the details to Logan that he hadn't scouted the cabin and ground hiding the ambushers in advance. He done the same fool thing outside Sedalia and got ten men killed then in an ambush."

Donovan's bearded head lowered and he stared at the diamond-patterned carpet at his feet. "The unnecessary loss of the Holloways, Shannon, and Owen soured things between Logan and Lance forever. There was a coldness between them that got harder and harder for everyone to swallow. The words they had to exchange to command the company resembled a spitting contest between two hopping-mad wasps, and Colonel Lawton wasn't around to cool them off. Lance took to openly bragging about lighting out on his own for North Texas. Then, during a skirmish with Yankee cavalry, Lance was seemingly knocked from the saddle by a hail of bullets, but despite a thorough search afterward by Captain Logan and the company, no one could account for his body."

"Do you think he survived, Lieutenant Donovan?" I asked after a quiet moment had passed.

Without any hesitation, Donovan said, "Yes, I do. Some men are damn hard to kill. It's almost like they can choose their time." Donovan did pause to snort. "Hell's bells, I been accused of that myself a time or two."

It intrigued me that Graham Donovan's coarse swearing didn't perturb Juliet Harris. But then I supposed every patient of a county doctor's practice wasn't a sweet-talking angel. Hadn't I learned that carelessness with one's language became more frequent when pain was raging inside you and your blood was flowing?

Marshal Bannister, always the steadfast investigator, asked, "Did Lance ever mention a particular place in Texas? A county? A town?"

Donovan's shaggy head nodded. "Yes, he raved about Sherman, Texas. Seems both Quantrill and Bloody Bill Anderson spent winters there when the bare trees of Missouri's woods make it difficult to hide from those hunting you with guns loaded and ready."

The broad smile on Marshal Bannister's goateed countenance was that of the child whose every want and dream were satisfied on his birthday. Lance might well be bound for the same destination as Frank McCabe and Henry Taylor, and Newtonia, the home of Sam Clifford, our fourth fugitive, wasn't far off the road leading to Sherman, Texas.

Lieutenant Graham Donovan's military training was so ingrained he couldn't delay men he realized were on a mission of importance to them. After nearly crushing my ribs with a good-bye hug while he wobbled on one foot steadied by his cane, he shook hands with Marshal Bannister, and insisted Juliet Harris show us to the door.

Untying his horse from the nose ring of Juliet Harris's stone pony, Marshal Bannister took note of the dark clouds forming on the western horizon. "Hard rain likely today, maybe snow, but it's easier to abide a wet saddle knowing you're not riding a shallow trail chasing rumors."

# CHAPTER 20

"HARD RAIN" FELL SHORT OF DESCRIBING WHAT CUFF PARKER thought the Bannister posse endured till near noon the next day. Cuff called the gray sheets of water pounding on our hats and shoulders "a shit cyclone of a downpour."

It wasn't just the rain. It was the rain combined with the wind that drove it eastward. We donned rubber ponchos over overcoats at the outset, only to find cold water still found its way inside our collars and down bare backs, gifting a rider the shivers normally associated with the aftermath of a fever. The horses kept shying, wanting to turn their tails to the brunt of the storm. As the Lord can attest, without John L. Whitefeather guiding us, we might have skirted Newtonia by ten miles, with not a posse member the wiser. The tracker's particular skills were rare as crown jewels.

The prairie storm slackened and fizzled out. We halted our horses on a tall bluff that overlooked Newtonia, Missouri, a hamlet of five hundred citizens situated on an extensive plain with open views in all directions, just like Sedalia. We sat watching smoke rise from what we would learn was the hamlet's steam-powered flouring mill, listening to Marshal Bannister detail how he wanted to proceed. "Owen and I will call on the law. Cuff, you find a warm, dry seat where townsfolk gather to eat and talk this time of day. Will and John L., ride around town and establish a camp along the southbound road. My hunch is anybody fearing the coming of Federal law will run for the Nations and Texas."

Marshal Bannister and I watched the rest of the posse descend the bluff on a public road scoured and rutted, fetlock deep on a horse, in places by flooding rainwater. He wanted Cuff and Will and John L. in place before we made an appearance in Newtonia. "I'm betting that if McCabe and Taylor know we're hunting them, so does Sam Clifford. Logic would tell you a bushwhacker wanted by Federal officers wouldn't hide out in his hometown, the most obvious of places. But that doesn't allow for the three-hundred-mile ride to Texas if Sam wants to keep company with his fellow lawbreakers. Maybe after two years of fearing today's the day a bullet kills you, living with a mostly empty stomach, hardly ever sleeping in a bed, and fearing the horse you're riding will falter, leaving you to face a hanging rope or imprisonment, maybe you chance staying put where family and friends will shelter you. I've learned over the years running from the law tires the fugitive more than it does the man wearing the badge. I can rest whenever I want, but the warrant never expires. Let's go see what fate hands us today."

Perhaps it was a stroke of luck or divine intervention, but Newtonia escaped the burnings so devastating to other towns, and the clash of General Price's army and Union forces in late October had occurred in the nearby countryside—the sole demand on the hamlet being makeshift hospital space for the wounded. Newtonia's private dwellings and commercial buildings were the standard mix of wood and brick with frame construction predominating.

All traffic—pedestrian, foot, horseback, and wheeled—was light on a weekday midafternoon. A two-story hotel and two-story courthouse faced each other across a small town square. A sign on a front corner of the courthouse at street level read POLICE & JAIL, with an arrow indicating one should travel the alley alongside the building to reach that office.

The jail was a separate stone structure opposite the rear door of the courthouse. The jail's barred windows and heavy wooden door looked substantial enough for its function. What caught Marshal Bannister's attention was the absence of a chimney. "Be damn cold serving time in there during the winter."

Chief of Police Ira Hooker's hand matched the pudginess of his body, and that roundness extended to the features of a forty-plus face, with dough-soft skin and the skimpy mustache and beard of a maturing youth. Hooker's appearance belied his approach to his duties. He wasted no time on charm or manners. Hands shook, he wanted to know our business, and when so informed, bent over the wanted posters Marshal Bannister laid out on his desk for closer scrutiny.

Hooker said, "Wish I'd seen these yesterday."

"Why's that?" Marshal Bannister asked.

Straightening up, Hooker pointed at the posters of McCabe, Taylor, and Sam Clifford, saying, "These three were in Saul Bartlett's saloon yesterday evening with another man."

A tinge of excitement invaded Marshal Bannister's voice. "Are they still here?"

Hooker's head swiveled and he yelled, "Brick, I need you!"

We heard, "Can't I ever get any sleep?" and a badge-wearing male stepped from a room off the chief's office. The badge bearer was half the size of his boss, with his forehead, Adam's apple, and the pistol hanging from his hip appearing overly large. The redness of his features fit his nickname.

Hand sweeping over Bannister's posters, Hooker said, "Have a close look, Brick. Three of these gents were drinking at Saul Bartlett's saloon yesterday evening, were they not?"

In short order, Brick confirmed the presence of the three fugitives at Bartlett's. "Are they still in town?" Hooker persisted.

"No, sir, they rode out short of midnight."

"'Rode out'?" Marshal Bannister said. "You were watching them at the time?"

"Yes, sir, all the way down Main Street to the city limits. They'd been drinking heavily and I wanted to be certain they didn't cause any trouble."

"Do you remember anything distinctive about their horses?"

"This one," Brick said, pointing at Frank McCabe, "was riding a red roan with a white blaze and three white stockings. They were all aboard top riding stock, including the one you don't have a wanted poster for."

Marshal Bannister's knuckles rapped on Chief Hooker's desk. I could almost hear wheels turning in his head and shared his frustration. The unknown man was most likely Mike Stafford, Charlie's brother. Our prey had at least a fifteen-hour head start on us, and the hours of rain after their departure would have destroyed their tracks for miles. It might now be impossible to overtake them before they crossed the Red River into Texas.

"Chief Hooker, I thank you and Brick for your cooperation and the information."

"Best of luck on your hunt, Marshal," Hooker said, extending his hand.

We were mounting our horses when I asked, "What now, boss?"

Marshal Bannister's brow knitted at my calling him "boss," something I'd never done before, but he made no mention of it. "We rode all night in the rain. We'll rest today and start out at daylight. I want Cuff to have a chance to ferret out any information suggesting Sam Clifford didn't leave town with his friends. No sense leaving a stone unturned."

Once around the courthouse, Bannister asked a passerby where we might find Bartlett's Saloon. The pointing of a long male arm accompanied "Three blocks west at the corner of Main and Kearny." Cuff's nondescript horse wasn't tied in front of the saloon. Bannister rode to the livery across the intersection and, sure enough, the stable boy remembered Cuff's mount. "He's out back with the other nags."

Satisfied his town spy was on the job, Bannister led me back to the town square, dismounted in front of a butcher shop, and waved for me to wait outside. He came out with his purchases wrapped in brown paper, passed them to me, and walked to an establishment with signage reading LEMAY'S GROCERIES, DRUGS, AND SPIRITS and emerged with a cloth bag whose shape indicated it contained two long-necked bottles.

John L.'s chosen campsite was a mile south of Newtonia. Together, he and Will had located sufficient dry wood to build a substantial evening fire. It was appreciated for more than its warmth when we learned Bannister's brown parcels contained large beef steaks and his cloth bag bottles of rye whiskey. John L.'s smile showed corn-yellow teeth. "Boss not forget ride in rain."

Will was an excellent open-fire cook. The salted steaks were pink in the middle, the biscuits piping hot, the rye whiskey smooth on the tongue, and the snores resulting from full bellies and tired bodies a chorus fit to wake the dead.

But the day that was over wasn't over. Running hoofs, muted by the muddy road next to our camp, were loud enough to awaken John L., who, I swore, was never more than half asleep.

He was shaking Marshal Bannister's shoulder as Cuff Parker, identifiable by his short stature despite the darkness, slid from the saddle. "Good news, boss, I have good news."

Bannister shed his blanket and lurched to his feet. "How the hell did you find us?"

"The embers of your fire haven't died out. They're visible for half a mile on this flat ground, and you told John L. to camp on the south road."

"All right, what's your news?"

"Clifford, McCabe, Taylor, and Charlie Stafford's brother were in Newtonia yesterday evening drinking at Bartlett's Saloon. They rode out of town round midnight."

"Sorry to disappoint you, Cuff, but Owen and I learned that from the police chief and his deputy this afternoon."

Cuff's white-toothed smile was that of the cat sensing the mouse was his for the taking. "What you don't know is Sam Clifford turned back at Dawes Creek."

Marshal Bannister demanded, "Who told you that, Cuff?"

"Carla, the girl at Bartlett's Saloon Sam's visiting at midnight tonight. Seems our boy needs to dip his wick a tad more before he takes up bushwhacking with McCabe again."

"Can this girl be trusted?"

"Much as any night gal. Carla's young, pretty, and busty. I lent her a sympathetic ear. She's convinced Sam's fond of her and won't disappoint her."

Bannister scratched his head, pondering. "Okay, we're already awake, dressed, and our powder's dry, so let's try and round up Sam Clifford. Might be, he can confirm McCabe's plans and keep us from chasing off in the wrong direction. Cuff, I don't like hunting like a blind hound. How does Saul Bartlett manage his girls?"

"The girls each have a room on the second floor. Once they have a customer frothing at the mouth, Tell Bowen records the customer's name and the girl's in a ledger at his desk under the stairs leading to the second floor."

"Is there any other access to that second floor?"

"There's an outside stairway at the rear of the building. Discreet customers who don't want to be seen inside the saloon can use the rear stairway by making appointments with Saul. If any trouble arises on the second floor, Moose Scanlon herds the offender out the back way, and the customers down below are none the wiser."

"Where is Moose stationed?"

"In the rear of the main floor. He has a chair on a raised platform that gives him a view of the entire saloon."

"Is he a formidable specimen for a bouncer?"

"Moose is the size of a bull buffalo and just as shaggy. He can lift an anvil over his head with one hand. He grunts rather than talks. He doesn't bother with a gun. If he wants you to leave, drunk or sober, it's best if you're fast on your feet. I'm told leaving the second floor through the air is a memorable experience. Needless to say, Moose doesn't have to leave his chair much, except to relieve himself."

Marshal Bannister clucked his tongue in admiration. "Sounds like Mr. Saul Bartlett owns and operates a very well-organized drinking hole and cathouse. Where's he stand with the police and Chief Hooker?"

"Long as there's no trouble, and there seldom is, the chief and town council look the other way. Nice to live in a town where a man can have a little fun and not be ragged about it at the dinner table, huh?"

The watching heads nodded, mine included, as if I was as well versed in what Aunt Emma deemed "male entertainment" as the other posse members. It had long fascinated me how young men would lie around adult men to avoid being shunned for lack of experience.

Marshal Bannister buttoned his overcoat. "Will, you hang here. We have to move fast. That bad shoulder of yours might be a hindrance to you. What's the time, Owen?"

Reading Laura Kellerman's watch by the last winking embers of our supper fire, I answered, "Ten minutes to midnight."

Bannister snorted. "Makes the time about right to catch Sam Clifford in the throes of his tryst with busty Carla."

We slowed from a trot to a walk past the first of Newtonia's private residences. Mud puddles reflected the faint light of a quarter moon. The stench of garbage and human waste was strong on the still air. Quiet abounded and not a dog barked with our passage, a rare occurrence.

Marshal Bannister's feel for his surroundings inside a town equaled Whitefeather's for the woods. We rode straight for six blocks, turned right abruptly, turned left two blocks later, then left again, and when we drew rein, we were smack before the rear door of Saul Bartlett's palace of pleasure.

After looking about, Marshal Bannister motioned for us to dismount. "Cuff, you scoot around to the front door and have a look inside. We need to know where Carla is. I'm hoping she's upstairs with Sam Clifford. You sure you can identify Clifford?"

"Yes, Carla bragged of his curly black hair and pointy beard, and she really liked his vest and tall boots decorated with silver conchos."

Cuff was gone a good ten minutes, long enough for the boss to mutter, "Must have had to find a chair to stand on."

Short-legged Cuff was huffing when he returned. "No Carla. No Sam Clifford."

"John L., you guard the horses," Bannister ordered. "Cuff, you and I will take the stairs. Do you know where Carla's room is located?"

"She said Room 2, with considerable pride."

"Damn, that puts her at the head of the stairs from the saloon. All right, I want the element of surprise on our side. You and I will work together. You identify Clifford and I'll put the cuffs on him. We'll march him down to the saloon and then ride over to the jail."

I was beginning to wonder what my role would be, if any. Marshal Bannister didn't disappoint me. "Owen, you follow us. I don't want any interference from customers from Carla's room to the back end of the hall. Fire a shot into the ceiling to discourage any nosy soul that sticks his head out a door."

Up the rear stairs we went. The door at the top was unlocked and opened to the outside. Three wall lamps lit the hallway. The carpeted floor muted the sound of Cuff's and Bannister's footfalls. They crept the length of the hallway, halted, and then barged into a room without knocking, both holding drawn pistols.

By that time, I had drawn my own weapon. A shot rang out, the report in those confined quarters as piercing as the high notes of a bugle. A door popped open at the midpoint of the hallway. The second a head appeared, I fired a shot into the ceiling. The patter of shattered plaster on the top of my hat reminded me of Marshal Bannister's deadly showdown at the Purcell hog ranch.

The door at my right elbow swung open, a hand grabbed me by the arm, and yanked hard. Taken by surprise, I had no time to set my feet. The yanking hand backed farther into the room and I went sprawling backside down on a hard bed, losing the grip on my revolver. Next thing that registered with me was the sight of a shapely, naked female breast turned golden by lamplight and hanging an inch from my nose. I distinctly remember the bulging tip of the breast's puckered nipple.

A high female voice ripe with excitement whispered, "I love a shooting man," cascading black hair surrounded a lowering face, and a wet tongue began licking my cheek. The licking goaded me into action. I braced a foot on the floor of the room, clasped the night girl's shoulders, and heaved upward. She left my line of sight faster than I'd entered the room and there in her place was the ruddy countenance of Marshal Forge Bannister.

"Christ Almighty, Owen, I don't remember saying you could knock off a piece while you stood watch," a grinning Bannister said, offering a hand to help me to my feet.

One good habit of Bannister's was his ability to put noncriminal events behind him quickly, particularly those of an embarrassing nature, and nothing could have pleased me more right then. "Clifford's in cuffs and waiting to be escorted to jail," Bannister informed me.

Without being asked, Bannister helped the night girl unscramble herself from the corner of the room and climb onto the bed again, giving me the opportunity to locate my dropped pistol. In the hallway, he handed me a deputy marshal's badge and said, "Pin that on your coat. We don't know the sentiments of the crowd downstairs and a show of force may be in order."

I noticed at the far end of the hallway that Cuff Parker was wearing the same badge. I couldn't help noticing also that the bulky body of Moose Scanlon filled the top of the saloon stairwell. "That pop gun of yours doesn't matter," Moose declared with a sneer. "Wasn't for that badge, I'd be dragging you to the back stairs."

Cuff stuffed his snub-nosed revolver in a coat pocket and said with a sneer of his own, "Tell that to Marshal Bannister."

Moose had nothing to say to a man nearly his size showing a Federal badge and backed down the steps ahead of us. The gunshots and Moose's charge to the second floor had Bartlett's regular patrons spellbound over what would come next. The effect of three Federal marshals descending the steps behind the unconquerable Moose Scanlon with drawn weapons and a handcuffed man in tow was akin to a wet blanket smothering a twig fire.

We walked out of Saul Bartlett's palace of pleasure without ever catching a glimpse of the owner and rode to Newtonia's police station with the handcuffed Sam Clifford riding double with Cuff. Marshal Bannister dismissed John L. and Cuff and they headed back to camp. He was pounding on the station door when Patrolman Brick spoke from behind us. "I'm here, Marshal. Saw you and your men from up the block. Figured you were in need of a cell."

"You don't mind, Patrolman, I'd like the use of your station for a few minutes. I need to ask Mr. Clifford a few questions."

"Certainly, sir, follow me. I'll light a lamp and get a fire going in the stove."

I swear, in the glow of Patrolman Brick's lamp, Sam Clifford's curly black hair, pointed beard, darting eyes, and sour expression had him appearing more like some kind of devil rather than the romantic swain envisioned by night gal Carla. An attack of nerves had Clifford licking his lips repeatedly.

Marshal Bannister placed a chair in front of the seated Clifford, positioning himself at eye level with his prisoner. "Sam, I'm tired, it's late, and I want straight answers, and I want them fast. Do you understand?"

With Sam Clifford's hasty nod, Bannister said, "I have word that you, Frank McCabe, Henry Taylor, and Mike Stafford were bound for Sherman, Texas, where Mike's uncle owns a cattle ranch; is that so?"

The surprised look on Sam Clifford's face vanished as he realized how intently Federal officers were hunting him and his comrades. His rapid "Yes, sir" answer to Bannister's question indicated he knew his days running free and loose above the law were at an end.

"Mike Stafford has been riding with you since you left Carthage?"

"Yes, sir, it was Mike and his stupid shit brother, Charlie, that ambushed you."

"We figured that's what happened that night. Now, what do you know about Mike's Texas uncle?"

"Mike said his uncle is gathering a herd of cattle he intends to drive to Sedalia at war's end. He needs hired help with the gather. We were planning on wintering with Mike's uncle and maybe heading farther south if the law came poking around. We didn't believe any law dog would be interested in riding three hundred miles to track us down."

"He might if the three of you are worth six hundred dollars of reward money and the marshal works for a stickler like Judge Appleby. Is Mike's father, Buck, living in Sherman?"

"I can't say. Mike didn't talk about his family around me much."

Marshal Bannister came to his feet. "Patrolman, this man is henceforth in your custody. If Chief Hooker will write to Judge Hiram Appleby, care of U.S. Marshals Office, Kansas City, Missouri, he will forward funds to have Mr. Clifford transported for trial. If the judge wishes, I will retrieve Mr. Clifford when I return from Texas, in which case you'll need funds to cover the cost of feeding him in the meantime."

Marshal Bannister unlocked the handcuffs on Sam Clifford's wrists, pocketed them, and said, "Patrolman, I much appreciate the cooperation of you and your chief. Please convey that to him. Come along, Owen; it's time for a council of war, come morning."

Marshal Bannister's council of war was a meeting with his posse over a second cup of breakfast coffee after the horses had been watered. "Gentlemen, one jailed, three to find. The evidence all points to Sherman, Texas. That's a fifteen-day, three-hundred-mile ride in ideal weather. I didn't say anything up front about such a ride. Cuff, you and Will have a decision to make. We agreed on a pay of twenty dollars a month, with horses and vittles thrown in at the government's expense. I can pay each of you what you're owed right now, with no hard feelings, and you can keep the horse you're riding. I want to hear from each of you."

It was a fair offer for services rendered. Cuff and Will mulled over Bannister's offer for a while. I was never certain they were serious about accepting it, believing, instead, it was their way of acknowledging Bannister's concern for their welfare, given the danger of hunting armed men. They weren't soldiers who had to obey his orders.

Cuff spoke first. "Hell, I'm getting used to being rode hard and put away wet, and my mother always said I was the child the Lord didn't give the brains he gave our goose, the fool animal that hung himself."

"I'll tag along too," Will said. "I like a full belly, and game for table food can grow scarce in the winter. I sort of like knowing Judge Appleby won't let me go hungry or horseless."

A smiling, obviously happy Marshal Forge Bannister dumped the last of his coffee on John L.'s morning fire.

"Then Texas it is, boys."

# CHAPTER 21

THE THINNING COLUMN OF SMOKE ROSE BEYOND THE UPHILL SLANT OF country we were climbing. John L. Whitefeather popped out on the crest of high ground like a toy jack-in-the-box. He waited there with his customary patience while we slogged to him and drew rain. John L. scouted ahead of us during the daylight hours, leaving us to follow his tracks. For him to halt with the sun shining meant something out of the ordinary was afoot.

We spread in a line on either side of John L. and our searching eyes looked where he was pointing. Smoke was still trailing from the burning remains of a prairie schooner. Two elongated lumps, one in front of the schooner and the other at the rear, were most certainly human remains. The contents of the long wagon, ranging from furniture to bedclothes, were scattered hither and yon. One horse of the schooner's team lay dead in his harness, rear haunch scorched by the fire. The other horse was missing, probably taken by the raiders. Brush surrounded the site of the attack, except for the narrow wagon track cutting through it.

Marshal Bannister leaned forward in the saddle to ease his hips and said, "What the hell were they doing this far off the main roads?"

"Trying to hide," John L. answered.

"From what? A child could follow the wheel ruts of that schooner by moonlight."

John L. said, "No ashes from campfire. Tracks say three men hunt them."

We were near the Nations, and Bannister had to ask the inevitable question. "White men or red?"

"Boot tracks and shod horses say your kind."

"Are there just the two bodies?"

"Body of young girl in bushes. Women not treated well before they die."

"Well, ain't nobody but us for miles in every direction," Marshal Bannister judged, "so let's get after what must be done before the buzzards show themselves."

Once we had descended the downward slope and pushed our horses through the thick brush onto the narrow wagon road, Bannister said, "Cuff, grab the shovel off the mule. Will, can you dig with that arm wound?"

Dismounting, Will said, "Yes, sir, I can manage."

"You and Cuff will take first turn at grave digging. Trench grave in the clear area to the side of the road behind the wagon will do. Use those blankets the bushwhackers threw away to wrap the bodies. John L., lead me to the young girl's body you mentioned. Owen, there's papers scattered everywhere. See if there's a name and address on one that will identify these people. Then we'll take our turn with the digging."

Averting my eyes from a dead woman's half-naked body, I slid around the blackened rubble of the burned wagon to where the ground was virtually covered by loose sheets of paper, two ledger books, and a pile of old letters dumped from a wooden box with a bullet shattered lock. Many envelopes were addressed to *Mrs. Cheri Evans, 92 Beal Street, Washington, Pennsylvania.* The return address was almost always *Claude Evans, General Delivery, Arizona Territory.*

The sound of loud sniffles spun me on my heels, facing the brush with the Russell Colt Navy on full cock. My surprise was genuine. Before me stood a yellow-haired, blue-eyed boy tall as my chest dressed in a loose blue shirt and trousers and high-topped brogans with untied laces. The blue eyes were red from much crying.

I lowered the hammer and holstered my pistol. I held up my hands, showing my palms. "We mean you no harm. You're safe now."

The boy's lower lip quivered, but he didn't break and run. I knelt down. "My name is Owen. Come sit down and tell me what happened."

The boy stepped from the brush and nearly collapsed at my feet. He reminded me of the night my father was hung and the two Unionists had delivered me to Uncle Purse's doorstep with silent tongues and hearts cold as stone. I swore as I gently grasped the distraught lad's shoulders and helped him settle into a sitting position that I would not let him succumb to the grief that had nearly destroyed me.

"What's your name?" I asked.

"Patrick . . . Patrick Evans."

"How old are you, Patrick?"

"I was nine years old, last Thursday."

I was afraid to mention his parents just yet, for fear he would start crying again. "Who burned your wagon, Patrick?"

"Three men."

"Did you know them?"

Patrick wiped his nose with the side of his hand. "They were the same men we saw at the stage station yesterday morning. Mama was afraid of them."

"Why's that, Patrick?"

"They carried many guns, like yours, and Mama said they looked mean. One of them, the one called Frank, kept staring at Molly. Mama told Molly not to look at him."

Frank? It seemed like a far-fetched coincidence, but Frank McCabe and his fellow lawbreakers were traveling the same direction as the Evanses' schooner. However, in light of their past crimes, Marshal Bannister would never discount the possibility of their involvement in the wanton killing of the family, except for Patrick.

The dead bodies and their positions would reveal to Marshal Bannister and John L. the details of what transpired after the arrival of the perpetrators. Had Patrick seen any of that? He was holding firm, but I suspected that was because I was blocking his view of what I hoped by then was his mother's blanket-wrapped body. He would surely ask about her any second.

"What did you do when you saw Frank again, Patrick?"

"Uncle Claude and Mama told me to run and hide till they called me. Mama pinched my arm hard to make certain I was listening."

"And you did as they told you?"

"Yes, sir, I ran through the tall bushes till my legs hurt and hid behind a big tree. I heard gunshots and screams, but I covered my ears and stayed put. After a while, I fell asleep. Someone woke me up, yelling, 'Forget the kid. Let's ride,' and I hid some more. Did I do right, Mr. Owen?"

A shadow loomed over me, the length of it identifying the owner. Patrick cringed a little. I quickly said, "Marshal Bannister, this is Patrick Evans. He's been telling me all that's happened to him today."

Perhaps the appearance of Bannister and the authority his badge represented caused the sobering of young Patrick's suntanned features, for his point-blank question was a real shocker. "Marshal, I heard your men digging. My mama is dead, and Uncle Claude and Molly, too, aren't they?"

I agreed with Bannister's forthright reply. "Yes, Patrick, there was nothing we could do for them."

Bannister's honesty had import beyond Patrick's mama and sister, Molly. Previous to that morning, despite the death and bloodshed wrought by three years of war, I had never heard or read of a single Missouri soldier, bushwhacker, or guerilla deliberately killing, abusing, or forcibly assaulting a female regardless of her age, ever. An unspoken rule had made women sacrosanct, not to be touched. It had taken a particularly evil trio of men to break that code of conduct. I had hope that Lance was less of a devil.

"Patrick, we have buried your folks and we must move along. If you decide to travel with us, I promise no harm will come to you. I guarantee your safety till we reach your family by mail and make permanent arrangements for you. Are you game for that?" Bannister asked.

Patrick bit his lip and nodded. "Yes, sir, I trust you and Mr. Owen."

He didn't so much as glance over his shoulder as we rode off. We found the horse missing from the Evanses' schooner grazing in a small meadow a mile down the narrow wagon track. He proved to be a dual-use animal, broken to both harness and saddle, and Patrick's ability to ride bareback gave him his own mount.

I agreed with Cuff's after-supper assessment of Patrick Evans. "He's hardy, knows how to eat, is sound of limb, has all his teeth, and isn't empty-headed. Sounds like a keeper to me."

In the night, Patrick snuggled tight to my backside, seeking the warmth of more than his blanket. I felt shaking shoulders later and he cried in earnest a goodly while.

I never heard him cry again.

After ferrying across the Red River at Denison, Texas, we met Deputy Sheriff DeWayne Tyler in the taproom of the Drover's Inn at twenty after eleven, per my silver pocket watch. The feed store calendar nailed to the wall of the taproom read: *December 17, 1864*. A surveyor's transom secured to the back of a packhorse tied in front of the roadside establishment was what caught Marshal Bannister's attention and led us to interrupt our long journey, just nine miles from Sherman, Texas.

"Might be a county surveyor and those gentlemen are usually a well of information about local folks and their doings."

We had only the information gleaned from Graham Donovan and Police Chief Hooker and Sam Clifford in Newtonia to undergird the expectation that our manhunt would succeed once we arrived in Texas. Thus, Bannister's desire for additional advance knowledge that might provide a clue as to what kind of reception we would receive from local officials who could aid or thwart our endeavors.

Grayson County surveyor Aden Craig proved polite but reticent, where Deputy Sheriff Tyler was effusive and anxious to please. The twisted tips of DeWayne Tyler's greased mustache extended four inches past the corners of his mouth like spear points. He wore his brow in the same fashion. His round Grayson County badge was trimmed with gold rope, and the huge Walker Colts resting in a twin holster rig appeared too heavy for his slim hips.

Green eyes blinking constantly, Tyler assured Bannister that Sheriff Hugh Ballard valued law enforcement over friendship and allowed no one, regardless of political or economic stature, to interfere with the performance of his duties.

Much heartened, Bannister pressed ahead. "Deputy, I'm carrying Federal warrants for Frank McCabe, Henry Taylor, and Lance

Wainwright for robbery and murder. McCabe and Taylor are traveling with a young man named Mike Stafford. I'm told Mike's uncle owns a ranch outside of Sherman."

Tyler enjoyed a sip of the brandy-laced coffee, courtesy of Bannister's purse, and said, "That would be Leland Stafford's Triple Can't Ranch."

Marshal Bannister's mug stopped short of his mouth. "'Triple Can't Ranch'? What the hell does that stand for, Deputy?"

"Leland Stafford got so tired of people telling him you can't find the cows or the men you need to build a herd during wartime, he named his spread Triple Can't and his brand is three *C*s."

Bannister's guffaw at that imaginative response to unknown naysayers he instinctively disliked plastered a smile on Tyler's lean countenance that had the points of his mustache standing at attention, and it was then I laughed. Thankfully, neither man was paying me any attention and my poor manners were overlooked.

"Is Stafford still in need of hands? Heard anything about his hiring more men lately?"

Tyler's mustache points stood a second time. "Damned if I haven't. The word made the rounds in the saloons last week, there were three to four new hires out at Leland's place."

"What kind of man is Leland Stafford? I have reason to believe his nephew and his nephew's brother, Charlie, tried to ambush my deputies and me. We killed Charlie. Will Leland object to my arresting Mike? He has no allegiance to McCabe and Taylor and Wainwright that I know of."

Deputy Tyler scratched beard stubble on his chin. "Leland's a proud cuss, loyal to his family, disappointed he was too old to bear arms for the Confederacy. Don't know how he'll view surrendering a nephew to a Federal marshal. He might not take to that. But then, he'll soon be subject to the laws of the Union, what with you Yankees winning the war and all that goes with it."

"Those new hands of his prove the ones I'm after, suppose your sheriff would assist me in serving my warrants?"

"If he chooses not to, he won't interfere with you doing your duty."

"Where is the Three C located?"

"Five miles south of Sherman on an open stretch of grassland.

Leland has his own orchard, vineyard, and truck garden. His ranch needs little help from outside. He and his two sons, both recovered from battle wounds, and Buck—that would be Mike's father—fended off a bunch of bushwhackers a month ago. Killed eleven of them."

"Then Leland's sons are able to get around?"

"Yes, crazy thing is, they were standing side to side on the firing line. One son lost a leg below the left knee and the other below the right. You know, given all the firepower available at Leland's disposal and Buck's secessionist fever, it might be best if you could work out a strategy for serving those Federal warrants with Sheriff Ballard."

The arithmetic wasn't particularly difficult. Leland Stafford, his two sons, Buck Stafford, and his son, Mike, plus possibly three other new hands, constituted a force capable of contesting smartly with Marshal Bannister's posse composed of a total of five men, if he counted me. I was certain Forge Bannister's pride wouldn't prevent him from accepting whatever assistance Sheriff Ballard might offer.

"I believe I'll hold a council of war with your sheriff," a standing Bannister decided. "Is he available this afternoon?"

"Yes, sir, his office is on the square next door to Sherman's log courthouse. Blind dog could sniff it out."

"Hotel for the night for my posse?"

"How many of you?"

"Four. John L. won't sleep under a roof."

"High Point, off the square on Rice Street, is the cleanest."

"Food and libation?"

"You mean roasted beef and best whiskey? Dag Harmon's saloon across from the High Point. Card games are straight. Sheriff Ballard can't abide cheats."

"Deputy, I thank you for your time, the information, and the advice. If you'll come by Harmon's this evening, I'll buy you a drink or two."

The two law officers shook hands; then Bannister and I walked outside. We found Cuff and Will slumped in chairs on the front porch of the Drover's Inn and John L. dozing in the shade of his horse. "Listen up," Bannister said, his tone commanding attention. "After eleven days in the saddle covering two hundred miles, we'll stay in town tonight. I have the name of a hotel and saloon close by each other. Don't wear badges tonight. There's a heap of sentiment for both sides of the war in North Texas, so tread softly. No trouble lest someone else starts the fight. Let's move out."

Bareback-riding Comanches couldn't have mounted faster.

We were expecting a peaceful evening. We were seated at a round table for five in the corner to the right of the front door of Harmon's Saloon. I was to Cuff Parker's right and Will to his left, giving Cuff a wide-angle view of the rest of the room, with nothing behind him but wall, the public seating arrangement preferred by Marshal Bannister for the safety of his charges. Surprise was Forge Bannister's least-favored action.

The food at Dag Harmon's saloon consisted of roasted beef, a corn pudding, halves of squash stuffed with bread dressing, and boiled onions that satisfied our rampant hunger. We lingered after dining, playing poker for the winner's pride with the pack of cards Cuff was never without. The shortest posse member seldom lost, leading Will to swear Cuff was a polygamist married to the queen of each suit.

Will was seating himself after refilling our beer mugs at the bar, when Cuff, dealing the next hand, said, "Trouble brewing. Owen, keep your head down and eyes on the cards."

Will dropped into his chair, gaze locked on Cuff. "How many?"

Cuff said, "I count four. They came in, one at a time, and spread out. They're watching us in the mirror behind the bar. Bloody Bills for certain."

Bloody Bill was a code word Bannister's posse used to designate any man wearing bushwhacker garb—pinned-up hat brim, large pocketed shirt, and tall boots—and carrying two or more pistols, the most dangerous bearer of arms west of the Mississippi.

We continued our poker game, Cuff's and Will's calmness restraining my anxious nerves.

"Why us?"

"We rode into town backing a man wearing a Federal star," Cuff answered. "That's all the reason Southern Rebels, who'll never admit they've lost the war, need."

Shuffling the cards, Cuff glanced in the direction of the bar. The nod of his head was slight but apparent to Will and me. "They're about to make their play. Owen, stretch your arms above your head, and then lower your hands to your lap so they're close by your pistol. Will, I don't think they intend to kill us, but I'm not inclined to let them beat us half to death either. If they're too stupid not to draw down on us, soon as I tire of their insults, this table is going up and over, so be ready."

Stealth was foreign to the four Bloody Bills. Anticipating we'd take no notice of them till they surrounded our table, they marched across the saloon, weaving among the tables that separated us from the bar, satisfied smirks visible on their bearded faces. They effectively walled us off from the balance of the crowd.

The broadest of them said, "We didn't expect the big man wearing the badge would let his posse out of his sight."

"Two old curs and a puppy is slim picking for four wolves."

"Yankees are best known for running from the fight, right, Buster?"

Buster's cackling laugh suffused Cuff's face with red. Gripping the edge of the table with both hands, Cuff snarled, "I wouldn't name a pet skunk Buster," and heaved with both arms.

The heavy round table went up and over. The center two Bloody Bills shied backward in alarm. The falling table crashed into the saloon's wooden floor. Two sharp cracks in succession resembled the snapping of large tree branches. The shying Bloody Bills crashed atop the fallen table.

Behind the fallen bodies stood Marshal Bannister and a ruggedly built gent with a star on his leather vest. Both lawmen had a bloody baton in their right hands and a revolver in their left. Will dispatched the third Bloody Bill with a chair to the head. The astonished Bloody Bill on my side of the table ceased reaching for his gun and froze in place when the cold metal of a gun barrel touched his ear. Marshal Bannister's deep voice, easily heard throughout a room gone dead silent, said, "Two seconds. Live or die. Your choice."

The fourth Bloody Bill's arms reached for the ceiling and a relieved sigh rippled through the watching crowd. Marshal Bannister's confident smile eased the tension, nailing my feet to the floor, and I sank back into my chair, surprised my right hand gripped a cocked Russell Colt Navy. I eased off the Navy's hammer, glad my hand on its butt wasn't shaking.

Bannister said, "You had him beat, Owen," a compliment that nudged me a small step closer to believing I was worthy of keeping company with the more stalwart members of his posse.

Aunt Emma held that when an endeavor was important to a man, he needed to persist with conviction, while keeping the Lord aware of its importance to him by prayer, creating the possibility that the Almighty might see fit to intervene by nudging the odds a bit in his favor with a twist of fate so subtle it defied belief. The Bannister posse had been in the saddle for four hundred-plus miles, netted one of four fugitives, and had solid leads as to the whereabouts of two others. What the posse lacked was information about the fourth fugitive, one Lance Wainwright, beyond his statement to his fellow scouts that he would seek refuge in Sherman, Texas, once free of his military duties.

The strange twist of fate that altered events in the posse's and my favor was the curiosity of Silas Hammer, a reformed drunk, jailhouse janitor, and sometimes jailer for the county sheriff Hugh Ballard. While his boss and Marshal Bannister were busy at Dag Harmon's saloon saving two posse members and me from a physical beating, Silas took note of Bannister's wanted posters on Sheriff Ballard's desk, poured himself a cup of coffee, sat in the sheriff's cherished leather chair, and studied them in detail.

According to Sheriff Ballard, sometime in the years previous to Silas's appearance in Sherman, the old drifter had acquired sufficient education to preach the Gospel to an unknown congregation and teach public school before a sturdy lass broke his heart and he lapsed into an existence ruled by his next drink. It was the wanted poster depicting Lance Wainwright that captured and held Silas spellbound, particularly its descriptive words: *Extra tall, red of hair, severe scar on right cheek.*

That precise description fit the rider, on a big, rangy black horse, who had asked Silas directions to Leland Stafford's Triple Can't Ranch in front of Nate Weekly's grocery the day before yesterday. Silas's belly had been sour that morning, but his mind had been sober and sharp. Otherwise, he wouldn't have remembered the rider with a stare that made his knees quake.

An excited Silas was waiting for Sheriff Ballard when Ballard, Marshal Bannister, Will, Cuff, and I marched our prisoners through the office to the cells lining the jail's rear hallway. The town harness maker and sometimes doctor came after us, summoned to sew up the head wounds inflicted by buffaloing lawmen.

By then, I had learned John L. had realized we were being followed from the moment we led our horses off Denison's Red River ferry. Bannister had sent us to Harmon's, while he conferred with Sheriff Ballard, hoping those having any sign of outside law headed for Sherman would make a play in his absence and they had.

Marshal Bannister had no sooner dismissed Cuff and Will for the evening when Silas's excitement overcame his patience. "I saw this one," Silas announced, stabbing Lance's poster with a forefinger. "Right here in the street."

Both Bannister and Sheriff Ballard stared at the old drunk. "You sure about that, Silas?" Ballard asked.

Silas puffed his chest. "Yes, sir, his hair was red as flame and the cheek scar a long white line through his beard. He looked like a tall giant riding that big black horse."

As I heard that news, my heart skipped a beat and I had to clamp my mouth shut to keep from gasping like a child. My fingers hurt from crossing them.

An equally roused Bannister turned to me. "Might be a long shot, but wasn't your brother riding a big black horse the day you were ambushed?"

"Yes, sir, he was."

Sheriff Ballard's inquisitive expression begged an explanation and Bannister obliged him. After introducing me, he recounted in sufficient detail the how and why of my becoming a member of his posse.

"Strangest tale I've ever heard," Ballard concluded. "Thought at first you were making it up."

"Has me scratching my head now and again too," Bannister admitted.

Ballard shrugged his shoulders, sighed, and said, "Silas, put a fresh pot of coffee on the stove. Marshal, you and Owen grab a chair. I have a proposition that might interest you and will benefit the both of us."

Out of the corner of my eye, I saw Silas's method of brewing a fresh pot of coffee involved throwing a handful of fresh coffee on top of the old grounds and adding water, which, in turn, produced a black liquid strong enough to float horseshoe nails and keep an imbiber awake half the night. Uncle Purse claimed emptying and cleaning of the pot with each brew was what made his Emma's coffee a magnet for morning, as well as evening, diners.

Sheriff Ballard leaned back in his chair. "Bannister, if Silas is right, you've accounted for all four of your fugitives, and that adds to the problem facing me. Leland Stafford's craving to build a spring herd, and be first to market in Sedalia, has resulted in his hiring in a season when most range men dismiss riders till springtime. His new hires are likely to go hunting for excitement before winter is out, and my guess is, they'll come to Sherman, a short five-mile ride away. The last thing I want is two or three dead citizens and half my town a pile of ashes."

"What do you have in mind?"

"I can count on DeWayne Tyler and four men here in town. Combine them with your posse and we'd have enough men to surround Leland's home and bunkhouse and demand your wanted boys give themselves up."

Bannister's body tilted forward, revealing an initial interest in what Ballard was proposing. "When would we stage this raid?"

"Too late for tomorrow morning, so right at daybreak, day after tomorrow. We call a meeting of our men tomorrow afternoon and lay out our plan. We swear everyone to secrecy. We'll ride at two a.m., putting us in position to surround Leland's place just as there's light enough to see, hopefully catching them still in bed. You've done this before, Marshal. With surprise on our side, the better the chance we succeed."

"Sheriff, Lance Wainwright and my other wanted men won't surrender without a fight. They know a hanging rope awaits them back in Missouri. I want your townsmen made aware of that."

"They'll be duly warned. I've hunted the Red River bottomlands with all of them at one time or another. They know how to stalk game animals and not expose themselves. They've served on posses with me."

"Any of them excel at long-range shooting?"

"Yes, Butch Carson."

"Good, we'll pair him with Will, my sharpshooter," Bannister said. "Now, there's one possible source of help we haven't discussed. Are there any Union troops stationed in your county?"

"Not at the moment," Ballard answered, "and from my experience, we would be a week to a month making the arrangements with their officers, even with you being a Federal officer."

Bannister grinned and nodded. "You're thinking the same as me. Leland Stafford has unknowingly brought together a bunch of border ruffians, not known for even tempers and love of hard work, from dawn to dusk—men accustomed to being on the run and enjoying whiskey and lifted skirts wherever they find them. Drudgery of any kind rankles them till they can't stand it another minute. Our wanted boys might not last ten days chopping firewood and helping Stafford build a spring herd buying cows and branding strays."

Sheriff Ballard said, "We're riding the same horse, Marshal. Being stuck in front of a bunkhouse fire in the winter can test a feisty man's temperament quicker than a year in prison."

Bannister accepted a tin cup of coffee from Silas, found its content lip-burning hot, and set the cup on the corner of Sheriff Ballard's desk. "Have you visited Leland Stafford's ranch?"

"Yes," Ballard said. "Last year, and just a month ago."

"I'd like you to draw a map showing Leland's home, the bunkhouse, outbuildings, barn, corral, and the surrounding ground, meaning high or low, brush covered or open. We can decide where to place our men. Might be possible to run off the horses in the corral straight off. Leaving our poster boys afoot to die by a sharpshooter bullet the moment they step outside will dampen their zeal for a fight."

Sheriff Hugh Ballard's salt-and-pepper beard signaled he'd lived a few decades. His demeanor suggested he was at home with firearms, the law, and the foibles of his fellow men; yet he recognized a superior mind in his field. "Bannister, I'm damn glad you don't hold a warrant with my name on it. I like to sleep at night."

The slightest hint of red on his cheekbones told me the unexpected compliment had embarrassed Forge Bannister. "Ballard, I'd trust you to back me in a weasel den, and that's true with damn few men."

We departed the Grayson County Jail for the evening on that high note of cooperation between the two lawmen that bode well for future joint endeavors. Two blocks down Rice Street, we entered the livery, where John L. was ensconced with the posse's horses, camping equipment, saddlebags, and Will's prized long-range rifles and their tripod.

The December evening wind had a sharp bite on bare skin. Night clouds obscured the stars. A warm body required a heavy jacket or overcoat. John L. sniffed the moist air and proclaimed, "Heavy snow tomorrow night."

Marching to the High Point Hotel, where we had booked overnight rooms upon our arrival, Bannister commented, "Snowstorm would work in our favor. It would pin our poster boys in the bunkhouse first thing in the morning. Make it harder to travel for anyone lucky enough to escape our net."

We passed a log cabin building whose signage read U.S. POST OFFICE. A separate building for mail service was rare. In most towns, a separate room in a hotel or business sufficed. I slowed for a few steps and an observant Bannister said, "Need to write to someone?"

The thought of writing Laura Kellerman had haunted me for days, but the posse hadn't stopped in one place long enough where I could acquire paper and envelope. In addition, I had no money for postage either. Bannister solved my dilemma in his usual straightforward manner.

"Hotel sells writing paper and envelopes, and I have money for postage. I have to forward a report to Judge Appleby before he thinks I fell off the earth. The old boy's nosiness is as natural to him as the bang of his gavel. Seems tomorrow could be your letter-writing day."

I didn't wait. Upon our return, the High Point desk clerk was only too happy to accept Marshal Bannister's money, and the room I was sharing with the boss provided a small table outfitted with a candle lamp and a chair. Boss's pen poised, I sat trying to decide what to say, and how to say it, while the pen's owner snored merrily away.

It slowly dawned on me that I wasn't about to become a poet, no matter what affectionate bromide I might eventually concoct, and I plunged ahead in the short and simple manner as I had previously.

*Laura: Expect to return home within a few weeks.*
*Remembering the store, your watch, and our kiss. Owen*

# CHAPTER 22

I AWAKENED IN AN EMPTY ROOM WITH WEAK SUNLIGHT AT THE WINDOW. A note on the table I'd used for letter writing read: *Harmon's 10:00 a.m. Bring Will & Cuff.* A small pocket Bible Bannister carried in a coat pocket rested beside the note. Was the Bible a hint I should pray for safe deliverance from the danger we would face on the morrow?

To be on the safe side, in case Bannister asked me at breakfast, I read passages from the Book of John till my pocket watch read quarter to ten. I washed my face and hands with the pitcher of water, basin, and towel provided each hotel room, used the thunder jug under the bed, strapped the Russell Colt Navy about my waist, stepped into the hallway, and rapped on the door across the way. Then Will, Cuff, and I hurried to meet the waiting Bannister.

Poached eggs atop beef hash, bacon, boiled onions, corn bread smeared with currant jelly, and piping-hot coffee, laced with brandy, as Marshal Bannister preferred, constituted breakfast at Dag Harmon's table. It was a day-starting meal that fit Bannister's rule that Judge Appleby owed his charges fine dining whenever available to make up for the cold nights on the trail when their fare was limited to beef jerky and creek water.

Over a second round of coffee, Bannister unrolled Sheriff Ballard's drawing of Leland Stafford's Triple C Ranch. All the elements Bannister had requested—main house, bunkhouse, outbuildings, barn, and corral—were carefully drawn with squiggly lines representing brush, puffy balls for trees, and upsweeping pen strokes to indicate the main house set on a higher elevation than the rest of the structures.

"Damnation!" Cuff exclaimed with a whistle. "Somebody, maybe the army, taught Ballard how to draw a map."

Bannister's immediate attention went to the location of the barn and corral well to the southwest of the main house, bunkhouse, and outbuildings. "Look at the brush and trees behind the corral," Bannister said. "Might be John L. could sneak in and flush the corral free of horses for us. Sans a chase, fugitives on foot are easier to rope and brand."

"How many of them are there versus our side of the roster?" Will asked.

"Sheriff and I count eight of them, if the oldsters Leland and Buck Stafford deal themselves in, to eleven of us, counting Ballard, his deputy, and his four townsmen. I figure Leland and Buck for the main house, their sons and our fugitives for the bunkhouse. Bear in mind, Leland and his sons may well decide they're not sacrificing themselves for fugitives on the ranch payroll for less than a week."

"Better odds than we usually enjoy," Will said.

Watching Bannister and his three deputies at work intrigued me. The four of them were older bachelors wedded to the enforcement of the law at their peril. The pay was low, the hours long, and the job required the physical endurance of younger men. They persisted anyway, buoyed by the stature and respect afforded a peace officer compared to that granted to those confined to working with their hands. It wasn't that Bannister and his deputies disrespected manual labor, but that they were thankful for the variety of their tasks and the authority and weapons to fulfill their duties.

Will asked, "Boss, when do we meet with Ballard's townsmen?"

"Four o'clock this afternoon, at his office. Wear your badges."

It was Sunday, and the day of the week, plus the warning signs of the coming winter storm, emptied the streets of Sherman except for churchgoers and a mule-drawn freighter loading at the rear dock of the warehouse beside the livery stable, populated by its owner and John L. Whitefeather. After breakfast, I checked the legs of our horses, the status of their shoes, and curried and brushed them, while Will and Cuff returned to the hotel to clean and oil their weapons. Once free of their leather carrying cases, Will's long rifles received particular attention. Having stood guard through the night, John L. piled fresh straw in an empty stall, wrapped himself in his blanket, and slept soundly without snoring. Marshal Bannister devoted the time in our hotel room finishing the report due Judge Appleby.

During that quiet afternoon, I discovered a fundamental truth about Owen Wainwright. It was hard for me to grasp at first how Forge Bannister and his deputies could pass hours so quietly. It was as if they were waiting to report to the local flour mill, instead of preparing to attempt the arrest of armed fugitives wanted for murdering their fellow men, and ready to kill again, rather than being taken alive to die at the end of a hanging rope.

No matter how much I respected the courage and nerve of Bannister and his deputies, I realized I was cut from different cloth. I had learned in a few short weeks that I didn't lack courage when it came to protecting my own life, and the lives of those around me, on short notice.

Surprisingly, neither did I find it cowardly to admit I didn't have the rare fortitude required to wear a badge, carry a gun, and enforce the law, day by day. I was more the soldier who would willingly fight the war, expecting that with the victory, I had earned the right to a peaceful life till my country needed me again. I could tolerate occasional battles, free of the constant danger a lawman had to confront.

Though six inches of snow had covered the ground during the night, at first light it had diminished to fluffy flakes fluttering on a light breeze. Everything to that minute had favored our expanded posse. Sheriff Ballard had had no trouble guiding us through the darkness of a moonless night to the gate on the lane leading to the dooryard of the Triple C. We dismounted and left our horses outside the gate, Leland Stafford's dislike of dogs of all breeds easing our fear that the slightest noise would betray our presence. Except for Marshal Bannister and me, the posse passed through the gate. Once we were alone, Bannister spoke in a whisper, with a restraining hand on my chest. "Owen, you stay with the horses. Tie their reins to the fence."

I opened my mouth to object, but Bannister shushed me, as he would a child. "A man never knows how the best-planned ambush will turn out. I don't want our horses scattered to hell and gone by a stray bullet. Watch me with your telescope. Lance and the boys get to their horses or scatter on foot, we'll need animals damn quick."

I should have guessed my role in advance. In the meeting at Sherman's jail, Bannister had employed Ballard's map of the Triple C and pointed out where each posse member was to station himself. When I wasn't mentioned, I assumed I would trail after Bannister as usual. My real mistake was failing to notice he had left the horses untended.

The single rough moment at the jail meeting was the suggestion from a townsman that the posse simply charge into the Stafford dooryard, kick in the doors of the main house and bunkhouse, and shoot anybody they saw without their hands in the air. Unperturbed, Bannister had patiently explained that no one knew how Leland, his sons, and his brother were going to respond to the invading posse. Did they know the hands they'd hired were wanted men? Would they side with them, once they knew? Then there was Leland's wife and daughter to consider. Of one thing, Bannister was certain: if the posse barged in unannounced, shooting was inevitable.

I ignored the creeping posse, tied the horses to the top wire of the fence near the gate with slipknots, and then braced my Dollond telescope atop a gatepost, shielding my body as much as possible behind the post.

I scanned the deserted yard, dwellings, barn, and corral looming ahead of the advancing posse, the scene reminding me of a wintertime painting evoking the beauty and peacefulness of country life. Movement ceased everywhere. The posse was in position.

A shadow stirring near the far corner of the corral flitted across the Dollond's lens. Once I zeroed in on it, the squat, short shape matched that of John L. With his push, the gate of the corral slowly swung open. Horses in the corral milled briefly before filing through the gate without a whinny or nicker, the snow deep enough to muffle the beat of their hoofs. John L. was a magician with horses. Will believed John L.'s smoky smell relaxed them.

Against the backdrop of the elevated main house, the huge barn, and the steep hill behind them, Forge Bannister's voice carried in the silent night as if he was shouting from the stage of a small theater. Firing a shot into the air, he let the echo die and shock set in before calling, "This is U.S. Marshal Bannister speaking. We have the place surrounded. Come out with your hands up."

A response after a long minute came from the bunkhouse: "Kiss your own ass, law dog."

The planned response to so much as a peep of resistance from the bunkhouse came from the posse's sharpshooters Will Strong and Butch Carson. Each put a bullet through the bunkhouse's two windows.

A booming shout originated in an upper-floor window of the main house. "Who the hell you after?"

Bannister had the stage and he took full advantage of the opening. "Frank McCabe . . . Henry Taylor . . . Lance Wainwright . . . and Mike Stafford."

What happened next I likened to the mind of a cunning animal trapped in his den having the wherewithal to acknowledge that to stay where he was meant certain death, and while any attempt to break free of his entrapment might also result in his death, to have any chance to survive he must put up a fight that at least brought his claws into play.

The front and rear doors of the bunkhouse swung open and armed bodies burst forth, holding fire till targets could be identified. Aware that his control of the situation was imperiled, Bannister yelled, "Fire," and long fingers of flame pointed at the fleeing fugitives. Those in flight scattered in all directions, pausing to return fire every few strides.

The fleeing fugitive that was a magnet for the lens of my Dollond was the one running in the direction John L. had shooed the corral horses. He was firing a gun in each hand while constantly on the move.

It was Lance.

Lance would have the quickness of mind to instantly figure the best and only chance of escaping justice was on the back of a horse. If he succeeded, his path would intersect the fence line southwest of the corral, where open prairie awaited him. I acted as I had the night of the attempted bank robbery in Waverly, without an ounce of forethought. I snapped the reins of the nearest horse free and stepped aboard, the Russell Colt Navy filling my hand.

I was serious about pursuing Lance, but I lacked the desperation of the man fleeing for his life, and he surprised me by putting his horse over the line fence in a leaping bound as I closed on him. The shoulders of our mounts collided, the crash throwing both of us from the saddle.

I landed and skidded through the snow on my backside, glad for no broken limbs or bones, retaining enough awareness of my circumstances to be thrilled I hadn't lost my grip on the Russell Colt Navy. I heard a wet sucking of breath and a body loomed over me with an uplifted arm, hand filled with a large rock.

John L. Whitefeather spared me the necessity of killing my half brother. The bullet from his flintlock rifle caught Lance in the back of the neck and he fell on top of me, blood from his wound dripping on my forehead.

I threw Lance off me and got to my feet, holstering my revolver.

John L. sidled next to me. "Tough men, good or bad, hard to kill."

It was an epitaph the family bastard didn't deserve.

I stood staring at a dead open-eyed Lance. Satisfaction that he was finally gone from my life took hold in my mind, but the final narrative had yet to be written.

John L. snatched the Russell Colt Navy from my holster, stepped astride Lance's body, and shot him twice in the heart. Stepping back, he returned the weapon to me butt first. "You shoot brother, no trouble. Me shoot him, maybe big trouble."

I couldn't fault John L.'s reasoning. Even with his being in the employ of the Federal government, a half-breed killing a white man in Texas might raise questions, should it become known publicly, and such a stain might dampen John L.'s usefulness as Bannister's deputy elsewhere.

The shooting in the Triple C dooryard had died out. A mounted Marshal Bannister came hunting us. From the saddle, he studied the long groves cut in the snow by sliding men and horses and the position of Lance's body and laid a raised brow on John L.

"Horses collide," John L. said. Pointing at Lance and me, he continued, "They fight. Owen shoot to save self."

Bannister's hard gaze found me next. "That the way it was?"

I suspected that during a lull in the Triple C shooting, Bannister had heard the crack of John L.'s black-powder rifle and then two distinctly different-sounding reports. I managed to keep a straight face. "Yes, sir, just as John L. said."

A satisfied Bannister thankfully stepped down. "All right, we're not chasing after loose horses. Drape Lance's body over my saddle and we'll walk him back to the main house."

En route, curiosity prompted me to ask, "Did the posse lose any men?"

Bannister's head shook. "No, thank the Lord. Taylor and Mike Stafford are dead. We can't account for Frank McCabe. One of Leland's sons claims McCabe and your brother here had an argument last night over who was cheating at cards and McCabe stormed off, helping himself to a good Stafford riding animal. No one tried to stop him. Seems the others had grown tired of his bad temper."

"The Stafford family stayed clear of the fight?"

"Not a shot was fired from the main house or by Leland's sons. Leland and his brother weren't totally satisfied with McCabe, Taylor, and Mike Stafford, once they'd settled into the bunkhouse, but decided they'd make do till spring, figuring any help was better than being shorthanded."

The Sherman members of our posse had businesses awaiting their attention at home and were chomping at the bit. Sheriff Ballard dismissed them after reminding them their $5-per-day pay would be available at his office. The Stafford family agreed to bury the dead, so long as a common grave didn't offend anyone.

My coldheartedness regarding Lance's grave not being marked didn't shock me. Beyond his service to the Confederacy, the world was better with him dead and buried without any recognition he ever existed.

Some evil deeds are not forgiven on this earth.

The long chase was over. The absence of the hustle and strain of counting every minute lost and won in pursuing fugitives around the clock felt as if the weight of a blacksmith's anvil had been lifted from our shoulders. Bannister himself admitted the ride from Otterville to Texas was the longest of his career and that it might be the last time he challenged a lower back growing crankier each winter.

Cuff Parker and Will Strong would survive the winter on their share of the reward money secured by sworn statements from Sheriff Ballard and the Grayson County coroner, who was called to the Triple C. Before the interment of the deceased fugitives, these two men verified that the deceased men matched the descriptions on Bannister's wanted posters and went by the names on the same.

John L. Whitefeather's devotion to Bannister went beyond his responsibilities as a deputy marshal and the pay it afforded him. Where Bannister was a bachelor, John L.'s Osage woman held fort on a small farm outside Leavenworth City, deeded to Bannister, and it was to that abode marshal and deputy repaired for rest and relaxation as their official duties permitted.

After riding for four hundred miles with them, I gleaned this personal knowledge of my companions during a congratulatory dinner that Monday evening in Dag Harmon's private dining room, courtesy of the boss and the unknowing Judge Appleby. Dag provided straightforward but delicious fare. Corn tortillas stuffed with beef and peppers hot on the tongue, fried beans laced with bacon strips, boiled brown rice, and pastries filled with canned peaches and spiced apples, all washed down with a full-gallon demijohn of brandy.

Full of belly, smile wider than that of a circus clown, Cuff Parker belched and said, "Boss, I finally know what my grandpa meant when he said, 'Cuff, my boy, we're shittin' in tall clover.' "

The laughter round the table lasted till tears ran. The merriment continued till the pourer at the time announced we had exhausted the demijohn. Boos followed Marshal Bannister saying perhaps retirement for the evening was in order, as Judge Appleby's budget was short on funds for hiring locals to carry us to bed, but we knew better than to buck the boss.

The night and the manhunt were officially at an end.

Or so we thought.

I fell asleep wondering if Lance had known who was chasing him down. The daily tension of making sure I didn't appear an immature oaf before men decades older than me was gone at last.

Thoughts of Lance gave way to dreams of the embracing arms, soft breasts, and velvet lips of Laura Kellerman. Lord, was she beautiful, and the joys I could share with her in bed, given her near-brazen forwardness, exceeded my imagination.

The urge hit me in the darkest hour of the night and refused to be assuaged. The only source of relief was a trip to the four-hole outhouse behind the hotel . . . that or suffer an insufferable outcome.

The wariness acquired riding with armed men searching for other armed men spared me. Despite the pressure building in my bowels, I took time to stuff the Russell Colt Navy behind my belt. I goose-stepped to the rear door of the hotel, stepped out onto the low stoop, and lunged for the star-decorated door of my savior.

Dropping my pants, I also dropped the Russell Colt Navy; fortunately, it fell to the floor of the outhouse and not down the hole beneath me. I'd started to enjoy the stupendous relief one derives from the realization a soul has won the most rewarding of races, and not your bowel, when a voice laden with a viciousness that chilled my heart said, "Come out of there, you son of a bitch. I owe you for killing my friends."

Had I never ventured beyond the city limits of Sedalia, I would not have survived that threat on my life. I was not that same naive young man unaccustomed to violence and bloodshed and unaware that a grown man looks to himself before he looks to others in desperate situations.

I swept the Russell Colt Navy from the floor of the outhouse and fired till the hammer clicked on an empty chamber, spacing the shots from the center to the bottom of the outhouse door. The slam of the shots in the narrow confines of the outhouse faded. I heard excited voices and lantern light shone between wall cracks. I lifted the latch and nudged the outhouse door open.

And there stood a familiar sight, with revolver in one hand and lantern in the other. Marshal Bannister grinned impishly and said, "You all right in there?"

I simply nodded. I wasn't hurt, not if you didn't count my embarrassment over being seen butt naked in an outhouse, with my pants around my ankles, holding a smoking pistol.

"Do we know the dead man?" Bannister asked over his shoulder.

Will Strong said, "Damned if it isn't Frank McCabe."

# EPILOGUE

*What I came to call my grand wartime adventure did not end with the outhouse shooting behind the High Point Hotel in Sherman, Texas, which became a part of Texas Civil War lore. At the time, I had no inclination how large those wild weeks and my memories of them would loom over me in future years.*

*We rode north two days after the demise of Frank McCabe with the sworn affidavits of Sheriff Ballard and the Grayson County coroner in hand, legitimizing our claims on the reward money due the Bannister posse. In Denison, Texas, the closest town to the Red River ferry, we retrieved young Patrick Evans from the widow in whose care we had left him on the recommendation of the local marshal, pending the completion of our business in Texas. Young Patrick had bonded with me, and the Bannister posse unanimously agreed that it would be best for his future if he were placed in the care of one Emma Wainwright, giving Marshal Bannister ample time to seek any living relatives interested in adopting him by mail, as we'd planned. In Newtonia, Missouri, much to the relief of Chief of Police Hooker, we assumed custody and responsibility for Sam Clifford, swore to him John L. would cut out his tongue if he couldn't keep his mouth shut, and continued our homeward trek.*

*The posse split up at Warrensburg. Marshal Bannister, John L., Will, Cuff, and prisoner Clifford continued on to Kansas City to meet with Judge Appleby. With Bannister's permission, Patrick and I sold our horses and purchased train tickets to Sedalia.*

*Our unexpected January 1865 appearance at the door of the Wainwright Hotel generated cheers of joy and much back patting. A healed Uncle Purse and Sam Benson insisted a now fully grown Owen Wainwright enjoy a toast with them at the hotel bar to welcome him home. Meanwhile, Aunt Emma was likely to smother young Patrick, holding him tight to her bosom, making sure he knew how welcome he was to join the Wainwright family for however long his stay might be.*

*My next stop was Laura Kellerman's millinery shop inside the Kellerman Mercantile building. At the door of the mercantile, I thought for a moment a bath and shave might be wise first, but the craving to see her was overwhelming. I pushed inside and heard the chatter of females. Hat in hand, I fought back the urge to run and entered the millinery shop at a gentlemanly pace.*

*Laura didn't share my concern about being embarrassed in front of her more genteel female customers. At the sight of me, her blue eyes widened, she gasped in disbelief, and then, accepting the fact those same blue eyes weren't deceiving her, she dropped the lace-trimmed nightgown she was holding up to a customer and charged across her shop. I had just enough time to brace my feet before she literally jumped into my arms.*

*She wound her arms around my neck, and ignoring the giggling and drawn breath of her astonished female customers, she kissed me hard on the mouth. She broke off her kiss, and lifting her mouth to my ear, she whispered, "I guess Santa didn't forget me after all."*

*Between breaths, I managed to ask, "Did you get my letter?"*

*"Yes, my darling stud," she said, forgetting to whisper, "and I'm dying to bed the writer."*

*With the pronouncement of a male nickname that reddened faces, her customers fled, leaving me alone in the shop with its passion-hungry owner, who smiled coyly and said, "Father is away." If a customer rang the clerk-calling bell in the mercantile that afternoon after the door of the millinery was locked, we didn't hear it.*

*We married a month later and moved into the suite on the second floor of the Wainwright Hotel at the insistence of Uncle Purse.*

*Laura continued to work for her father at a salary, and I helped with whatever chores needed doing at the Wainwright and undertook a serious reading for the law under Master Schofield, financing my studies in part with my share of the Bannister posse reward money.*

*By late spring, it became obvious Marshal Bannister's inquiries mailed to Pennsylvania and Arizona Territory on Patrick Evans's behalf wouldn't locate any living relatives, and Patrick, already occupying my old room on the first floor near the rear door, became a permanent resident. He soon began an apprenticeship under Sam Benson and Titus Culver after each school day.*

*Early that summer, with the April surrender of the Confederacy long signed by General Lee at Appomattox Court House, an unsettling feeling began to nag at me, the notion that I had left something undone, a failure that slighted someone who had been close to me. Restless nights beset me.*

*The answer to my unease came as unexpectedly as had my first sensing of it. On a beautiful clear Sunday afternoon, Laura asked me to take her for a buggy ride north of town.*

*During her weekly horseback rides, she had noticed a three-year old chestnut horse frolicking in a roadside pasture and decided he would be a perfect gift for a horseless young Patrick.*

*Laura's judgment was dead on target. The young chestnut was sound of limb and his conformation excellent by every definition. Laura arranged to buy him at a fair price and we were to bring Patrick to claim him the following Sunday.*

*My revelation occurred during our drive home. The contrast between the beautiful, lively Laura and the solemn quiet and loneliness of the Sedalia cemetery as we trotted past it struck a dual chord of love and pain in me that shortened the breath in my lungs and quickened my heartbeat. Ridiculous as it sounds, Morgan Holloway was suddenly seated next to me, instead of Laura, and she was saying,* "Nothing lasts forever. Remember this night when you think of me."

*Laura yelped as wheels slid in loose gravel at the edge of the road and the buggy slewed sideways. I sawed on the reins, bringing the buggy back onto the road and slowing the team to a walk. A concerned Laura touched my arm. "Are you feeling ill, dear?"*

*I shook my head and sat silently till we were past the graveyard, and then I had to tell her. I'd vowed there was to be no secrets between us. I halted the buggy beside the road under a tall shade tree and told her the whole story of Morgan Holloway, from my looking down the barrel of her shotgun in the woods outside Sedalia, to the moment that the welling of blood on her back during the Yankee ambush told me she had perished. I left nothing out. I ended my story with how and where she was buried.*

*I sat staring at the buggy's dashboard, gripping the buggy reins so tightly my knuckles turned white. Laura tugged on the sleeve of my coat. When I looked at her, love and concern welled in her eyes. "We can't have your memories of her tearing you apart. I won't have that. May I make a suggestion?"*

*I nodded my head.*

*"You believe you abandoned her. You didn't, but that's what you believe. She's gone and you can't change that. But you could bring her here to Sedalia, where you can visit her grave and let her know she's not been forgotten."*

*"You wouldn't have a problem with that?"*

*"No, darling, I truly don't. It takes a special kind of man to feel the kind of responsibility you do toward Morgan Holloway. It's not in your nature to take advantage of any woman. It's one of the reasons I love you so much. I never feel alone, even when you're not with me."*

*Laura leaned close and kissed my cheek. "But there is one condition."*

*She laughed at my frown. "Sam Benson must accompany you. I hear Father's customers and my gossipy millinery ladies talking about how unsettled things are in southern Missouri and North Texas, almost like the war hasn't ended there in some places."*

*With Uncle Purse's blessing and plucky Patrick assuring us he could handle the hotel chores in our absence, Sam Benson made the journey with me. Traveling beyond the railroad, we shared the road with wagon trains and freighters bound for the West and Southwest till we passed beyond Little Santa Fe, near the junction of the Missouri and Kansas state lines. Our horses being broken to both saddle and harness, we purchased a flatbed wagon and a lead-lined coffin in Hickman Mills.*

*I had no problem locating the swale where Dayton Foster's men had ambushed Lance's detail. A homesteader and his family had moved into the cabin, but they had no objection to our removing the blanketed remains beneath the grave marker flying a scrap of red bandana. At the end, Sam Benson made me wait in the cabin while the homesteader helped him finish the digging and placed Morgan's body in our coffin. I must have thanked Sam Benson a hundred times for his insistent thoughtfulness on our return trip to Sedalia.*

*The interment of Morgan's body in the Sedalia cemetery was my last overt act stemming from my grand adventure in the autumn of '64, till the retirement of Marshal Forge Bannister ten years later. I built a successful law practice during those intervening years, which led to my appointment as the youngest circuit court judge in the history of Pettis County. Age had finally forced Forge from the saddle, and John L. had passed on to what Forge jokingly called "Teepee heaven."*

*Forge was still a healthy man at retirement, so long as he kept his feet on the ground and drove a buggy. Never concerned about pride or appearances, he took a room at the Wainwright Hotel and offered to serve as my court clerk and bailiff for whatever the position might pay. It was an offer I couldn't refuse. I forgave him for his calling* me *an undeserved "boss" on occasion.*

*I have thanked the Lord many times while seated with gavel in hand for granting me the privilege of meeting Forge Bannister, Brett Logan, and Dayton Foster and witnessing the honesty, respect, and fairness with which they treated every man they commanded, regardless of his origin, monetary wealth, or skin color.*

*I've tried my best to treat every soul appearing before me in court with the same unspoken creed, no matter the opinion of the body public, for it is my most fervent desire to stand before my Lord on Judgment Day humble and free of fear.*

*Written by hand this date, October 30, 1881,*
*Owen Wainwright,*
*Attorney-at-law*

# DISCUSSION QUESTIONS

1. To this day, the Civil War has been the deadliest, the most economically disastrous, and the most controversial conflict in American history. It is also the event that abolished the atrocity of slavery. How did the portrayal of the Civil War in this book reinforce or contradict your understanding of this history?

2. What other works of fiction have you read or watched that focused on the battles of the Civil War? How did this book compare or differentiate?

3. The long-lasting impact of the Civil War still resonates throughout America today. Can you think of examples of how this is true?

4. This novel portrays many characters. What character experiences particularly resonated with you? Are there any whose perspectives you could not relate to? Are there any groups of people whose perspectives you thought were missing from this story, and you would have liked to see included?

5. During the Civil War, strong sentiments for the Union and the Confederacy divided the state of Missouri into two warring groups. Owen Wainwright supports the Union cause, but finds his loyalty to that cause is tested when he is fairly treated by his Confederate captors. Did Owen reconcile this conflict in a manner that didn't betray his true loyalty? What does this say to you about the nature of political and ethical loyalties? Can you think of another example of when a person's ideology has been tested against their physical reality?

6. Honor in War is a theme found throughout this novel. How has our idea of Honorable Warfare changed since Owen's

time? How has it remained the same? Do you feel that war is ever truly justified?

7. Confederate forces were able to break through Union defensive lines during their siege of Sedalia, Missouri, Owen's hometown. What weapon gave the advantage to the Confederates and spearheaded their advance? The use of technology in warfare has changed dramatically since the Civil War; what do you see as some of the pros and cons of this evolution? How does technology change the nature of modern-day warfare, and what are the moral implications of these changes?

8. The Wainwright Hotel in Sedalia was renowned for the food served in its dining room. How much appeal does the Wainwright menu have compared to modern-age fast food?

9. Homer's *The Odyssey* is one of the first works of western literature to portray the tragedy of war, and conversely the unique bond between dog and man. In *When the Missouri Ran Red*, Morgan Holloway unexpectedly acquired a canine friend. How did the hound, Jacks, survive life in an army constantly on the move and to what extent was he willing to risk his life protecting his adopted master? What did the portrayal of the animal-human bond in a time of war mean to you? Did it draw any parallels to your own life, news events, or other works of fiction? Is there an irony in animal and human forming a bond, in the midst of war? Who was the more loyal character, the human or the dog?

10. U.S. Marshal Forge Bannister was known for enforcing the law violently, but fairly. Was his philosophy a proper approach for his era? Would Bannister's philosophy fit with modern law enforcement?

11. In the novel, Owen Wainwright falls in love with two totally different women and must deal with his feelings for them. How did he arrange his life so he could live with one lover while cherishing the memory of the other? Do you think such a thing is possible? How do you think the nature of relationships and love has changed from Civil War times to the present?

12. This novel features protagonists in their late teenage years who are making adult decisions. How has the role of youth changed in our society since the Civil War? When do we consider teenagers adults? What are the benefits and/or possible drawbacks of this change? How do you feel about the fact that many soldiers today are still teenagers?

13. A theme of the novel is the impact of war causing instability on civilian populations, even if that war is far away from the general population. Do you see a similar impact in modern day? Can you give examples?

14. Historical fiction often offers the reader parallels into their modern life. Can you think of ways this is true for this book?